PRAISE FOR ONE DEATH AT A TIME

"Staying sober and getting along while trying to nab a killer is no picnic, but this amateur detective duo pulls it off with wit, style, and plenty of laughs." —*People*

"Waxman's mystery is a sly female-bonding manifesto: It's *Thelma & Louise* without booze or Brad Pitt." —Oprah Daily

"Delightful characters, funny moments, and a quirky mystery combine in Abbi Waxman's new page-turner." —*Woman's World*

"[A] fun, clever tale." —AARP.org

"An absolute roller-coaster ride of a mystery! Loaded with hilarity and heart . . . it is impossible not to get attached to this snarky dynamic duo and their shenanigans."
—Jenn McKinlay, *New York Times* bestselling author of *Booking for Trouble*

"A fabulous mystery, characters with depth, and a total hoot, too. More, please!"
—Alison Goodman, *New York Times* bestselling author of *The Benevolent Society of Ill-Mannered Ladies*

"Abbi Waxman has done it again. This book has everything you could want: a cast of funny, flawed, feisty characters; a deliciously irreverent, hilariously high-octane murder mystery plot; and a huge amount of heart. I absolutely loved it."

—Freya Sampson, *USA Today* bestselling author of *The Busybody Book Club*

"Sparkling prose; quirky, well-drawn characters; laugh-out-loud dialogue; and a murderous 'curse.' This is a total winner with a satisfying ending."

—Kathleen West, author of *Making Friends Can Be Murder*

PRAISE FOR ABBI WAXMAN AND HER NOVELS

"Abbi Waxman is both irreverent and thoughtful."

—Emily Giffin, #1 *New York Times* bestselling author of *Love You More*

"Move over on the settee, Jane Austen. You've met your modern-day match in Abbi Waxman. Bitingly funny, relatable, and intelligent, *The Bookish Life of Nina Hill* is a must for anyone who loves to read."

—Kristan Higgins, *New York Times* bestselling author of *Look on the Bright Side*

"Waxman's wit and wry humor stand out."

—*The Washington Post*

"Abbi Waxman offers up a quirky, eccentric romance that will charm any bookworm."

—*Entertainment Weekly*

"Brilliant. Simply brilliant."

—Karen White, *New York Times* bestselling author of the Royal Street series

"This novel is filled with characters you'll love and wish you lived next door to in real life." —Bustle

"Waxman's voice is witty, emotional, and often profound."

—*InStyle* (UK)

"An aptly and hilariously titled novel. . . . Waxman again delivers with her signature wit and laugh-out-loud writing, offering us authentic characters who feel like people we've met and loved in our own lives." —Shondaland

"Funny and insightful." —Book Riot

BERKLEY TITLES BY ABBI WAXMAN

The Garden of Small Beginnings

Other People's Houses

The Bookish Life of Nina Hill

I Was Told It Would Get Easier

Adult Assembly Required

Christa Comes Out of Her Shell

The Mason & Mann Mysteries

One Death at a Time

Deadly Does It

DEADLY DOES IT

Abbi Waxman

Berkley Mystery
New York

BERKLEY MYSTERY
Published by Berkley
An imprint of Penguin Random House LLC
1745 Broadway, New York, NY 10019
penguinrandomhouse.com

Book design by Alison Cnockaert

Library of Congress Cataloging-in-Publication Data

Names: Waxman, Abbi author
Title: Deadly does it / Abbi Waxman.
Description: First edition. | New York: Berkley Mystery, 2026. |
Series: Mason & Mann Mystery
Identifiers: LCCN 2026018093 (print) | LCCN 2026018094 (ebook) |
ISBN 9780593816691 trade paperback | ISBN 9780593816707 ebook
Subjects: LCGFT: Fiction | Novels | Detective and mystery fiction
Classification: LCC PS3623.A8936 D43 2026 (print) | LCC PS3623.A8936 (ebook)
LC record available at https://lccn.loc.gov/2026018093
LC ebook record available at https://lccn.loc.gov/2026018094

First Edition: July 2026

Printed in the United States of America
1st Printing

To Jack, for helping me find the plot and turn the page.

We will not regret the past, nor wish to shut the door on it.

—Page 83 of *Alcoholics Anonymous*

(commonly referred to as "The Big Book")

DEADLY DOES IT

1

IT WASN'T THAT Mason was vain. It was just that if anyone was going to mess up her face, she wanted it to be her. She already had two piercings in one eyebrow, two in her nose and multiple holes in her ears, but the guy approaching her with a slender but very pointy ice pick seemed to think something more central was going to really pull her look together.

Not that aesthetics were his primary concern.

"I'm going to hurt you," he said, his breath a little ragged. Mason had just punched him in the gut, and he'd taken it badly. "I don't give a shit who your boss is. She's going to have to find a new pain in the ass to help her out."

Mason was wearing a tiny earbud in her right ear, and it spoke to her.

"Need a hand?" it said.

"Yes, hurry," Mason replied.

The guy raised his eyebrows and grinned. "Oh, no," he said, "I'm going to take my time."

Mason put up her fists and took a step back, settling into a wider stance. Her nose was bleeding, her eye was starting to swell, and she hadn't enjoyed any of this conversation so far. However, her natural exuberance was far from exhausted.

"Bring it, Halloran," she said. "We know you have the diamonds, we know where they are, and the police are on the way."

"Bullshit," replied Halloran, taking a step toward her. "We're all alone and I'm going to cut your tongue out."

A tongue piercing had been on Mason's list of considerations, but she drew the line at complete removal. She leaned back on her left foot and raised her fists higher, pulling her elbows close to her body. Smaller target.

A loud noise outside the warehouse drew the guy's attention for a moment and it was all she needed. She took two quick steps forward and swung her right, aiming for his jaw and following through with a lot of commitment. She connected, but he'd been more ready than she thought and grabbed her arm.

He pulled her close enough that she could smell the vodka he'd been drinking. For a split second she flashed on all the nights she'd had too much to drink, the scent of her own skin rank as her body struggled to process the alcohol, then she twisted in his grip and brought her bootheel down on his instep. He folded a little, and she folded with him, grabbing the arm with the ice pick and pulling it tight against her own belly. Still twisting, she unbalanced him and got her ass tight against his lower abdomen, bending almost double now and pulling his body up and over her own back.

The arc he made in the air was quite beautiful. The sound he made when he hit the ground was not.

Mason put her foot on his wrist and leaned all her weight

on it. His hand opened, the ice pick dropped out, and she swiftly kicked it away. Having focused her attention on that, she was somewhat surprised when his other hand grabbed her ankle and pulled her foot out from under her. She overbalanced, but managed to shift her weight as she fell, coming down on top of the guy. Which would have been fine as a strategy had he not immediately wrapped his arms around her and rolled on top of her, pinning her to the ground, her face against the concrete.

"Bitch," he said, getting one hand on her head and slamming it down. "That hurt."

"It . . . was . . . meant . . . to," muttered Mason, struggling to get her arm out from under herself, trying to push up against his weight. Halloran was so big it was hard to move, and as her head hit the ground a second time, she began to see stars. He was using his weight to hold her top half down, but she managed to pull one leg free and lever herself up a little. It was all the room she needed to get one arm loose and brace herself. She tried to throw him off, but he probably had sixty pounds on her and she wasn't getting very far.

Suddenly, he slumped against her back, lifeless. This didn't help—he was now two hundred pounds of deadweight—and Mason's head hit the ground for a third time.

"You alright, Mason?"

There was a pause, then the man's body was pulled or pushed off her. It was hard to tell from underneath. She lay there for a moment, gathering herself.

"The police are nearly here," said her rescuer, "but it seemed like maybe you needed assistance more quickly than that."

Mason rolled onto her back and looked up.

A very elegant woman in her mid-sixties looked down at her, a crowbar in her hand. "Do you think I should hit him again?" Julia Mann, Mason's boss, shifted the crowbar from hand to hand, looking like a bride getting ready to throw a bouquet. Graceful was just how she rolled.

Mason turned her head. "No . . . I think you nailed it the first time." She reached out a shaking hand and checked the guy's neck for a pulse. "He appears to be alive, but I doubt he's going to wake up anytime soon."

She could hear sirens. She felt a wave of nausea as the adrenaline started to dissipate and physical pain took its place. "I don't feel so good."

Julia took a step back. "Don't throw up on my shoes, please."

Mason looked at her shoes. Stilettos. Peep toes with a creamy flower at the ankle. She couldn't see the red bottoms, but she assumed they were there.

"Those are your fighting shoes?" She pushed off the ground with one hand, and for a moment her head swam. The sirens were getting closer.

"No, I was waiting in the car, but it sounded like things were getting heated, so I came to your aid."

"Thank you," said Mason weakly, getting up onto her hands and knees. She was going to rest here for a second.

"These are my whacking shoes," said Julia, obviously pleased with herself.

Halloran groaned and started to stir. Julia stepped closer to him and raised the crowbar again.

Mason got to her feet. The sirens were outside now, the flashing red dappling the interior of the warehouse like the world's dustiest disco.

"Drop it," said the first cop through the door, gun drawn.

Julia tossed the crowbar away and turned to face him. There were three of them now, and as Mason watched, hoping she wasn't going to pass out, a pair of plainclothes detectives followed the uniforms in.

There was a pause as they took in the scene.

"Good evening, Julia," said the first one. "Mason."

Mason raised a shaky hand in greeting.

"You've looked better," said the detective.

"I haven't," said Julia, "and I have dinner plans. You don't need me, do you, Brooks?"

"Nice try," replied Brooks, a redheaded woman with a deceptively peaceful expression. "You're both coming downtown."

"Mason probably needs a hospital," said Julia. "She got a pretty serious knock on the head."

"We'll have the EMTs check her out," said Wilson, the second detective. He and Brooks were familiar with Mason and Mann but weren't exactly fans of their work. The uniformed cops had the guy in handcuffs now, although he wasn't completely conscious yet. "Once they finish with this guy."

"It's possible Mr. Halloran has forty thousand dollars' worth of diamonds in his pocket," said Mason, "I didn't have time to check."

"Thanks," said Wilson, unfazed by the news. "We'll take a look."

Mason started walking toward the detectives, but a wave of nausea overwhelmed her, and her knees buckled. She turned to Julia.

"I think I'm . . ." she said.

Julia caught her as she fell, managing to hold her off the

ground until the cops came over to help. Once they had Mason between them, Julia dusted off her dress and sighed.

"I need to make a phone call."

Wilson shrugged. "Calling your lawyer?"

"No," replied Julia Mann, pulling out her phone. "Canceling my reservation."

2

EARLY THE NEXT morning, the assembled team regarded Mason with a mixture of sympathy and amusement.

"Why is it always your face?" asked Claudia, Julia's housekeeper, handing Mason a bag of crushed ice. "You need to work on defense. Or get better at ducking. Something."

"She leads with her face." This from Archie, Julia's agent and sometime lawyer. He grinned. "More specifically, her mouth." He privately was very attracted to Mason's face, including her mouth, but didn't need to mention that. Everyone knew.

"Her mouth looks largely unscathed today," said Will Maier, Julia's legal assistant and good friend, and the resident know-it-all. "It's the hugely swollen eye and scraped-up forehead that give me concern. Did you go to the hospital?" He shifted uncomfortably on the persimmon sofa stretching a good way across the length of the office. He didn't enjoy the physical aspects of their work—they made him queasy. He picked an imaginary piece of fluff from his rumpled corduroy pants and shuddered.

Mason shook her head, carefully. "They checked it out at

the scene and let me go. I don't have a concussion. It's just cosmetic. I'll be fine in a week or so." She shot Archie a glance. "And I don't lead with my face. I just fight my corner. Yours, too. Didn't notice you running in to help."

Archie turned up his hands. "I was miles away, at a movie premiere. Working," he added, "not having fun." Although he'd helped a lot with Julia and Mason's last case, he wasn't a regular member of the team. He'd made up a reason to come over when he'd heard Mason had been hurt and was hoping no one dug too deeply into what had brought him there so early in the day.

"Sure."

"I would have tried to help," said Will, apologetically, "but I was back here, tying up the paperwork that will hopefully seal Halloran's fate. Legal fate, anyway. His moral fate is in the hands of the gods." He looked up, faux piously, then shrugged.

Julia laughed. "Not sure which gods he follows, but they were not in evidence last night. Mason was struggling with gravity and the hardness of concrete, but I sailed in and made everything OK again." She preened. "Damn, I crush, as the young people say."

Will clicked a button and the giant screen that covered the far wall of the office flickered into life. "And he had the diamonds on him?"

Julia nodded. "In his pocket, ready to sell."

"The client must be happy."

Another nod. "Yes. He's wiring payment this morning."

Julia's legal and investigative business broadly fell into two categories: Finance and Fun, which are somewhat self-explanatory. The diamond case fell into the Finance category, because it had been straightforward and highly remunerative.

Fun cases often involved someone they knew, or a friend of someone they knew, and frequently made them very little money. However, those cases often got someone they liked *out* of trouble, got someone they didn't like *into* trouble, or got Julia's name in the papers. Occasionally, all three things happened. Finance supported Fun, Julia liked to say, and Fun often led to increased Finance. She claimed it was a virtuous cycle, but Mason had yet to be convinced. Cycle, sure. Virtuous? Depends who was asking.

Julia had been an award-winning and headline-stealing actress who'd gone to jail for murdering her husband (she always said she didn't do it) and then got sober and became a lawyer while she was behind bars. Mason and she had met when a dead ex-boyfriend showed up in Julia's pool and her subsequent drunken running from the police (in a Lamborghini, because why not) had made her look guilty. Mason had stepped in as her interim sobriety sponsor . . . then her temporary assistant . . . then her permanent sidekick. So far it was working well for both of them. Apart from the occasional beating up, which, to be fair, only ever happened to Mason.

The young woman stretched, then regretted it. "I'm going to a meeting," she said. "Get my busted head on straight. Any takers?"

As a sober alcoholic, Mason regularly attended AA meetings, and as both Julia and Will were also sober, they often went together. Right now, though, both of them shook their heads.

"I went on Zoom this morning," said Will. "I need to close out the Halloran case and finish filing all the paperwork."

"I'm good," said Julia. "I might go later."

Mason stood up, nodding. "Got it."

"Wait," said Julia, "there's something else we need to discuss." She held out her arm, which was dotted with red spots. "There are fleas in the house, and I blame you."

Mason raised her eyebrows. "I don't have fleas, Julia."

"Maybe, but Phil does."

Phil was Mason's cat. After their first case together, Mason had moved into one of Julia's guesthouses, and Phil had obviously come along.

"How do you know it's not Lorre? Dogs get fleas, too." Lorre was Julia's dog, also a relatively new arrival on the scene. He was sitting under one of the Eames loungers and perked up when he heard his name. His bulging eyes gleamed as his plumy tail moved some dust around. He was not an athletic dog, more of a character actor than a superhero, but he was comfortable in his milieu and really liked living with Julia, who had strong opinions about high-quality dog food.

"Lorre is regularly medicated." Julia reached out as the dog emerged from under the chair and docked his head with her hand. "Aren't you, baby?" The dog said nothing, but it was nonetheless true.

"So is Phil."

"And yet I have fleabites."

Will cleared his throat. "You know, fleas have been around for a very long time. Dinosaurs had fleas. Some fossilized fleas have been dated to at least 165 million years ago."

Julia smiled at him. "While that's fascinating information, Will, those are not the fleas I'm concerned about."

"They would have been much bigger, obviously, with mouthparts strong enough to bite through dinosaur skin." Will was keen to share the details.

"Of course. Which would make them easier to see, I guess." Julia pointed at Mason. "You need to keep Phil out of my house, Mason."

Mason shrugged. "He is not my employee. If anything, I am his. He has a cat door, he roams the grounds at will, I have no control over him. I tried keeping him indoors, but he wailed and paced for two days solid and my nervous system couldn't take it. Maybe beef up security over here."

"I don't let him in."

"Well, someone does."

There was a silence. Claudia got to her feet and started to leave. "If you guys have finished this pointless debate, I'm going to go get dinner started for tonight."

"Fix it, Mason." Julia's voice was firm.

So was Mason's. "We'll move out. I've only been here a few months and my subletter is month to month."

Julia's mouth tightened. "No, I don't want you to move out. It's very convenient having you here. I just didn't count on two thousand fleas coming with you."

"You know," said Will, "a flea can lay fifty eggs a day."

They all gazed at him.

"And jump a foot in the air, which is like 150 times their height . . ." he said, his voice trailing off.

There was a pause. Mason clapped her hands. "OK, this has been real. I'll keep medicating the cat and watch your windows and doors. For now, I'm off to my meeting."

Julia scratched her arm. "Bring back a flea collar. And flea spray. And maybe some miniature barbed wire."

Mason nodded, and left, trying not to scratch her own fleabites as she did so.

After a moment, Julia turned to Archie. "I have no idea why you're here, but she's gone now, so I guess you'll be on your way."

Archie thought for a moment about launching into his "reason" for being there, but then just shrugged and got to his feet.

"Always nice to see you," said Julia, as he left the room. She turned to Will. "Hopeless."

Will shook his head. "On the contrary," he said. "Very hopeful."

"HEY, MASON . . ." ARCHIE came loping out of the house just as Mason reached her car.

She turned back, her hand on the door handle. As part of Mason's job, she had access to the seven vintage cars that Julia Mann owned, and enjoyed driving all of them (except the Rolls; she hated driving the Rolls). But she had her own car, a beat-up Corolla in a shade of burgundy that reminded her of teenage afternoons on old basement sofas, and which listed to one side regardless of how often she got the wheels balanced.

She looked at Archie and raised her eyebrows. "Need a lift?" This was a joke; his Audi was parked nearby, looking quietly confident, as Audis will. Archie was also quietly confident. And tall. And good-looking. And well-dressed. But Mason made him feel nervous, not that she knew it.

Archie didn't answer until he was next to her. "No, thanks. I was wondering, actually, if you would like to go out sometime? Maybe lunch tomorrow?"

Mason stared at him for a moment but didn't immediately answer.

A little background: Archie and Mason had always had chemistry, but as it tended to come out in squabbling and sarcasm, it hadn't been as clear to them as it was to everyone else. However, recently Archie had started popping up at the house a little more, and Mason had an increasing tendency to send him funny memes she saw online. Though she'd noticed both of those things (she was very observant, as her job required), she hadn't expected today to be the day that Archie shot his shot, so to speak. But if she could take a thrashing from a diamond thief and keep ticking, she could handle this little surprise.

"Like a date?" she said, nonchalantly. Or at least, she hoped she seemed nonchalant. She felt perspiration break out between her shoulder blades, which was definitely chalant.

Archie, for his part, hadn't been intending to ask Mason out at that particular minute, but when he'd opened his mouth, that's what his brain had sent down.

"Uh . . . yeah," he said, unable to control himself. "A lunch date."

Mason pulled hard on her car door, which had a tendency to stick, if tendency applies when the door sticks one hundred percent of the time. She yanked, and the door flew open, nearly hitting Archie, who jumped back. Her shoulder blades got sweatier.

"Tomorrow I'm going to Alexa's fashion show thing."

Archie paused. "Oh, wait . . . is that the mayor's fashion show thing?"

"I guess. I think of it as Alexa's, you may think of it as the mayor's, but either way, it's a fashion show thing downtown."

"Yes, OK. So let's both go to that at the same time, and eat lunch while we're there."

"So . . . less of a date and more of a coordinated eating?"

"Yes. Simultaneous feeding."

Mason made a face. "That sounded creepier than coordinated eating. Let's stick with that."

"Alright. Around noon?"

"That was my plan."

"My plan, too."

"Great, now it can be our plan."

That felt too datey, so Mason slid into her car to cover her confusion. She was feeling feelings she didn't usually like: embarassment, excitement, embarassment again. She put the key in the ignition and turned it. As always, the car started. Honestly, the 2013 Corolla was a fucking workhorse of the first order, and despite the fact that it leaned to one side, it rocked her world.

"See you tomorrow lunchtime, then," said Archie, moving toward his car, which probably opened less aggressively.

Mason nodded casually, then waved as she pulled the car around and headed out of the gate. It was a moment of perfect cool . . . until she hit a small pothole in the driveway, banged her hand on the top of the window and made an involuntary noise like a stepped-on cat.

Whatever.

THE PHONE RANG as Mason was driving down the hill toward Hollywood. Probably Julia, making additional demands.

Mason answered without looking. "Dude, there's really nothing I can do about the fleas."

"You have fleas? Honestly, Natasha . . ."

Mason closed her eyes, briefly. "Hi, Mom."

"Hi. How's it going?" She paused. "Apart from the fleas."

"It's going well, thanks." Mason slowed for a light. "All good with you?" This part of a conversation with her mom she could handle. The basic exchange at the beginning, the newsy part, the part she could expand to several minutes if she inquired about each family member in turn, including the pets. Her parents had lots of pets. Usually, by the time she got to the last dog, she'd have killed nearly ten minutes.

"Well, no, actually."

Needle scratch. That wasn't how this part was supposed to go. Everyone needed to be fine for it to work.

"What's wrong?"

"It's your dad. He's had a heart attack."

Mason automatically flipped on the indicator, checked the mirror and pulled to the side of the road. "I'm sorry, Mom, what did you say?"

"A heart attack. A small one, but one nonetheless."

Mason looked out the window. A mother and her small child were negotiating over a Popsicle. The child appeared to be winning, insofar as he had his hand on the Popsicle.

"Mason, are you still there?"

"Yes, Mom." Mason's vision was a little cloudy, her ears were ringing, but she was there. "Is he OK?"

"Yes, he's OK. We went to the emergency room yesterday, he has an appointment with his cardiologist tomorrow, it's fine." Again, a hesitation. "I just thought you should know. In case you, you know, wanted to come visit."

There it was. There was always an ask, with an implication that Mason wasn't going to give, whatever the ask was. *If you'd like to visit . . . which we both know you don't like to do.*

"Is he home? Can I talk to him?"

"He's sleeping right now." Her mother hesitated again, which was unusual for her. Mason braced herself. "Louise is here."

Louise was Mason's sister, which explained the hesitation. There was a metaphorical clunk, as the other shoe dropped.

"Oh yeah? When did she get there?"

"Yesterday. I called her from the hospital."

"Why didn't you call me?"

"I thought you'd be busy."

"But not Louise? She's a lawyer in private practice. She hasn't had time to talk to me in two years."

"Well, I called her, and she got on a plane."

"Good for her." Mason looked in the rearview and got ready to pull back out into traffic. She noticed the deep groove between her eyebrows looked even deeper than usual and tried to relax her forehead. It didn't work. Maybe she'd hit a drive-through Botox clinic. This was LA—there was bound to be one somewhere. "I'm on my way to a meeting. I'll call you later. Hopefully, Dad will be up."

"Alright, Mason. Fit us in if you can."

Oh my God.

"OK, Mom. I'm glad Dad is OK. Talk to you later."

Mason hung up and tried to squeeze into traffic. No one was letting her, and she found herself leaning on the horn. As she pulled away, she noticed she'd scared the kid into dropping his Popsicle. She knew she should feel worse about it than she did, but that's what talking to her mother did to her.

3

HER SPONSOR RAISED an eyebrow. "I doubt he had a heart attack to mess with you, Mason. Yes, you're having an experience with it, but he's the one whose heart nearly conked out."

Mason smiled ruefully. "True."

They were sitting in the coffee shop across from the church where the AA meeting had been. There were several other ex-drunks sitting around, many of them meeting with their own sponsors, or just shooting the shit with one another. *Fellowship*, they called it, the company of people who've burned the same bridges and jumped from the same boats. It's one of the mainstays of any 12-step program, and Mason loved it. Mostly. Some of her fellows she could live without, but her sponsor was amazing.

Alexa was in her mid-fifties, still very vibrant and youthful, and sober for well over a quarter of a century. She had long, wavy dark hair shot through with gray, large hazel eyes and laugh lines that told of a life she hadn't taken too seriously. Mason knew she'd burned through her twenties like a forest fire, done things she wasn't proud of, started and ended relationships in a variety of disastrous ways, and wound up with a serious drinking problem that nearly cost her everything. But she'd gotten sober and worked her program hard, sponsoring half a dozen women and living a life marked by serenity rather than anxiety. Mason had been working with her since her first month in AA and loved her.

The sponsor-sponsee relationship is an unusual one. They're your friends, they care deeply about you, but they won't hesitate to call you on your shit. In fact, that's their job. They take you through the 12 steps, each one a variety of reading, writing, reflection and conversation. They give you homework. They follow the details of your life, know your whole backstory, share theirs, understand your triggers and challenges, and will fire you in a minute if they need to, or if you're somehow threatening their own sobriety. It is a very specific role, and each sponsor does it slightly differently. Alexa moved back and forth between hard-ass and jelly roll, as needed.

Now she leaned back in the booth, her dark hair contrasting beautifully with the deep red of the vinyl, and regarded Mason thoughtfully. "Are you going up?" Mason's family was in Berkeley, Northern California.

"I don't know." Mason played with her spoon, spinning it on its rounded side, her finger pinning it down. There was a small spill of something on the tabletop, so the spoon's circle was erratic.

Alexa watched her. "When was the last time you spoke to Louise? Properly spoke to her."

Mason shrugged. "Couple of years. Maybe more. She works all the time, she's five years older, we don't have much in common." The spoon came to a rest; she flipped it over, slid it away.

"Does she drink?"

"Like a regular person." Mason was the only one in her

immediate family who'd developed a drinking and substance problem, though there was an infamous aunt who no one saw anymore. They called her Aunty Tipple, and Mason had always enjoyed the stories about her when she was a kid, even as she didn't fully understand why this clearly Most Fun Family Member never came around anymore.

Alexa nodded. "But you'll call back later? Talk to your dad?"

"If Mom stops gatekeeping."

"She wasn't gatekeeping. You're projecting. He was asleep."

"So she said."

Alexa tipped her head slightly to the left. "Call your dad this afternoon, see how he's doing, make a decision about visiting later on." She reached into her bag and rooted around. Pulling out a pill case, she popped something into her mouth and reached for her water glass. "It's bullshit that my cholesterol is high. If I'd known I was going to live this long, I would have eaten more carefully."

"OK." Mason had come to accept that Alexa's counsel was usually sound. She'd told Mason never to accept criticism from someone you wouldn't take advice from, someone who didn't live a life you wished you had. Mason loved her mom, but her mother's life, with its endless committees and volunteering and activity, would make her break out in hives. She'd tried to pin Mason down a lot as a teenager, and it had made her flap her wings all the harder. Some of those feathers still hadn't quite grown back.

Alexa pushed her bag away and folded her hands on the table. "What else is new? How's things with Julia?"

Mason told her about the fleas, and added, "The rebuild is taking longer than Julia would like, but I think that's often the case." At the end of their first case together, a murderer had set fire to the house, and one wing had been extensively damaged. An architect and a contractor were mutually tearing their hair out over the reconstruction, but it was moving along.

Alexa nodded. She herself lived in Glendale, about thirty minutes from where they sat today. "Yeah, it always takes longer and costs more than you want."

Mason shrugged. "Never had to redo a house myself, so it's all new to me. What's new with you?"

Alexa picked up her phone. "Not much. I went to that wedding with Jennifer a couple of weekends ago. That was good." She flipped the camera around, showed Mason photographs of her and another of her sponsees, dressed up and dancing. "Up in Ojai, at some vineyard. Why do people get married at vineyards? Why not clothing factories or other scenes of production?"

Mason grinned. "Because all the T-shirts you can eat just isn't as compelling as wine by the bucket?"

"Fair point. Are you going to Jennifer's opening this weekend?"

"Yeah, I think so. Julia and the gang were surprisingly enthusiastic about it." Jennifer Desposito was a restaurateur. With two successful locations under her belt, she was opening her third, and there was a big party for opening night. Julia and Claudia were huge fans of the other restaurants and had leapt at the chance to preview the new one. Mason was generally antisocial but was open to getting dragged along as long as there was free food. "Are you going?"

"Probably not. The fashion show's going to wipe me out, and I think I'd like a quiet weekend." Alexa looked at her. "You're coming tomorrow, right?"

Mason raised her eyebrow. "I said I would, didn't I?"

Alexa grinned. "You're not one hundred percent reliable."

"I'm at least eighty-seven percent reliable. But yes, I'll be there. Do you need actual help working the show, or just emotional support?"

"The latter. I like seeing friendly faces in the crowd, you know . . . Jennifer will be there, too. She's catering, which is amazing considering the restaurant is opening this weekend, but that's Jennifer for you. When she commits, she *commits*, right? She's had quite the year, what with divorcing Edward and having to move house and everything, but she's got enough energy for, like, three people. Not sure about Iris or anyone else." Iris was Alexa's newest sponsee, and Mason didn't know her very well.

Outside of her sponsoring duties, Alexa ran an event planning agency, though that was understating it. She organized events, she coordinated security, she handled PR and marketing . . . She'd been in business for longer than she'd been sober and was well respected and highly sought-after. She was the living embodiment of that truism that if you wanted something done, you gave it to a busy person, and the chances of her having a quiet weekend were remote. It was even unusual for her to want such a thing.

Mason, watching her, realized something was off and, as was her way, decided to push.

"Is everything OK? You seem a little . . . something."

Alexa sighed. "Nah, I'm good. Just tired in anticipation of tomorrow, if you know what I mean."

"Sure." Mason looked for the waitress and signaled for the check. "So, you think I should go up to Berkeley?"

Alexa spread her hands on the table and looked at them. "I

think you could talk to Louise. Find out what's going on, then get on a plane and see for yourself." She looked up at Mason and smiled. "But the other option is to find out what's going on and then pause and do nothing. Doing nothing is always a good option, at least at first."

Mason scrawled her signature on the check and stood up. "Thanks, Lex." She stretched, and Alexa watched her affectionately.

"Keep me in the loop," she said. "And come find me when you arrive at the show tomorrow, OK?"

"Will do," said Mason.

She walked away, her long legs and firm stride turning more than one head as she left the coffee shop. She didn't notice . . . she never did.

4

AS WAS OFTEN the case, Mason drove up the driveway to Julia's house pinching herself. Located at the top of one of the hills that backdrop Los Angeles, the house was a mid-century masterpiece. Wide two-story wings straddled the canyon and gazed down at the city with an air of indifference and maybe a whisper of pity. The entire front of the house was glass, and you got the impression it was holding very still so the photographer could get the perfect shot. Like its owner, it knew it was beautiful and didn't care if you judged it one way or another. Mason had found it intimidating at first (again, like its owner), but now it felt almost like home. Almost.

When Mason walked back into the house, she thought maybe a party was underway. There was loud music coming from the office, and it was of the disco variety. Julia loved music, and played it all the time, but "We Are Family" was a little touchy-feely for her.

Mason pushed open the door and stopped short.

Claudia was dancing.

Claudia was Julia's housekeeper, but Mason had quickly realized she was much more than that. To start with, she and

Julia had met in prison, and although Mason hadn't had the nerve to ask her why she'd been there, Claudia clearly had a past. She was an incredible cook, and Mason had gained a lot of delighted weight in the last few months. The risk of losing access to her sauces had been more than enough reason for Mason to mind her tongue.

Claudia was also, it turned out, a total and complete disco queen.

She had company, a complementary disco king, a tall man wearing a pale yellow linen suit of immaculate cut, a silk shirt that he was totally pulling off, and a face of middle-aged handsomeness that made Mason think of the classic actor Peter O'Toole. Bony, angular, sexy.

What the actual fuck?

Mason came the rest of the way into the room and realized no one else was paying any attention to the dance party. Julia was sitting on the sofa, scanning something on the huge main display screen, and Will was on his phone at the other end, totally engrossed. The two dancers looked like they'd been rehearsing a lot. They were coordinated, sexy, professional. It was amazing, and Mason was amazed. She stood there, transfixed.

The song came to an end, and Claudia and the guy stopped dancing and began kissing. Also with a degree of coordinated professionalism.

Mason was starting to think she'd fallen through a rift in the space-time continuum and entered an alternate reality, when Julia looked up and spotted her.

She laughed. "Judging by the expression on your face, you're worried you dropped acid accidentally on your way home. It's OK. Claudia is a multifaceted person, and you just haven't seen all her facets yet."

"No one has," said Claudia, catching her breath. She looked at the tall guy, who was still standing very close. "Except maybe you, baby."

He grinned. "I like to think there's still plenty to discover, and I plan to take my time uncovering it."

Claudia raised her eyebrows and laughed in a way that made Mason embarrassed. She wondered if maybe she should go out and come back in again.

"Mason, this is Teddy Kettleman, also known as Teddy the Kettle, a long-con practitioner extraordinaire, and more recently a private investigator with whom we collaborate."

Teddy bowed to Mason, gravely.

"Plus, he's my boyfriend," added Claudia, unnecessarily.

"The long con came first, then the boyfriend status, then the private investigator."

"With the boyfriend title being the most important." Teddy kissed Claudia again. Then he kind of leaned into it, and everyone else in the room looked away, politely, as one.

After a moment, they broke apart and Claudia turned around.

"I think we're making everyone hyperglycemic, and none of them are diabetic. Let's cut the sugar, baby. I got to get back to work."

Teddy laughed. "OK. See you later." He slapped her gently on the bum as she turned to leave, and she looked back over her shoulder at him, grinning.

"OK, Mason," said Julia, turning away from the screen, "now that the nauseating display of joy and affection is over, I want to talk about something else."

Mason made a face. "Is this still about the fleas? I picked up a flea collar on my way home."

"No, it's about you finishing your degree, like we talked about."

Mason made a different face. "I thought you wanted me to go to private investigator school?" Julia had suggested this career path to Mason a few months previously, and Mason had been privately warming up to the idea ever since. She was a slow warmer, generally, but she'd been turning it over in her mind like a pebble and liking it more and more.

Julia waved her hand. "I do, but I just want to talk it over a minute. Keep your hair on. I had Will look into it."

Will cleared his throat and looked at the ceiling, which Mason knew meant he was consulting the giant notebook in his brain.

"In order to become a PI in California you need to have a law degree or a police science degree and four thousand hours of related experience. Or you could *not* have one of those degrees but then you need six thousand hours of experience. As you have a portion of a *political* science degree, that means the latter."

Mason stared at him. "How will I get the hours of experience?"

Will shrugged. "You're already doing it. Working as an investigator for Julia."

"I'm an investigator? I thought I was an assistant."

Julia chimed in, "You assist with my investigations, ergo you're an investigator. Stop being pedantic. Plus, I was thinking of farming you out a bit, which is why Teddy is here."

Teddy smiled at Mason. "I can always use a sidekick. Company on stakeouts, help with research, muscle on occasion." He indicated her face. "I can see you're a fighter."

"She's more of a fightee," said Julia, dryly, "but she's game."

"You should have seen the other guy," said Mason, without hesitation.

"I'm sure," said Teddy, clearly not sure at all.

"Anyway, the point is, it's going to take you several years to get the experience you need, and I wanted to give you the option of completing your undergraduate degree at the same time. One year of undergraduate, assuming you can stay awake through whatever credits one needs to finish a political science degree. Then you can decide if you want to go to law school as you originally planned, or become a PI, once you've got your however many hours it was Will said."

"Six thousand," said Will.

"It gives you more choices." Julia examined her fingernails. "I mean, I don't care what you do, and you being a licensed PI would be more useful to me, but you know . . . you might want the option."

There was a pause as Mason considered this. A thought occurred to her.

"Not sure I can afford to go back to school." She blushed. "I mean, you pay me very well, I'm not . . ."

"I'll pay your tuition. I'm sure I can claim it as a business expense or something." Julia looked shy, which was almost unprecedented. "It's totally up to you, I realize it's a big commitment to . . . well, to us . . . to working with us, and it's only been six months and you did just get beaten up, which has happened several times, actually . . ."

She went quiet. Mason looked at Will, who grinned at her and turned up his palms. She looked at Teddy, who shrugged.

"Think about it," said Julia.

"Alright," said Mason, who was suddenly fighting tears. It

was a huge vote of confidence, this offer. And it had been a while since anyone had any confidence in her, or since she'd had much in herself. "Thank you, Julia."

Julia attempted insouciance, and largely pulled it off. "You're welcome." She waved her hand again, either wafting away her own emotion or dismissing Mason's. "Let's get back to the work at hand. We have a potential new client coming in at three. Teddy's going to sit in."

"Fun or Finance?" Mason asked.

"I think Finance, but we'll see. The bank balance is healthy right now, so if it's only Finance I might say no."

Will cleared his throat. "The bank balance could be healthier. And I was hoping we could maybe talk about upgrading the projector system."

"Didn't we get a new system a few years ago?"

"Yes. But there have been advances."

Julia made a face and turned to Mason. "Did you eat breakfast?"

Mason nodded. "Some. With Alexa." Julia and Alexa hadn't met, but Julia knew who she was, of course.

Julia sighed. "I need to eat something. I'm feeling angsty and aggressive, which isn't a good combination."

Everyone stood up.

"To the kitchen!" said Teddy. "Any excuse to see my beloved." He left the room, quickly.

Mason looked at Julia and Will. "Is he always like that?"

They nodded. "He's smitten," said Will. "They both are."

"It's like that at the beginning," said Mason. "It'll wear off."

Julia laughed. "Shows how much you know about love," she said. "They've been together twenty years."

5

AS MASON WAS following the others to the kitchen, her phone rang. She looked at it and cursed.

Julia paused. "Problem?"

"No, but I have to take this. I'll be along in a minute." Mason turned and went back into the office, answering the call as she went. "Louise?"

Her sister's voice came through as loudly and clearly as ever. Louise always spoke as though she was addressing the court, and Mason felt the edges of the witness stand closing in around her. "Hello, Natasha." Her family called her by her given name. It was the people she liked who called her Mason.

She tried to keep her voice calm. "Hey there, Lou. How's Dad?"

"He's doing OK. Up and about a bit, which is fine. The doctors told him to take it easy, and he is, or at least his version of taking it easy."

Mason perched on the arm of the sofa and started plucking bits of thread off a cushion. "And Mom?"

"She's fine, too. Are you coming up?"

Mason gave the cushion a break and thought about it. "Maybe this weekend? I'm working this week."

"You couldn't work from here?"

"No." Mason fought the desire to say more, to explain herself. Louise always put her on the defensive. "I'm needed here, in person. But this weekend I can come. Saturday morning."

"Text me flight details. I'll meet you at the airport."

"OK." Silence fell. Mason pushed herself. "And you? You're well?" It was like talking to an old school friend, or someone you didn't know very well, rather than someone you'd grown up with, loved, celebrated birthdays and ridden ponies with. The sisters had had periods of being friendly, but longer periods of not.

"Of course," said Louise, briskly. "Work is very busy, but I can do much of it from here. My team is handling things on the ground."

"Your team . . . that's nice." Mason made a face to herself; she could hear she sounded sarcastic, without wanting to be.

"Yes, my team. I made partner last year, did I tell you?"

"No, but Mom did. Congratulations."

"Thanks." Another silence. This one stretched. "Alright, well, I'll see you this weekend. I'll let you know if anything changes here. With Dad, I mean."

"OK, thanks."

They said goodbye and hung up. Mason felt the usual mild nausea and anxiety she got after talking to Louise. She always felt . . . It was hard to put into words. Dumb. Clumsy. Childish. Yes, that was it. Louise made her feel like an awkward little kid because she was so polished and completely grown-up. Mason always felt like a clod.

She shook herself and caught sight of her reflection in a framed print on the wall. Bruises. Scabs. But still definitely a fully grown woman.

She straightened up and headed to the kitchen, where hopefully someone would have fixed her a snack.

"WHO WAS THAT?" asked Julia, as Mason entered the kitchen.

"My sister," replied Mason, walking over to help herself to coffee. "Her name is Louise."

"You have a sister?" Claudia sounded shocked. "What else haven't you told us? Isn't that pretty fundamental information?"

"Look," said Mason, sitting on the edge of the kitchen table, "that's rich, coming from you—how is it possible I've known you six months and am only now finding out about Teddy, a boyfriend you've had for twenty years?"

Claudia looked over at her boyfriend, who shrugged. "He was out of the country, working."

"And you completely forgot he existed? You didn't mention him once."

Teddy sighed. "Seriously, it's out of sight, out of mind with her. It's a constant battle, trying to keep a woman like that interested. She has so many suitors, so many options . . ."

Claudia snorted. "You didn't tell me you had a sister, I didn't tell you I had a boyfriend, I say we call it even." She slid a platter full of sliders onto the middle of the table, and everyone started to help themselves. "It would have come up eventually, as it did today. I am a woman of intense privacy. There are many things you don't know about me." She shrugged and turned back to the oven. "For example, how I make tiny burgers so well that each is a kiss from me to you."

Mason moved to sit down in an actual chair, across from

Julia, and reached for a plate. It was true—Claudia's burgers were transcendent.

Julia took a bite and waved the remaining half at Mason. "So, spill it," she said. "What's the deal with your sister? What other family members have you neglected to mention?"

"I wasn't being neglectful," said Mason, lifting the top bun and admiring the teeny, flower-shaped pickles. Claudia made everything small, so the proportions were right. "It just never came up before."

Claudia snorted. "See? Easily done."

Mason continued, "I have one sister, five years older. She's a lawyer, like you, but unlike you she's more interested in money than crime. As far as I know, anyway. She lives and works in Chicago." She took a bite. "I don't know if you guys have siblings. It's not like we sit around and show home movies."

"I have two sisters," said Will, "and one younger brother who died of a drug overdose a few years ago." He made a face. "Stupid."

"I'm sorry," said Mason. "That sucks." It was also common as dirt, especially considering the number of addicts and alcoholics they all knew. But that didn't make it any easier.

"I have two sisters also," said Julia, "but sadly they're both still alive."

Mason grinned. "Not close, then?"

"Not close enough to kill them. They're older. Hopefully, they'll fall off the perch shortly."

Claudia clicked her tongue. "Don't believe her, Mason. She loves at least one of them."

"Maybelle," said Julia. "I like Maybelle. Probably because I never see or hear from her. She lives in Florida in one of those huge gated communities for incorrigible old people, the ones with shuffleboard and rampant STDs. The other one is called Phyllis. Phyllis I hear from twice a year, when she calls to see if I've accepted Jesus Christ as my Lord and Savior, and I have to inform her that, no, I haven't. That I haven't accepted *anyone* as my Lord and Savior, and if I did, it would be unlikely to be him and more likely to be a strapping thirty-year-old lifeguard in a Speedo, and that's usually where the conversation falters." She laughed, suddenly. "I really enjoy those chats. I don't know what I'm complaining about."

"I have a brother," offered Teddy, "but he's still in prison."

"I am an only child," said Claudia, sweetly, "because my parents realized they couldn't improve on me and broke the mold."

"And what was your sister calling about?" asked Julia, gesturing with her cup for more coffee.

Mason sighed. "My dad had a heart attack."

Julia nearly spilled her newly full cup. "What? When? Jesus, what else aren't you telling us? First you have a whole sister we never knew about, then you had a father . . ."

"Well, of course I have a father. Everyone has a father . . ."

Will opened his mouth, but Julia rolled over him. "And then you apparently nearly didn't have a father. I assume he's still alive, or you would have phrased that differently."

"Insofar as I would have said he was dead?"

"Exactly."

"Yeah, he's not dead. My mom said it was minor. I might go up and see them this weekend, if that's possible."

"Of course. The Bay Area is only an hour away by plane. Go today if you want. Family is important." Julia looked at the skeptical faces around the table. "Or so I'm told."

"No," said Mason. "He's OK. There's no need to panic. I'll go up Saturday." She looked around, much as Julia had done. "Hey, I love my dad, but my mom and sister are also there, and I'm not keen on the excoriating personal examination and dissection that comes with each visit with them."

"Wow," said Will, "that was quite a sentence. Not a relaxing vibe, then?"

Mason shook her head, a lock of her short hair falling over her forehead. "No. I'm a big disappointment."

"Not to me," said Julia, getting to her feet. "Well, not consistently, anyway. The fleas are a bit of a downer." Mason frowned and started to speak, but Julia raised her hand. "Save it. I need to go get dressed."

"You are dressed," said Mason. Julia was wearing a vintage wrap dress with a vivid black-and-white pattern.

"This is my first-thing outfit, my morning ensemble. I had a different vision for the afternoon."

Mason raised her eyebrows. She had today's clothes on, some of which were yesterday's clothes and several of which would probably be tomorrow's, too. When she had visions, clothing was rarely the subject. "OK. Knock yourself out."

"I usually do. See you in a bit."

And with that, Julia swept out of the room.

Not ten seconds later there was a soft thump as Phil the cat jumped through an open window above the sink and landed gently on the counter. Everyone stared at him, but he couldn't have cared less. He only had eyes for one person.

"Hey, baby . . ." Claudia walked over to him and let him butt her gently in the upper arm. Then he sat and curled his tail tightly around his toes, gazing at her in patient expectation. Claudia turned, opened the fridge, and brought out a dish of finely chopped meat. Then she pulled out a quail's egg, which she cracked onto the . . . Mason goggled, realizing it was steak tartare . . . and delivered it to the cat. The cat squeezed his eyes at her and tucked in.

Will was the first to speak. "It's you. You're the one letting him in."

"We're in love," she replied. "Phil likes Mason well enough, but that was before he met me." She looked over her shoulder at Mason. "Sorry, Mason." Then she looked at Teddy. "Sorry, Teddy."

They both shrugged.

Teddy said, "I can't get jealous of a man who's that hairy, has only three legs, and stands nine inches tall on tiptoe."

Mason said, "He and I practice consensual non-monogamy. It's OK. I regularly pet other cats."

Will snorted. "Julia's going to have a fit if she discovers you're encouraging his visits."

"She won't," said Claudia. "Phil is the smartest cat I've ever met. He knows and anticipates her every move. He's a ninja."

"And yet he's managed to infest the whole house with fleas."

"The fleas aren't ninjas, they're a rabble. I try and keep him in the kitchen at least, but I did catch him on Julia's bed once." She stroked the cat's head, and his purr could be heard from the table. "He's a warrior. He enjoys a little risk. Julia was out of the house at the time."

Suddenly, Phil's head popped up, and like a shadow fading out in a beam of sunlight, he was up and through the window in an instant.

The kitchen door swung open and Julia appeared. "Claudia, do you have any idea where my . . ." She stopped and narrowed her eyes. "What's going on?"

"Nothing," said everyone at once.

Julia looked around, swiftly, then her eyes fell on the plate Claudia appeared to be guarding. "Claudia, you didn't want to cook your burger?"

"Trying out a new recipe," replied her friend. She reached out for a nearby fork and delicately scooped up a mouthful of what had only moments before been cat food. She ate it and looked thoughtful. "Needs salt."

6

THE NEXT DAY dawned bright and clear, with a sky the shade of eggshell blue that promised heat later in the day. Mason took one look and dressed lightly. The fashion show was close to downtown, not her favorite part of the city, but she loved Alexa and was going to show up for her, oppressive heat and the smell of spoiled milk be damned. She wondered if Alexa's other sponsees would be there, then remembered that Jennifer was catering, so that was at least one compatriot on hand. Iris had been invited, of course, but whether she would make it or not remained to be seen. Mason frowned at herself; she didn't like Iris, and she needed to interrogate that. Not now, though. Now, she was going to focus on Alexa.

Navigating the one-way system downtown always put her in a bad mood. Los Angeles wasn't big on one-way systems; generally, it was a little too East Coast–coordinated for the city's devil-may-care approach to traffic, but downtown was the exception. There were also several points where you entered a street with about twelve feet in which to cross several lanes to exit again, and by the time Mason arrived at the venue she was cross and sweaty. She paused for a second before walking in, petting a familiar adorable scruffy dog who was tied up outside (with a bowl of water—this was LA), and took a moment to mutter the Serenity Prayer to herself. It helped, but only a little. She tried smiling at the guy checking bags, and realized she recognized him from meetings, which is to say she knew his name and that he'd once brought a sheep to a bar.

"Hey, Mason," he said, reaching to take her bag.

"Paul," she replied, angling her body to show him she didn't have a bag to inspect. Or a sheep. "Traveling light today. Is Alexa already here?"

"Since before I got here," he replied, grinning. "Always on the grind, that one."

"True story," she replied, bumping fists as she walked past him and into the venue. It smelled like a farmers market, and once she was in, she realized why.

The event, which was a fashion show raising money for the city's main food bank, was being sponsored by some kind of produce consortium: West Coast Fruits and Vegetables. Mason couldn't tell if they were a union, a farmers group, or merely deeply committed fans of tubers and legumes. Whoever Alexa had hired to decorate the venue had embraced the theme in a big way. Barrels of apples, several complete orange trees, waitstaff with Carmen Miranda–level fruit hats . . . you get the vibe. Mason took a few steps into the room and looked up.

Wow. Mason had lived a full life, despite being so young, but she'd never seen a zucchini as big as that one. Easily fifteen feet long, it hung above the runway, in the company of an enormous cob of corn, a giant green bean, and several clementines the size of Mini Coopers. She turned on her axis—

giant fruits and vegetables hung all over the room. They were shiny and fulsome, as if Jeff Koons and the makers of American muscle cars had met up in a paroxysm of inspiration in the produce aisle. Never had a turnip oozed so much sex appeal. Never had asparagus radiated so much speed and power.

"They're amazing, right?" A familiar voice made Mason turn, and she grinned to see Jade Solomon, an actress she'd become friends with on the case that'd brought her and Julia together.

Jade was a very beautiful woman, and one of *Vanity Fair*'s hottest "Young Hollywood" stars. She had a face and figure that suggested partying might be her middle name, but actually, she stayed home a lot reading books, watching movies and eating breakfast cereal, about which she was obsessive. Jade had saved Mason's life, then Mason had saved Jade's, and that kind of thing tends to cement a bond. Mason hugged her, then stepped back again to take in the aerial vegetable show. "Yeah, 'amazing' is the word. I had no idea a cob of corn the size of a minivan was going to be so impressive, but it really is."

Jade looked earnestly at her. "You know, giant anything is usually a win. If you think about *Honey, I Shrunk the Kids*, or *Alice in Wonderland*, or that amazing Miyazaki movie based on the *Borrowers* books . . ." She nodded. "And predating the movies, of course, *Gulliver's Travels* used size as a satirical device, playing with scale as an allegory for power and influence."

Mason nodded slowly at her.

"Besides," the actress continued, "who doesn't love a giant everyday object, and the delightful dissonance it creates?" She was wearing a linen shift dress in a shade of butter yellow that contrasted so beautifully with her dark eyes and hair that for a moment Mason just let herself be dazzled. Then she slowly allowed her eyes to cross and the tip of her tongue to poke out of her mouth and Jade started laughing.

"Am I doing it again? Talking too much?"

"You never talk too much," said Mason. "You're always interesting. But sometimes the combination of the way you look and the things you say blows my gourd. I'm a simple creature." She looked up again. "Speaking of gourds, I'm not sure dissonance is what this giant zucchini makes me think of, but maybe I have a filthier mind than you do."

Jade opened her mouth but closed it again to smile at someone over Mason's shoulder.

"I'm not sure what I just walked into," said Archie, leaning over to hug Jade hello, and grinning at Mason, "but those are some seriously big vegetables."

"Right?" Mason stared up into the rafters of the building. "They're probably not as heavy as they look."

"Not at all," said Alexa, appearing suddenly, walkie-talkie in hand. "The designer told me they're made of foam, covered in fiberglass and sprayed with layers of acrylic. He apparently does a brisk trade in giant vegetables, and could also have offered us enormous insects, household utensils or a variety of cloud formations."

"Well, the clouds at least make sense," said Archie, looking at the green bean with a quizzical expression on his face. "How do they stay up?"

Alexa looked at him. "Magic."

"No, but really."

Alexa shrugged. "Mostly magic, but also electromagnetism. The designer installed these powerful bases, and the sculptures are attached to them with very strong cables and can be installed and removed fairly easily. You should have been here yesterday, when I watched him and the clothing designer argue for three hours—three hours I will NEVER get back—about the precise placement of everything. The corn was in the wrong place. The clementines clashed with the beets. The grapes were . . ."

". . . full of wrath?" asked Jade, unable to help herself.

"Well, the grapes themselves were mellow, but the two creative professionals were pretty ticked. They sorted it out in the end, but you haven't lived until you've seen two grown men directing a team of other grown men as they bicker over the perfect height for an eighteen-foot carrot."

"Sounds fun," said Archie. "I spent yesterday discussing contracts and residual agreements, so placing hilariously oversized fruit sounds way better."

"Yeah . . ." Alexa shrugged again. "It looks great. I'll give them that." Her walkie-talkie buzzed, and she gave it a worried look. "Did you guys get some canapés? We did tastings yesterday while they arranged the vegetables. Ms. Desposito outdid herself."

"Not yet," said Mason, looking around for someone carrying a tray, "but I'm determined. Is she around? I thought I saw her dog outside . . ."

Alexa looked at her phone. "She might have left already, but she also might be raising hell behind the scenes. I'm not sure. The show should start in another ten minutes or so. I have to run."

"Need any help?"

Alexa shook her head. "No, it's all in hand. The mayor and his wife will be here soon, the food is circulating, the designer's having a conniption about the surface of the runway, which is better than freaking out about the vegetables, so just another day in paradise." Her walkie-talkie hissed at her, and she pressed a button. "I'm here, go ahead."

Mason turned to see that Jade and Archie had already headed in the direction of the best seats in the house (bar the ones that were being saved for the mayor) and went to join them. On the way, she snagged a couple of canapés, which, she was amused to see, were bite-sized pastry bowls with miniature vegetables in them. Playing with scale again. Jade would be amused.

THE SHOW STARTED only a few minutes late, and Mason simply copied Jade, who had clearly been to more than her fair share of fashion shows. She angled her body just right, she occasionally glanced at the program thing and even made little notes in the margins . . . she was to the manner born, so Mason followed suit. The clothes themselves were largely uninteresting to Mason because she liked to wear things that could be fallen over in, whereas all these clothes looked like a stiff breeze might be end times for them.

"Ooh . . ." said Jade, in response to a slip dress that barely obscured the model's body it was hanging on. Mason wondered if it was made of fabric at all, or if they had simply wiped the model down with a damp cloth and then puffed colored chalk on her until enough of it stuck to call it decent. She turned to look at Archie, but strangely, he was looking at her rather than at the essentially naked women who were ambling down the runway. Surprised, she smiled at him.

He leaned over. "While I'm sure you would look beautiful in any of these, they don't strike me as your kind of thing."

"Not really . . ." confirmed Mason, then added, "What's my kind of thing?"

"Fighting clothes," he whispered. "Clothes that don't need thinking about."

Mason made a face. He was right. She wasn't sure how she felt about it and was about to point out that she didn't end up in a fight *every* single day, when there was a ringing snap and something big and red broke loose from its mooring and hit the very end of the runway with a giant cracking sound.

It was an enormous tomato, of course. Mason disliked tomatoes. The tomato in question (a cherry tomato, fortunately, not the beefsteak variety) had a diameter of about three feet and narrowly missed (and highly traumatized) a young woman who would never look at a crudités platter the same way again. Mason thought about it for a second: These vegetables were made of polystyrene and covered with a fiberglass shell and several layers of acrylic paint and high-gloss lacquer, so they were light . . . but not that light. If the tomato had hit the woman directly, it would have been . . . bad. Mason looked up as another snapping sound heralded the launch of a bunch of grapes, which fell somewhere behind her. This was a different sound, as you might imagine, as the stem itself cracked upon impact and some of the individual grapes shattered like Christmas baubles, while others simply rolled over their fallen comrades and across the floor. Louder than all of that was the yelling of the crowd as everybody realized this was a food fight only a giant could win. People stood. People ran. And people screamed.

Jade yelled in Mason's ear, "Which way?" She sounded excited.

"How do you mean?" Mason had assumed a fairly classic half crouch as she looked up and evaluated the smorgasbord of potential crush injuries. She was also looking around for Alexa and had taken a firm grip of Jade's arm. She could sense Archie was close behind her, while most of the other people in the room were moving.

"Well," said Jade, "I tend to run away from trouble, but you tend to run toward it, so I was waiting to see which was happening now." She looked at Archie. "What about you? Toward or away?"

"I'm following her," he replied, ducking as a clump of high-gloss beets hit the deck about five feet away from him. He hadn't been anticipating this outcome, but he thought he was handling it well. He wanted to grab Mason and protect her, but he knew that was both futile and unwelcome, so he just kept a close eye on where she was going next.

Mason spotted Alexa leaping onto the runway, presumably so she could see better. She was frantically yelling into her walkie-talkie, and as Mason looked around, she could see all of Alexa's staff starting to converge, directing people away from the runway, and trying to clear the room. The mayor and his wife were surrounded by their own security detail and were attempting to remain calm. This was a losing proposition, because if there's one thing that's going to put a crimp in your calm, it's being aerially attacked by glossy crucifers. Especially in an election year.

There was another snapping sound, and Mason looked up in time to see one end of the giant cob of corn, which hung lengthways down the runway, come free and start to swing with increasing speed toward the top of the runway, where Alexa was standing. Mason moved as fast as she could to beat the corn to Alexa, but physics is a cruel taskmistress. Alexa saw the cob coming, as it were, and tried to get out of the way, but the enormous vegetable weighed about eighty pounds and swiped her off the runway like she was a ladybug. She landed in the mayor's arms, knocking both of them onto the floor, and the cob, on its return swing, snapped its remaining cable and landed with an enormous crack on the runway itself. It was chaos, as the mayor's security didn't know whether to help Alexa or arrest her for assaulting the mayor, and no one wanted to tackle the cob of corn, which was rolling toward the edge of the runway at a rapid clip, individual kernels shattering like light bulbs. Mason and Archie threw themselves at the corn, but it had quite a head of steam at that point, and they ended up sprawled across the runway as the corn rolled off and straight at the group of people with the mayor. Alexa appeared to be unconscious, but the mayor, who was made of sterner stuff than anyone had expected, picked her up and ran out of the way just in time, as the corn took out five rows of wooden folding chairs and still had enough speed to crash spectacularly into a stalk of celery, bringing it to a complete stop.

As Mason and Archie picked themselves up, the remaining produce—a rutabaga, a red pepper and an avocado, the official state fruit of California—crashed from the ceiling into the remaining seats, which could have been deadly if everyone hadn't already cleared the room in a panicked mob.

Mason took a deep breath and looked around for Jade.

Jade was standing on a chair some fifteen feet away, holding her phone at the perfect angle, completing a panoramic sweeping shot that was going to be the lead footage on every single news show and social media site in about ten minutes.

"Wow," she said, hitting the button to stop recording. "Wasn't expecting to see that today."

"Giant vegetables crashing all over the place?" asked Archie.

"No," she said, climbing carefully down off the chair, "the mayor putting someone else's life before his own. His agent is going to be thrilled." She laughed. "Only in LA, baby."

7

"IT COULD HAVE been so much worse," said Will the next morning.

He, Julia and Mason were sitting in the office, recapping the events of the day before. Up on the main screen was the front page of the *Los Angeles Times,* with the headline *Mayor Creamed by Corn* stretching much of the way across all the columns. A subhead, *Guests Crushed by Grapes*, showed that the serious journalists of the *Times* had seen the event as the gift it was and let their hair down as far as it would go.

"You know, it's a fascinating physics challenge, working out the various forces that were at play."

Julia and Mason looked at Will as he reached for his tablet and shared its screen to the main screen at the front of the office. He pulled out his pen and started drawing.

"For example," he said, "that first tomato weighed about twenty-five pounds and was being held up by a very powerful magnet that wasn't under any kind of strain. But someone turned off the power to the system, so it just plummeted, with considerable speed and force. If someone had been right underneath it, it would have been disastrous. Possibly fatal."

Mason said, "Are we sure someone did it on purpose? Couldn't it just have been a glitch? A technical problem?"

Will shook his head. "No, because the system was programmed very carefully, and each electromagnetic base had its own switch. It says in the *Times* that the designer claims the tablet that controlled everything was stolen, although the police found it when they were clearing the scene. No idea if anyone's going to be held liable; the police are still investigating. Someone had it and carefully flipped each switch, one by one. First everything above the runway, then a set behind the chairs, and so on." He started drawing the cob of corn, carefully adding in length and height. "The cob of corn was essentially hollow, although the fiberglass shell and the acrylic paint added considerable weight, as did the metal plates inside it that were there specifically for it to be rigged and held magnetically, so it probably netted out around a hundred pounds, and then, when only one end released, it swung, so then it had momentum, so"—he started doing math, which was giving Mason a headache—"basically a beam rotating kind of problem, so gravity times length, times three . . . square root . . . something around ten meters a second when it hit her, no wonder she flew into the mayor." He looked up. "Physics is so fun."

"You're so weird," said Mason.

"It's really amazing no one was seriously hurt or killed." He looked at the headlines again. "The only real damage was to Alexa's reputation. The mayor came out of it a hero, and Jade Solomon is getting props for her cinematography."

The front doorbell rang, and after a moment or two Claudia opened the door to the office. Alexa was with her, and Alexa's husband, Scott.

Mason knew Scott relatively well, but she was pretty sure she'd never seen him looking as upset as he did at that moment. He was not a tall man, but he was a tough cookie, and right then he looked ready to kill someone.

Mason stood up. "Julia, I don't know that you've actually met Alexa before, and this is her husband, Scott."

Julia stood and extended her hand. Today she was wearing a vintage Pucci jumpsuit that was so vibrantly patterned in purple, black, white and turquoise that Mason had exclaimed involuntarily when she'd entered the room. Now she walked toward Alexa looking like a surreal jungle cat and smiled the smile that had won her fans the world over during her successful acting career. "Alexa, it's a pleasure to meet you. Mason speaks of you often, and highly."

Alexa smiled and shook Julia's hand. "She speaks of you often, too. It's strange we haven't met before."

"I doubt her reviews of me are as glowing as yours."

"Oh, you'd be surprised." Alexa smiled but didn't offer anything more. The conversations between a sponsor and her sponsee aren't privileged in the legal sense, but they are private.

Julia turned to Alexa's husband and shook his hand also. "Scott, a pleasure. Welcome to my home."

Scott looked around in mild amazement.

"What an incredible room," he said.

Mason looked, too, though she'd seen it a hundred times. When she'd first come to Julia's house, she'd been shown into the living room, but as that was currently under construction, the office was pulling double duty. The living room had been a study in mid-century concrete and glass, all air and angles. The office was an airy room, too, but two walls were lined with bookcases containing hundreds of volumes, magazines, DVDs, and various other information, while the third wall was covered with an enormous screen. The final wall was all glass, draped with soft orange curtains that filtered the light and gave the room a glow that was inviting, and also very flattering to Julia's skin tones. It was, as Scott had pointed out, an incredible room, and Mason loved it.

Julia turned to Will. "Mason you already know, and this is Will Maier, my legal assistant. Anything you can say to me you can say to him. He's the soul of discretion." She sat back down. "How can I help you?"

Scott and Alexa sat down, and there was a pause as they clearly decided which of them was going to speak first. Or maybe at all. As Mason studied her friend and her husband, she realized Alexa was—as she had been the other day—under some kind of stress.

Scott cleared his throat. "So, you know what happened yesterday." He looked at Mason. "You were there."

Mason nodded.

"Alexa calls me from the hospital, right, and I head over there to get her. She's her usual calm self, OK, like, yeah, this was a disaster for her professionally, but at least no one got badly hurt, apart from some bruises and scrapes, and she's insured, and the venue was insured, and the designer was insured . . . all good, right?"

Mason and Julia both nodded, waiting. He was a fast talker, and he was getting there.

"So, she asks me to get her something from her purse and I'm in there, OK, looking for whatever it was, it doesn't matter, and I find this." He pulled a folded piece of paper from his pocket and handed it to Julia.

She took it, unfolded it. Read it out loud.

"*Open your mouth, and I'll destroy you.*" She looked at Alexa. "Typed. Unsigned, obviously. When did you receive this?"

"Day before yesterday. In the mail. Regular mail."

Julia looked at Scott. "But she didn't mention it to you?"

He shook his head. "No. Nor did she mention the one that came last week."

"This wasn't the first?" asked Julia.

Alexa shook her head and reached into her purse. She handed Julia an envelope, from which Julia pulled an identically folded piece of paper. She read this one out loud, too.

"*Silence cuts both ways. You know what you did.*" She refolded the paper and looked at Alexa. "You mention this to the police?"

Alexa shook her head. "I see why Scott's upset. I see the connection. I'm just not . . ." She ran her hands through her hair and shook it back. "Scott made me come. I don't really want to make a big deal of this."

"What are they talking about?" asked Mason. "In the letter? What do they think you did?"

Alexa shrugged. "I have literally no idea."

Scott spoke again. "Whoever sent the letter must have been the one who caused the chaos yesterday. Alexa could have been killed, anyone could have been. I know you help people. We want to hire you to help us."

Alexa moved slightly, her hand clenching. Mason wasn't so sure she was on board with this plan.

Julia was watching Alexa. "Well, why don't we start small. If you have a dollar, you can hire me and then everything we discuss will be under attorney-client privilege."

Alexa smiled tightly and pulled a dollar from her wallet.

She handed it to Julia, who waved it at Mason. "Mason, please draw up a receipt for Alexa and enter her into the books as a new client."

Julia waited till Mason had written a quick receipt and handed it to Alexa, then she handed both notes to Will. "What do you see?"

He took them and put on his glasses. "Typed on an actual typewriter—that's interesting. Maybe they thought Alexa might recognize their handwriting." He flipped the papers over, glanced at the backs, held them up to the light, then returned to the content. "Anonymous is strange. Typed is strange. Let's face it, sending physical mail is somewhat strange these days."

"It has to be someone she knows, right? Or at least, someone who knows her." Scott was clearly very worried. "Alexa knows a lot of people, in and out of the program."

Julia nodded. "In all likelihood, yes. But it's still an unusual choice. First, the typing. There aren't that many typewriters around these days. Everyone prints everything." She shrugged. "But maybe they couldn't face setting up their printer to take this smaller paper. I know if I have to change the settings from fucking portrait to landscape it puts me into a decline for days." She waved the paper. "It's nice paper, actual letter-writing paper. For some reason that makes me think of an older person, but maybe I'm underestimating the younger generation."

"Generations, plural," muttered Mason.

Julia laughed, which was lucky. "Yes, you're right, of course, generations. I'm a boomer, right?" She pointed at Alexa—"You're Generation X"—then at Will—"You're a millennial"—and finally at Mason—"And you, child, are firmly Gen Z, bless your seamless socks and extensive therapy." She looked at them, one after the other. "So, tell me, do your generations still enjoy writing letters by hand?"

Will cleared his throat. "The sales of quality stationery have been steady, actually, over time. While it's nothing as common as it used to be, handwriting letters is still popular, particularly as it now carries the additional weight of being a deliberate choice, and something that requires effort. People often choose to handwrite invitations, special announcements, that kind of thing."

"Do you do it?"

He shook his head. "No, although I have taught myself to write in Klingon and Elvish, so I have special paper for that." He paused. "Klingon I only write using the standard Roman alphabet, but I write in Tengwar for the Elvish, obviously."

"Obviously," said Julia, calmly. "Much prettier."

"Exactly," replied Will. He hesitated, then added, "I have a special pen."

"Of course you do," said Julia. She turned to Alexa. "And you? Do you handwrite letters?"

"No, although I do handwrite my gratitude list, my daily tenth step, and other step work. I find it helps me connect with it." Alexa blushed. "That sounds very New Agey, but for me it's true." The tenth step is a daily reflection about things you might regret saying or doing, self-examination about things you might do better the next day, and is often shared with a sponsor. "I encourage my sponsees to do the same, but they don't always follow my suggestions." She looked at Mason, who grinned.

"One hundred percent text, all day, all the way." She raised her hands. "I think I can still write by hand, but on the few occasions I have to, it looks like a centipede has done two lines of coke, stepped in a tiny pot of ink and scrambled across the page in a hurry to get to somewhere else. Not exactly legible."

There was a pause.

"Thanks for the colorful image, Mason," said Julia. "Not sure who would sell a centipede the minuscule amount of drugs they could take, but your rich and vivid imagination will eventually come in handy, I expect."

Mason rolled her eyes.

"Alright, so someone made a choice to type the note, for reasons that will doubtless become clear. More importantly, the content." She looked at Alexa. "What are they referring to? You really have no idea?"

"I'm not sure," said Alexa, looking at her lap. "I've done plenty of stuff I'm not proud of—they could be referring to any number of things. And I don't have a lot of secrets. I talk pretty openly about my story. In meetings, with fellows, sponsees." She flicked a glance at her husband, and Mason wondered how much of an open book she was with him.

Julia regarded her thoughtfully. "You know, whatever you tell us is confidential."

As if reading Mason's mind, Scott spoke. "I can go for a walk."

His wife looked at him and made a face. "You know everything. It's not that."

Julia shook her head. "I think it is that. I think you do know what they're referring to."

There was a long silence. Then, "I really don't. But I can tell you a few things that might be it." She took a deep breath. "I was married and divorced in my twenties, twice. Both ex-husbands are still alive, and maybe one of them might still be pissed, even all these years later."

"Why?"

"Because I cheated on him with husband number two, who happened to be his best friend and, more importantly, his landlord and cocaine dealer."

"His dealer?" Julia raised an eyebrow. "Unforgivable."

Alexa nodded. "At the time we were living in a small town in Northern California. He was one of only two cocaine dealers in town, and the other was a violent asshole and, worse, a capricious overcharger."

Julia made a sucking noise with her teeth. "Painful."

Alexa laughed. "Yup. But I doubt Richard, the first husband, still gives a shit. It was a long time ago."

"And the second husband?"

"Dave. We're not in touch. When I last heard of him, he was still active, still drinking. I got sober, he didn't, we split up, didn't talk anymore, and eventually we divorced at a distance. I was a lot, back then. We had moved to Oakland after I left Richard and were totally chaotic for a year or so. Fucking or fighting, you know, that old two-step. We partied a lot, saw and did plenty, you know how it is."

"You lived at the Albatross then, right?" Scott frowned at her. "The building that burned down?"

Julia raised her eyebrows. "Why is that name familiar to me?"

Mason answered her. "Because back in the nineties it was a big story, certainly in the Bay Area. An old warehouse, turned into illegal artists spaces . . ." She paused. "The artists weren't illegal, the spaces were, you know what I mean. The owner was completely absent, the guy that theoretically ran the place was kind of a flake, and the day-to-day super was stoned most of the time. The place was a death trap, and during a big party, it became one." She looked at Alexa. "Were you there that night?"

"I was," said Alexa, shuddering. "It was dreadful. That place was nuts, a huge mess inside, walls made of art, salvaged furniture, electrical cables all over the place . . . and in the dark, and in the smoke, it was a maze nobody could navigate. Thirty people died." Her eyes clouded. "I lost friends."

"Was it arson?" asked Julia. "I remember it vaguely, but no details."

"It was ruled an accident," chimed in Will. "But the criminal and civil cases stretched on for years."

Alexa shook herself. "It was the end for me, actually. I left Oakland a week or so later and went into rehab in Southern California."

"Not the end," said Scott, putting his hand over hers. "The beginning."

Julia turned to Mason. "Are you making a list? We'll need to talk to all these people."

Mason sighed and opened her phone. "OK, two husbands, check. Big fire, check. I'll get the names and details once she's done. I have a feeling we have plenty more to go."

"Sadly," said Alexa, "we do. I left a lot of wreckage."

"We all did," said Julia, calmly. "I doubt you were as terrible as you think."

The office door opened, and Claudia came in, followed by Teddy. She was carrying a coffeepot, and he was carrying a large plate of cookies. Mason could smell them from where she was, and half rose from the sofa without meaning to.

Peanut butter cookies, for sure, and maybe something else.

Claudia smiled at Alexa. "You said you didn't want anything, but I thought you might have changed your mind.

Talking to Julia can wreak havoc on your blood sugar. And I made cookies—no nut allergies?"

"No allergies at all, except to hard work." Alexa grinned. She seemed to be relaxing.

"The prevalence of peanut allergies in adults is around one to two percent," said Will, reaching for a cookie. "Slightly higher in children, but not too much. And while peanuts are of course legumes, the rate of tree nut allergies is also somewhat similar. And the two can coexist, obviously."

"Obviously," said Mason, around a mouthful of peanut butter cookie.

"Alexa," said Julia, "this is Teddy Kettleman. He's a private investigator we work with extensively. If it's OK with you, I'd like him to sit in on the rest of this conversation, as I have a feeling we'll need to share the load."

Alexa nodded.

"Great, so let's continue with husbands and lovers."

"Fine." Alexa rubbed her hands on her pants, then reached for a cookie. "You're right, my blood sugar is getting low."

"Low blood sugar contributes to anxiety and dysregulation in a variety of interesting ways," said Will. "Lack of glucose impairs brain function, obviously, and also triggers the release of cortisol and adrenaline, which stimulates the release of stored glucose but makes you feel anxious and shitty. Furthermore, low blood sugar also reduces the synthesis of dopamine and serotonin, so you feel less calm and happy, and finally leads to physical symptoms such as shakiness or weakness that make you feel desperate and panicky. It's really a cascade of very bad things." He took a third cookie. "My own blood sugar level may explain why I'm having trouble not babbling about low blood sugar, in a probably irritating way."

"You're always informative," said Julia, pouring coffee. "And only very, very rarely irritating."

Will smiled around the cookie and reached for another.

"What else should we be looking at?" Mason brushed cookie crumbs from her lap and picked up her phone again.

"Um, I stole from a couple of employers, but I paid them back when I did my amends." Amends are part of the process of doing the steps, a practice of examining where you've been at fault and then trying to undo it, as best you can. Sometimes it's just acknowledging what you've done, apologizing for it and then changing your behavior; sometimes it's literal reparations, like repaying money or replacing totaled cars. "But, you know, they might be pissed. Can't imagine they'd be pissed enough to mail me weird threats, though."

"Probably not," agreed Julia, "but let's write it all down anyway. What about family?"

"My mom's passed on, my dad's in assisted living in Florida, I have a younger sister who's still active with alcohol, some cousins I was close with as a kid but not really anymore . . ." Alexa trailed off. "There's not much family left, to be honest. Most of my family is program people."

"And what about that?" said Julia. "What about people you've annoyed in meetings? There must be some. You can't be sober as long as you and not irritate some delicate flower."

Alexa thought about it, munching. "No one that springs to mind."

Julia frowned. "It's going to be a challenge, investigating people in the program. There is a serious and reasonable expectation of privacy in the rooms, and we're not going to break anyone's anonymity or ask anyone to gossip about anyone else. It'll be a delicate process."

Everyone turned and looked at Mason.

"What?" she said. "I can be delicate."

"Can you? I think the conversations in and around meetings might be better left to me," said Julia. "You can do other things."

"Like?"

"Like talk to the ex-husbands and employers." She turned back to Alexa. "Apart from Mason, do you have other sponsees?"

Alexa nodded. "Yes, I have two others right now. I'll ask them if it's OK for me to tell you their names and information." It was common practice to not share contact information or details about other members of AA without first getting their permission. It's not a secret society; it's just doing its best to be considerate. "I'm sure they'll help if you need them."

"Do they know about the letters?"

Alexa shook her head. "No. It's not something I wanted widely shared. I'm not sure I feel comfortable with you investigating at all." She looked at Scott.

"I don't feel comfortable with doing nothing," he said. "These are threatening notes, someone sabotaged your show, you could have been killed." He paused. "And even though you weren't, your business is damaged, and this kind of scandal can ruin your reputation."

Alexa smiled. "It's amazing I even have a reputation, considering the misspent youth I had. I can probably handle it."

Mason leaned forward. "Maybe I should come to meetings with you for the next few weeks, see if anyone looks suspicious."

"Everyone at meetings looks slightly suspicious," said Will. "And they won't like it if they think they're being observed."

Mason raised her eyebrows. "Well, I'll also be attending the meeting, right?"

There was a silence. Julia frowned. "No, let's keep it away from actual meetings. The purpose of attending meetings is staying sober. I don't want you to be doing anything other than that when you're there, and it doesn't feel right to be there with any other ulterior motive."

"People go to AA meetings for all kinds of reasons," argued Mason. "Aren't we just trying to help Alexa?"

Alexa reached over and put her hand on Mason's. "I appreciate that, baby, but as your sponsor and friend, I'm going to agree with Julia. Meetings are for you, and for everyone else there, to feel safe and work on staying sober. Let's keep this away from meetings as long as we can."

Mason made a face. "Fair enough, but if someone comes at you in a meeting, I'm going to throw hands."

"Totally reasonable. I won't stop you." Alexa smiled. "Not that it's a requirement of a sponsee, defending their sponsor, but you'd clearly do a better job than I would."

Julia was looking at Alexa thoughtfully. "I think you'd do just fine, actually. I imagine you were quite formidable in your youth."

Alexa sighed. "I was. Nothing like the woman I am now. Much more energy, for a start, and an aggressive commitment to being 'authentic' and 'creative,' which showed up in the form of partying with other people who called themselves artists and ignoring the rules of society. Things like paying rent or getting a job. Or being reliable. Or considering other people's feelings. And that's the tough part, right? The things we did when we were drinking are very often things we'd never do sober, but we can't change the past. We neither 'regret the past nor wish to shut the door on it.' It's one of the Promises."

The Promises is a section of the AA literature that talks

about the benefits of being sober, and not looking back in horror is one of them. Which, considering the things drunks and addicts get up to, is quite a big promise.

"Yeah, I'm not that woman anymore." She turned to look at her husband, who smiled gently at her. "But I have a sneaking suspicion she's coming back to haunt me."

8

WHEN MASON RETURNED after walking Alexa out, the office was empty, so she headed to the kitchen. Claudia was throwing grapes from one end of the table to Teddy, who was catching them in his mouth with a surprising degree of accuracy. Will was counting and had reached twenty-something, so this had clearly been the main activity since Mason had left.

Julia was sitting midway down the table, writing a list. She looked up as Mason came in.

"Alright, I'm dividing so you guys can conquer. Will's going to look into the friends, or ex-friends. Teddy is going to check employers and run a basic background check to make sure we're not missing anything." She paused. "And to make sure she's being straight with us."

"She's very honest," replied Mason, hearing a slightly defensive tone enter her voice.

"We're all honest," said Julia, looking back down at her list, "but that doesn't mean we're completely forthcoming. You can be honest but still leave shit out."

Mason shrugged. "And what about me?"

"Well, you're going to check out ex-husband number one. Will looked him up already. He's still up north."

Will nodded. "His last known address is only a year or so ago, so he's probably still there. He lives in Orinda. Do you know where that is?"

Mason nodded. "It's through the tunnel." She thought about her childhood in Berkeley, how people still talked about the Caldecott Tunnel fire, an incident that killed seven people after a gas tanker crashed and the tile-lined tunnel acted like a kiln, causing an incredibly hot fire. Clearly, fire was today's theme. "I seem to remember it's kind of fancy."

"Orinda is home to the oldest building in the East Bay," replied Will.

"Well, that one's probably not fancy," said Julia, "but thanks for the information."

"Did you just happen to know that," asked Mason, "or did you somehow google it in between counting grapes?"

"The latter," said Will, blushing. "I have a compulsive Wikipedia habit. I can't help it."

"There are worse habits," replied Mason.

"Many of which I also have," said Will, "but the wiki one is at least not potentially fatal."

"You have to go up north to see your family anyway," said Julia, "so it seems appropriate to have you do a little work while you're there. In fact, I already bought you a ticket. I bought two, actually." She raised her eyebrows at Mason. "If you think I'm missing out on a chance to meet the people responsible for your upbringing, you're delusional."

"Wait, you're coming with me?"

"Wouldn't miss it for the world," said Julia. "We'd go today, but we have the restaurant opening . . . which we can now write off as a business expense because we will talk to Jennifer, as well as enjoying her food." Jennifer and Iris had both texted Alexa back to confirm they'd be happy to talk to Julia, if it would be helpful at all.

"I'm not sure that's a good idea."

"Talking to Jennifer?"

"Coming with me to Berkeley."

"And yet I'm doing it. Some of my worst ideas have led to some of my best times, not going to lie. I have a feeling you and me are going to be in each other's lives for a while. I might as well get to know your family."

"I don't know yours."

"Well, if either of them ever come visit, I'll make sure you meet them. Don't sweat it, Mason, I'll be polite and charming. I promise."

"You're not the part I'm worried about."

"I'm sure your family is delightful. They produced you, didn't they?" She got to her feet. "I need to go change my clothes. I've been wearing this for too long."

They all watched her leave, then Mason turned to everyone else.

"My father has owned the same two pairs of shoes since I was in elementary school. My mom likes to wear one color at a time. I'm not sure this meeting is a very good idea."

"Oh, it'll be fine," said Claudia. "Julia never met a social situation she wasn't equal to."

"Like I keep saying," said Mason, "she's not who I'm worried about."

Teddy turned to her. "Hey, fascinating though this discussion of clothes and shoes is, I wanted to ask you about something: Claudia told me you'd received a box of letters and information that might clarify what happened to Jonathan Mann. Is that true?"

Jonathan Mann was Julia's late husband. He'd died or been killed (depending on who you asked) decades earlier, and Julia had been accused and convicted of his murder. She'd spent a decade and a half in jail, during which time she'd made some lifelong friends, gotten sober, and taken a law degree. When Julia and Mason had met, it had been just after Jonathan's old business partner, Tony Eckenridge, had been killed, and Julia had been accused of that murder, too. Solving that crime had brought them together.

Mason looked at him in surprise. "Yeah . . . several months ago, a few weeks after Tony's funeral. He'd packed up all this stuff to send to Julia if he died, and eventually it found its way to us. She wanted to throw it all away, but I managed to snag it before she could." She frowned at him. "How much do you know about Jonathan's death?"

Teddy shrugged. "Probably more than you and less than Julia. I didn't know her, or him, at the time, of course. I came into the picture much later, after she became friends with Claudia."

"You knew Claudia first?"

"I've known Claudia since we were kids, although we weren't in touch much in the years before we both ended up in prison. We kind of reconnected once we were out."

Mason nodded. "And she and Claudia met in prison."

"Yes. Became friends there, stayed friends after, then Claudia came to work for her. She and I reconnected before that, so I knew of Julia before I actually knew her. And I guess I'd always assumed she'd killed Jonathan, because she went to jail for it. But I don't think she did, actually. I've offered to sniff around for her, offered to look into it hard, in fact, but she doesn't want me to."

"No, she was pretty clear with me, too."

There was a pause as the two of them looked at each other.

"So," said Teddy, "I'll assume you've ignored her just as I have?"

"HUH," HE SAID, four minutes later. "That's pretty impressive."

Mason lived in one of the guesthouses farther up the hill behind Julia's house. Hers was the smallest, with just one bedroom up a spiral staircase above the living room, but what the bedroom had in spades was wall space. And that wall space was at least partially filled with everything Tony had sent her after his death. Newspaper clippings, letters, diaries, photographs.

"You went the whole hog with pins and string," noted Teddy. "It's always so pleasing."

"Sure," said Mason, reaching over and plucking one of the colored threads that connected a photo of Julia in rehearsal with a movie ticket for the premiere of *The Codex*, the movie she and Jonathan had been filming just before his death. "But I don't think the strings are actually in the right places at all. I just started doing it and then I couldn't stop."

"Totally relatable," he replied. "It feels good, connecting things."

"Yeah, and it looks awesome." Mason stepped away from the wall, which did indeed look like a very impressive detective movie set, or one of those TV procedurals everyone loves so much. There had been a tough first day or two, as Phil had been thrilled by this big new cat toy she'd installed for him, but they'd sorted it out.

Teddy stepped close to the wall and looked at some of the diary entries Mason had xeroxed. "Jonathan wrote about himself in the third person?" he asked.

Mason shrugged. "Sometimes. It's strange—he did when he was talking about his work, but less when he was discussing Julia or some other private life kind of thing." She pointed to another xeroxed page. "He refers to himself as The Director sometimes, other times just Mann . . ."

Teddy frowned. "Does it seem like he saw himself as separate people?"

"No idea. I spent weeks on this when the stuff first arrived, trying to put things in chronological order, trying to work out all the other people in his life, what mattered to him, et cetera, but then I ran out of steam. We got involved in other cases, other clients . . . and Julia really won't talk about any of this with me. She says she already did her time for the murder and talking about it now feels like extra weeks being added to her sentence."

"Sounds like Julia," said Teddy. "I think chronology is important. I like how you've started that process . . . but don't forget that history repeats itself, so look for patterns of behavior as well as dates."

"How do you mean?"

"Well . . ." Teddy started walking along the wall, pointing at things. "Are all these girls in the photos girlfriends? Affairs? Or just friends?"

"I believe they're all girlfriends, mistresses. Julia said their marriage was very open, that they both had other partners, although she's not volunteering anything much more than that. But most of these girls were actresses or crew . . ." She poked her finger at one of them. "This one was a makeup artist, that kind of thing. And I worked out who most of them were, reverse image searching online, or surreptitiously asking Will, who seems to know every face he's ever seen . . ."

"It's a curse," said Teddy, absently. "Imagine not being able to forget stuff you don't need anymore."

"And then looking through the diaries and desk calendars, I worked out that most of them lasted about six to eight weeks, and then there would be some kind of public spat, and then he would go quiet for a few months and then it would repeat again, new girl."

"Right," said Teddy. "So the pattern repeats."

"Yes," said Mason. "And it also waxes and wanes depending on where he was in the process of making a film. If he was in preproduction, he didn't have any side relationships; he was totally focused on work. Then once the filming began, he started to look about for entertainment, or distraction, or whatever, which doesn't make any sense to me, but then why should it? I would have thought he would be too busy for anything else, but apparently not."

"And you didn't find anything that suggested a motive for him to kill himself? Because that's what Julia always claimed, right? That he jumped off the balcony out there."

Mason nodded. "Yes, but Tony implied, in the letter that came with all this stuff, that the Mob had something to do with it, that he owed them money he had no way of paying back."

They both stood there a moment and stared at the wall.

"But there weren't any accounting books or ledgers or anything like that," said Mason. "Tony handled all the business of the studio. Jonathan was the creative guy, right?"

"So presumably Tony would have been the one who knew

all about the money stuff." Teddy looked around. "Is everything he sent here on the wall?"

"No," said Mason. "The rest, and the original diaries, are in that box over there. Help yourself."

Teddy went over and knelt down. "The first thing we need to do is catalog and list out all this stuff. Did you do that?"

Mason shook her head. "No."

"Well, that's job one. If you're going to be a PI, you'll need to get organized and detail driven. You'd be surprised how many cases get cracked because of a receipt, or a bill that got paid, or a parking ticket from the wrong place. All those little pieces of paper can be very important. An accurate calendar can be a hardworking friend."

"But there's so much less paper these days than there used to be," said Mason. "It's all digital now."

Teddy nodded. "Yup, but I still end up making lists. Whether they're in my Notes app or on my desktop, it's all a question of keeping track." He stood and pushed the box with his foot. "Start by listing every piece of evidence in here, organize them chronologically, then cross-reference everything so you can see how it all fits together. The wall is good, visual is good . . . but a detailed breakdown of data is better."

Mason sighed, and he laughed. "There's no rush. This case couldn't be colder, right? But it's good practice for you, and you can start doing it on Alexa's case, too. Pretty soon it'll just be a good habit."

"Huh," said Mason. "Never had one of those before."

9

JENNIFER'S NEW RESTAURANT was in Eagle Rock, a hip neighborhood with several excellent restaurants already. But in order to compete, you need to get in the race, and Jennifer was not one to turn down a challenge. Mason didn't know her all that well, but Alexa had shared details, and she'd heard Jennifer tell her own drinking story once or twice. Mason knew she was from Northern California, had lost a sister and both parents when she was young, had been homeless for a while and then gotten lucky with a job in a kitchen where the chef took an interest. Showing a natural aptitude for speed and accuracy, she rose to line chef and then saved enough money for culinary school. Too much drinking, too many drugs, too many jobs lost: Getting sober in the restaurant business is a challenge, but after a decade of trial and error, she made it. Now sober for a long time, she'd started working with Alexa a year or two earlier, not long after Mason had. She was friendly without being particularly warm, giving the impression she always had a pot on the boil somewhere else, which of course might literally have been true.

Tonight, Jennifer was working the room, greeting guests both personal and professional, and making sure everyone was within reaching distance of food at all times. The room was large and high ceilinged, with big wooden trusses under the roof, from which a hundred different office light fixtures dangled. The decor was eclectic, with booths and tables in cubicles, like an office had been taken over by a chef and an interior designer, which is essentially what had happened. The space had been an accountancy firm, and the designer had decided waste not, want not was the theme. Filing cabinets doubled as wine carts, typewriters and classic computers were dotted here and there, and the waitstaff wore green eyeshades and sleeve gaiters. The restaurant was called Oficina, and if the opening-night crowd was anything to go by, it was going to print money.

The gang was sitting in a booth, with Will tasked with making sure the food kept coming. For someone with more than a dash of social awkwardness, he was a king at attracting a waiter's attention. The advantage of being sober at events like this one was that you could keep eating, steadily and with complete control of your taste buds.

"The short rib flautas for the win," said Claudia, wiping her chin.

"Mushroom gorditas," argued Julia. "Or the masa cake with aioli."

"I like the guacamole," said Will, his mouth full.

Mason said nothing. She was still chewing.

Most people were drinking, of course, but their table was laden with a variety of nonalcoholic drinks and mocktails. Being sober, Jennifer had really leaned into the latter and offered nearly a dozen mixed drinks with no alcohol. As Mason gazed around at the littered plates and glasses, a waitress read her mind and arrived to clear the table.

"You guys OK?" Jennifer was right behind the waitress and smiled around. "Need anything at all?" She was tall and slim, with a head of enviably wavy blond hair and a strong nose that made Mason think of racehorses every time she looked at her.

Julia shook her head and smiled back at her. "Everything is delicious, the space is fun, I'm sure it's going to be a roaring success."

"Thank you," said Jennifer, watching the waitress stack glasses with an apparent disregard for the laws of physics. "Thoughts about the mocktails?"

"The one with plum and fresh ginger was amazing," said Will. "I had several of those."

Jennifer grinned. "Yeah, that's a good one. We're obviously stocking a lot of local wines and spirits, but I want the non-alcoholic drinks to be just as interesting."

"All local?" asked Claudia.

"Yeah, all California and almost all organic and biodynamic," said Jennifer. "I hired a sommelier who does it all for me, as obviously I can't taste the booze. She's great." She looked around. "There she is now. I'll introduce you."

She beckoned to a young woman standing with an older man, and in the end both of them came over.

"Hilary, meet Julia Mann and her lovely crew."

Everyone shook hands and smiled, and then Jennifer made her excuses, and she and the sommelier melted away. The older man stayed, though, and leaned over the booth, extending his hand.

"Julia Mann, it's really a pleasure to meet you. Justin Avermore. I'm a huge fan." He raised Julia's hand to his lips, lightly.

Julia smiled up at him. "How lovely."

Mason looked over at Will and rolled her eyes. He grinned at her. She'd had less time than he and Claudia to get used to this part of working for Julia. Julia's movies still played on classic movie channels all the time, and her Academy Award for one of them meant she was a permanent member of Hollywood royalty. She was frequently recognized when they were out and about, and Mason still found it slightly cringeworthy.

But Julia had no such issues.

"And are you a restaurateur as well?" She gazed up at the man, who was, now that Mason took a closer look, handsome and elegant, with a smile that cast a glow of charm over the whole table. He appeared to be younger than Julia by a decade or two, but the way he was looking at her suggested age was not only just a number, but also an irrelevance.

"No, I own a vineyard, just up the coast in Ojai. Jennifer was kind enough to include our wines on her list, and I came down to deliver a few extra cases for the party. This new restaurant is a wonderful opportunity for my vineyard. I appreciate it more than I can say." He looked knowledgeably over the glasses the waitress was carrying away. "Not a wine drinker, Ms. Mann?"

"Not a drinker at all, Mr. Avermore, and please call me Julia."

At this Will rolled his eyes back at Mason and then looked down at the table. Julia in full-charm mode was eye-watering, like looking directly at the sun.

"Alright, Julia. And please, call me Justin."

Julia dimpled, and Mason had to resist the urge to make a furball noise.

"Time to dance," said Claudia firmly, sliding out of the booth. Mason didn't dance, nor did Will, but they followed her out in order to give Julia some space.

They'd cleared a central area for dancing, and Claudia waded into the small crowd without a backward glance. Mason and Will made for a quiet corner and started snagging dessert bites from passing trays.

They watched from a distance as Justin and Julia talked and clearly flirted. They could hear her laughing and almost feel the breeze from her eyelashes. They couldn't look away; it was like a car accident. A bottle of wine appeared on the table in front of Julia, and Mason turned to Will.

"Do I need to worry about that wine?"

Will looked and shook his head. "No, she's good right now."

Julia had been sober a long time, but off and on. More off than on, and she'd been drinking when Mason first met her, six months earlier. Relapse can happen to anyone, at any time, and Mason found herself feeling nervous as Justin opened the bottle of wine and poured himself a glass. He offered Julia a sniff, but she shook her head.

"See?" said Will, holding a tiny tartlet between his fingers. "She won't even play. Don't worry, she's solid right now. Going to meetings, talking to her sponsor, doing the deal. It's OK."

Mason had been sober for nearly five years and knew sometimes there were signs that suggested a slip, or relapse, was imminent. Not going to meetings. Not calling other sober people. Not talking to your sponsor. But at the same time, you could be doing all of those things religiously and then suddenly the urge to get drunk or high would be stronger than the urge to stay sober and you were off to the races. They said there would come a time when you would be powerless over the first drink and only good habits and a strong faith in a higher power would save you. She watched herself every day, and she watched Julia now.

Jennifer came by with a small platter of desserts, which she handed to Will.

"I saw you grabbing the occasional passing sweet treat and thought I'd save you the effort. Here is a complete set." She paused, and pointed. "I recommend the Mexican s'mores."

Silently, Will and Mason took her recommendation.

"So, what was it you and Julia wanted to talk to me about?" asked Jennifer, watching them chew happily.

"What did you think about what happened at the fashion show the other day?" asked Mason.

"The vegetable puree? I watched the video, like, twelve times. Who knew the mayor had that kind of spring?"

"I thought you were there," said Will. "You were catering, weren't you?"

"My company was. I'd been there the day before checking setup, doing last-minute tasting adjustments, but I'd already left that day when the vegetables started flying. My people had it under control."

"I'm not sure if she's mentioned this yet, but Alexa has received some threatening notes . . ."

"Yeah, she said." Jennifer's attention was briefly drawn away by a waitperson, but she looked at Mason. "And you think that has something to do with the vegetables breaking?"

"I don't think they broke, in the classical sense. I think it was sabotage."

"Why?"

The same waitperson returned, somewhat breathlessly. "We need you in the kitchen, Jen."

Jennifer nodded, and shrugged at Mason and Will. "It seems a little far-fetched, to me, to go to all that trouble just to mess with Alexa. And it didn't really mess with her, right? No one was hurt, nothing bad happened." She grinned. "The s'mores are awesome, right?" She started to move away, then added over her shoulder, "If you have more questions or whatever, just yell, OK? Anything for Alexa."

And then she disappeared into the crowd.

Will licked his fingers. "Why aren't all s'mores made with cinnamon like that?" he asked.

"S'mores are America's greatest contribution to world cuisine," said Mason, airily. "I've always thought so."

"Not cheeseburgers?" asked Will. "I think an argument can be made for cheeseburgers."

"Nope," said Mason. "Cheeseburgers are just a variation on a meat-and-cheese sandwich. S'mores are wholly original, and often the thought of them is the only thing that keeps me going on a dark night."

"I had no idea," said Will.

Mason slowed a passing waitperson and grabbed two more. "It's a true story."

And then there was peaceful silence. Peaceful, slightly sticky silence.

IN THE CAR on the way home, Mason decided it would be fun to tease Julia.

"So, did Justin ask you out on a date?"

There was a pause. The temperature in the car dropped a little, and Claudia made a warning cough. Mason looked in the rearview mirror and saw Will shaking his head in the back of the car.

Julia was gazing out the window. "He invited me out to dinner, yes."

"On a school night?"

Another pause.

Then Julia said, "Are you attempting to make a joke about the fact that Justin is younger than me?"

Mason grinned. "Only a very small one."

"Yes," said Julia. "I see that. Hilarious. Were the genders reversed it wouldn't even cross your mind to question it."

"Yes, it would," replied Mason. "A serious age gap is comedy gold, in either direction."

"You're clearly not familiar with actual gold."

Mason wasn't going to be cowed by the ice queen. "He seemed very smitten."

"He was charming and intelligent. Well traveled. Successful. Interesting. Why wouldn't I want to go out to dinner, if only to see if my initial impression was accurate?"

"No reason at all."

"Right."

"And so you're going to?"

"Yes. Next week."

Mason bit her tongue, but it escaped. "Assuming his mother gives him permission."

"Mason, while I usually enjoy your lack of self-control, this would be one of those times where a little more of it would come in handy. As your colleagues will tell you, I don't enjoy or invite commentary on my romantic life, sexual life, or indeed personal life of any kind. We are friends, in the broadest sense of the word, and we are colleagues, but I would no more comment on your romantic proclivities than I would offer pointless fashion advice."

"Well, that's a load of . . ." said Mason hotly, thinking about the frequent comments Julia and the others made about her and Archie, but Julia held up her hand.

"No, save your breath. Let me be even clearer: Don't comment on my dating life. Don't ask questions, don't expect answers, don't speculate or hypothesize, and certainly don't make judgments."

"Alright." Mason subsided. She turned onto the steep canyon road that led to the house. "He seemed very nice."

"You barely spoke. Back off."

"It's nice for you to get out. Play with the other children."

Claudia started winding down the rear window. Apparently, in case she needed to jump out. Will began whistling under his breath.

"Mason."

"He might have had posters of you up in his bedroom in high school." She giggled.

"Mason."

"OK, I'm done." But as they pulled through the gateposts at the end of the driveway, she spoke again. "I'm forty years younger than you and I can barely keep up. Not sure a decade or two is going to give him the advantage he needs. Men don't have the stamina women do."

She pulled up in front of the house and had barely killed the engine before Will and Claudia were out of the car. She turned and grinned at Julia.

"I'm just glad you made a new friend."

Julia stared at her. Then she leaned forward and said, "Mason, what you know about romance would scarcely fit in a bottle cap. You know more about fashion, and you know nothing about that. I'll give you a pass for tonight, because this is the first time it's happened, but be warned. I don't want to hear another word about Justin or anyone else I choose to date, of any age, at any time. Understood?"

"Sure. Are you going to text him good night?" Her eyes were dancing. "Because it might be past his bedtime."

Julia sighed and got out of the car.

"Last warning, Mason."

Mason watched her boss walk into the house and grinned as she put away the car.

Challenge accepted.

10

YOU CAN, IF you want, get to the Bay Area by flying from LAX to SFO, the San Francisco airport. But sensible people choose to fly from Burbank (a small, delightful airport) to Oakland (same). Besides, Julia and Mason were going to the East Bay and would hopefully be able to avoid San Francisco altogether. (The relationship between San Francisco and Los Angeles is somewhat fraught: It's like two cousins, one of whom is studious and self-satisfied, and the other is fun-loving and debonair, and the studious one is all bent out of shape that the other one is so happy, and the other one . . . forgets they even have a cousin.)

Julia had rented a car, so once Mason had gone to pick it up and returned to get Julia (who had spent the intervening time sitting on a bench by the terminal, reading a book, never one for extraneous energy expenditure), they headed toward Berkeley.

"You presumably let your family know you were coming, right?"

Mason nodded. She navigated the ramp onto the 580, which at this time (and every other time) was a glinting river of barely moving vehicles. As an LA transplant, Mason had become a connoisseur of traffic, and the 580 always felt like a freeway that wanted to be part of the LA snarl but had to content itself with destroying the hopes of East Bay residents instead. It curves through Oakland and into Berkeley and points beyond, hugging the Bay, giving its occupants incredible views of San Francisco and its bridges, and the lovely hills of Berkeley . . . which they have plenty of time to enjoy, seeing as it takes approximately two weeks to go twelve miles.

Eventually, Mason exited the freeway and headed up into the hills, trading multiple lanes of traffic for the two-lane parking lot that was Ashby Avenue.

Julia was looking around with interest. "It's pretty here," she said, with some surprise. "I mean, it's small, but I like it."

"You don't know it. It's insufferably smug."

Julia raised her eyebrows.

"I babysat a lot when I was a teenager. Try giving a kid refined sugar in public. You'll raise a chorus of tutting tongues so loud you'll think you wandered into a tap-dancing convention. Everyone here has an opinion they're dying to share, and the only thing they agree on is that their way is the only way to do it. Regardless of what it is."

"And you *love* being told what to do."

"You know it."

"People have opinions in Los Angeles, too. I myself have strong opinions."

"Sure." Mason waited to make a left across traffic, heading up a steep residential street. "But when people share them, it's just to hear themselves talk, not to actually change behavior. Angelenos couldn't care less if you do what they suggest; they're too busy thinking about themselves. And the Bay Area has a pretty dark side: Zodiac Killer, Night Stalker, Golden State Killer, that murderous landlady in Sacramento, can't remember her name . . . the list goes on. Everyone thinks of LA as a big, dark city, and Southern California as the home of lunatics and fanatics, but Northern California has its fair share."

Julia laughed. "You sound like Will. I didn't realize you were such a true crime fan."

Mason shrugged. "I'm more interested in it than I feel is healthy, but you can blame podcasts . . . Some of them are just so good." She shot her boss a look. "What about you?"

"Nope," she said. "I've known too many true criminals to not just feel sad about the whole thing." She looked out of the window. "Are we nearly there? These twisty streets are making me nauseous."

The street wound up and up, climbing the hill in the switchbacks and tight curves so familiar to Mason. How many times had she driven this street? Thousands. Finally, she reached the turnaround at the top of the street, spun the car around and pulled into a space in front of her childhood home. It sat at the top of a path of stone steps that cut their way down the hill, a pedestrian shortcut only the healthiest attempted. Half a dozen houses sat on the flight itself, reachable only on foot, all inhabited by the same families Mason had grown up with. People rarely left these Berkeley staircases. Moving was just too damn exhausting.

Julia got out of the car and stretched, gazing at the view. "Well, that doesn't suck."

The Oakland hills to their left, the city of San Francisco directly in front, and the Golden Gate and Marin headlands to the right. A full panorama, all lying across the carpet of trees and variegated rooftops of Berkeley itself.

"Yeah," snorted Mason, "it's pretty." She grabbed the bags from the trunk. "If you like that sort of thing."

"Natural beauty and thoughtful engineering?"

"Whatever."

"You're so cranky, Mason."

Mason led the way to the gate to her house, muttering under her breath, "I don't like being home."

"I see that." Surprisingly, Julia put her hand on Mason's shoulder and squeezed. "I'm here."

Mason said nothing and led the way down moss-edged steps to her front door. At one point, she'd walked out of it hoping to never come back, yet here she was.

She raised her hand and rang the bell.

"OH MY GOD, what happened to your face? Are you drinking again? Did you get into a fight?"

Mason's mother, Barbara, was standing in the doorway, apparently waiting for an answer to her question before letting them into the house. Mason, who had forgotten her bruises, took a second to answer.

"No, I'm not drinking, and yes, I got into a fight, but it was for work, and you should have seen the other guy." She hesitated. "Can we come in?"

Barbara nodded, but her eyebrows were still set in a straight and uncompromising line. Then she looked at Julia and smiled, transforming her face.

"And you, of course, are Julia Mann. What a lovely surprise to see you, too. I'm a huge movie buff. *The Codex*, of course, but also *Angel's Flight*, *Seven for Hugo* and even that TV series you did, such a guilty pleasure."

Julia was still shaking her hand as she said all this, and as she dropped it, she raised one eyebrow. "Do you mean *Coffee Grounds*? That lasted one season. You might have been the only person watching it."

"Oh, I'm sure not. Everyone loved it."

"Well, not that they demonstrated by tuning in. It was an easy show to make, a nice cast, friendly people . . . and I needed the money."

"You'd just gotten out of prison, of course." Barbara's face looked sympathetic and interested, the neutral but supportive regard so familiar to her therapy clients. Mason's mother never hesitated to say the things that were on her mind. She saw it as refreshingly honest.

Julia went still for a second, but Mason saw it.

"That's right. I wish it had lasted longer, but them's the breaks." She paused. "The show, not the prison. That lasted plenty long enough."

"You don't act anymore?"

"Not for money, anyway."

Mason's mother wasn't sure what to do with that, so she just smiled enthusiastically. "My husband will be so happy you joined Natasha. He used to have such a crush on you."

Used to? Ouch. Mason frowned at Julia, but she seemed unbothered.

Mason's mom stepped back into the living room and waved her hand around. "Well, you're very welcome here. It's not every day we have a movie star in the hills." She looked at Julia and smiled. "I love your outfit."

Julia was wearing a vintage Pierre Cardin shift dress with polka dots around the hem, knee boots and a short cape with a fur collar. Pretty standard, for Julia. No hat, for once. Julia loved a hat.

Mason's mom was wearing L.L.Bean, top to toe. Soft pants, a functional T-shirt in, doubtless, pima cotton (no wrinkles!), and a matching cardigan. Suddenly and surprisingly, Mason felt a wave of affection for her mother, followed immediately by a sensation she couldn't quite put her finger on. It wasn't regret, exactly, but it was some flavor of sorrow. So much of her relationship with her mother had been about disagreeing over every little thing. Mason didn't know what to call the feeling, but she could certainly call it familiar.

"I'm very happy to be here, Barbara," replied Julia, looking around quickly for the location that would show her off to the best advantage and picking (accurately) a soft gray chair near the window. "When Mason told me she was rushing home to see you and her dad, I jumped at the chance."

That was somewhat revisionist, but Mason wasn't about to correct her.

Louise came down the stairs, stopping short as she walked through the wood-lined arch into the living room.

"Oh!" She looked at Mason. "What happened to your face? Fighting again?"

Mason sighed, but her mother answered for her. "She was, but only for work."

"Oh, that's so much better." Louise looked at Julia. "I see you brought reinforcements."

Louise was very tall, like some ancient relative no one could remember, because the rest of the family were pretty average. She stepped forward to shake Julia's hand, much as her mother had done. Unlike Barbara, hers was all business.

"This is Julia Mann, Louise. My boss."

"Good to meet you," said Louise. "You have my sympathy."

Julia got to her feet and took her hand, smiling. "I don't need it but thank you."

"I can't imagine having Natasha working for you is all that easy. She's not very . . . compliant."

Julia cocked her head to one side, slightly. "I don't actually require compliance from my colleagues. I require intelligence, bravery, out-of-the-box thinking and a certain element of je ne sais quoi, a freedom of spirit. Mason has all of those things in buckets."

Mason bit her tongue. Her throat was tight, suddenly.

Louise was wrong-footed but recovered quickly. "Well, you know your business." She looked over at Barbara. "Mom, Dad is awake. He's asking for coffee."

Barbara frowned. "Well, he can't have it." She headed toward the stairs. "Excuse me. I'll let him know you guys are here, but he's not really supposed to get up." She looked over her shoulder at Julia. "I might wait to mention you. Not sure if I can contain him if he knows there's a beautiful woman in the living room."

"I imagine he's used to it." Julia smiled.

AFTER HER MOM had disappeared up the stairs, Mason turned to Louise.

"So, what did the cardiologist say?"

"That he'd had a warning, that it was time to change his lifestyle, start exercising more, eating less red meat and butter, that kind of thing. You know."

"And less coffee?" Mason raised an eyebrow. Their father

was an inveterate caffeine fiend, regularly starting the day with a triple shot and going on from there.

Louise nodded. "He agreed, theoretically, but the practical application of that agreement hasn't sunk in yet. He asks for coffee more than anything else."

"Some things are harder to quit than others."

"You would know."

Mason nodded but didn't rise to the bait. Louise liked to needle her, but she wasn't going to let it get to her in front of Julia. Strangely, Julia did it for her.

"You've never had to give up anything, Louise? No bad habits you wish you'd never started?"

Louise laughed. "My first marriage. But apart from that, no. I try not to get involved in stuff that I can see is going to end in tears. I like to think things through to their logical conclusion, plan ahead, you know?"

Julia nodded, rearranging herself on the chair to better deflect the midday light pouring through the windows. "Sadly, it's not always possible to see that conclusion at the outset, but I agree that's the best policy. Not one that I myself have ever followed, but I hear it works."

There was a minor commotion on the stairs, and Barbara appeared, accompanied by a man who did not in any way look like he'd just had a heart attack, minor or otherwise.

Tall, straight-backed and with a shock of white hair, Mason's father was a psychiatrist and professor at Berkeley, used to being listened to and attended to. However, at that moment, he was blushing and stuttering as he approached Julia.

"My goodness, what a pleasure. When Natasha told us she was working with you, we were quite enchanted. Your work has brought us so much joy over the years."

Julia stood and took his hand, smiling and giving the full star wattage she was capable of turning off and on so easily.

"Mr. Mason . . ."

"Please, call me Doug . . ."

Mason's eyes met Louise's, and they both rolled them simultaneously. Dr. Douglas Mason was only very rarely Doug. Their mother called him Dougie, but only in the privacy of their own home, and his students and patients called him Dr. M. But clearly, this was an important moment for him.

"Doug," said Julia, "thank you so much for the wonderful job you did raising Mason. She's been an invaluable addition to my team."

Mason was slightly taken aback. It was always nice to hear you were appreciated, and she was glad Julia wasn't mentioning the flea issue, but she wondered why her boss was laying it on so thick. Maybe it was just her habit to charm.

Doug laughed. "Well, I'm sure she's happy to be working." He walked over to Mason and gave her a hug. "How you doing, sweetheart? What happened to your face?"

Mason shrugged. "I was doing my job. I'm more interested in how you are."

"Oh, I'm fine, this was nothing. Everyone's making an unnecessary fuss. Do I smell coffee?"

"No," said Barbara, "that's just wishful sniffing on your part." She got up and left the room, adding, "I can get you some decaf." She paused at the door. "Regular for everyone else?"

Nods around the room. Mason's father groaned, "Is decaf coffee really even coffee? Maybe you should just bring me a cup of hot water with some twigs in it."

"Do you mean tea?" asked her mother.

"Sure," he replied, the fight visibly leaving him.

"Had you been feeling bad for a while?" asked Mason. "Or did this come out of the blue?"

Her father shrugged, an unconscious precursor to Mason's own habitual response to most questions. "You know, the usual stresses. Work has been a little challenging of late." He sat down heavily on the sofa and sighed. "I feel fine." As every line of his body radiated exhaustion, this was in no way convincing, but maybe it felt good to say it. "The doctor said it barely registered as a heart attack, really. More of an *episode*."

Louise snorted. "That is not what he said. He said it was a mild heart attack, but that you should think of it as a warning shot, with every possibility of further shooting to come. It's time to talk about retirement, Dad."

Mason's eyebrows flew up, and she looked at Julia without thinking. Julia's expression was calm but interested, a familiar look for her. She said nothing, but Mason couldn't help herself.

"Retirement? Is that what you want, Dad?"

"No, of course not," he replied. "It's a ridiculous idea. Internal politics at the department have made things a little rough lately, but I'm sure they'll calm down. The basic work of the job is still what it always was, students and lectures and essays, and I can handle all that with no problem at all."

Mason was conscious of an undercurrent she didn't quite understand, as though Louise and her father were talking about something they weren't saying. "What internal politics?"

"Oh, just the usual back-and-forth, sweetheart, nothing out of the ordinary. I guess I just let it get to me a bit."

Mason opened her mouth to ask more questions, but just then her mother returned with a tray of coffee cups.

"What are we talking about now?" she asked.

"Nothing," said Louise, firmly.

"Dad's stress at work," said Mason, equally firmly.

Barbara made a moue of disapproval. "We need to keep things quiet and calm right now, Natasha. No need to bring up uncomfortable subjects."

"I didn't bring it up, actually . . ."

"Your father needs to rest. He doesn't need to get all worked up again."

"So, he was getting worked up?" Mason looked at her father. "To the point that it triggered a heart attack? That worked up? What's going on, Dad?"

"Really, Natasha, there's no need to take that tone with your father . . ."

"Mom, I'm not taking a tone. I'm asking a question, born of concern, that's all." Mason took a deep breath.

"It's being handled," said Louise, clearly. "We're handling it."

Mason felt a flare of injured anger, yet another familiar feeling in this context. "And you don't need my help?"

"No," said Louise, "insofar as your help usually comes in the form of lighter fuel on a barbecue. You never met a problem you didn't instantly escalate."

"That's unfair," replied Mason, stung. "You barely know me these days."

"And yet," replied her sister, indicating Mason's bruised and battered face, "leopards clearly haven't changed their spots."

There was a pause. Julia cleared her throat.

"Delightful coffee, Barbara," she said. "Colombian, if I'm not mistaken?"

And that was the end of that.

11

THAT AFTERNOON, JULIA and Mason got back in the car and headed inland to Orinda. Will hadn't been able to turn up a phone number for their quarry, Alexa's first husband, Richard Streppo, but he was still getting services at his address, so Julia had decided they should just go and see for themselves if he was there. Mason was still peevish about the conversation with her family and was more than happy to flee the scene. She could feel her tension dissipating. She always felt better when she was on the move.

They got through the tunnel without incident and turned off to Orinda. It was a classic Northern California small town; Craftsman houses dotted the hills alongside more modern homes, and pulling into downtown was like stepping back in time. Not all that far, but back to when a lovely movie theater might be the heart of a Friday night.

"I need more coffee," said Julia. "There must be a Starbucks or something."

Mason drove around downtown, which didn't take very long, until she spotted the familiar chain logo. Running in, she was surprised by the crispness of the air, the coolness of the season. She always forgot how much cleaner the air was up here, she was so used to the smog. Los Angeles feels sparkly because of the sunshine, but you can see the pollution every time you fly in or out, and she took a deep breath and could taste the difference. Clean air wasn't enough incentive to live here, but it was pleasant. She carried the beverages back to the car and got in.

"Alright," said Julia, taking a big swig of her iced cold brew. "Do you have the address?"

Mason nodded. "It's like two minutes away. Are you ready or do you want to drink your coffee first, go pee, fix your make-up, whatever?"

Julia frowned at her. "Let's go."

Richard Streppo's house was a seventies ranch, anonymous in its similarity to its neighbors. There was a tricycle outside, a swing set that didn't look like it got much use, and a variety of chewed dog toys. A family house, clearly.

Mason pulled up a little way past the drive. There were no cars parked, no signs of life. She turned to Julia.

"What's the story here?"

"How do you mean?"

"Well, what are we saying? Hi, we're here to talk to you about an ex-wife you haven't thought of in over twenty years, just in case you've been sending her hate mail?"

Julia nodded. "Yes, basically. Wherever possible, just go with the truth."

"Really?"

Julia swung open the door. "Yes, really."

There was no answer to their knock, but as they stood there, they became aware of the distant sound of hammering and, fainter still, a radio playing seventies soft rock.

"Around the back?" Mason asked.

Julia nodded and turned to lead the way. Mason marveled at how she always looked like a model at the end of a runway, spinning elegantly to show off her clothes. It was just part of who Julia was, factory installed, baked in. Mason clumped after her, a Clydesdale following a racehorse, and grinned to herself at the image.

The driveway curved around the house, and they followed it. The air was cool with a slight dampness that suddenly made Mason shiver. Behind the house was a detached garage, its double doors open. A car was up on blocks, and a pair of legs stuck out from underneath with, hopefully, the rest of a man attached to them.

Julia stopped about ten feet away and spoke. "Hello? Mr. Streppo?"

Both feet jumped, which was satisfying in a comedic way, and after a moment of scrabbling, a man slid out from under the car, on one of those wheeled platform things mechanics use for precisely this purpose.

Richard Streppo, assuming it was him, was a still-very-attractive man in his mid-fifties. Tanned, high cheekbones, a shock of dark hair barely touched with gray. A wide mouth, a nose with a charming bump in the middle. He frowned and sat up.

"Yes, hello? I wasn't expecting anyone."

"Yes, I'm sorry, we couldn't locate a number for you. I'm Julia Mann, and this is my associate Mason."

"Just Mason? Like Prince?"

Mason grinned. "Natasha Mason, but people only rarely call me Natasha."

He nodded, folding his legs up and resting his arms on

them. Despite the suddenness of their arrival, he seemed to have recovered from his initial surprise. Now they were just three strangers talking, nothing unusual to see here.

"And you're looking for me?"

Julia nodded. "Yes."

He smiled and put down the socket wrench he'd been holding. It made a faint clink on the ground, the air still around them. "How can I help you? I hope you're not selling anything. I'm not buying."

"No," said Julia. "We're up here from Los Angeles. We're looking into a situation that concerns an old friend of yours, Alexa Rousso."

Richard was still smiling, but now his face froze in thought. "Alexa?"

Mason nodded. "You and she were married."

His face relaxed, suddenly, and he laughed. "Yes, I remember. It was a long time ago, and feels even longer than it was, change being what it is. I'm not that man anymore, and I doubt she's the same woman, either."

"She would say not," said Julia, shifting her weight. "Is there somewhere I could sit down? I would be more comfortable."

Richard Streppo jumped to his feet, easily. "Of course, I'm so sorry." He pointed over to where a small café table and chairs sat under a tree. "Let's go there. Would you like some coffee or anything?"

"A glass of ice water would be good," replied Julia, eyeing the chairs, which were wrought iron, "and maybe a cushion of some kind for my bony butt."

Richard laughed and headed into the house. Julia and Mason sat and looked at each other.

"He seems very relaxed," said Mason.

"He does," agreed Julia. "And why not? We're not very threatening."

"You scare the crap out of me on a regular basis," said Mason.

"Ah, that's because you know me."

Richard came back out of the house carrying a pitcher of ice water and three glasses, a seat cushion tucked under his arm. Offering it to Julia, he put everything else on the table and poured them each a glass of water.

Then he sat, a glass in his hand, and smiled at the two women. "OK, so what's going on with Alexa? I haven't heard from her or spoken to her in over two decades. Is she alright?"

"Yes, largely," said Julia. "But someone is sending her threatening notes and may have thrown giant vegetables at her."

"I'm sorry?"

"They weren't real." Mason made a reassuring face.

"And we're trying to help her discover who and why that might be."

"And she thought it might be me?" He tipped his head, quizzically, thinking about it. "I don't have access to giant vegetables."

"They weren't real," Mason said again.

He stared at them both. "Well, regardless of that, I guess we ended things pretty badly, to be fair. I was angry as hell with her. But back then I was angry about almost everything." He shrugged. "Like I said, not that person anymore."

"Would you be able to get in touch with Alexa if you wanted to?" asked Mason. "Do you even know where she is?"

"Well, you just implied she's in Los Angeles, and I guess I knew that already. But I don't have a number for her, or address or anything." He grinned. "Although these days you can find anyone online and addresses are kind of old-school, right?"

"They are," said Mason. "Do you follow her on social media?"

He shook his head. "I don't really have it. I mean, I have it, but I don't use it much. My kids and I watch TikToks sometimes." He laughed. "Cat videos, that kind of thing."

"How old are your kids?"

"Ten and twelve."

"Peak age for cat videos."

He nodded. "My wife knows I was married before, but we haven't talked about it much." He squinted up at the sky, despite there not being much sun. "I got sober twenty years ago, changed everything about my life. I left a lot of things behind, and Alexa was one of them. I'd actually love to reconnect, see how she's doing. Is she well?" He paused. "Apart from the vegetables."

Mason nodded. "She's good, but a little worried." She hesitated, wanting to tell him Alexa was sober, too, that she was happy, that she was a sponsor, a sober woman at peace, but the program frowns on that kind of disclosure. She closed her mouth.

Julia drank some water and looked thoughtful. "What do you remember about that period of time, the time you two were together?" she asked. "The person who's threatening her has implied she did something in the past she should be ashamed of or should take responsibility for. Can you think of anything they might be referring to?"

Richard laughed. "It depends on your definition of 'shameful,' I guess. We drank all the time, cheated on each other, sold drugs for more money than they were worth, stole from convenience stores, stole cars, borrowed things from friends with no intention of returning them, that kind of thing. In fact, we could have done all of that in a single day. We were not in any way good people back then." He made a face. "I like to think I'm a good person now, but if I don't remember my capacity for bad behavior, it tends to reoccur."

"What about people you used to hang out with? What about the man she left you for . . ." Mason looked at her phone. "David McGann. Are you still in touch with him?"

Richard laughed. "Dave? My God, I haven't thought of him in decades, and there was a point in my life where I would happily have gutted him like a fish." He raised his hands. "Not literally. Dave was my dealer, our dealer, and Alexa running off with him kind of put a crimp in my supply for a while. I wonder what happened to him." He made another face. "Dave was much more hardcore than I was, more literally criminal, rather than just feckless and addicted. He hung out with a heavier crowd, and I guess Alexa did, too."

Julia smoothed her hands on her lap. "Hopefully, we'll find out. He's on our list. They were together for quite a while, then lost touch."

"Dave's crew was pretty eclectic," said Richard. "There was a guy named Fuzzy, I remember that."

"Well, Fuzzy is a memorable name," replied Julia, smiling.

"It was a bad name for him, because he was a cranky asshole and not in any way a soft or appealing person. He used to sell drugs to Dave; he was the next up in the food chain, if you follow me. He ran girls, he could get rid of stolen cars, he could find you someone who would beat someone for money, that kind of thing. At the time it felt dangerous and exciting, you know, like we were all too cool for school, living on the edge. He was also a graffiti artist, with a lot of talent and a reasonable amount of street cred." He made a wry face. "But the whole thing was just sad and kind of lame. Small-time criminals, living in a small town, doing small shit and dreaming of making it big in some amorphous, creative way. Fuzzy did a lot of work for some rich kid whose name I forget." He laughed. "This was when we were all living in a nothing town near the coast, up in Sonoma: Tomales. Being the baddest baddie in town was nothing to brag about, but Lex and I thought we were Bonnie and Clyde." He rubbed his hands through his hair, shot a look over at the car, waiting patiently for whatever work they had planned together. "She and Dave moved to Oakland, and I think Fuzzy did, too, and a few other people. They needed a bigger city." He glanced at his watch. "Is this going to take much longer?"

"I doubt it," replied Julia. "Apart from Fuzzy, anyone else spring to mind?"

Richard pondered, looking at the ground. "There was a woman named Lisa Rawlings that Alexa used to pal around with. She was more into the sex part of sex, drugs and rock and roll. Lex and I were all drugs and rock and roll, if you know what I mean. No judgment. We all do what we need to do to stay afloat, right? But she helped Fuzzy with the girls sometimes, you know. She might know something. No idea where she is. She might still be there, for all I know, or long dead." He shrugged. "They might all be dead. Addicts and criminals aren't known for their longevity, right?"

"Not usually, no." Julia stood and stretched. "Thank you for your time, Mr. Streppo. Mason will give you our number, if anything else occurs to you."

"Will you give my number to Alexa? Tell her I'd love to reconnect, catch up. It's been a long time, plenty of water under the bridge, you know?"

Julia smiled. "If you give us your number, we certainly will. Whether or not she'll reach out, I can't say."

"I owe her an amends," he said ruefully. "I didn't make her life any easier back then. Mind you, she didn't do a lot for mine, either. We loved each other as best we could, but our best was pretty shit." He stood up, stretching like Julia had done. "I hope you find what you're looking for."

Mason wrote their contact details on a card and gave it to him, nodding. "We hope so, too. She's worried."

"She was never a bad person, Alexa. She did bad things from time to time, we all did, but her heart was usually adjacent to a good place, at least."

"She's still a good person," said Mason, turning to follow Julia up the driveway. "She means a lot to me."

"That's nice," he replied, watching them leave. "She meant a lot to me, too, despite everything."

BACK IN THE car, Julia called Will and put it on speaker.

"Here's a fun one for you. I need you to track down a guy named Fuzzy, who operated various criminal enterprises, and I use the term loosely, back in the nineties in and around Tomales, Northern California. And then later on in Oakland."

"Tomales is where they filmed *Bandits*, a largely unsuccessful Bruce Willis movie, also featuring Cate Blanchett and Billy Bob Thornton."

Mason frowned. "There is no way you had time to wiki that. You already knew it."

There was a silence on the line. Then, "Yes, sadly, I already knew that. I can't control the contents of my head." He paused. "But I wiki'd it now and it turns out several other movies were at least partially filmed there, including *Village of the Damned*."

"Well," said Julia, crisply, "while that is fascinating from a movie buff's point of view, it's not really germane to this inquiry, is it?"

"No," he replied, softly.

"So, returning to the matter at hand, we need to track down Fuzzy, and a woman named Lisa Rawlings, also active at the time. Check arrests for prostitution or related offenses. And look for known associates. Alexa's ex remembered Fuzzy working for some rich kid but couldn't remember his name." She paused. "I assume it was a guy, but I guess a kid could be either."

There was the sound of typing. "OK, got it. I'll see what I can do. Tomales is a very small place. I may widen the search to nearby Petaluma, which is a much bigger city, and down to Oakland. Petaluma isn't a big city, but definitely big enough to support various nefarious industries. Apart from chicken production, which was one of its main industries for many years, giving rise to the nickname Chickaluma, and making it the 'Egg Capital of the World' for a while."

"Focus."

"I'm focused. I'm just focused on multiple tasks at once. My neurodivergent superpower."

"Fair enough. I can hardly complain when that superpower is so often helpful to our endeavors."

"Winona Ryder's from Petaluma."

"Fantastic. Good for her. Mason's going to write up notes

from our conversation with Richard Streppo and send them to you."

"I am?"

"You are. Will, were you able to track down Dave McGann? Alexa's second husband."

"Yes, and you're in luck, he's also still in Northern California. Oakland, right along from Mason's house."

"My parents' house, not mine."

"Thanks for the correction, yes, your parents' house."

Julia looked at her watch. "Send us his number. We'll try and see him today, too. I want to get back to Los Angeles as soon as I can."

Mason looked at her. "I thought you were smitten with Berkeley's verdant, relaxed charm? Its counterculture vibes, its wholesome atmosphere."

"It's fine," said Julia, tapping her fingers on the car door. "It's fine. I just get antsy when the air is too clean. My lungs aren't used to it."

Seeing as she'd been thinking much the same thing, Mason said nothing.

12

THERE WAS NO answer when they called Dave McGann, so Julia left a polite message and turned to Mason.

"Well, we have some time to kill, assuming you want to avoid hanging out with your family. What shall we do?"

"How about a meeting?"

Julia gazed out of the window, but Mason could hear her eyes rolling. "Sure, that would be the right thing to do. I was thinking we could get matching tattoos on Telegraph Avenue, but OK, you can be sensible."

"Well, I'm driving, so you'll have to look up times." Mason handed over her phone. "There's an app. Look for the icon of a folding chair."

Julia busied herself with the phone, commenting caustically on the sheer number and variety of apps Mason had, then fell silent, scrolling.

"Huh," she said, "there's actually one soon, but it's outdoors."

Mason nodded. "In Tilden Park?"

"Yeah, is that close?"

Mason nodded again. "Is it by the trains? I've been to that meeting before. But that was a Sunday morning."

"Well, then you're in luck, because there's one today, too. I'm hungry, though."

"On Sunday they have food . . . people bring baked goods. It was always a feature. I remember a pumpkin loaf that was worth staying sober for all on its own."

TILDEN PARK IS two thousand acres running along the ridge of the Berkeley Hills, and it was one of Mason's favorite places growing up.

"I'm telling you, I spent months of my life, cumulatively, at the Little Farm," she told Julia, as they drove through the park. "I spent hours every weekend watching the chickens and goats and whatever. I think my parents thought I was nuts. I mean, kids love animals, right? But I was OBSESSED."

"I can see that," said Julia, mildly, the corners of her mouth twitching. "Is it still there?"

"I think so," said Mason.

"Well, maybe we can go after the meeting."

Mason shot her a glance, but her face was innocently radiating supportive enthusiasm. Mason narrowed her eyes. She wasn't fooled for a second.

"You? At a farm?"

"Why not?" asked Julia. "I can handle a few feathers, even if they're not ostrich." Her phone chimed and she flipped it around to read the text. Mason flicked her a glance and caught the edges of a smile.

"Huh . . . new boyfriend?"

Julia frowned at her. "We covered this, Mason. Keep your beak out of my business." She paused. "But yes, that was a text from Justin confirming dinner. I like a man who confirms, don't you?"

Mason shrugged. "As you yourself pointed out, I don't have a hell of a lot of experience with romance, and even less with traditional dating. The men and women I go out with tend to have mutual interest as their sole selling point. I'm not looking for a relationship. I don't think I'm actively looking at all."

"Except for Archie."

"I have no idea what you're talking about. That lack of beakiness cuts both ways, Julia."

They pulled into the parking lot adjacent to the steam trains and quickly found a space. Luckily, both of them were ready to drop the personal discussion.

Walking through the parking lot, they saw a few other people heading toward a raised area at one end, surrounded by trees. Fortunately, when they reached the meeting, there were many unoccupied chairs, and they were able to sit. After, that is, Julia had raided the fairly substantial snack table, snagging a slice of banana bread and a cup of coffee.

"This is very civilized," she muttered to Mason, settling herself down and taking a bite. "NorCal drunks are clearly more domesticated than SoCal ones." She went to put the banana bread on her knee but realized her dress would get a mark, so she put it on Mason's knee instead.

"Look, my home group meeting has donuts all the time. And the Saturday evening meeting has pizza." Mason took a corner of the banana bread. Knee tax.

"Yes, but is it homemade and delicious?"

"Not homemade; yes, delicious." Mason frowned at her. "It's not a contest." She looked across the circle at the view of the hills behind the park, with Mount Tamalpais in the distance. There were still a few minutes until the meeting started, and people were chatting quietly and greeting one another. The soft curves of the hills were every shade of green, the birds were singing, the afternoon sun was spangling each leaf with gold . . . She couldn't wait to get back to Los Angeles.

JULIA HAD HER phone silenced during the meeting, but when it was over, she discovered Dave McGann had called her back. She hit speaker.

"Hi . . . this is Dave McGann returning your call. I've got nothing to say about Alexa Rousso, I haven't spoken to her in decades, I know nothing about her life now and I'm happy for it to stay that way. End of story. Thanks for calling. Don't do it again."

Julia looked at Mason and raised her eyebrows. "Charming."

"Well, to be fair, he has no idea who we are, and why should he care about Alexa after all this time?"

"Sure, but wouldn't you be curious?"

Mason shrugged. "Perhaps he's just not the curious type."

"Or perhaps he's still mad. We need to talk to him." She turned the phone to face Mason. "Here's the address. Let's go."

Mason looked at the time. "We're going to hit late-afternoon traffic getting to Oakland and then early-evening traffic coming back."

"So?"

Mason pursed her lips. "OK, you're the boss."

ALEXA'S FIRST EX-HUSBAND seemed like he'd landed on his feet after her. Dave McGann, not so much. Of course, decades had intervened, and who knows what choices and decisions had brought him to this shitty corner of downtown Oakland, but let's just say he hadn't stuck the landing.

Mason stood in the street and checked the address. "Well, this is the right place. It doesn't look like anyone actually lives here." She looked at the stack of labeled doorbells by the door. "His name's not listed."

"You have the apartment number, right?"

Mason nodded.

"Press it, then."

Mason did so. They waited, and Mason listened to the sounds of the city. Oakland really is a city, in a way Berkeley is not. Broken everything, trash everywhere, it was much more comfortable for Mason than Berkeley was. She leaned on the bell again, giving it a bit more emphasis.

"Fuck off," said a voice. "Fuck all the way off."

Mason grinned. "He's home."

"Christmas came early," said Julia. "Press it again."

"No, really," said the voice in response, "fuck off to the end of the street, turn the corner, then fuck off all the way down THAT street."

"I like this guy," said Mason, stepping out into the street and looking up at the windows. She didn't even know if the apartment had windows on the street, but she was hopeful. "You press it now. My finger is tired."

A window flew up and a man stuck his disheveled head out, glaring down into the street. "Who the hell are you and why aren't you going away?"

Mason stuck her hands in her pockets and gazed up at him, grinning. "Hi there! Having a tough day?"

"Having a tough life, so I repeat, fuck off. I'm not buying anything from anyone."

"We're not selling," replied Mason, as Julia joined her in the street. She looked over her shoulder. The occasional passersby were slowing to see if this was about to turn into a show. She hoped it wasn't.

"Hello there," said Julia. "Are you David McGann?"

He squinted at her. She was obviously still wearing the dress and boots combo she'd had on this morning, and standing on the Oakland street, she resembled a flamingo wandering through a parking lot.

"I am. Are you the woman who called me earlier?"

"Yes," she replied. "I'm Julia Mann. This is Mason, my colleague. We wanted to talk to you about Alexa Rousso."

Full-on scowl. "I've got nothing to say about that bitch. We were finished decades ago."

"And you're clearly over it," said Julia calmly. "Someone is threatening her, and we're trying to find out who."

"Why would it be me?" he said, scoffing. "I have nothing to say about her and even less to say to her."

"Could we maybe talk about this inside?" asked Julia. "Looking up at you is giving me a pain in the neck."

"You're a pain in the neck," he replied. Then he sighed. "OK, come up. This day couldn't get any shittier." He slammed the window.

Julia looked at Mason. "We'll see about that," she said.

DAVE McGANN HADN'T been lying. He was clearly having a tough life. Walking into his apartment reminded Mason of walking into an animal shelter: the smell of desperation, antiseptic and an underlying peat layer of cat shit.

And there was a cat. Sitting on the table in a beam of

sunshine, sleek and well-fed, a Siamese with perfect seal-point coloring. Gorgeous, glossy, proud without being showy, you know the kind. She curled her tail more tightly around her back legs as the strangers came into her world, ready to accept whatever offering they'd brought her.

Her owner stood uncertainly in the center of the room, rumpled and anxious underneath his obvious anger. He had probably once been as good-looking as his cat—his bones were good, his eyes were a deep and pleasing blue—but the years had been unkind. Time and whatever else he'd done to himself. Deep grooves ran from his cheekbones to his puffy jawline, his brows were drawn together in a rictus of self-protection, and the smell of poorly metabolized alcohol came off him in almost visible waves.

A drunk. Still active, still caught in the jaws of his addiction. Still losing the daily fight, and unclear if tomorrow was going to be worth fighting for.

Mason looked around for somewhere clean enough for her boss to sit and spotted a chair that might serve. It was covered in a pile of bills, but she lifted them off and placed them carefully next to the cat, who didn't turn a hair. She blinked, but that was the only sign she wasn't carved from marble.

Dave said nothing as Julia made her way to the chair and sat, arranging her legs to her comfort and turning a beaming smile at him.

"We appreciate you making time to talk to us, Mr. McGann."

Now that they were here, the man seemed ready to capitulate to whatever shit was coming his way. "You can call me Dave."

"Alright, Dave. We won't take up too much of your time. You and Alexa Rousso were married back in 1997, correct?"

Dave looked around for somewhere to sit himself and decided the corner of the sofa would do. Mason was leaning against the wall, between him and Julia, just in case.

"Yes, that's right. I think. Not so good at dates, you know?"

"I know. That's fine."

"You guys are detectives? Cops?"

"No. I'm a lawyer. Mason is my associate. Alexa is our client."

Dave nodded slowly. He was clinging to the thread. He slumped lower on the sofa, and Mason watched the color drain from his face.

"Have you eaten today?" she asked, suddenly.

He turned and looked at her numbly, shaking his head. Mason walked into what she assumed was the kitchen, based on the presence of a fridge. She pulled it open. Literally empty. She looked around. The surfaces were clear, but not clean. She pulled open a couple of cupboards, which were as bare as the fridge apart from a stack of cat food, each individual foil-topped portion promising high-quality protein from organic sources, balanced nutrition, and a dining experience your beloved cat would enjoy. Somebody in this place was being taken care of.

She walked back into the living room. Julia looked at her questioningly, having paused to wait for whatever it was Mason was doing.

"Did you eat yesterday?" she asked Dave.

He shook his head again. He was deathly pale, a sheen of sweat had broken out on his brow, and Mason frowned. She turned to Julia.

"He needs to eat something, and so do I. I'll be right back."

"I'll take a latte and something small but sinful," replied her boss, reaching out for the cat, who butted her hand with regal acceptance. "We'll wait here." She turned back to Dave, who was barely holding on at this point. "So, tell me, Dave, how did you come by this incredible cat?"

Mason left them to it.

SHE RETURNED FIFTEEN minutes later with three coffees, two pressed ham and cheese sandwiches and a lemon cupcake. She'd also stopped at a convenience store and bought coffee, a loaf of bread, a jar of peanut butter, a jar of jam, milk and butter. She didn't know why she was doing it; she just did it. There was nothing friendly about Dave McGann, nothing charming or even interesting. But he was a fellow drunk, and he was on his last leg. She remembered, and she bought the milk.

Julia was still talking when she walked back in, still on the topic of cats, a subject Mason knew she didn't know a lot about. But she was winging it in high style.

"They always seem like they're barely tolerating your existence, then they come over and sit on your lap and it feels like you've been singled out by a god. Amazing." The Siamese was indeed on her lap, sitting in classic Egyptian cat style, facing her, allowing a constant stream of petting and cooing. "You really are such a princess, aren't you?"

Dave McGann looked like his earlier anger had taken his last calorie, and when he started eating the sandwich, there was a moment when it seemed as though he might not be able to keep it down. He stopped, looked up, closed his eyes, and both the women in the room knew exactly what he was feeling. It was a struggle, but he breathed deeply and pushed through, and once the sandwich was down, his color started to get better.

Mason was back against the wall when Julia began her questions again.

"So, Dave, yes, you were married to Alexa for several years in the late nineties . . . Ring a bell?"

He nodded. He hadn't been sure today wasn't going to be his last, but things were improving. "She went off and got sober. I think. She went away to rehab anyway."

"And you?"

He raised his eyebrow at her. "You're joking. Rehab's for pussies."

"On the contrary, Dave, rehab is for warriors, but you're entitled to your opinion. What can you remember about those years? Whoever is threatening Alexa seems to think she did something bad. Maybe it was when you knew her."

Dave nodded. "We did plenty of bad things. I was selling drugs, she was doing them, you know?"

"Do you remember a guy named Fuzzy?"

He laughed. "Of course. Fuzzy was my dealer and, to a lesser degree, my friend. Not a very nice friend—it wasn't like I could owe him money or anything—but we knew each other."

"Do you still?"

"No. I think he's dead. Probably."

"Do you remember the guy he worked for?"

Dave shook his head. "No."

"He was rich."

Dave shrugged. "So? Fuzzy worked for lots of people, all of whom had more money than he did, otherwise they couldn't have afforded to hire him, right?"

"I see," said Julia. "What about Lisa Rawlings?"

"Sure, although I haven't seen her in forever. I think she got arrested. She worked for Fuzzy, too, and he wasn't keen on getting involved if you got busted for anything. He was good at evaporating, you know what I mean?"

"I do. Were Alexa and Lisa close?"

Dave shrugged. "As close as people got back then. Close when you were high, less close when you were jonesing . . . unless the other one was holding, in which case you were the best of friends."

Julia nodded. "Was Lisa usually holding?"

Dave frowned. "She was, actually. She had plenty of cash, plenty of drugs, plenty of friends. She was nice, in her way. Friendly until she wasn't."

"And what would make her unfriendly?"

"Not getting her way. She liked to run the room, let's just say that." He looked at his hands. "I haven't thought about any of this in a long time. It seems like another life ago."

"You're living a different life now?" Julia's tone was neutral.

He shook his head. "No, same life. Different body. It was a lot easier to be fucked-up and twenty-five, you know what I mean? Now I get hangovers for days, can't eat, can't sleep . . . Back then I could drink into a blackout, do an 8 ball or two, fuck a woman, sleep for three hours and wake up ready to do it all again."

"What an entrancing picture," said Julia. "But yes, age gets us all in the end."

"Might have been better if I'd died back then."

"Yes, maybe, but here you are now. You can always stop. You know that."

He eyed her. "What, you're going to save the poor sinner

from himself?" He looked at Mason, still leaning against the wall. "What is this, a fucking intervention?"

"Hardly," said Mason. "We're helping a friend, and you happened to be on the way. But I will say that I used to be where you are right now, and when I stopped drinking, things got better."

He stared at her. "I've been sober. It's not better."

She shrugged. "You do you."

Julia said, "Dave, is there anyone else we haven't mentioned that you remember from back then? Someone who knew Alexa, friendly or otherwise?"

"Her first husband, Richard, was pretty angry with her. And with me, but mostly with her."

"We've spoken to him. Like you, he hasn't had any contact with Alexa for many years."

"Yeah? How's he doing?"

Julia smiled. "He's well. Sober. He seemed happy enough."

"Good for fucking him." Dave shot a glance toward the window. People's voices floated in from the street, apparently calling to him. "Are we nearly done here?"

Mason caught Julia's eye. He was feeling better. He'd eaten, he'd caffeinated. And now he wanted to hit the liquor store. Time was ticking on.

"Yes, I think so. Mason will leave our contact information with you, in case you think of anything else."

"Is Alexa scared?" Dave asked, suddenly. "She was always so tough, that girl. We got caught in that big warehouse fire, do you remember?"

Julia shook her head. Mason nodded hers. "The Albatross? I was just a kid, but it was big news."

"I was sitting outside, thank God, but the second it started to go down, Alexa appeared, and we beat it out of there. A huge section of wall collapsed exactly where we'd been sitting." He shook his head. "She was smart, and quick thinking, you know? Scanned a room the minute she walked in and had it all down cold. Remembered everyone, everything, names, dates, you know. Even when she was fucked-up." He squinted at them. "And now she's scared?"

"She's concerned. Receiving threats will do that."

Dave nodded. "Sure."

Mason handed him a piece of paper with their information on it. "Call us if you think of anything."

"Yeah, will do." He stood up, wobbled, then steadied himself. "Thanks for coming."

There was a pause. He seemed to hear how ridiculous a thing that was to say, and was aware that it came from a polite, well-brought-up place inside him he thought he'd lost forever. "I mean, you know . . ."

Julia was up, placing the cat gently back on the table. "We know, Dave. Thanks for talking to us. If we have further questions, we'll be in touch."

"Alright." He looked toward the window again. Getting antsy. Forgetting the pain of waking up, ready to escape again, rolling the dice that this time maybe the high would last forever. He clicked his fingers, getting impatient, the craving curling through his nervous system like fire licking the onionskin pages of a bible.

Julia headed toward the door. "Don't forget to feed the cat."

"I never do," he replied. "She's the only good thing I have."

"And you are hers," she said.

Mason followed Julia out the door, feeling the cat watching her all the way.

13

THEY WERE HALFWAY back to Mason's parents' house when Julia's phone rang. It was Will, with information.

"Hi there, away team."

Julia frowned. "Are you making a *Star Trek* reference?"

He paused. "Would it be bad if I was?"

"No, it would be very on-brand."

"Well then yes, I am. Claudia and I are the mother ship, you are the away team, down on the planet. If one of you is wearing a red shirt, you might not make it back."

"Neither of us is in red. Please get to the point." Julia shifted in her seat. Not a huge *Star Trek* fan.

"I was able to track down Lisa Rawlings. Well, mostly."

"Mostly?"

"It was easy at first, because she got arrested a lot back in the nineties. Solicitation, minor assault, disorderly conduct, public intoxication, the usual suite. I could track her pretty easily. Then she was arrested for extortion in the early '00s and went away for a while."

"Extortion? State or federal?"

"State. Central California Women's Facility at Chowchilla.

Few years, sentence reduced for good behavior. I guess she pulled it together on the inside."

"People do," said Julia, dryly, having done so herself.

"She got out and I lost her for a while, but sadly, she popped back up in 2011, arrested once more for disorderly conduct, although apparently she moved south. This was in Palmdale."

"Where's that?" Mason asked, slowing for a red light as she crested over the hill into Berkeley.

"About sixty miles north of LA, in the Antelope Valley. It's hot as hell. You wouldn't like it."

"I don't mind the heat."

Julia clicked her tongue. "Focus, you two. So, what happened to Lisa?"

"She was released without formal charge but got arrested once more in Palmdale and then hit Los Angeles. She went dark again for nearly a decade, but popped up five years ago in Central Court, here in the city."

"What was she arrested for that time?"

Will cleared his throat. "Assault in the second degree."

Julia raised her eyebrows. "Well, shit."

"Did they put her away?" asked Mason. Second-degree assault is pretty significant.

"The victim dropped the charges."

"And where is she now?"

"Running a brothel near Las Vegas. It gets very good reviews on Yelp."

Mason snorted. "You can rate a brothel on Yelp?"

Will made a surprised noise. "You can basically rate anything on Yelp."

"Who would put their name on a brothel review?"

"They're largely anonymous. Why is this bothering you?"

Mason sighed. "No idea. Please continue."

"That's pretty much all I have on her."

"It's excellent work," said Julia. "We'll be back tomorrow. We'll pay her a visit very soon." She turned to Mason. "And we can spend the night in Vegas. That's always fun." She turned her attention back to the phone. "Anything else?"

"Yes," said Will. "I dusted the notes for prints and got what you'd expect. Hers, Scott's, Mason's and yours."

"OK. So they wore gloves, no big surprise there. Everyone knows about prints these days."

"Yeah," said Will, "but it was fun because paper can be difficult, obviously. I used ninhydrin and DFO."

"I would expect nothing less," said Julia, turning to Mason and making a face that made it clear she had zero idea what he was talking about. "Good for you. Anything else?"

"One funny thing, although only in the widest sense of funny. A load of people who were at Jennifer's opening last night got sick. Really sick. Hospital sick."

"Well, that's unfortunate. Not the best way to open a restaurant, a food-poisoning scandal. How did you hear about it?"

"It was in the news. Not big news, local news online, but still."

"I think we sampled everything on the menu. I felt fine, did you?"

"Yup. The health department is investigating, and they're closed for the time being. What time will you be back tomorrow? Do you want me to pick you up?"

"Midmorning and no," said Julia, her mouth turning down. "We left the car at Burbank. We're all good." She paused. "Any other disasters? Are they making progress on the house?"

"Uh, they ran into some difficulties with something this morning. I'm not entirely clear what happened, but there was some broken glass."

Julia tipped her head. "You're lying about something."

Will blustered. "What makes you think that?"

"Your voice. The way you're speaking. The words you're using."

"Oh." He paused. "Yeah, well, what happened was the glaziers were carrying a huge piece of window glass across the hallway, probably for the living room windows . . ." He tailed off, and there was an almost audible sound of mental gears turning. "Do you know they make large panes like that using a method where they float glass at fifteen hundred degrees or so onto an enormous bath of molten *tin* . . . ? That just blows my mind for some reason."

"Possibly because your mind lives to be blown," said Julia. "What happened to the glass, Will?"

"They tripped and lost control of it. It's mostly cleaned up now."

"They tripped?"

"Um-hmm."

"Over what?" The entryway was a large, airy space with no rugs or anything on its granite floor.

Will mumbled.

"I'm sorry, what did you say?"

"Phil."

"They tripped over Phil?" Julia turned her head to glare at Mason, who felt the heat of it but kept her eyes on oncoming traffic. "What was the blasted cat doing in the house?"

"That's unclear, but he was crossing the hallway at that exact moment and managed to get underfoot."

"Was he hurt by the glass?" Mason still wasn't looking at Julia, but cat ownership has its responsibilities. Which hopefully didn't extend to replacing enormously expensive sheets of glass.

"No," said Will. "By the time the noise had died down, he was nowhere to be seen." He paused. "The noise was incredible."

Mason and Julia drove the rest of the way to Mason's childhood home in silence.

JULIA CHANGED FOR dinner, because of course she did. She came downstairs at Mason's house wearing a vintage Halston halter top dress in emerald green, but barefoot, just in case anyone thought she wasn't cottoning to the hippie vibes of the Berkeley Hills.

The way Mason's dad's eyes bugged out suggested Julia might have considered his delicate cardiac health before getting dressed, but he calmed down pretty quickly. Inspired by their glamorous guest, Mason's parents had also dressed up: Douglas Mason was wearing a tie and Barbara had upgraded from L.L.Bean to J.Crew. Thankfully, there are many clothing retailers who use initials.

In honor of Mason being home, they were eating deep-dish pizzas from Zachary's, the best Chicago-style pizzas on the West Coast (Mason's opinion) and her favorite tradition. They can be picked up half-baked and then finished in the oven at home, and the smell always made Mason feel like a kid again.

Louise was having salad.

"Not sure how you stay so skinny when you eat so much," she said to Mason. "It's a mystery."

"Judging another woman on both her body size and her appetite is soooo twentieth century, Lou. What the hell?" Mason chewed her pizza. "Honestly, you're such a throwback."

Louise looked at her mom, who shrugged. "You're not just another woman, you're my sister. The gloves came off at birth, no?"

Mason shook her head. "You wouldn't comment on Julia's appetite, or anyone else you didn't know very well. Why does familiarity have to breed contempt?"

Doug cleared his throat. "Family dynamics are so hard to break free of. They're our earliest conditioning, our most deeply ingrained habits. Often our roles within the family are set very early, and changing them challenges both our sense of self and our sense of safety within the familiar confines of a pattern we're used to." He looked at Julia. "Please excuse my daughters. They love to bicker." And he couldn't help sounding like a college professor, clearly also a familiar confine.

"Well, we bicker. I'm not sure we love it," said Mason, reaching for another slice. "Sorry, Julia, we apparently feel comfortable enough with you to show our dysfunction openly."

"Oh, who doesn't love dysfunction?" said Julia, easily. "Tell me, Louise, what kind of law do you practice?"

"Tax litigation, mostly."

"Fascinating," said Julia, although she couldn't possibly have thought that was true. "Mostly domestic?"

Louise nodded, spearing a piece of celery. "Largely, although we have been working on a complicated case lately involving a Swiss national. They have an interesting set of tax laws with regards to foreign income, and of course the IRS has a strong opinion, too. Really compelling."

"More pizza, Julia?" Barbara pushed the platter closer, and

Julia snagged another piece. "Are you working on anything interesting right now? Do you miss making movies?"

"Not at all," said Julia, with her mouth full. "It's short periods of intense stress interspersed with stretches of mind-numbing boredom and self-criticism. Criminal law is much easier."

"But more dangerous, surely?"

"Not usually. Film sets can be dangerous places, sadly, and most of my work is conducted in the safety of my own home." She angled her head toward Mason. "I try to outsource the dangerous parts as much as possible."

Everyone swiveled to look at Mason, who waved her slice. "Like I keep saying, you should have seen the other guy."

Barbara looked back at Julia. "Natasha was always one for confrontation, even as a child. Other little girls played with their dolls or stuffies, you know, in fake family groupings, or reenacting social dynamics they were working through themselves, friend groups, that kind of thing. It's developmentally appropriate."

Mason rolled her eyes.

"But Natasha," continued her mother, "used to set up opposing gangs and stage elaborate battles, with deadly consequences."

"Who could forget the Barbie Wars of 2007?" half joked her dad.

"Not me," said Louise. "Those were my Barbies."

"For a while we thought maybe she was interested in the medical aspect of these things, you know, maybe she wanted to fix up her toys, grow up to be a doctor, nurse, something like that. But she just left them to die." Barbara looked at her daughter. "She had a lot of . . . anger."

"You had a lot of . . . judgment," said Mason, mimicking her mother. "You loved a gender norm."

Doug adopted his instinctive instructional tone. "While Judith Butler's work on gender performativity would suggest children learn gender roles from the culture around them, and Eckel and Grossman's work advocated . . ."

". . . and you treated me like a science project," continued Mason, feeling her temper start to flare. "I was just who I was. I don't think I was a problem."

"You fought all the time at school."

"The other kids were morons."

Her mother turned to Julia. "She was expelled from two preschools. It was embarrassing."

"It's embarrassing they couldn't . . ." Mason's voice was rising.

"All my friends knew she was my sister . . ." Louise sounded like she was still pissed about it.

"You sent me away."

"You were doing drugs."

"Barrie Thorne, on the other hand, discovered through her work that gender dynamics can be negotiated in creative ways . . ." Doug wanted to keep it theoretical—safer ground for him.

"Well," said Julia, cutting through the argument with a clarion tone, "whatever she was like as a child, she is a force to be reckoned with now, and those particular bruises were earned defending herself while recovering stolen diamonds, earning us a fat fee and the satisfaction of our client, so I, for one, am grateful for her occasionally combative approach. She saved my life a few months ago, mine and another woman's, using no physical skills at all, so she's hardly a one-trick pony."

The room fell silent.

"She did?" said Louise.

"She did." Julia beamed around. "Is there another pizza somewhere? I'm pretty sure I have room for another slice."

LATER THAT NIGHT, after everyone else was asleep, Mason padded down to the kitchen and found her dad sitting at the kitchen table. A glass of wine was in front of him, and as she walked in, he looked around, startled, and made a feeble effort to cover the glass with his hand.

She laughed.

"I can see the wine, Dad. You've never been one for pretense. Don't start now."

He made a rueful face at her. "There was never much point in pretending in front of you, anyway. You were too sharp." He sighed. "All you women are. I've lived my life surrounded by perspicacity."

"Wow," said Mason, pulling out a chair and joining him at the table. "That's a big word for late at night."

"Well, 'snoopy nosy butts' doesn't have the same ring to it."

"No, good point." She got up again and got herself a glass of water.

"Do you miss it?" asked her dad.

She knew what he meant, but asked all the same: "Drinking?"

He nodded. She shook her head. "Not really. I mean, sure, occasionally the thought pops into my head that it would be nice to relax with a glass of whatever they're having, but then I think about it for a moment longer and remember that one always led to two, or four, or six, that a pleasant evening would be ruined, and that I would spend the next day in agony of several kinds, waiting for the hangover and remorse to pass. That's what it always meant to me, and I don't miss that."

He nodded and took a sip of his wine. "I know I'm not supposed to have this, but I was feeling rebellious."

"Relatable," said Mason, reaching out to squeeze his hand. "I won't tell."

They sat in silence for a moment, listening to the condenser in the fridge doing its thing, the sound of the boiler turning on and off in the basement. The smell of Zachary's from earlier still lingered, and Mason wondered idly if there was any left.

"So," she said, after a minute or two, "are you going to tell me what's going on at work, or do I have to ferret it out of Mom in the morning?"

Her dad sighed and made a defeated gesture with his shoulders. "There's not much to tell. A colleague wants my position, and as there is no budget for another professor at my level, he is trying to push me out. He's made some unpleasant insinuations about my level of familiarity with my research assistants, implied I'm losing my memory . . . It's been distasteful." He shrugged, ruefully. "I have no idea what I've done to piss him off, but maybe I'm just the oldest in the herd and so he's decided to winnow me out as the easiest target." He took another, longer, sip of wine. "I don't believe I've done anything untoward, I feel like my memory is still good, but when someone insists the opposite, you do end up questioning yourself. It was worrying me a lot, and now that I've had this . . . episode . . . it'll be more fuel for his fire. The department told me to take a leave of absence while I recover, but I fear there won't be a job waiting for me when I'm better." He sighed.

"Your mom and sister think I should retire, but that feels like giving up and I don't like it."

"You hadn't been considering it?"

He shook his head. "No, not at all. I'm only in my mid-sixties. I've got another decade at least to teach, or so I thought. I like teaching," he added. "I like the students, I like continuing to learn from them . . ." His voice tailed off a bit. "I like my work."

"Who's this guy? The one who's harassing you?"

"His name is Roger Eberling. He's a smart guy, a very capable teacher, and more of a politician than I ever was. He has strong ties in the department and in the college at large. He's a lot younger than me, but still a fully credentialed, tenured professor. I liked him, always have. I still like him. I just don't know why he's doing this." He shrugged. "After decades in this field, I still struggle to understand people's motivations sometimes."

"And how do you feel yourself? I mean, physically?"

"A little scared, to be honest. I don't want to keel over at the podium and frighten the children."

Mason laughed. "Is that a possibility?"

"More than it was a week ago."

"Have you talked to this guy, this Eberling, directly?"

"No," said her dad, draining his glass. "The whole thing has been whispers and rumors. Maybe that's why it's been so effective. But perhaps I should. Once I'm better."

"Louise said she was handling it. What is she doing?"

"I think she was going to write a letter or something. Talk to the Faculty Association. We don't have a union, per se, us tenured professors, but the FA helps out." He stood up. "It won't do any good, but Louise likes to go through channels, you know?"

Mason looked up at him. "I could just go beat him up for you."

He laughed. "That might be satisfying, but hardly helpful."

"Well, the offer stands."

"Thanks, Natasha. Good night, baby."

"Good night, Dad."

Mason watched him leave the room, moving more slowly than he used to, looking older than she remembered. And then she sat there for a while longer, thinking about her family, and smelling the remnants of wine in his glass.

14

MASON AND MANN headed back home early the next morning, to the relief of both of them. Mason was unpacking her overnight bag when her phone rang.

"I got another letter." Alexa's voice was low, lacking its usual vibrancy and with a new note Mason hadn't heard before, a certain bafflement. "Meaner, this time."

"Read it to me," said Mason, lobbing clothes into the laundry hamper. She tried to keep her little guesthouse tidy. "Tried" being the operative word.

"I don't really want to," said her sponsor.

"Do it anyway."

Alexa sighed. "*You're good at staying quiet. But it won't keep you safe anymore.*"

"Huh, that's definitely a more explicit threat."

"Yeah. Maybe I woke up in a bad place, but it's starting to wear on my nerves a little."

"Is it time to go to the police? It's a criminal offense, sending threatening letters."

"No. I want to handle it myself. Well, I want your and Julia's help, but I don't want to go to the police. It's only words right now. No sticks or stones."

"Those vegetables were pretty real. I mean, not literally."

"But nobody was hurt."

"Apart from your reputation."

There was a pause, then Alexa said, "It's OK. Scott says I can stand being a little less busy. Only a few things have been canceled, and no press is bad press."

"I don't think that's true. I worry you're going to get hurt."

"You sound like Scott. Quit it. I don't know if it's wise, but it's what I want to do." Alexa paused. "I'm getting together with my other sponsees tonight, at the diner. You want to come?"

"Working or fellowship?" Working in the context of AA means reading, writing, discussing specific topics or readings. Fellowship is just . . . hanging out.

"Just fellowship. I haven't gotten all my chickies together in a while. You barely know Iris."

Alexa currently had two other sponsees, in addition to Mason. Having multiple sponsees was common; working the steps happens in a variety of ways, some intense, some very long-term. Everyone works it differently, and some never work it at all.

"Sure, I'll come. Usual diner, or are we trying something new?"

"Usual. Seven o'clock work for you?"

"Yeah. And, Alexa, bring the new note, OK? Will's going to want to test it for fingerprints."

Long sigh. "OK. You can keep it. I wish I'd never seen them, but I can recite them all from memory." She paused. "I didn't see you at the eight forty-five this morning."

"I was up in Berkeley, no time to log on. I went to an in-person yesterday."

"Alright. I'm thinking of switching meetings anyway. These notes are flipping me out. I can't help thinking the person sending them might be in the room, you know? Watching me. You see the same people all the time."

"Where will you go instead?"

"No idea. Other Zoom meetings, maybe, or switch it up and go in person in a different neighborhood. Downtown, perhaps. There used to be a great women's meeting by the train station. It might still be there."

Covid had had an impact on AA, as it did on everything else. One thing was very positive—AA meetings had migrated onto Zoom within a few days of the general lockdown being announced, and now there were thousands of meetings online every hour of the day. People had gotten sober completely online, never going to in-person meetings at all, and referring to themselves as "Zoom babies." Now some of the in-person meetings were suffering from a lack of attendance, and some had closed down completely. Anyone can start a meeting, but you need people to keep coming back if you want to keep it open.

"Let me know. Maybe I'll join you," said Mason. She said goodbye and hung up, frowning. She loved Alexa and hated to hear the tension in her voice. She was glad she could do something to help, even if so far nothing seemed relevant.

Phil jumped up onto the bed and chirruped a jaunty greeting, as if he hadn't caused a major problem only the day before. Cats are easy forgivers . . . of themselves. Shat in your slippers? Let's agree to move on. You moved the sweater they were sleeping on? Carved in stone until the last star flickers into darkness.

"Hey you," said Mason. "Thanks for causing problems in our living arrangement. Don't tell Julia I said so, but I actually like living here. Please try not to get us thrown out."

Phil shrugged without moving a muscle, another cat specialty.

WILL WAS PLEASED to hear there would be new material to analyze. He pulled images up onto the screen.

"There was a week between the first and second letters, and now only a few days before this new one." He waved his palm. "They're ramping up. I'm assuming the postal service did their usual job of delivering the most recent one. Of course, I'll have to see the envelope to double-check when it was mailed." He turned to Julia and Mason, who were sitting on the sofa, Mason with a piece of toast halfway to her mouth. "The envelopes are the most interesting thing about these letters, as is obvious to all of us."

Mason chewed and swallowed before taking the bait. "Not to me. Go ahead."

"The sender purchased Forever stamped envelopes."

Julia frowned. "So?"

He looked surprised. "Well, it's relatively rare. You have to get them at an actual post office, largely. You can get them occasionally at a big office supply store, like Staples or something like that, but it's unusual."

"What about a retail mail store? Like a mailbox place."

"Sometimes, but not reliably. It's most likely they went to a post office."

"And why is that important?" Julia sounded like she was ready for a clue of some kind, and this seemed promising.

"Well, although they're treated and processed much the same way as any other letter, in practice they often don't get postmarked or canceled the same. I don't know if it's a policy decision or an artifact of some other subsystem within the postal service, but you can see there's no location stamped on these envelopes. We assume they came from Los Angeles, because we're assuming the sender is someone who knows Alexa well, ergo probably local. But the envelopes don't confirm the letters were sent from here." He wandered over to the desk and scruffled around for a moment, finally waving another envelope in the air. "This utilities bill is stamped Los Angeles, but these letters to Alexa merely have the date. However, the gap between postmark and delivery tells us they are almost certainly local because they took two or three days to arrive." He paused. "Although local in this context also stretches to the rest of California, at least on the face of it, because a letter could conceivably make it here in three days from anywhere else in the state, too."

Mason gazed at him. "So, the envelopes are interesting because they *don't* contain useful information, but the gap between being mailed and being received narrows the sending location to somewhere within California anyway?"

"Exactly."

"It's a big state."

"Yeah . . . and to be fair, the post office would claim that a letter sent from adjacent states would also take one to three days. They say three to five from the East Coast, and of course that's entirely dependent on factors no one can control."

Julia looked disappointed. "I realize you think the envelopes are interesting, but I'm not seeing it myself. Maybe the sender didn't think about it that deeply?"

Will shook his head. "Doubtful. They went to the trouble to type the letters on an actual typewriter, so there is no digital file anywhere to discover. That was purposeful. I think the envelopes are meaningful, too. Who goes to the post office by choice? I mean, I do, but in-person visits to the post office are a relatively small portion of the USPS's business. They serve around seven million customers a day in person across the nation, with around thirty-four thousand post offices, so let's call it approximately two hundred people a day, and of course that's an average, and Los Angeles is a very dense urban environment with over a hundred post offices . . ." He tailed off.

"That's too mathy for me," said Mason.

Julia said, "And not helpful anyway, if I can be blunt. This person may have taken the envelopes from someone else, may have purchased them months or even years ago, may have used them out of habit rather than on purpose and may have pretty safely assumed that no one was going to be scrutinizing them as closely as you are."

"Few people would," Mason added.

"But I love your attention to detail and always have." Julia sighed. "We didn't learn all that much in Oakland. Neither husband seems to be harboring a resentment, neither seems to know what secret Alexa might be keeping—it was a big, fat waste of time."

"We went to a nice meeting," said Mason.

"Yeah, and I got to meet your family, which added some context I found illustrative."

"In what way?" Mason said, feeling her hackles getting ready to rise.

"In the way that explains why you dislike categorization as strongly as you do. Because your family has cast you in a role you didn't enjoy then and actively reject now. That, like many families, you're all stuck in the relationships and personae you had twenty years ago and will struggle, like many families, to change them."

Mason frowned at her. "And so?"

"So nothing. I've only known you six months, and meeting your family just helped fill in some background. You don't need to get defensive."

Mason opened her mouth to protest, and realized that would prove the point and closed it again.

"I'm going to dinner tonight with Alexa and her other sponsees. I'll be home later."

"Great. Report back. I'm interested to learn more about the other people in Alexa's life."

"OK, will do."

There was a pause. Then Julia said, "Have you thought any more about your plans for the next year or so?"

"About going back to school?"

Julia nodded. "Yes. Unless you're planning on joining the circus."

"Not going to do that." Mason shook her head. "I haven't, no. I will."

"No pressure."

"Well," said Will, "there is some pressure. Registration for classes will open in a few weeks."

"Alright, gentle pressure, then," said Julia. "You can always do it next year."

Mason sighed. "I don't want to let anyone down. I don't want to overcommit and fail."

"Reasonable," said Julia. "But you'd be letting yourself down if you never moved forward, right?"

"I guess." Mason felt uncomfortable. "I'm going to go finish unpacking."

She got up and left, and Julia and Will watched her leave.

"Twenty dollars she won't do it," said Will.

"I won't take that bet," replied Julia. "I don't think betting against Mason is ever a good idea." She stretched. "I still think she and Archie are going to get together, even though you and Claudia say not."

"I'm not betting against Mason on that front; I'm betting that Archie will fumble." Will laughed. "I love Archie, don't misunderstand me, but Mason needs gentle handling, and I don't know if he has the finesse."

"She's a delicate flower?" Julia's tone was incredulous.

"No," said Will, "she's a hand grenade."

MASON HADN'T OVERHEARD the conversation between Will and Julia about Archie, but he was on her mind as she walked toward her guesthouse. Mason hadn't been on all that many first dates, but the ones she had been on hadn't been interrupted by the sound of crashing sculptures or the imminent threat of being squashed by . . . squash. She opened her messaging app and hovered over his name.

What would she even say? *Sorry about that ridiculous first date*. . . She wasn't sorry—it's not like it was her fault. Um, *Hey, wanna try another lunch without the threat of vegetable-related concussion?* Nope.

But in the way these things often happen, as she was standing in her living room staring at her phone, a message appeared. From Archie.

That was not the lunch I was hoping for, it said. Maybe we'd have better luck at dinner?

There was a pause.

Not a vegetarian place.

Mason smiled. She hesitated for a second, then sent a link for a well-known steak house.

THE DINER LOOKED as though it had been built in the 1950s, but actually dated from the early 2000s, which meant it was both historically accurate and technically efficient. Most importantly, the food was excellent and reasonably affordable, a fantastic combination for anyone, but especially for broke people in recovery. Mason had sat in a booth every day for the first year of her recovery, drinking a chocolate malted and eating a grilled cheese, and still loved everything about the place.

The waitress knew everyone by name and leaned down to give Alexa a hug before grabbing them all some water.

Jennifer looked stressed and was clearly wound very tight. She kept checking on her dog, who was tied up outside, and was generally constantly on the move. She'd check her phone, check the dog, take a drink of coffee, check her phone . . . The tattoos on her arms were a blur, the orange flowers dancing as though they were in a breeze.

To give her a moment, Mason said, "Jen, I heard about the issues with the restaurant. I'm so sorry. That must be a challenge."

"It's a fucking disaster. Two people are still in the hospital, but out of danger. The only thing they all had in common was one of the wines. I'm working with the health department, and we'll be able to put out a press release soon clarifying it wasn't the food, but who knows if that'll make any difference, if anyone will even notice. They'll just remember the restaurant name and food poisoning."

"Well, at least they'll remember the name . . . ?"

Jennifer grimaced and shrugged. "It's not good, but it's OK. All part of the universal plan, I guess. Trying to not spin out. It's out of my control, right? This whole year has been out of my control, what with the divorce . . ." Mason noticed the E tattooed on her arm; she'd met Jennifer's ex-husband, Edward, a few times—he was also sober—and she wondered what had happened between them. The waitress returned to take their orders then, and Jennifer looked up at her. "Can I get a burger and fries, American cheese, Diet Coke?" She looked over at Iris. "You hungry, Iris?"

Iris was new. Young, maybe a year or two older than Mason, and still in her first year. There are certain traditions about the first year of sobriety, and Iris was working hard to get a perfect score (no one's keeping score). No relationships in the first year. No major changes. Find a sponsor. Start the steps. She sat close to Alexa in meetings, probably called her every day, sat quietly and listened. Mason was jealous of her but wasn't sure why. She herself spoke to Alexa daily, mostly followed suggestions . . . She shrugged, mentally. Iris was just the new girl at the party and Mason had work to do on herself. It didn't help that Iris was pretty in the way Mason wished she was: elegant, cool, blond. She was a ballet dancer and every move she made was beautiful; even reaching for a fork looked like the beginning of a pas de deux. She ordered a cup of soup and a glass of water. Mason wondered if she was too broke for more. Who knew how much money a ballet dancer recovering from a wine and heroin addiction was bringing in?

She looked up at the waitress. "And I'll have a grilled cheese and a chocolate milk shake, please."

"Wow," said the waitress, teasing. "You'll excuse me if I sit down from shock." Mason ordered the same thing every time. Maybe one day she'd amaze the waitress by changing it, but the repeated order gave her half the comfort she felt from being in the diner. It was a superstition, a covenant she kept with herself. Eat a grilled cheese in this diner whenever possible, and it will help you stay sober.

Alexa ordered and then sat back and looked around the table.

"So, how is everyone? Iris?"

Iris shrugged. "OK, I guess." She shrugged again, although her shrug was more of a ripple that started at her shoulder and went down to her narrow wrist and out through her fingertips. "I talked to my ex the other day, which was an error on my part."

Alexa raised her eyebrows. "Why?"

Iris turned up her palms. "Because there's nothing there for me anymore. He's still using, doesn't want to stop. If I go back to him, I don't know . . . But I miss him."

"What do you miss about him?" asked Jennifer. She was watching the younger woman with kindness, but also awareness. Everyone at that table had been where Iris was now, in the early days of sobriety when you don't have a lot of experience doing the usual things in an unusual way, without any substances on board. They call it sober reference, the knowledge that you can do holidays, work, relationships, shopping, putting your socks on the right feet, without being hammered or high to do it.

"He made me laugh. He practiced with me." She paused. "He fucked me." She looked at the other women. "I think it's just as well you're not supposed to have relationships the first year. I'm pretty sure I won't know how to do it without being drunk."

"It'll come back to you," said Jennifer, dryly. "The moves are the same, the feelings are different—you'll get it."

Iris looked dubious. "Anyway, we talked for a little bit, just general catching up, then he had to go." She sighed. "It's always him that ends conversations, always was. He always had somewhere else to be. It made me anxious. I always felt needy." She played with a sugar packet. "Less than."

The women nodded. Another familiar feeling.

Jennifer spoke next, when it was clear that was all Iris was ready to offer. "I'm freaking out, for obvious reasons, but it'll be OK."

"Sure," said Alexa. "It's a lot."

"I think my nervous system just likes dysregulation. I'm going up the coast to look at a vegetable provider's operation tomorrow, then I have a private party at my first place, Invernadero. It's a vegetarian restaurant, right, but they wanted salmon and we had a little back-and-forth . . ." She ran her fingers through her hair. "Sorry, it seems like there's always a new fire to put out, so I feel myself going into every situation anxious before I start, and then of course that makes it worse."

"Going to meetings?"

Jennifer nodded. "Three a week."

Alexa squeezed her hand. "Keep it simple, right? Just do the next appropriate thing, the next right action. One day at a time." This was standard program advice, classic AA phrases, but she meant them. Mason knew her own tendency to complicate things often made life more difficult than it needed to be, and sometimes the best thing to do was less. Sometimes the best thing to do was nothing.

The drinks arrived and they fell silent for a minute. Mason stirred her milk shake and watched Alexa's face. Her fidgeting had ceased. There was no sign of the stress she was under, no hint that she was worried someone was out there, hating her. It was admirable, but also . . . Mason wondered for the first time whether she knew Alexa as well as she thought she did.

After dinner, Jennifer offered to take Iris shopping, and they headed off together. Alexa and Mason watched them go.

"It's nice when you guys become friends, too," said Alexa, calmly. "I mean, you share a sponsor, but you might not have anything else in common."

"Apart from a desire to drink?" asked Mason. "A general feeling of not being OK in our skin? A sense that everyone else got the manual for life but we got passed over? An inability to control our impulses on occasion? A feeling of mild panic pervading our every waking moment?"

Alexa looked at her and laughed. "Yeah . . . apart from that."

"It's not surprising we band together," said Mason. "We're all clinging to the same log." She hugged Alexa. "And you're our log."

"Awesome analogy," said Alexa, dryly. "Who doesn't want to be compared to a log? Are you heading back to Julia's place?"

Mason nodded. "Gym first. I need to do a little boxing, thrash out my feelings."

"Fair enough." Alexa turned to leave, then turned back for one more hug.

Mason watched her walk away and felt the usual flood of gratitude for her sponsor. She knew Alexa was going through it right now, but she also knew that in helping her sponsees she was escaping the confines of her own head, at least for a while.

Mason was going to do the same. Through violence, to be fair, but everyone has their thing.

15

THE NEXT MORNING, Julia woke up in a black mood, for no reason anyone could see. She snapped at Will for talking about shale, snapped at Mason for asking a follow-up question, and started to snap at Claudia for the speed with which she was dishing up breakfast.

She didn't get very far.

"Hey!" Claudia was standing at the table with a spatula in her hand, and she raised it a little. "Don't start with me. I'm sorry you woke up with your panties in a bunch, but I am providing you with a delicious breakfast that will almost certainly improve your mood, and if you raise your voice at me, you're going to be wearing it."

Julia frowned at her.

"Furthermore, I was very interested in what Will was telling us about shale, because who knew?"

"I didn't even get into how feldspar, which is a constituent mineral in shale, is used in glass production, but I was going . . ."

Julia slapped the table. "Will! I understand the glass breaking the other day has triggered a compulsive cycle of ever deeper investigations into glass production, but the bottom line is that enormous windowpane cost me more than I pay you every year and the blasted cat broke it."

"Well, not actually . . ."

"Yes, actually."

The phone rang, which was a relief to Mason, who was starting to wonder if she could slide under the table without anyone noticing.

Claudia answered it, her voice softening very quickly. She hung up.

"That was Teddy. He was wondering if Mason was available to help him this afternoon. He has a stakeout and it's easier with two."

"Why?" asked Mason.

"Less peeing in a bottle."

Mason thought about that for a second, then looked at Julia. "Am I available?"

"Yes," she said, "I'll be happy to see the back of you." She looked at Claudia. "Is Teddy in his office?"

"I think so. I don't actually have a tracker on him."

"OK, let's finish eating, then do a quick status on Alexa's case. We'll give Teddy a call from the office." She forked up the last bite of her breakfast and stood up. "Let's go."

Claudia smacked the table much as Julia had done earlier. "They haven't finished."

Will stood up, holding his piece of toast. "No worries. When she's in this mood I like to move quickly and keep my head down."

Mason was already out the door.

~~~

"WHERE ARE WE at?" Julia threw herself down on the sofa and crossed her legs. She was clearly feeling better and no longer shooting daggers at Mason. Mason pulled a cushion in front of herself, just in case. Teddy had been called and was currently regarding them from a Zoom window on the big screen.

"Yeah," he said, now. "What happened up in Berkeley?"

"Well," said Julia, "we talked to ex-husbands Richard Streppo and Dave McGann, neither of whom seem all that pissed with Alexa anymore, and got leads on Lisa Rawlings, Fuzzy, and someone Fuzzy worked for whose name no one remembers."

Teddy looked surprised. "Can you call it a lead if you don't have a name?"

"Well," said Mason, "maybe Will found a name?"

Will shrugged. "Nope. I got a little lucky on Fuzzy. It's a regularly used alias for a guy named Michael Jones."

"Mike Jones? How did he arrive at Fuzzy?"

"Unclear. He was indeed a medium-time crook in the nineties, but he went to jail in 2010 and has been there ever since. He might be coordinating mail from there, but it didn't sound like he and Alexa ever really had serious beef, so maybe that's all there is to it."

"Fair enough. And the guy he worked for?"

"Nothing. There are half a dozen names, maybe more, associated with him at that time, but no one consistent, at least not that I've found yet."

"What about her old employers, Teddy?"
~~~

Teddy cleared his throat. "I have contact information and an address for one of them. She's a therapist now; still working on the others."

Julia nodded. "Will can call her today and make an appointment. We'll do it this week. This afternoon you're going to be helping Teddy." She gestured to Mason, then looked up at the Oz-like head on the screen. "What do you have in mind for our girl? Please tell me it's sewing mailbags or something."

Teddy raised an eyebrow. "Why would it be that? Are you in a cranky mood, Julia?"

Silence.

"Did she eat?" he said to the other two. They nodded.

"Is it because of your date? That's tonight, right?"

Mason and Will looked at Julia. Who stared at Teddy and said nothing. Pointedly.

He cleared his throat. "Alright, well, moving on. It's a straight tailing job. I'll teach her the finer points of surveillance as we go." He shrugged. "I've been doing it for a couple of days on my own, but the steering wheel's getting tired of my material."

TEDDY'S STAKEOUT WAS in West Hollywood, on a residential side street. He parked six or seven houses away and leaned his seat back, getting comfortable.

Today he was wearing a different linen suit, a different silk shirt, and the same relaxed, good-humored expression.

"Have you ever done a stakeout before?" he asked.

Mason shook her head. "I've watched suspects from a distance. Does that count?"

"Sure. The obvious part is not to be seen yourself, but mostly it's light clerical work with associated muscle fatigue. I've spent the last several days establishing what is a normal schedule for our bird, when she usually goes to work, when she usually comes back, when she walks her dog, when she goes to the store, et cetera. Most of us, particularly those of us who work a regular job, have a pretty set schedule. We settle into routine and, if we're lucky, feel secure and contented within it. For some of us, me included, a regular schedule is eventually a vise that closes about our neck, choking off the air of inspiration and curiosity. But some people love it, and what can you do?"

Mason looked at him. "I have a checkered relationship with routine, so I hear you. There are things I like to do regularly."

"Sure."

"Like working out and going to meetings. But if things get too predictable and consistent, I get a little squirrelly." Mason thought about it. "But to be honest, my life hasn't been very predictable or consistent, so it's never really been a problem. Not yet anyway."

"How long have you been working for Julia?"

"About six months."

"She said you saved her life."

"Once."

"Well, that's nice."

"Yeah." There was a pause. "Mind you, she saved mine a week or so ago, so I think we're even."

"That's a nice exchange. Keep that shit up."

"So," asked Mason, "who are we watching and why?"

Teddy stretched and rolled his shoulders. "I'm getting a

little old for all this sitting. We are watching a woman named Clarice, who doesn't actually have a regular job, but who does have a long-term boyfriend."

"Who thinks she's cheating on him?" Mason frowned. "Do you do a lot of domestic stuff?"

"He isn't sure she's cheating on him; he just suspects something is going on."

"Can't he just ask her?"

"He has. She says everything is fine."

Mason was quiet. "Don't you feel weird, getting involved in people's private lives? Doesn't she have an expectation of privacy?"

"She does, and actually, California explicitly protects that privacy to a greater extent than the federal government. However, public spaces, which is what this street constitutes, are fairer game. He's not wiretapping her house, or having me break into her phone; he just wants to know where she goes when she leaves the house." He turned and looked at Mason. "And yes, you could argue that a relationship where you need to hire a PI to get answers to very personal questions has a problem, and maybe it does. But most of the work I do is domestic in nature. If investigating infidelity bothers you, PI work might not be your jam."

Mason thought about it. "I guess I hadn't really thought about what I thought, if you know what I mean."

"Julia does mostly criminal work. PIs mostly do domestic. Infidelity, child custody, insurance fraud, that kind of thing. We largely do work that confirms someone's suspicions, if you follow me. They think their wife is cheating, or they think their ex isn't taking good care of the kids, or they suspect someone's repeated claims of back injury are an exaggeration. It's a little bit dispiriting at times, because everybody lies."

"Everybody?"

"Everybody." Teddy's tone was firm. "Not all the time, not even necessarily a lot, but everybody lies about something, sometime. We do it casually, when someone asks how we are and we say fine; we do it seriously, when someone asks where we were last night and we say at home when actually we were at a bar; and we do it for profit, manipulation and gain."

"That's a dark point of view."

"Based on extensive evidence." Teddy shrugged. "And most of the time it's fine. Lies are lubricant, they keep the peace. But sometimes . . ." He broke off. "There she is. Jeans and yellow baseball hat."

A young woman was coming out of a house a little way down the block. Mason spotted her and nodded. "OK, now what do we do?"

Teddy was opening the car door. "We follow."

Clarice was walking down the street at a pace that suggested she had somewhere to go, but no particular urgency about getting there. Mason and Teddy were half a block behind, and Teddy was teaching as he went.

"Obviously, you need to keep your target in sight while staying out of sight yourself, which is harder than you might think. However, most people don't think for a second that anyone is following them, especially on a crowded street, so it's not too challenging." He sped up a little. "Clarice hasn't looked behind her even once, so it's probably pretty safe to assume she has no idea we're here." He looked ahead. "There's a four-way junction coming up. I want you to cross to the other side of the street and close the gap a little, so if she turns you will be able to maintain line of sight longer than I can. We'll regroup after the crosswalk."

Mason nodded and crossed the street. She sped up a bit until she was almost level with Clarice, and when they reached the junction, Clarice did indeed turn left. Mason kept an eye on her as she turned, and Mason crossed back to the other side of the street where Teddy was just drawing level. He'd pulled on a baseball cap, and for a minute she hadn't been able to spot him. He handed her a beanie.

"See?" he said. "Because you were closer and farther away at the same time, physics being what it is, you kept sight when I couldn't. It's a lot easier tailing with two. Put on the hat. It helps to change your appearance a little every so often."

They were still half a block behind Clarice, who had put earbuds in and sped up a little.

"She's walked this way several times before, but never did anything interesting. Not sure why, but I feel like today might be the day . . . I want you to cross the street again and get ahead of her. We're coming up on Santa Monica Boulevard, and I want you to get there first. Wait on the far side of the street and be there before she turns the corner."

Mason shook her head. "I'll never get ahead of her without running."

Teddy looked at her. "You're wearing leggings and a sweatshirt, so run. She's got earbuds in, she won't hear you, you'll be on the other side of the street, so she won't see you, and if she does look over, you'll just look like yet another jogger."

"In Doc Martens?"

He shrugged. "Solid parked cars on both sides. She can't

see your feet. You only need to get ahead a little bit to beat her to the corner. Chop-chop."

Mason made a face but jogged across the street and ran to the corner of Santa Monica Boulevard, turning and crossing to the far side. She was in luck: The traffic light was with her. Once on the other side, she stopped and turned back to watch.

Clarice came around the corner and went into a drugstore. Teddy was right behind her, and followed her in, after signaling to Mason to stay put.

They ended up following Clarice for another twenty minutes, as she ran errands. Teddy would follow behind, and have Mason go ahead, then switch, then one of them would cross the street . . . It was a lot more involved than Mason had expected, and she found it amusing and interesting. Especially because Teddy apparently had an endless supply of hats and kept changing them. Finally, Clarice entered an office building, and they stopped across the street.

"Go look at the list of companies in the building," said Teddy. "Text me a photo."

Mason looked up at the building, which was a midsize seventies undifferentiated, nothing special, with stores on the ground floor. "It looks like the kind of building my doctor has an office in. Mixed-use, right?"

"Yeah, but this neighborhood it's mostly medical, as you say. Go take a look."

Mason did as she was told and sent him a photo of the list of companies. They were, as he had said, mostly doctors and therapists, some specialists, the occasional single name with no indication as to service, that kind of thing.

As she was standing there, Clarice came out of a bathroom

on the ground floor, just behind her, and walked over to the elevator.

Damn.

There was no one else in the lobby, so Mason couldn't call Teddy, and didn't have time to text him before the elevator arrived. So she impulsively joined Clarice, and the two women stood there for a moment, waiting for the elevator.

Clarice shot Mason a look, and gave her a small, polite smile. Mason smiled back, then returned to gazing at the floor indicators. The elevator was on its way, steadily ticking down from the fifth floor.

The doors opened, and they stepped in.

Clarice pressed three, then turned to Mason with her finger near the buttons. "Which floor?"

"Also three," said Mason, praying there wouldn't be follow-up questions.

Her phone pinged in her pocket. She stepped to the back of the elevator and pulled it out of her pocket. Teddy. What gives? Where are you?

They reached the third floor before she had a chance to text back, so she shoved the phone into her pocket and followed Clarice out of the elevator. Clarice turned right. Mason turned as if to go left and discovered there was no left. Not literally; she could turn left, but there were no doors in that direction. Fuck.

Clarice was walking down the hall, when suddenly she turned back to Mason.

"I'm sorry . . . are you my three p.m.?"

Mason paused. "I'm sorry?" Dammit, Teddy was going to be furious. Avoid eye contact at all costs, he'd said. Eye contact makes you memorable. What about actual conversation? Not good, presumably.

"Are you here for photos? I have a three p.m. appointment, and suddenly thought it might be you?"

Mason had often gotten herself into trouble due to her inability to control her impulses. It was a major feature, in fact. And here she was, about to do it again.

"Yes," she said, firmly. "I'm here for photos."

Clarice smiled. "Great. Come on in. We'll get started." She opened a door, and Mason followed her in, trying to look like someone who was here to get photos. Photos of what, she didn't know, and what she was going to do when Clarice's actual client showed up, she also didn't know, but here she was, and she was going to roll with it.

Coming into the room, Mason realized she was walking into a photography studio, which tracked.

"You can get changed over there," said Clarice, pointing to one of those old-fashioned screens. "I pulled a load of options based on the sizing you sent me . . ." She paused and looked at Mason more carefully. "Although, now that I look at you, I think I must have misunderstood. You said you were a 14–16 . . . You look more . . . You look less . . ."

"Yeah," said Mason, "I must have mistyped. I'll make it work."

"Well," began Clarice, but Mason went behind the screen and started looking through the clothing that was there, realizing as she picked up a red silk camisole that she'd made an egregious error heading down this path. It was all underwear. Fancy underwear. Mason was a solid all-cotton, Fruit of the Loom, boy short–wearing underwear person, with not a single piece of lace or underwire in her collection, and this array of lacy, boned and ribboned lingerie was freaking her out. Time to improvise. Or rather, re-improvise.

She stepped out from behind the screen. "I'll be honest," she said, lying through her teeth, "I'm having second thoughts."

Clarice had been setting up her camera, attaching lenses, or whatever it was one does with a camera. She turned to look at Mason and smiled. She put the camera down.

"That's entirely normal. I understand. Most people are nervous their first time, but I promise you I'll make you feel comfortable."

Mason looked around. A chaise lounge. Pillows. Long ostrich feather boas. Fans.

"Can we just talk for a minute? Maybe I'll calm down."

"Sure," said Clarice. She sat on the chaise and patted it. "Have a seat."

"So . . . how did you get into this?"

"Boudoir photography?" Clarice laughed. "I sort of slid into it sideways. I studied photography in college, then couldn't really find work afterward, and then I did some photos for a friend. She wanted something sexy for her boyfriend, but it's hard to take good sexy selfies. It's an art." Clarice shrugged. "Much easier to get a friend to do it, so that's what she did. And they turned out great, great enough that she showed our other friends, and then I started doing it more."

"And do you enjoy it?" Mason asked.

"I do," said Clarice. She hesitated, then she said again, "I do."

Mason raised her eyebrows and waited. She'd found that people didn't like silence all that much and would often say things they'd usually keep to themselves, simply in order to break it.

"My boyfriend . . ." said Clarice, then stopped.

"Thinks it's great?" suggested Mason.

Clarice shook her head. "He doesn't know about it."

"How come?"

"Oh, I don't know . . ." Clarice looked uncomfortable. "If I'd told him right away, it wouldn't have mattered, he doesn't give a shit, but now it's been over a year and I have an entire business and so the secret got too big to share."

Mason nodded. "Yeah, little lies have a way of growing."

"It's not like, 'Oh, I didn't tell you about this,' it's 'I didn't tell you about this FOR A YEAR,' and it's the year that matters." She looked at Mason, carefully, took a breath and changed the subject. "What made you want to get pictures taken?"

"Uh . . . it was just an impulse."

"You have a very casual aesthetic," said Clarice. "I can understand why you might want to get dressed up a bit. It's fun to explore different sides of yourself. My clients want to see themselves in a different way, or just sometimes want to see themselves as they feel they actually are, if you know what I mean?"

"No, what do you mean?"

Clarice sighed. "We tell ourselves stories about ourselves, right? We're this person, we do these things, this is how our life is. And sometimes it feels hard to change that, that we've worn a groove in our life and are just moving along with the sides getting higher and higher. Doing something slightly risqué, like openly displaying a more sexual side of ourselves, a more objectified side, shakes us up a bit. Pushes down those walls."

"Do your clients ever regret it?"

"I don't know. It's funny . . . women talk to me very intimately in the sessions, reveal themselves, but I never hear from them again. It's like they're embarrassed that they came to me, like I'm a hooker or something." She shrugged. "No judgment."

Distantly, Mason heard the elevator bell. She stood up. "I think I'm going to come back another day," she said, grateful she hadn't gotten undressed and re-dressed as a French maid or whatever, because it would have made this sudden exit a lot harder. "Sorry, I'm just not . . ."

Clarice smiled at her. "It's OK, just text me and rebook when you're ready."

Mason nodded and made it to the door and through just in time to step aside to let a more curvaceous woman enter.

"Hi," said the woman. "I have an appointment at three o'clock?"

Mason was down the hall and onto the stairs too quickly to hear Clarice's response, but as she took the stairs three at a time, she thought about what Teddy had told her: Everybody lies. She'd just done it herself.

16

TEDDY FOUND MASON'S story highly amusing, and as he drove her home, he said he looked forward to telling Julia and the gang all about it.

"Do you have to?" asked Mason, uncomfortably. She watched his face as he drove up the canyon, the light playing over his cheekbones. He was very handsome, and she wondered how helpful that was in doing his job. People tend to find attractive people more trustworthy, more likable, despite ample evidence to support the "not judging a book by its cover" concept.

"Whyever not?" he said, tipping his head back and regarding her thoughtfully. "You winged a difficult situation, discovered why our target was lying to her boyfriend, where she was going and what she was doing, and managed to keep your shirt on and get away all on your first day. You're a natural. I would have thought you'd be shouting it from the rooftops."

"I feel weird about lying to her," said Mason, not sure herself why she felt that way.

Teddy grinned. "You improvised and played with the truth a little. You were doing your job, and you did it well. No harm, no foul."

"Well, she's going to wonder what the hell that was, right?

Why a total stranger followed her into her studio and pretended to want photos taken when she didn't." Mason drew her eyebrows together. "I would be freaked out, personally."

Teddy thought about it. "The question is, is it going to alarm her sufficiently that she comes clean to her boyfriend? I'm not entirely sure why she was keeping it a secret anyway. It's not that big a deal."

"I get it," said Mason. "The secret itself gets away from you, and the length of time makes it so much worse than the content of the lie itself, right? She said it herself; it's not that she didn't tell him about it up front, it's that she kept *not* telling him for so long. So each time she didn't tell him sort of compounded the lie."

"Like you not telling Julia you're still investigating Jonathan's murder?"

Mason shot him a look. "Or like you not telling her?"

Teddy laughed. "She scares me—I'm not afraid to admit it." He headed up the hill toward Julia's house. "How's the organizing coming along?"

"Slowly," said Mason.

"Keep at it," said Teddy. "The littlest thing can crack a case, so you need to get your head around the little things. You should pull together a timeline for Alexa, too."

"Of the case?"

"Of her life. The notes suggest it's something from the past, right? You need to go back to the beginning."

"OK. I know where she was born, and more or less when. I guess I can ask her the rest."

"Well, you know when the fire happened—that's public record. And you know when she got sober, because you presumably know her sobriety date?"

Mason nodded.

"And you might know her wedding anniversary."

Mason nodded again. "Yes, because she always throws a party."

"Great. You'll be surprised how much you know already, and then you can get her to fill in the blanks." He turned into the long driveway to Julia's house, clouds of dust rising up from the wheels. "What we do is who we are, so work out what she did, and when and where she did it, and look for patterns."

Mason nodded. "Are you going to call the boyfriend and tell him?"

Teddy nodded. "Yeah, after I drop you off, before she beats us to it."

"Do you have to?"

"Yes," said Teddy. "That would be the entire point of the exercise, right?"

"But she doesn't want him to know."

Teddy frowned at her. "I would argue that she does want him to know, she's just not sure how to tell him. You're going to need to think about this if you want to become an investigator. You routinely break people's privacy, their secrecy, because someone else is paying you to do so."

"Do you always tell the client what you see?"

Teddy paused for a moment, then shook his head. "No, not always. One time I had a client who had me tail his wife because he said she was cheating, but it turned out she was seeing a lawyer in order to file a restraining order and leave him. He was abusive, controlling, and once I worked out what was going on, I kept silent. I gave her time to pull it together and make it out, and then I told him." He shrugged. "He refused to pay me and threatened to take me to court, but he couldn't prove when I knew anything, so he didn't have a leg to stand on. And when he shoved me, I shoved back, which of course he wasn't used to, the bully. Our business arrangement ended less than amicably."

"So why can't we do that here?"

"Because in my opinion, the client deserves an answer to his question, and I wouldn't be surprised if they work it out just fine. He's not going to be happy that she kept a secret, but I think he'll get why, and I think he'll get over it."

"You can't know for sure."

"No, but that's the position the job puts you in: You use your discretion and judgment, and you have to be OK with that. If you're not, then maybe PI work is not for you."

They pulled up to the house.

"You coming in?" asked Mason, as she opened the door.

"No, although if I'm lucky, I'll get invited back later." Teddy grinned through the car window at her. "I'll let you tell Julia about your triumph yourself."

"It doesn't really feel like a triumph."

"Well, it was. Go have dinner, Mason. You did good."

Mason wasn't so sure, but as she got changed, she looked at her underwear with a slightly critical eye. That red camisole had been so soft . . . She wondered for a second about Archie's opinion of underwear, then shook her head like a dog getting out of water and pulled herself together.

IT TURNED OUT Julia had already left for dinner with Justin Avermore, so Mason spent a couple hours trying to come up with a timeline for Alexa. Teddy had been right: She knew quite a lot. She knew when Alexa had been born, and where. She knew approximately when she'd moved to Oakland, because she'd said it had been a year or so before the fire, and she knew when she'd headed south to Los Angeles, because she'd said it had been the week after the fire. As she filled in approximate dates and locations, she started to get a better sense of who Alexa had been, as a young woman, not much older than she herself was now. She sat back and looked at the big piece of paper. Maybe she could start a new wall, with more string and pushpins?

Her phone rang.

"Hey there." Her sister's voice, quiet.

Mason was surprised and said so. "Hey, Lou, I'm surprised to hear from you. Is everything OK with Dad?"

"Yeah. He's insisting on going back to work, and I'm not sure it's a good idea. I thought maybe you could talk to him?"

"Me? Since when does he listen to me?"

Louise snorted. "You've always been his favorite, and you know it."

Mason literally took the phone away from her ear and stared at it. "Firstly, no, and secondly, how could I know it when it's not true?" She paused and took a breath. "Are you OK?"

"I guess . . ." Louise sighed. "I don't know what to do about Dad, and Mom is bugging me to help him, and it's all a bit much."

Wow. Mason wasn't sure what to say. Louise's defining characteristic had always been certainty.

"Well, what have you tried, with Dad?"

"I wrote to the department and suggested legal action might be forthcoming."

"On what grounds?"

"Harassment. Defamation of character. Slander."

"And what did they say?"

"They said they had no idea what I was talking about. So then I went back to Dad and asked him if he was sure this Eberling guy had been talking smack about him, and he got all affronted and asked if I was suggesting he was getting paranoid delusions, which I wasn't, but you know how he gets."

"I do."

"And I wrote to the union, such as it is, and they said with no proof, there's nothing much I can do."

"Do you want me to help?"

"I don't know."

"I can talk to the guy."

"He'll probably deny it, too." Another sigh, heavier this time. "I'm not good at direct confrontation."

Mason thought over her entire life with her sister and raised her eyebrows. "You're not? You were always pretty damn good at confronting me."

"You're different. I'm not scared of you." She paused, then said, "Tax law isn't very dramatic. It's not like I go into court on a regular basis."

Mason laughed. "Fair enough." She thought about it. "I'm sure I'll be up again soon. This case we're on seems to revolve around the Bay Area. Let's get together and work it out, OK?"

"Yeah . . ." She fell silent.

Mason was perplexed. Her sister didn't sound right. "Lou, what's going on?"

There was a long sigh. "I don't know," she said, eventually. "Being home is wigging me out, I guess. I'm . . ."

Mason waited.

"I'm sorry, Mason."

"You're sorry? For what?"

"For always busting your balls. Mom was needling me this morning, and I suddenly had the epiphany that it's what I do to you, always getting at you for this thing or that thing, some childhood issue, and that I don't like it when she does it, and I bet you don't like it when I do."

"You're right, I don't," said Mason, really quite taken aback. "But it's OK. Like Dad said when Julia and I were up there, families fall into familiar patterns."

"I guess . . . But I want you to know I actually think you're kind of a badass. You've always just been yourself, and I'm not sure I've ever been as brave as you. I've just done what's expected, what's right. And now I'm in my early thirties, alone, with a career that doesn't really interest me and no personal life at all. It's not an excuse, but . . . I think that's why I've acted the way I have."

Mason wasn't sure what to say. "Lou, I . . ."

"I just wanted to say that, is all. And maybe next time you come up we can hang, and I'll try not to be such a bitch. And maybe you can come and visit me in Chicago."

Mason found herself grinning. "Sure. Or you can come to LA. It's warmer here for sure, and Julia's life is well worth visiting."

"Yeah . . . I guess that's part of it. Seeing you with her, I realized you kind of have it going on right now. You're sober, you're building a life, you work for a movie star . . ."

Someone scratched at Mason's door, making her jump. "Hey, Lou, much as I'm enjoying this surprise lovefest, I gotta go. Someone's here."

"OK." A small pause, then, "Thanks, Natasha."

"You're welcome, Lou. We'll talk soon." Mason hung up, shook her head to clear the weirdness of that conversation, then got to her feet to see who was at the door.

"Jesus wept, Julia," she said, finding her boss outside. "You scared me."

"Bonus," said Julia, sweeping in. She was wearing a very elegant dress, high necked but tight waisted, with little buttons up the back.

"Nice outfit," said Mason, closing the door. "Sort of sexy schoolmistressy."

"Not exactly what I was going for, but that's OK," replied Julia, throwing herself down on Mason's sofa, which was squishy green velvet. "It's Norma Kamali, vintage eighties, not that you care."

"I care," said Mason, sitting back down on the floor. "Or at least, I'm trying to care."

"Doubtful," said Julia.

"I just had a very strange conversation with my sister."

"Strange how?"

"Strange, friendly," replied Mason.

"Huh. That's unexpected. But nice, right?"

"Sure. How was dinner?" Mason was a little too tired to tease Julia, but she was always down to hear the tea.

"Meh," said Julia. "He's charming, and certainly handsome, but I don't know . . . there's something not quite right."

"Apart from poisoning all those people?"

Julia shrugged. "He says it wasn't his wine. He got quite heated about it, actually. It was part of what put me off. I don't mind a temper, in men or women—I have one myself—but he got a little personal about Jennifer in a way I didn't like.

And . . . oh, I don't know. I just wasn't feeling it." She looked at Mason. "How was your afternoon with Teddy?"

"I enjoyed it. I liked learning to tail. I like being competent, you know what I mean?"

"Totally. I think you'll make an excellent PI, if that's what you decide to do." She looked at the big piece of paper on the floor. "What's all this?"

"Teddy told me to make a timeline for Alexa, so that's what I've been doing."

Julia flipped the paper around. "How are you feeling about this? About digging into Alexa like this?"

"OK, I guess. I mean, I don't want her to get hurt."

"She's not being completely honest with us, I don't think."

Mason made a face. "Teddy says everybody lies."

"He's right. Usually to protect themselves, not to prevent other people from helping them."

"I guess it doesn't feel that way to her."

"Right. Which means either it's a big enough secret to be worth keeping, even if it hurts her, or it's so insignificant that she doesn't see its importance. I guess that's what we're trying to find out." Julia got to her feet. "Well, I'm glad the afternoon went smoothly."

"I'm sorry the dinner didn't."

"It's fine. Like I said, I like to keep my private life private, and one way to do that is to not have much of a private life at all." She walked to the door. "I've always been happy on my own, anyway."

"Me, too," said Mason.

"You should go out with Archie, though," said Julia. "I think you two might be good for each other."

Mason leaned on the door and watched her boss walk into

the starry night. “I think you just have money on it,” she replied.

“Will cannot keep his mouth shut,” floated back Julia’s voice.

“True story,” said Mason, closing the door.

17

IN THE MIDDLE of the night, Mason came awake like a meerkat, sitting up in bed and grabbing her ringing phone in one fluid movement. The time caught her eye as she answered the call: two a.m. She was half-awake, but getting all the way, fast. Her first thought was her father.

"Yes? Mom?"

"No . . . it's me." Alexa. Sounding both very far away and very close, all at once. "Sorry to wake you."

"It's OK . . . What's up?" Mason realized she was hot and sweaty, and pushed the covers off, revealing Phil curled up by her knees. He blinked at her reproachfully, then put his head back down. "Are you OK?"

"No . . . I think someone's in the house. Scott's not here."

"Call the cops."

"No . . . I'm . . . not sure. Something woke me up, but I've been sitting here for ten minutes in a panic and there haven't been any more noises, or anything . . ."

Mason swung her legs over the side of the bed. "I'm on my way."

"No . . . it's OK . . . I don't even know why I called you. I'm just freaking out about nothing."

Mason was already pulling on her boots, having thrown on sweatpants and a sweatshirt. "Lex, I'm out the door. Wait for me. I'll be there before you know it."

MASON HAD ACCESS to Julia's extensive collection of cars and grabbed the keys to the 1955 Porsche Speedster. She didn't want to get pulled over by the police on her way to Glendale, but she wanted to be quick. She headed up the canyon to the top of the crest and was on the freeway heading to Glendale in a matter of minutes. At two in the morning there was very little traffic, and she kept it at eighty pretty much the whole way. Swooping up the hill to Alexa's house, she killed the lights as she approached and looked carefully at the street. Nothing unusual to see: Alexa's car was in the driveway; her husband's was not.

Mason knocked on the door and found it ajar. She wished she had a weapon of some kind to pull, but she didn't, so she just raised her fists and shouldered the door open. The house was dark, apart from a couple of those plug-in earthquake lights people in Los Angeles tend to have, and she couldn't hear anything.

Alexa's house was open-plan on the main floor, with a view across the hills from big picture windows. Right now, it was a scattering of bright lights against an inky night, and Mason's eyes adjusted very quickly. She moved carefully to the center of the room, making out the edges of the kitchen island ahead of her, the pale rectangle of a pull-down projector screen to her right.

No sound. No movement. No nothing.

"Mason?" Her sponsor's voice was surprisingly close, and Mason jumped.

"Alexa? Where are you?"

"On the stairs."

Alexa's house had the bedrooms downstairs, as was common for hillside homes, and Mason found her sitting huddled halfway down the enclosed staircase, a baseball bat propped against the wall next to her. She was very small as she sat, and probably cold, wearing a nightgown with nothing on her feet. Mason flicked on a lamp in the living room and sat next to Alexa on the stairs, tucking her feet under her and pressing up against her friend.

"Can I get you a blanket? You're going to freeze."

"I'm OK," said Alexa, blankly. "Was there anyone here?"

"Not that I could see," said Mason, "but maybe there was, and they left. The door was open—did you open it?"

"No," said Alexa. "Scott's away. He usually locks the doors at night. Maybe I forgot . . ."

"No Bear?" Bear was Alexa's enormous dog.

"No, Scott took him."

"That's unusual, right?"

Alexa shrugged. "Not very. He went up to the cabin." Alexa and Scott had a cabin in Lake Arrowhead, a few hours north of the city. "So, there was nothing? I dreamed it all?"

Mason squeezed her knee. "Come on, stand up. Let's get some tea." She stood and tugged Alexa to her feet, leading her up the stairs and into the kitchen.

She plonked Alexa on a stool and went to turn on the kettle. She pulled mugs down from the cabinet, doing the things her sponsor had done for her so many times in this very room.

She didn't say anything until she put the tea, heavily honeyed, in front of Alexa.

"Tell me exactly what happened."

"I don't know." Alexa shrugged. "I was asleep and then I wasn't, and I was completely convinced there was someone in the room. My heart was pounding. It felt like waking up from a nightmare, but I was definitely awake."

"Did you turn on the light? Say anything?"

Alexa shook her head. "I was frozen. But I swear someone was there. I couldn't catch my breath. I was panicked." She hugged herself tighter, but it didn't seem to help.

"Did they move? Say anything?" Mason was keeping her voice low and listening hard at the same time. She could hear the wind outside, she could hear the ticking of a heating system, but she couldn't hear anything else. She had no sense there was anyone in the house besides the two of them, but she kept her antennae extended, just in case. She looked around at the windows, wished she knew more about how to evaluate a scene, wished Teddy was there to help them both.

Alexa answered her. "No . . . it was like they just faded away. One minute I felt there was someone there; the next I realized there wasn't." She reached for the tea, and her hand was still shaking. Mason ran downstairs and brought back her dressing gown, draping it around her shoulders. Alexa was sipping the tea, calming down.

"When I felt there was no one in the room, I called you. Then I thought I heard the door opening and suddenly I got some balls back and got up to go investigate."

"Bat in hand."

Alexa tried a smile, but it wasn't super convincing. "Yes. But there was no one here, nothing."

Mason got up and reached for the bat. "Well, let me just check outside."

She started to the door, but Alexa reached out her hand. "Mason, just close the door. Maybe it was the wind."

Mason raised her eyebrows. "It gets breezy here, but not enough to open a dead bolt." She went to the door and took a quick look at the lock. No scratch marks or anything she could see, not that she was an expert. Again, that slight frustration that she didn't have the skills she needed to be more effective. She pulled the door open, cautiously, even though she herself had just come through it, and stepped out into the night.

It's cold at three in the morning, even in Los Angeles, and Mason could see her breath as she walked carefully down the driveway. She stood in the street and listened. Willed her heart to calm, so she could hear above its insistent thumping.

Nothing. Distant traffic on the 134. An owl, almost as far away. She looked up the street: no cars had their lights on, no sound of cooling engines ticking, apart from her own. She rested her hand on her car hood, feeling how warm it still was. She walked up the street, touching cars as she went, but for half a dozen in each direction, all was cold.

She turned back to the house and heard a sudden rustling in Alexa's garden. She froze, then slowly raised the bat.

"I can hear you," she said, surprised at how firm her voice sounded. "Come out."

No response.

She stepped closer to the shrubbery, smacked her booted foot down hard on the cement. "Come out!"

A sharp movement, a coil of muscle. There he was.

They looked at each other for a moment, then the coyote blinked and turned to trot away.

MASON WENT BACK into the house, still surprised. "There was a coyote. Do you see them a lot?"

Alexa nodded. "All the time. I lock the cats in at night. Sometimes they knock over the trash, but that could be raccoons. Nothing else?"

Mason shook her head.

"Maybe I dreamed the whole thing."

"The coyote didn't open the door," replied Mason.

"Maybe I opened it after all. Maybe I was just half-asleep and don't remember."

"You said you thought you heard the door, and you probably did. Let's do a quick walk around and check."

Alexa looked at her. "Can I stay here? I'm not feeling very good."

Mason went over and hugged her. "Of course. I'm sure if there was someone here, they're gone. I just want to make certain. Then we can call the cops."

"No."

"Why not?"

"Because I'm tired and maybe I was just having a bad dream."

"What about the door?"

"No, Mason." Alexa got up and reached for her bag, which was sitting on a nearby chair. "I'm going to take half a Xanax and go back to sleep." She smiled at Mason. "Don't worry, they're prescribed." AA makes a clear distinction between taking drugs that are prescribed by a doctor, taken as prescribed, and those used and abused by so many addicts. Prescription drugs are dangerous, but so is untreated depression and anxiety.

Alexa rustled around in her bag and there was a familiar clinking. She paused, frowned. Mason had been walking toward the stairs, but she stopped and looked around. She knew that sound, knew it in her bones.

Alexa drew out three small bottles. Miniatures. Like you get on an airplane. Vodka. She looked at Mason.

"These . . . these aren't mine."

Mason looked at her. Alcoholics lie; it's a defining feature. Was Alexa lying about the vodka, or was she as surprised by its appearance as Mason was?

"And you're sure they weren't in there earlier?"

"Of course. After twenty-eight years of not drinking, I'm unlikely not to notice myself carrying alcohol, right?" She placed the bottles on the table in front of her and stared at them. "I didn't buy them, and they weren't there when I went to bed."

"So, someone broke into the house in order to put booze in your bag?" It didn't sound very plausible, but then neither did Alexa drinking after so long. But there was a nagging worry at the back of Mason's head. She started to walk toward Alexa, intending to take the bottles and bring them back for Will to check for fingerprints.

Alexa shrugged, clearly shocked. The tiny bottles seemed so out of place in this kitchen, where sober people lived and cooked and laughed. Suddenly, Alexa reached for one, twisted it open. She stood and carried it to the sink, pouring it out, then did the same with the second, and the third, turning her head to avoid the smell. Then she opened the kitchen window behind the sink and threw them, hard, arcing into the night into her garden below.

"I don't even want them in the trash," she said, firmly. "Not today, Satan."

18

AS MASON DROVE over the top of the ridge heading back into the canyon, she could see the beginnings of light in the sky. The moon was still very clear and high, but the stars were twinkling out. She thought about the many times she'd stumbled home at this time, bars finally closed, fights over, just the slightly out-of-control walk home as the light changed.

She'd checked Alexa's house, tucked her sponsor into bed, then locked the dead bolt from the outside and posted the keys through the mail slot. She took photos of the lock, which seemed pointless, but she knew Will was going to ask if she had. And now, as she put the car away and walked into her guesthouse, she wondered again about the vodka.

Alexa had been a vodka drinker—she knew that from hearing her share in meetings, and from knowing her story. Many drunks describe themselves as "garbage heads," happy to drink or swallow anything as long as it will change their mood, and while Alexa had certainly tried everything going, she had settled into a long and abusive relationship with vodka that ended only with her sobriety. So, either she was drinking again, or considering it, or someone was trying to mess with her head by offering her drink of choice. All seemed unlikely, but people drink after decades of sobriety all the time. Why had Alexa emptied the bottles like that, then thrown them away? They were evidence, but maybe they were evidence she didn't want investigated. And with that in mind, why hadn't Mason herself stopped Alexa in her tracks and salvaged bottles two and three? No, she'd just stood there and watched Alexa throw them away, unwilling to intervene. She frowned at herself as she got undressed and into bed, lowering her blinds against the rising of the sun.

It was nearly lunchtime when she woke again, and when she wandered into the kitchen, only Claudia was there, cooking something that smelled rich and delicious.

"Hi," she said, walking over to the stove to take a look. "Is that lunch or dinner?"

"Neither, for you," said Claudia, watching her take a spoon from a drawer and sample the stewing mix of meat and vegetables. "It's cat food."

Mason made a face but swallowed anyway. "It tastes great. Not sure he's going to appreciate it."

"Oh, he loves my cooking. Do you know how much crap there is in commercial cat food? It's hideous. This is much better for him. It'll make his coat all glossy and cut your vet bills."

"That's a stretch, but OK. It's very nice of you to . . . uh . . . care for him."

"I never had a cat before. They're nicer than I thought. Interesting. Friendly. Soft."

Mason looked at Claudia and wondered about her, as she often did. She didn't know her very well, despite seeing her almost every day for the last six months or so. She knew she'd met Julia in jail, so presumably not an angel, but then again, who is? And she knew she cooked like a celestial being, and now she knew she had a boyfriend she adored and was fond of at least one cat. Slowly, a picture was emerging, but it was still murky as hell.

"Where is everyone?"

"Julia is getting her nails done, in the office, and I think Will might be there, too. Teddy is at work, not here."

"Alright, I'm going to check out the traveling nail salon and report to Julia about my strange night."

"What happened?"

Mason told her. When she got to the part about the miniature bottles of vodka, Claudia sighed.

"Alexa's under a lot of stress right now. Maybe she thought about drinking, even got so far as to buy the bottles, then needed to lie about it when you were right there."

Mason didn't want to admit she'd had the same thought. "I don't think so. It seemed like she was telling the truth, that she was as surprised as I was."

Claudia stirred the stew, and said, "You know how that goes, Mason. If you want to fool others, you need to fool yourself first, and that's all there is to it. She might have been lying to you, but there's every chance she believed the lie herself." She lifted the spoon and tasted. "Hmm, needs less salt." She looked at Mason and smiled. "Did you know cats can't taste sweet things? They don't have the taste buds for it."

"Did Will tell you that?"

Claudia nodded. "But I told him it was because they had so much sweetness in their hearts they didn't need it on their tongues." She smiled to herself, then looked suddenly at Mason. "If you ever tell Julia I said that, I'll poison your food."

"You, madam, are a softy."

"Watch it."

Mason walked out of the kitchen.

WHEN SHE REACHED the office, Julia was waving her hands gently in the air and Will was getting his toenails done.

"Ah, Sleeping Beauty finally arises," said Julia, looking over and raising her eyebrows. "Up late working?"

"Yes and no," said Mason. "Someone broke into Alexa's house in the middle of the night, and she called me. I got back early and grabbed a few more hours of sleep."

"Huh, interesting. Tell me everything," said Julia.

"There's not much to tell. She woke up suddenly, thinking someone was in the room, but eventually she decided there wasn't, and when she went to look at the rest of the house, there was no one there. However, when I arrived, the front door was open." Mason pulled out her phone. "Yes, Will, I took pictures of the door, but it won't tell you anything." She handed over the phone. "And then she went to get something from her bag, and someone had put three miniatures of vodka in there."

"In her bag? Not just out on the counter?"

Mason shook her head.

There was a pause while Julia pondered this. "If someone was trying to make a statement, I feel they would have left them in the open. A nice big bottle. Are you sure she didn't just get them herself?"

"After twenty-eight years of sobriety? Why now?"

"Why any day? People relapse all the time. She's under a lot of stress."

Mason shook her head. "Claudia said the same thing, but I don't think so. She seemed as shocked as I was."

"Did you bring the bottles?" Will looked over. "I can check them for prints."

Mason made a face. "I'm sorry, no. She emptied them out and threw them out the window."

"Maybe because she bought them herself and didn't want us looking." Will's tone was calm, but clear.

"No," said Mason, starting to feel defensive, "she was just acting in the moment, getting rid of them. She didn't want them in the house. I wouldn't like it, either."

"Alright, keep your hair on. It's just a lot of trouble to go to, for no clear reason."

"Well, the reason is to mess with her, right? Someone is trying to upset her, and they're succeeding."

"Or maybe she's dancing around a relapse, and you don't want to see it."

There was a pause. The lady doing Will's toes sat back and declared herself satisfied. He held his feet up—hot pink polish with blue flowers.

"Festive," said Mason, somewhat grumpily.

"For spring," he replied. "No one can see them—it's not like I wear sandals or walk around barefoot—but they make me smile when I take my shoes off."

Julia said, "What about you, Mason? Want to get your nails done?"

Mason shook her head. "No, thanks. I want to get to work. I want to figure out who's messing with Alexa."

"Fair enough," said Julia. "We have an appointment in a couple of hours with her old boss. You've got time to eat some breakfast. Or lunch. Whatever you want to call it."

"What makes you think I didn't eat?"

"Your charming frown and lighthearted demeanor," replied her boss, sourly. "Go back to the kitchen and eat. We'll leave for Santa Monica in an hour."

Will came with her to the kitchen, claiming that he was ready for second breakfast, which led to a digression about Hobbits that Mason didn't completely follow. As they sat peacefully together at the table, eating fresh brioche and Nutella (Mason needed the sugar), she thought about Alexa, about the serious emotional debt Mason owed her. Alexa had brought her through the 12 steps of AA, had helped her stay sober, had spoken to her almost every day for the last five years. Was she who Mason thought she was? As her mind wandered over the previous evening, she found herself wishing again for more skills, more experience in this new line of work she'd found herself in. Maybe she should take Julia up on her offer, go back to school and learn how to be a real detective. Teddy seemed to always know what he was doing, and she envied that competence and confidence. She chewed her brioche, and watched as Claudia opened the window for Phil.

The cat jumped onto the counter and stood for a moment, presumably ascertaining whether or not the coast was clear.

"You know," said Will, in the tone he reserved for useful information, "cats' hearing is supremely sensitive in a variety of ways; it's not that they simply hear better. They hear a much wider range of frequencies, they are better at isolating sounds, they can hear much softer sounds than we can, and they can angle their ears 180 degrees to pinpoint where all those sounds are coming from." He watched as Phil settled down to try Claudia's latest offering. "If he could talk, he could tell us where everyone was in the house, what they're doing, and probably whether or not they're heading toward or away from us."

Mason privately thought that that level of granular information would probably be interesting to Will but not really anyone else. Regardless, Phil seemed relaxed, which meant Julia wasn't within overhearing distance.

"Will," she said, "do you think I should go back to school?"

Will looked at Claudia, who kept her back turned. She'd set out three little dishes of food and was watching to see which Phil preferred.

"I think it's always good to finish things you've started, and you only have a few credits left to get your degree. You can do that and then see how you feel. You don't need to swallow the whole thing at once. You can take it a bite at a time."

"Right." Mason thought about this. "I guess I'm already gaining hours of experience, just doing my job, and I can finish my degree in the evenings."

"Yeah, Julia had me look at all the local community colleges. There's lots of options for evening classes."

"She did?"

Will nodded. "Yes, she didn't want to make the offer if it wasn't possible to actually do it." He paused. "You know Julia pretty well by now, but maybe you haven't fully realized that she doesn't like to promise things she can't deliver. That's why we don't take on every client that comes to us. If she thinks you're fucked, and doesn't see how she can un-fuck you, she won't take the case."

"So presumably she thinks she can help Alexa."

"Yeah. Although it would be easier if we knew what it was that Alexa supposedly did. We could work from that to determine who cares about it coming out." He looked carefully at Mason. "Do you think she knows and isn't telling us?"

"I don't know." Mason popped the last bite of brioche into her mouth and chewed. "I don't think she does, but maybe she just hasn't remembered yet. Sometimes I get memories from when I was drinking that were simply lost until suddenly they weren't, do you know what I mean?"

"Yeah, like when a piece of a dream suddenly comes back to you. I get it." Will licked his fingers. "OK, let's get back to work." He looked over at Claudia. "Thanks for breakfast, Claude."

"You're welcome," she said, absently. "He really likes the liver, dammit. Julia hates liver. It's going to be hard to explain why I'm suddenly cooking so much of it." She sighed. "I'll think of something."

19

WHEN PEOPLE THINK of Los Angeles, they often think of the beach. Which is reasonable, thanks to TV and movies largely portraying Angelenos as surfing stoners in bikinis and roller skates. However, the beach they visualize most frequently is actually Santa Monica, which is a separate city of its own. And for Mason, who was an Eastsider by choice and inclination, it might as well have been a different continent.

For a start, Santa Monica is clean. It's attractive and coordinated. And the office Julia and Mason were entering was a classic of the Santa Monica lookbook: natural fibers, eclectic art, a ridiculously soft rug, a vintage coffee table.

Julia raised her eyebrows. "Nice. I guess whatever damage Alexa did wasn't too catastrophic. This woman seems to have recovered."

"She's a therapist?"

"She is now. She wasn't when Alexa worked for her. She ran a vintage clothing store."

There was a small sign by a door with the name Jane Perdian on it, with a switch next to it, and a little light. Mason, familiar with therapists' offices from both her childhood and ever since, went over and flicked the switch.

"And now we wait?" asked Julia.

"Yes. You've never been to therapy?" Mason couldn't keep the note of incredulity from her voice, and Julia raised her eyebrows.

"No, unless you count the somewhat forced counseling one gets in prison. Those conversations were mostly geared around getting me sober and into acceptance about the fact that I was in prison." She shrugged. "They did that."

"And nothing since?"

"Nope. I don't find talking about my problems very helpful. I like dressing up and pretending everything is OK, or being angry, or acting out, or relapsing, as you know." Julia flicked open one of the glossy books on the coffee table. "I find most therapists are simple creatures, whereas I am a complicated and multilayered individual."

"I bet you'd find it helpful," said Mason.

"You'd lose that bet," replied Julia.

The inner door opened, and an attractive woman poked her head through. "Julia Mann? I'm Dr. Jane Perdian. It's a pleasure to meet you." Her long blond hair was tied up in one of those effortless twists that took hours to perfect, along with multiple YouTube tutorials. Mason was secretly jealous of anyone who could do it and thought for a moment about the long hair she used to have. She preferred her buzz cut, but got hair envy every so often. Only human.

Julia nodded. "The pleasure is ours. This is Mason, my assistant. Thank you for making time to see us."

"Of course," said Dr. Perdian, leading the way back into her consulting room. This was even more neutral than the waiting room, if that were possible. Shades of flax, oatmeal and beige competed to be the least competitive, and the simple illustrations on the walls served to reinforce that there were no windows to fling yourself out of. Although maybe that was just Mason's impression.

"You wanted to talk to me about Alexa Rousso?"

"Yes. She's experiencing some challenges that seem to be related to her past, and she thought maybe you could remember more of that past than she could." Julia smiled. "I know she's spoken to you since she got sober, and made amends, but we were hoping you might remember a little more about her than she can."

Jane Perdian nodded. "It really was a long time ago, but I remember it pretty well. I ran a vintage clothing store in Venice, and Alexa came to work for me when she was out of rehab." She paused, delicately. "The first time. She was very cool. I'm sure she still is. A fantastic dresser, a great eye for clothes and accessories . . . I was stoked to have her in the store and often took her with me when I went to appraise collections, you know." She turned to Mason, as though assuming she knew less about fashion than the older woman wearing Balenciaga in front of her, and Mason couldn't fault her for that. "Someone passes on and their heirs want to clear their collection. I would buy what I knew I could sell for more. Alexa was especially good at spotting the pearls. She would take a ten-second look and know the three pieces that mattered."

"Alright. So, what happened?"

"Well, I got a call one day from one of these people, a daughter who'd sold us a great many pieces from her late mother's collection. She'd traveled a lot in Europe, had some really beautiful things. But the daughter was concerned about something else: a jewelry box had gone missing, and a little china teapot that had actually already been appraised by a dealer and was waiting to be collected. Probably if Alexa had picked other things to steal she never would have noticed, but her good eye meant she picked what was most valuable, so she got caught."

"She'd taken these things while you were buying the clothes?"

"Yes, exactly. While I was packing up the garments she went to the bathroom, but actually just eyeballed the valuables and took a couple of things she knew she could pawn for ready cash." Jane looked at her hands. "She was drinking again, and using cocaine, and she needed more money than I was paying her."

"Did you call the cops?"

Jane shook her head. "No. She still had the items, so I returned them and explained a little bit of the situation to the daughter, and she accepted it." She looked at Julia. "I am not a vengeful person. I was more sorry for Alexa than mad. In fact, seeing how she struggled helped solidify my decision to go back to school and become a therapist. People think addicts and alcoholics are morally bankrupt, and maybe some of them are, but the majority are just dealing with a disease that pretends it's their friend. Perhaps you understand?" She looked at Mason and Julia in turn, smiling the smile Mason recognized from her own mother.

"We do," replied Julia, neutrally. "So, you fired Alexa?"

"I had to. There need to be consequences for the choices you make, otherwise you keep making the same mistakes."

"True story," said Julia. "And do you remember what happened after that?"

"I believe she went back into rehab pretty soon after that. A couple of years later she reappeared at the store, which was lucky because I was in the process of closing it, and made a formal apology for that incident, and for the several hundred dollars she'd pilfered from the cash register that I had been completely unaware of." Jane laughed. "She paid me back, and she tried to track down the daughter, too, to apologize, but I don't think she ever found her." She looked thoughtful. "She had some wonderful pieces, that woman. There was a Pierre Cardin suit that sold for nearly a thousand dollars, and a classic Burberry trench that I regretted selling because I wanted it for myself." She smiled at Julia. "I still dream about those clothes, you know? I love working as a therapist, but I miss the fun of dressing up."

"Presumably you could wear whatever you want now?"

Jane shook her head. "I try to remain neutral. Simple, classic. Too much of my own personality makes it harder for my clients to feel safe with me, which is an important part of the client-centered process."

Julia nodded. "Do you remember anything else about Alexa at that time? Friends who hung around, that kind of thing?"

Jane shook her head. "We talked a little bit about her past, and she was very honest about being fresh out of rehab, but I got the impression she was trying to leave a lot behind her. She didn't seem to be in contact with anyone from up north."

"You remember she was from Northern California?"

"Yes, I went to Cal, in Berkeley, so we knew some of the same places, although I seem to remember she was originally from farther north. I know she'd been living in Oakland for a while, but not much beyond that. She'd come to Los Angeles to get sober, and she'd been in rehab for nearly nine months, you know. She'd missed a lot, had been very much in her own bubble, which is common in rehab. She hadn't seen any of the big movies, she knew nothing about Bush v. Gore, the whole recount thing. Not that it mattered. I thought she was doing really well: She seemed to be going to meetings, she had a sponsor, I remember that."

"Name?"

"Nope, long gone. She had a boyfriend or two that used to come around the store, but no one serious. And no, before you ask, I don't remember any names."

Mason leaned forward. "Was that one incident, the one with the teapot, the only one you remember?"

"Yes, although as I said, she had been skimming from the register. It's a funny thing"—and here her eyes got cool—"addicts are such skillful liars. She looked me straight in the face and denied stealing those things, and if I hadn't already searched her locker and known she had them, I would have completely believed her. It's not that they're immoral; it's that they firmly believe that telling the lie is going to get them what they need, whatever that is, and their desire to get their own way smooths over any conscience or guilt they might have. It's supreme self-interest, almost childlike in its purity. Apart from the fact that it often has very grown-up consequences, and not just for them, but for the people they lie to. I've learned to accept it." She shrugged. "They can't help it. Once they're sober, they can fight it in themselves, they learn to pause and think before they lie, to play the tape all the way through and see the consequences, but many clients have told me they still feel no compunction about lying, there's no friction internally."

"They can also, in my experience, be brutally and rigorously honest, too," Julia said.

"Yes," replied the therapist, "but often there are consequences to that, too, and they can be blind to those. It's a fascinating thing, addiction."

"For sure," said Julia, getting to her feet. "Well, thank you so much for your time. If anything else occurs to you . . ."

"Oh, wait, I just remembered something. She had one girlfriend that used to come around all the time. Her name was Lisa. Don't know if I ever knew her last name. She was trouble, though—would be drunk when she got to the store, so I asked Alexa to stop her from coming. I'll let you know if I think of anything else."

Mason stood up and handed Jane a card with their contact info. She smiled, wondering if the other woman was leaving anything out.

"Good luck to you both," said Jane Perdian, showing them to the door. "And good luck to Alexa, too. I always liked her, despite the mistakes she made. Hate the sin but love the sinner, right?"

"Ideally," replied Julia. "But it can be hard. You have a forgiving nature."

Jane stood at the door and smiled at her. "I don't think of it as forgiveness. I think of it as hope."

20

MASON'S PHONE RANG as they reached the street, and she turned the screen to show Julia.

"Speak of the devil," she muttered, and answered Alexa's call. "What's up?"

"Where are you right now?"

"Santa Monica," replied Mason. "Why?"

"Because I'm worried about Iris but I can't leave where I am. Are you able to go to her place?"

"Which is where?"

"Venice."

"I'll call you back. Two minutes." Mason hung up and turned to Julia. "Alexa is worried about Iris."

"Why?"

"I didn't ask her that. I just assumed she had her reasons. Iris lives in Venice. Can we swing by and check on her?"

Julia nodded, and Mason called Alexa back as they headed to where she'd parked the car.

"We can go there. I'm with Julia. What's going on?"

"Well, we were supposed to have a call last night, as usual, but I didn't hear from her. Then this morning I called and she didn't answer."

"And this is unusual?"

"Totally. She rarely misses a call in the evening. It's our standing arrangement."

Mason felt her brows contract and took a split second to interrogate her own feelings. What was that tightness in her chest? Jealousy, no question. She was jealous that Iris got Alexa's attention, and she needed to work on that shit.

Alexa was still talking. "So I texted and called again, just now, and the call went straight to voicemail, so I think her phone must be dead and, I don't know, I just have a really bad feeling about it."

Mason and Julia had reached the car, and Mason clicked the key to unlock it. Sliding behind the wheel, she said, "Text me the address. We're not far. I'll call you as soon as we've made contact. I expect she's just sleeping."

"I think she relapsed."

"I think you're worrying too much. I'll call you back."

Mason put the car into gear and pulled out into traffic. She turned to Julia and handed her the phone. "Alexa is going to text the address. Will you map it and give me directions?"

"Certainly." Julia looked out the window. "Do we think Iris is drinking again?"

Mason shrugged. "Hopefully not."

"Why don't you like her?"

Mason looked at Julia. Was it that obvious?

"I think I'm just jealous because Alexa likes her." Mason swerved around two kids on an electric scooter. "And because she's blond. And skinny. And elegant."

"But apart from that," said Julia, dryly, "there's nothing standing between you and best friendship."

"Right."

Julia directed Mason along the oceanfront, and into the flat and winding streets of Venice Beach. Iris's place was an apartment in a 1950s building, referred to by local architects as "dingbats" because they often sported a stylish (in the 1950s) piece of star- or planet-shaped sculptural decoration under their building name, which would be something like "Excelsior" or "Capri" in elegant serif font over their back-in, under-cover parking.

Iris's was called the Fleur-de-Lis and had a—you guessed it—golden fleur-de-lis decoration over its name, which was rendered in wrought iron painted gold. It was a classic of its type, and Mason pulled up in front and leaned down to look across Julia at the building.

"You're blocking the parking," said her boss.

"We're not going to be here long enough for it to matter," said Mason, swinging open the car. "Which apartment is it?"

"First floor, rear," replied Julia, waiting for Mason to come around and open her door, which she did. Julia exited as regally as always and then leaned against the car. "As I don't know Iris, why don't I wait here? If someone needs to get out, I'll holler." She looked at Mason. "Off you trot."

Mason nodded and headed around the back.

The wrought iron balustrade wobbled under her hand and the pebble-dashed steps harbored some rusty water on their inner edges. Typical of the dingbat, which suffered from structural weaknesses of all kinds, and which had been outlawed by zoning and the seismic improvements in the seventies. The buildings had a tendency to collapse in earthquakes, and Mason was confident it wouldn't take much to bring this one down. Probably two tenants with simultaneous coughing fits could do it.

Iris had painted her front door yellow, presumably in the hopes of giving the place a little whimsy, but it hadn't worked. Mason could see brushstrokes in the paint as she approached and felt herself judging again. What the hell was wrong with her? She was cursing herself when she paused suddenly, realizing the door was ajar.

"Welp . . . that's not good," she muttered to herself. She knocked, gently. "Iris? You here?"

Silence.

Mason waited for a second. Should she call the police? Should she call Julia? She pulled her phone out of her pocket and weighed her options. Then, being Mason, she suddenly just pushed the door open and walked in.

It was a classic stucco box apartment. A rectangular room, with a kitchenette at one end and a flat-screen TV at the other. No smell of cat or dog, so Iris lived alone. Something smelled sweet, though; maybe Iris baked cookies for herself and sat and contemplated her life choices with chocolate on her chin.

"Iris?"

Still silence. Mason walked carefully across the room and into the tiny hallway that angled off the middle of the room, just next to the kitchen counter. She could see the corner of a dresser through the bedroom door, which was ajar.

She pushed it open. And stopped.

Iris was dead, that was instantly clear. No question one way or another; no one that color could still be alive. She was bluish-gray, though not uniformly; her legs were mottled where they hung off the bed. There was a needle in her arm, still held by the tautness of her skin, and probably helped by the scab that had formed, a tiny amount of blood around the crook of her elbow.

"Fuck," said Mason, pulling her hand off the door. She hesitated. Should she check to be certain Iris was dead before calling the police? She stepped into the room and felt suddenly sick. She had just been dissing this poor girl, and now she had OD'd, and Mason felt terrible. She walked over and touched Iris's arm. Cold. Stiff. She was wearing a white vest and a pair of pajama pants that Mason herself also owned. Target classic tartan. Peach and blue. Flannel. She'd pulled them on without any idea that these were the clothes she was going to die in.

Mason stepped backward and then noticed the note propped on the bedside table.

"Mom" on the envelope. Loopy, childish handwriting.

Mason reached out toward the envelope but stopped herself. She didn't know enough. She didn't have gloves. She pulled her phone out of her pocket and spent a few minutes taking a lot of photographs. Iris. The envelope. The layout of the bedroom. The contents of the fridge (no, she didn't know why). Mail, some of it pretty old, spread out on the kitchen counter (Mason used her elbow). She wanted to empty Iris's coat pockets, her purse . . . but she wasn't a PI yet, and she didn't know what she was doing. She went back into Iris's bedroom and stood there a moment.

"Did you call the cops already?"

Mason jumped a good two feet in the air and whirled around. Julia was standing in the bedroom doorway. She pointed at Iris.

“She’s not going anywhere, but if anyone saw us pull up in front nearly twenty minutes ago, they might tell the cops, who are going to wonder what you’ve been doing all this time.” She noticed the note on the bedside table. “What have you been doing all this time?”

“Taking photos,” said Mason, dialing 911. “But now I’m calling the cops. Go back to the car.”

“Way ahead of you,” said Julia, pausing to hold out her hand. “Keys, please. You’re going to be a while.”

21

THE COPS HAD lots of questions, most of which Mason could answer. She'd known Iris for a while. She had friends in common. Yes, she'd known she was a drug addict, although no, she hadn't expected her to OD. She'd called Alexa while she waited for the EMTs and cops to show up, and it hadn't been an easy call.

"Why didn't she call me? You're supposed to call your sponsor . . ." Alexa was crying.

Mason sighed. She herself hadn't relapsed, not yet, not today anyway, but she knew from observation that when someone had made the decision to relapse, they were hard-pressed to stop themselves. The last thing you want is to be talked out of it.

"And there's a note for her mom?" Alexa seemed stuck on this, kept returning to it.

"Yes, or at least there's an envelope marked 'Mom,' so that's what I'm thinking it means. Do you know her mom?"

"Nope, I thought they were completely estranged. I'm not even sure where she is. I know Iris was from some small town in Wisconsin, but I don't know if her mom is still there, or if there's more family, or really all that much. We hadn't reached the fourth step yet, which is where all that detail usually comes out."

The fourth step is where you do a "fearless and searching moral inventory of yourself," a kind of accounting of trouble you caused, resentments you had, people you hurt, people who hurt you, all that kind of thing. But Iris hadn't reached that point.

"I imagine the police will be able to track her down. They have resources we don't, obviously."

"I just . . ." Alexa broke down. Mason was at a loss. She heard the sirens outside and made her excuses.

And then she waited until two big guys came in, EMTs ready to save the day.

Sadly for them, this was not their day to save.

BEFORE HEADING HOME, Mason went to the diner, where Alexa was waiting for her.

"The cops might call you," Mason said, sliding into the booth. "I gave them your number. I hope that's OK."

"Of course," said Alexa, her face pale. "I still can't believe it." She looked around at Jennifer, who was sitting with her. "Had you spoken to her lately?"

"Apart from the other day with you, I saw her at a meeting last week," said Jennifer. "But she didn't see me, and I didn't speak to her." She looked at Alexa, apologetically. "I was in my own head. I didn't have space for anything else. Now, of course, I wish I had. Maybe it would have made a difference. But she looked OK. And I took her shopping the other day—remember, after we all got together?"

"Did she say anything at the meeting?" asked Mason.

"No, she just listened." Jennifer shook herself. "There was no sign at all that anything was going on with her. But then again, you never know with people, do you? They can look completely calm and normal and be all kinds of messed up inside." She shrugged. "She burst into tears in the changing room when we went shopping, but to be fair, I usually feel that way myself when trying on clothes, so I didn't think that much of it."

Alexa's voice was low. "We spoke most days, and honestly, she seemed good. We talked about the first step. She seemed to be happy about it, pleased to be making progress." The first step is the only one they say you need to do perfectly, because it's the one where you look back over your drinking life and see how powerless it made you, and how unmanageable your life became. It helps to clear the denial about having a problem, helps you start moving forward. Alexa frowned. "But maybe she started thinking about how she'd messed up her life. Maybe it all got too much for her."

Jennifer looked at Alexa. "Maybe . . . You were pretty pushy about my first step. You wanted me to get everything down I could remember. I had to think about some pretty painful stuff."

Alexa just shook her head, helplessly. "I don't think I was too pushy." She looked at her lap. "I was just trying to help."

Jennifer shrugged. "I'm just saying . . ."

Mason shook her head. "Don't blame yourself, Alexa. People do what they're going to do, right? We can't control them. She could have called you, talked it through."

"Not if she felt I wasn't going to be helpful." Alexa was distressed. "She clearly thought so." She reached for her water, and Mason noticed her hands were shaking. "I let her down."

There was silence. Then Jennifer kind of jumped a little. "Oh, I nearly forgot, I printed some pictures for you, Lex." She rootled around in her bag and pulled out an orange envelope. "From the wedding we went to, plus there's one of you with Iris, which is what made me think to bring it today." She handed it over, and Alexa flipped through the photos, putting them down on the table.

Mason craned her neck to look. Beautiful scenery, happy people in pretty dresses. "Wow, gorgeous wedding."

Alexa nodded. "It was . . ." She tailed off, having gotten to the photo of her and Iris. She held it up, the two of them grinning into the camera, waving fancy iced coffee drinks, Iris proudly displaying a 90-day chip, the small token sober people give each other to mark lengths of sobriety. "This was a happy day. She'd really started to feel physically so much better, you know?"

Everyone nodded.

Mason looked at Jennifer, who was watching Alexa. "Is that when you met Justin Avermore? At the wedding? Or did you know him before?"

Jennifer shook her head. "No, I never knew him." She looked at Alexa and seemed to be about to say something, but then added, "But that's when I decided to put his vineyard on our wine list, and what a mistake that turned out to be."

Mason remembered what Avermore had said to Julia. "It was his wine that caused the food poisoning?"

"Looks like it. It was the one drink all the customers who got sick had in common."

"But presumably more than those people drank it. Did everyone who drank it get sick?"

"Hard to tell," said Jennifer, looking hopeless. "All we can know for sure is that they all ate lots of different things, but they all drank that wine. I'm clutching at straws, obviously." She looked at Alexa again. "I'm sorry, side problems. We're here to talk about Iris."

Alexa reached across the table and covered her hand. "It's OK. Life goes on, right? We lose people and life trundles on, uncaring."

"Sometimes," replied Jennifer. "It depends, probably, on who you lose and how."

Alexa nodded. Mason wondered what she was thinking, if she was thinking about the fact that somebody hated her. She wished Alexa would remember what she could have done to inspire such venom, but apparently she was as in the dark as everyone else.

22

THE NEXT DAY, Julia, Mason and Will were sitting in the office comparing fleabites when Claudia opened the door, carrying a large bouquet of flowers.

"These came for you. And the cops are here."

Julia took the flowers and read the card. She smiled, but simply asked, "Street or detectives?"

"Detectives. The usual two. I think they have a crush on you."

"Wilson and Brooks?" Julia shrugged. "Always nice to see old friends. Even if they're not very friendly." She waved a hand. "Where did you put them?"

"I left them on the stoop."

"Huh. Speaking of unfriendly."

Claudia did indeed look cross. "I'm getting tired of not having a living room to park people in. And letting the cops in and leaving them unattended in the foyer felt . . . ill-advised."

"Understandable. Although I can't see Wilson and Brooks rifling through the silver while your back is turned."

Claudia made a face. "I'm not in the habit of trusting the

police." She turned and left the room, and Mason looked at Julia.

"Best guess as to why they're here?"

"I'm going to say they're fishing. I'm further going to bet it's about Iris's death, but that's because that's top of mind for us now. It could be totally unrelated. They could have a new case for us. They could be returning a borrowed book."

"Did we loan them one?"

"No, which makes that less likely."

"Who sent flowers?"

"Mr. Avermore. He's very persistent." She paused. "He's running for mayor of Ojai, did I mention that?"

Mason's eyes opened wide. "You did not. Way to bury the lede. He really is a boy wonder, isn't he?"

Julia was about to retort when the door opened and Wilson and Brooks came in, with an air of being slightly herded by Claudia, who was right behind them. Apparently, she was worried if she took her eye off them for a second they were going to start shoving valuables in their pockets.

"Good morning," said Julia, regally. "Mason, move your butt." Possibly she was irritated by the boy wonder comment.

Mason frowned at her but moved to the end of the long sofa. The two detectives sat, Brooks throwing herself into the corner and Wilson perching on the edge.

There was a silence. It lasted ten seconds longer than Mason was comfortable with, but she knew her boss too well to interject. Eventually, Julia sighed.

"You guys came to me. I assume you have a reason to be here? I'm still sober these days, so I'm pretty confident I didn't drunk dial you in the middle of the night."

"Yes. We wanted to talk to you about Iris Buchanan."

Julia flicked a look at Mason, who pulled out her phone to take notes. She knew that look.

"I didn't know her last name, but I'm assuming we're talking about the same Iris. She died yesterday."

"Yes."

"Drug overdose."

"Is that a question?" Wilson inched a little farther forward on the sofa. "Seeing as Mason was the person who discovered her body, you should know."

"It wasn't a question, no. Should it have been?"

Brooks shook her head. "No, that's certainly what it looked like. But we did all the usual forensic work we always do in the event of a suspicious death, and something strange showed up."

"Is a drug addict dying of a drug overdose suspicious? Isn't it sadly routine?"

Brooks shrugged. "Just because it's common doesn't mean we don't care about it. And in this case it was good that we looked, because there was some fingerprint weirdness."

"Weirdness? Is that a technical term?" Julia looked skeptical.

"No," replied Brooks, evenly. "It's a descriptive term, applied in this case because the fingerprints that were on the syringe weren't exactly in the right position for self-injection, and there was no thumbprint on the plunger. There was nothing at all."

Julia nodded. "Weird indeed."

Brooks continued, "And her ex, family and several other friends expressed deep dissatisfaction with the idea that Iris would have suddenly gone back to intravenous drug use after nearly a year, simply in order to die. The medical examiner found no other evidence of recent IV drug use, none at all."

Julia said, "People throw themselves off buildings in order to die, having never done so before."

Wilson laughed, surprising himself. He shut it off quickly and looked embarrassed.

Brooks looked at him, then back at Julia. "And Iris's mother made some very serious allegations against Iris's sponsor, Alexa Rousso, who, it turns out, is a friend of yours." She looked at Mason. "Or at least, of Mason's."

Mason raised her eyebrows. "So?"

"So, we're here. This isn't our first rodeo with you two," said Brooks, "and when I saw Mason had found the body and that she knew Alexa Rousso, it seemed reasonable to take a little drive."

"What did her mother say?" asked Julia.

"I'm not able to give details, but let's just say that the note found with the body did not paint a favorable picture of Alexa Rousso."

"Hmm," said Julia. "Alexa is my client, so I can't discuss details any more than you can, but I can tell you that we're working for her, investigating something that we don't think is related to Iris's death, but I can't completely rule it out. I'm not ruling it in, either. We're wondering about it, same as you."

"Well, we're more than wondering. We're opening a homicide investigation."

Wilson spoke up. "One question we wanted to answer is how come you came to discover the body, Mason? I mean, your statement said you were concerned about her. But it also said you weren't close, so we were wondering how those two things went together."

"Which two things?" Mason looked confused.

"That you weren't close, but you were concerned enough to go to Venice to check on her."

"I was in the neighborhood."

"Fortunately."

"Coincidentally." Mason pondered for a second, then decided to go with the truth. "Alexa was concerned, and she called me. She wasn't able to go check on Iris herself, so she asked me to do it."

"What exactly is your relationship with Alexa Rousso?"

"She is my AA sponsor, and my friend."

"I see." Brooks made a note in her little notebook. "So you headed over to Iris's. Did you expect to find her dead?"

"Not at all. I expected to find her asleep."

"Or high?"

"No. Asleep."

"Yet Ms. Rousso has stated that she was worried that Ms. Buchanan had relapsed."

Mason turned up her palms. "She was worried, which is why she asked me to check on her. We covered this already."

"And once you arrived at the crime scene you called 911?"

"I didn't know it was a crime scene. I thought Iris had accidentally OD'd. That's still the likeliest scenario, right?" Mason swallowed. "I called 911 because she was very clearly dead."

Julia said, "Who are you thinking might have killed Iris?"

"We're just beginning our investigation. We simply want to know what you know."

"And in return you'll share what you know?"

"We just did, that's the whole bag. Forensics came back. We opened the case and headed over here." Brooks looked around at Mason and Will. "You guys have a tendency to show up when cases are complicated."

"What can I say?" asked Julia. "We enjoy a challenge. I can ask my client if she feels comfortable sharing details of how we're helping her, but for now all I can share is that Alexa was as surprised by Iris's death as anyone else and deeply upset by it. If you can tell me more about the contents of Iris's note, maybe I can be more forthcoming about how it might tie into what we're investigating."

Brooks and Wilson exchanged a look. "The implication is that Alexa was highly discouraging, suggesting that Iris would never be able to remain sober."

"That's ridiculous," said Mason. "Alexa is always supportive. The thought of her being aggressively discouraging is very, very out of character. No sponsor would ever say anything like that."

"Was the note typed or handwritten?" asked Julia.

"Typed," said Brooks. "There was a printer in the apartment. Why?"

"Just curious," said Julia. "If our investigation turns up anything that we think is related to Iris's death, we will of course let you know. And I trust you will do the same."

"Sure, if we knew what you were investigating. How could we possibly know if what we find out is relevant to what you're doing, if we have no idea what you're doing?"

Julia inclined her head an inch south but said nothing. This wasn't her first rodeo, either.

ONCE THE DETECTIVES had left, Mason turned to Julia in some consternation.

"I totally respect attorney-client privilege, and I understand why you didn't tell them anything, but surely, the letters to Alexa are related to Iris's death?"

"How?" asked Julia, calmly.

"Someone is threatening Alexa. They sabotage her event and nearly kill her . . ."

"Unproven."

"Someone breaks into her house and plants alcohol."

"Unproven."

"Now her sponsee is killed, and she is implicated."

Julia snorted. "Implicated in what way? For being a bad sponsor? Not, the last time I looked, a crime or anything close. And the word of an addict who was about to take her own life and was looking for someone to blame . . . not super compelling. I can see a reasonable argument for it being totally coincidental." She turned to Will. "What do you think, Mr. Maier?"

Will turned up his hands. "I see both sides. I've been looking into Iris a little bit more, but there isn't that much to find. She was so young, she hadn't really had time to cause a lot of devastation, and she had no connection to Alexa at all until this year. It hurts Alexa personally to lose her, and maybe a few judgmental assholes in meetings might mutter about her losing a sponsee this way, but the police aren't going to be able to build a very strong case that it benefits her at all, and you need a motive to kill someone." He paused. "I mean, usually. Obviously, sometimes the motive is purely . . ." He stopped when Julia held up her hand.

"Doubtless this is about to be a fascinating dive into the motivations of sociopaths, but let's not go there. Let's just agree that it would be out of character for Alexa to kill Iris and leave it at that."

Mason's phone rang. "It's Alexa," she said, answering it. She was silent for a moment, then said, "Read it. I'm going to put you on speaker." She hit a button and dropped the phone on the sofa. "She got another letter."

Alexa's voice was shaking, but this letter was very brief. "*One down, two to go. Then it's your turn.*"

Julia spoke into the silence. "Well, shit." Then she sighed. "Alexa, it's time to let the police know what's going on. They literally just left, and I was able to convince myself and them that what we're doing for you and Iris's death were unrelated. Now that's no longer plausible."

Alexa didn't answer right away. Then, "Let me talk to Scott. If it's going to turn into a shit show, he's going to get it on his shoes, too. I'll call you back."

Mason hung up and looked at the others. "Well, that's not great."

Julia shook her head. "Not for her, not for you."

Mason frowned. "Why me?"

Will snorted gently. "Because, you doofus, you're one of the two left to go."

23

A FEW HOURS later, Archie showed up in the kitchen, which was a pleasant surprise for Mason. She was sitting there helping Claudia when he walked in. She was aware that seeing his face made her feel . . . good. She was OK with good, and maybe even interested in seeing if good could get to great.

"Hey," said Archie, tipping his head a little as he walked toward her. "Everything OK? You look a little worried."

"I do?" She was tearing the ends off green beans, and kept doing so. "Yeah, everything's mostly OK."

Claudia looked over her shoulder at the two of them but said nothing.

"Mostly?" replied Archie, taking a handful of beans.

"Largely," said Mason.

"'Largely,'" said Archie thoughtfully, "in combination with 'mostly,' suggests there is an area of undefined size that is not OK. It might not be the majority, but it's still very much there."

Mason sighed. "The case we're working on is somewhat close to home, and someone might be trying to kill me. Or at least is open to the possibility of doing so. Maybe."

Archie was silent for a moment. Then, "How close to home?"

"A good friend." She shook her head at herself. "My sponsor. I don't know why I'm beating around the bush. You know I'm sober."

"I do," he said, "and I'm proud of you."

Mason was always mildly irritated when people said this about her, but she let it slide. "Anyway, someone is threatening her, and we're trying to find out who, but now one of her other sponsees OD'd and the police aren't convinced it's an accident."

"And they're worried you're next? Or you are?"

"Well, I wasn't, but my sponsor got another threatening letter that made it very specific."

"What does Julia think?"

Mason made a face. "She wants to go to the police with it. We're waiting for permission from the client to do so."

"That seems like a good idea. And in the meantime, I assume you're being extra careful."

"As careful as I usually am."

He laughed. "That's not very reassuring."

Julia and Will walked in. "We still haven't heard from Alexa."

Will said, "You have the right to break attorney-client privilege in order to prevent a crime. You could go to the police without her permission."

Julia shook her head. "I think it works if you think the client is going to commit a crime. Not sure it covers this particular situation."

"Aren't you withholding information pertinent to an ongoing criminal investigation?"

"You could argue that."

Will nodded. "Well, then I do argue that. The last letter made a pretty clear admission of guilt in the case of Iris and made a distinct threat to other people. I think you have to take it to Wilson and Brooks."

Julia frowned. "I'll give her overnight. If she doesn't call us in the morning, I'll call her and make my argument a little more forcefully and see where we end up." She looked across the table at Archie. "Hello there, Archie. What brings you to this neck of the woods?"

Claudia spoke up. "I invited him for dinner."

Mason finished the beans and carried the bowl over to Claudia. "I was bringing him up to speed on the case."

"Kind of," he said, "but I'm still a little sketchy on the details." He looked at Will. "Can I get a special Will recap?"

"Sure." Will cleared his throat. "Mason's sponsor, Alexa, has received four threatening letters, anonymously, typed, difficult to trace origin. They warn her, imply she's keeping guilty secrets, and now threaten her and two others directly."

"One of whom is Mason?"

"One of whom is Mason, indeed. Alexa was involved in small-time criminal activity, mostly related to her drug and alcohol addiction, thirty years ago in Northern California, but says there's nothing she can think of that would cause someone to come after her like this. Mason and Julia spoke to two ex-husbands and an ex-employer and found nothing of much note. Alexa was present at the Albatross warehouse fire, which you might or might not remember, but left immediately after to go into rehab, where she was for nine months. One of her sponsees just OD'd, and the police found evidence of foul play. Slight, but not totally insignificant. Alexa then received another letter that claimed responsibility for that OD and threatened her remaining sponsees and herself. We're currently waiting to tell the police about it." He turned up his palms. "That's about it."

"I remember the Albatross warehouse fire. Nothing there?"

Will shrugged. "She was a resident, and she was present the night the fire broke out, but that's all. The legal cases are long over and done with. A couple people were found liable and served sentences, and they're both out now." He paused. "I can look into it harder than I have. I didn't think there was much point."

Archie looked at him. "There might not be. I just remember it, not even sure why."

Will nodded, and looked at Julia. "OK with you if I dig a little deeper?"

"Yes," she said. "Look everywhere. I don't want to lose Mason. Good help is so hard to find."

Mason's phone rang. "Sorry," she said, "it's her, it's Alexa."

"Put it on speaker," said Julia.

Mason did so and slid the phone to the center of the table. "Hey there."

"Mason?"

Mason raised her eyebrows. "Yeah, you OK?"

Alexa's voice was higher than usual, faster than usual. "No . . . I don't know what's wrong. I can't calm down, my heart is racing, I'm freaking out. I think I'm losing it." She paused. "My voice sounds weird, am I on speaker?"

"Yeah," said Mason, "we're all here."

"Take me off speaker," Alexa said, tightly. "Take me off right now. I don't want to . . ."

Mason hit the button and picked up the phone. "It's OK,

you're off. What's going on?" She looked around the table. Everyone was watching her. She stood and walked out of the room.

"I don't know . . . I don't know . . . I went to a meeting with Jennifer, we had coffee after, everything was fine, then I was talking to Scott about what we should do and suddenly I realized I was talking too fast and too loud. I'm having a panic attack, I think. I'm losing my mind. I can't believe someone killed Iris and is now threatening you and Jennifer."

"You're not losing your mind," said Mason, calmly, heading out the front door and turning toward her guesthouse. "You've got a lot going on. It would freak anyone out. I'll come over."

"No, no, don't do that. I just don't know what to do. Maybe I should take a Xanax."

"Sure, you could do that." Mason paused. "Is Scott there? Can I talk to him?"

"Yeah . . ." There was a pause.

But Mason never got to talk to Scott, because it was at that moment that someone started shooting at her.

MASON HIT THE dirt. The space alongside the house, where you took the path up the hill to the guesthouses, was pretty open and there wasn't much cover. The first shot hadn't come close—she'd heard it ricochet off the house somewhere—but she didn't want to give them a second chance. Archie's car was parked a little ahead of her, so she started scrambling toward it. A bullet slammed into the ground about twenty feet away, causing her to change direction rather sharply, but she kept going. Whoever this was, was not a great shot, so that was some consolation.

"Mason?" Archie's voice, loud and panicked, as he came running out of the house, followed by everyone else.

"Get back," she yelled. "I'm OK." She raised her voice even higher. "They're a fucking lousy shot."

As if to prove it, another bullet hit the ground somewhere to her left.

"I called the cops," yelled Will. "They're on their way."

Mason reached Archie's car and crouched behind it. She peered through the windows and scanned the hillside. The shots had come from there, but where exactly? "One more shot, baby," she muttered to herself. "Show yourself."

She got her wish, and as the shot echoed across the canyon, she saw the briefest of muzzle flashes. *I got you now, motherfucker*, she thought, as she stood, rounded the car at a flat-out run and took off up the hill. It was hard going; the ground was very dry and almost vertical, the shrubby bushes not allowing much purchase. Her boots scrabbled on the ground, and the sound of her cursing was a distraction.

"Man down!" yelled Julia, behind her. "Man down! Will, ambulance."

Mason slipped on the hillside as she turned, losing her footing completely.

Archie was lying on the ground, not moving at all.

And above her, someone on the hill started to run.

24

IT WAS DIMLY lit, the hospital room, but Mason could see every detail of Archie's face where it lay against the pillow. She could hear Julia and Will talking in low voices in the hallway, with the occasional interjection from Wilson or Brooks, but she wasn't all that interested.

Archie stirred, and she got closer.

"Hey there . . ."

He opened his eyes. "Hey . . ."

"You got shot. Sorry about that."

He smiled and turned his head toward her. "I did kind of run into the line of fire."

"Yeah, about that . . ."

"You said they were a lousy shot."

"Well, they were. If they were trying to hit me, that is. If it turns out they were after you the whole time, they nailed it."

Archie moved his arm and winced. "Shoulder?"

"Yeah. Through and through. You'll be fine. You'll have a cool scar." She reached out and touched his bandage, softly. "Sorry."

"No worries," he said, watching her face. "The ladies love a scar."

She looked at him, and for a moment there was silence.

"I assume they got away?"

"Yeah. I was heading in their direction, although not sure what I thought I was going to do, seeing as I was unarmed, but I turned around when you went down."

He clicked his tongue. "Eye on the prize, Mason. Stay on target."

She raised her eyebrows. "Are you making a *Star Wars* reference?"

"I might have been." He looked past her as Will, Julia and the detectives came in. "Hello, everyone."

Wilson spoke first. "I guess you have nothing to add to the statements all your colleagues have made, Mr. Jacobson?"

"I doubt it," he replied. "We were inside the house when we heard the first gunshot. Will called 911 and we all ran outside. Mason was heading toward cover, and I headed toward her. A bullet hit the ground between the house and where she was, and I was running in that direction when I got shot. I don't remember that part very well."

"We have forensics at the scene now," said Brooks. "We recovered one bullet from the side of the house and hope to find the other two."

"Pistol?" asked Will.

"Yes." Brooks nodded. "Probably a Glock 9, based on the highly preliminary opinion of the forensic guy." She sighed. "One of the most common handguns in the States, but there you go."

Will cleared his throat. "Small enough for easy concealed carry, reliable and less prone to jamming than most other guns, favored by law enforcement—it's popular for many reasons."

Archie winced. "Why doesn't that make me feel better?"

"I spoke to Alexa," said Julia, "and she gave me permission to tell Wilson and Brooks about what's been going on."

"It would have been nice to know earlier," said Wilson, deadpan, "as maybe we could have been watching your house and prevented Mr. Jacobson from getting knocked on his ass."

Julia shrugged. "I couldn't tell you earlier, as you know. But now you know and can keep an eye on the players."

Brooks nodded. "And talk to Ms. Rousso, which we will do tomorrow."

"With me present," said Julia. "You can talk to her at my house."

"Actually, she can come to the precinct."

"No, she's not a suspect of any kind. There's no need to drag her anywhere. I'll make my client available for questions at eleven, Detectives. We'll be happy to host you."

There was a pause, then Brooks nodded.

"Will there be cookies?" asked Wilson.

ALEXA WASN'T AS calm with the cops as she had been without them, which was reasonable. It had been a long time since she'd broken the law, but old habits die hard, and as her hands twisted in her lap, Mason wondered if she wanted a drink. Or something else.

They had had a few minutes before the cops arrived, and she'd had a chance to ask Alexa about the previous evening.

"It was the weirdest thing," her sponsor had said, frowning. "I was just freaking out. My nerves were totally jangled.

Scott was getting worried I was having a heart attack." She made a face. "I'm not that old, but not so young that it's out of the question."

"The average age for a first attack is early seventies for women," said Will, helpfully. "You've got a ways to go."

"Sure," said Alexa, "but who knows what damage I did with all the drugs and smoking and alcohol, so I do worry about it. My doctor says I'm fine, but I don't know . . . I was so wound up. And then when you dropped the phone and I could hear yelling, I thought something terrible was happening, which it was, and then I thought maybe I was having a premonition before." Alexa was originally from New York, but her long years in California meant she occasionally came out with somewhat left-field assertions. "You know, feeling the energetic vibes."

Mason raised an eyebrow. "That seems unlikely. And you felt better this morning?"

"Yeah. I feel nervous, but that's because I'm about to talk to the cops."

But now, sitting in front of Wilson and Brooks, Alexa looked reasonably calm.

"So," said Wilson, "the first letter arrived a couple of weeks ago?"

Alexa nodded. "Yes. Then another last week and two this week."

"When Iris Buchanan OD'd, did you assume the letters had something to do with it?"

"No, not at all." Alexa sighed. "I still want to believe there's no true malice behind them. They seem somewhat . . . childish. I thought everyone was making too much of a fuss."

"They're a form of harassment," said Brooks, "especially in

a series like that. A one-off, furious letter? We can all imagine getting that angry, being that impulsive. But to send a series, and to be so specifically threatening, is far more serious. Do you have them all?"

"I have copies for you," said Will, handing over a large manila envelope. "Except for the last one. I took prints. I've included what I got in the package. Only Alexa's, Scott's, Mason's and Julia's, and Mason and Julia handled them for the first time only a week or so ago."

"Or so they claim," said Brooks, acerbically. She opened the package, shaking out the letters and spreading them out on the coffee table. "Typewriter, interesting. Prestamped Forever envelopes, interesting." She flipped them over. "And they taped down the flap, so no saliva." She paused. "Although that can be hard to get, but someone's being very careful." She looked at Alexa. "And you have no ideas at all about what they're referring to? No skeletons? Big secrets you'd like to tell us about?"

"I have plenty of skeletons, but nothing big enough to warrant this, I don't think." She gestured at Julia and Mason. "They've been looking into it."

Julia nodded. "So far we haven't found anything major. We still have to talk to a woman named Lisa Rawlings. You guys were friends."

Alexa looked surprised. "My God, I haven't thought of Lisa in decades. I'm kind of surprised she's still alive."

"As far as we know," replied Mason. "She runs a legal brothel in Nevada, a very successful one." She paused. "According to Yelp."

Wilson made a note. "Were you ever convicted of a criminal offense?"

Alexa shook her head and looked slightly embarrassed.

"Not convicted, no. I got arrested a couple of times for public intoxication, I got caught shoplifting a few times, but I never got charged for that, got rounded up in drug houses a couple of times . . ." She turned up her palms. "Just your usual drunken bullshit."

Julia said, "We talked to two ex-husbands, an ex-employer. The former had nothing really bad to say, the latter spoke of stealing that was paid back as part of Alexa's recovery process. None of them seemed to have outstanding complaints. We still have Lisa to talk to, of course, and more leads to chase up."

"And I'm following up on the Albatross warehouse fire," added Will. "Alexa was there that night, and there were long criminal and civil proceedings afterward." He turned to her. "Were you directly involved in either of those?"

Alexa shook her head. "Mind you, I came to LA and went into rehab right after that," she said. "I was there for nine months. I missed a lot of it."

"The case went on for years," replied Will.

She shrugged. "Without me paying much attention, to be honest. I was in early recovery, living down here, working and trying and failing, going back into rehab, that kind of thing. I was totally self-obsessed, like we all are." She looked at the two detectives, who spent their lives helping other people. "I mean, like most of us."

Wilson nodded. He turned to Julia. "Have you put her under surveillance of any kind?"

Julia shook her head. "We've been a little bit dancing around the obvious conclusion that the sender of the letters is someone in AA, right? It's fairly likely to be someone who knows her pretty well, and most of the people she knows are in the program. We can't surveil in meetings. It feels wrong."

"Alright, but what about coming and going? Consistent people, people who follow her, that kind of thing?"

"We hadn't yet." Julia sounded slightly irritated. "Maybe we were treating it a little lightly."

"Wait, we didn't tell you about the other night." Mason slapped her forehead, literally. "She woke up and thought there was someone in the house."

"But there wasn't?" Wilson's pen was poised above his pad.

"Well, I don't know," said Alexa. "When Mason arrived, the door was open, but I'm not totally sure I didn't open it. It was the middle of the night, and I was confused."

"And then we found little bottles of vodka in her bag."

Wilson's pen made contact. "And that's unusual?"

A chorus of snorts around the room. "Yes," said Julia. "Alexa is sober. She's not in the habit of buying vodka anymore."

"And if I did," added Alexa, "it probably wouldn't be miniatures."

"I don't know about that," said Will, conversationally. "I've known several people in recovery who existed entirely on those little airplane bottles, because it helped them with the denial that they had a problem. 'Oh, they're only little bottles; the fact that I'm drinking ten of them every day is irrelevant.'"

They all looked at him.

"Just saying," he said.

"Anyway, the point is," said Mason, "Alexa didn't buy them, didn't know they were in her bag, and that would suggest that someone definitely was there, in her house."

"And where are those bottles now?" asked Brooks.

“In my garden somewhere,” said Alexa. She looked at the detectives and watched their expressions change. “I can maybe go out and find them?”

Brooks shook her head. “You can if you want to, but the chance of forensic evidence still being there is slim.”

“Our guy is too careful for that, anyway,” said Will. “Typed the letters, taped the envelopes . . . unlikely they would have left prints on the bottles.”

“Well, last night wasn’t very careful,” said Mason. “They sat up on the hill outside the house and waited for me to come out. What if I’d been in for the night? And then they missed completely. They might be careful, but they’re not super professional.”

“Nothing about this says professional,” said Wilson.

“Nope,” said Brooks. “This is clearly personal.”

25

IT WAS LATER that afternoon, as Mason was sorting through Julia's extensive collection of vinyl, that Will suddenly gave an exclamation.

"Huh," he said, one of his favorite exclamations. "That's interesting."

Julia looked up from the sofa. "Explain yourself."

"Alexa is listed as a material witness in the original court filings of the Albatross warehouse fire."

"But she said she didn't testify."

"She didn't . . ." Will was studying something on his screen. "A material witness warrant was issued for her, but she couldn't be located, and she doesn't appear on any subsequent lists." He looked up. "I guess she was material until she wasn't. Maybe they found someone else who had the same information."

"She was in rehab in Southern California," said Mason. "I guess they gave up on her."

"Call her," said Julia. "Put her on speaker." Alexa had left to go to lunch after the police were done with her, and several hours had passed.

But Mason couldn't reach her. "I'll try again later." She frowned. "I can text Jennifer. She might be with her."

The door opened and Claudia came in. "Your sponsor is back," she said to Mason, "and honestly, she's not looking too hot."

ALEXA WAS STANDING in the hallway, gazing up at the ceiling. She was tapping her toe and clicking her fingers in two different time signatures, which is a challenge.

"Hey," said Mason, coming out of the office door. "You good? I just tried to call you."

"I think I lost my phone," said Alexa. "I thought maybe it was here. Although I did hear something ringing a few minutes ago." She laughed. "Maybe it's following me . . ." She took a few steps toward Mason and then stepped back. "I have a lot of energy right now, but I also don't feel great. I'm not sure why I'm here. I should probably be at home."

Mason frowned. "We were calling to ask about the Albatross fire. Why don't you come into the office?"

Alexa nodded. "Is there any coffee?"

Claudia had just come out of the office, and she nodded. "Are you hungry? Did you have lunch?"

"I did, a nice fellowship lunch. I'm not hungry. But I am thirsty." She passed Mason on her way into the office and suddenly took her hand. "Do you feel how fast my heart is beating?" She put Mason's fingers on her wrist but didn't wait for a reply. "Maybe I should have tea instead. Maybe it's that heart attack coming back."

"OK," said Claudia, shooting a look at Mason. "Tea it is."

Alexa sat on the sofa and smiled at Julia and Will. "Hey

there! Mason said you had questions? Is it me or is it hot in here?"

"It's seventy-two degrees in the room, but I could open the sliding doors if you're too hot," replied Julia, who liked the place to be warm. "I can probably find a wrap of some kind."

"Thanks," said Alexa, who did indeed look flushed. "I get overheated—could be a hot flash. I'm at that age."

"Hot flashes are fascinating," said Will. "The fluctuations in hormones cause the hypothalamus to get dysregulated, sensing even minor changes in body temperature as greater or smaller than they are, making it dilate the blood vessels, which gives rise to the sudden hot flash sensation, then triggering the autonomic nervous system to think it needs to cool the body down so it sweats . . . I always think of it like a panic button, pressed unnecessarily."

"Do you think about hot flashes a lot?" asked Mason, nonplussed.

"I think a lot about the hypothalamus. It's my favorite neuroendocrine organ."

They all looked at him for a moment. Then Julia walked over to the glass doors and slid one open. Immediately, a steady breeze entered the room, stirring the curtains. Julia walked out of the room and returned with a cashmere shawl the color of tamarind.

"OK," she said, settling herself in her chair. "Are you more comfortable?"

"Yes," replied Alexa. "Sorry about that. My temperature is all over the map today."

"You came here yourself," said Julia. "What did you need to talk about?"

"I'm not sure," said Alexa. "The police were very nice, but I was still a little nervous, so I went to a meeting with Jennifer, then we had lunch. Everything was fine, although obviously I'm still very upset about Iris, and about the letters, and about your friend getting shot, and about everything, but then I was driving and I got the sudden urge to come here and see if you were making progress, and then I was here. I kind of lost a bit in the middle." She wiped her hand over her face, which had gotten to a more normal color. "Have you made any progress?"

"Sort of," said Julia. "The Albatross fire keeps cropping up. Did you know you were a material witness in the criminal case?"

Alexa shook her head. "I was?"

"You were."

"But I didn't testify."

"No. You were in rehab in Los Angeles during the first part of the trial, and you apparently weren't needed after that."

Alexa shrugged. "I remember some things about that night very well, but others are a bit of a blur. Sort of before and after the drugs, you know." She shivered. "I'm cold now. Can we close the door?"

Julia frowned very slightly, but looked at Mason, who sighed and got up to close the door. God forbid Julia stir herself twice.

Claudia came in with a teapot and, of course, some kind of tiered dish with a handle. "It's teatime," she said, "so I decided to do afternoon tea. There's English clotted cream and jam, scones of course, some cookies, and a few small sandwiches."

She put down the tea stand, and they all stared at it. Tiny sandwiches with the crusts cut off, a plate of little things Mason assumed must be scones. She wasn't sure how you were supposed to eat them, but hopefully someone would show her the ropes.

Surprisingly, it was Will. He hurried over. "I love scones," he said enthusiastically, taking one and splitting it in half. He spread jam on it, then topped it with a dollop of cream. "The English are responsible for a lot, both good and bad, but afternoon tea is definitely good."

Julia waited for someone to pour her some tea (it was Claudia), and then pressed Alexa a little. "Can you tell us everything you *do* remember about that night?"

"Well," said Alexa, settling back on the sofa, then sitting back up again . . . then settling down, "it was summertime, and I had been living there for about six months. People came and went all the time, you know—it was kind of a loose situation." She looked at Mason. "You would have liked it, actually. There were a load of cool and kooky people there, artists and dancers and inventors. It was kind of like the Burning Man crowd."

"I've never been to Burning Man," said Mason, unaccountably affronted by the assumption.

"Oh yeah?" Alexa looked at her, and for a moment her eyes became unfocused, her expression confused. "Maybe I'm mixing you up with someone else. Sorry. I'm kind of all over the place today. Anyway, it was a weekend, and we had friends down from Tomales. It was a scene."

"Who was there?" Will was ready to take notes.

"Lisa was there, the woman you found. I'm kind of fascinated to see how she is." She turned to Mason. "She was kind of like a madam, in a way. She used to do sex work herself but quickly realized the real money lay in management." She laughed, suddenly. "So she used to find girls who were younger than her, stupider, less experienced, you know, and turn them out, get them into sex work. She'd take care of overseeing, making sure they were relatively safe, fed, dressed, et cetera. She had a big apartment and there were always half a dozen girls there, but they didn't work there; they went out to clients or worked on the street."

"She ran the whole thing herself?"

"No, with Fuzzy . . ." Alexa stopped. "My God, I haven't thought of Fuzzy in twenty years. I wonder where he is now, if he's even still alive."

"He's in prison," said Will, helpfully. "We might have to go and talk to him."

"Oh yeah?" Again, that sudden lack of focus . . . then she snapped back. "So, he was there, and Lisa was there, and that guy he worked for, Birdman, the rich kid." She paused, and shivered. "I didn't like him. He . . ." She looked around. "You know when you meet a guy and the hairs on the back of your neck stand up? Where you suddenly feel like you get wider vision, like you're always checking your peripheral?"

The women in the room nodded.

"Well, he was that guy. And he could tell I didn't like him and mostly left me alone."

Will was still taking notes. "His last name was Birdman?" He flicked a glance at Julia; now they had a name.

Alexa shook her head. "No, that was just a nickname. Not sure I ever knew his actual last name—like I said, we weren't friends. But man, did he love the girls. He was always heading off with one or another of Lisa's little protégés." She shivered again. "Poor things. But he had lots of money, always flashing the cash. And driving fancy cars. He had one with him that night. I remember seeing him get into it after the fire started." She paused, as though she had another thought, but then she shrugged and stayed silent.

"How did you know fire had broken out if there was no alarm system?" Will was interested.

"Screaming," said Alexa, simply. "There was a sort of DJ going on in the space outside the warehouse, but people were in and out all the time; like I said, it was always kind of fluid. So, there was music inside, music outside, everyone was high, it was a scene. But my husband Dave and Fuzzy and Lisa and I were outside, right, and we suddenly heard people screaming from inside." She looked out of the window and her face changed color again. "It was hot, too, almost immediately, even outside. There was a door nearby, and people started coming out of it, panicked. We could smell the smoke then, too, and then suddenly no one was coming out of the door anymore; they were just screaming inside. So, we beat it. Fuzzy and Lisa went one way, Dave and I went the other, the girls kind of scattered, it was bedlam. It took a little while for the fire department to arrive, and once they did, it got crazier; they pushed us all out of the way and started fighting the fire, but I swear it wasn't much of a fight. Half an hour, forty minutes maybe, and then the roof collapsed and there wasn't any more screaming. Dave and I walked to a park nearby and slept there, then I went back the next morning to see if any of my stuff had survived, but dude, there was nothing left but part of one wall. It was all just rubble. And people had been using mannequins for art projects inside, it was like a feature, so there were all these blackened mannequin limbs sticking out every so often, totally grotesque, because you knew there were dozens of bodies in there somewhere." She closed her eyes for a second. "Damn, I'm too hot again."

Mason got up and slid the door open again, thinking to herself that menopause must suck. She liked a well-regulated temperature, man; this hot and cold thing was a drag.

"But I talked to this guy there and asked about the mannequins and he said real bodies didn't look like that after a fire, so the firemen didn't even notice." She paused. "He was nice. I don't remember his name. He wanted to know what it had been like inside the building, how people were situated, you know? I helped as much as I could, but to be honest, I was kind of hungover and freaked out. They wouldn't let me look for my stuff, and as I was standing there looking at it, I realized if I didn't get my shit together, something like that was going to happen to me. That I could easily have been inside that building, getting high. I suddenly decided to blow Oakland, head south to LA, where I had some friends, and try to get sober. I left the next week, and I've actually never been back to Oakland since." She looked at Mason. "You're from the Bay Area, right?"

Mason nodded. "Yeah, but Berkeley, not Oakland."

"Same difference," said Alexa, pulling her jacket tighter around her and shivering. "It's all kind of the same."

Mason opened her mouth to argue, but it wasn't worth it. Alexa was in such a weird mood.

"And you don't remember anything about the criminal or civil cases that followed?"

"Nope, I was in rehab. You know what it's like; it's like a bubble. You just keep the place clean, go to meetings, go to work . . . then I was working at a vintage clothing store."

"Yes," Julia nodded, "we talked to your boss."

"Jane?"

"Yes."

Alexa looked thoughtful. "She was nice to me, nicer than she needed to be. She fired me, but nicely, you know what I mean?" Then she stood up. "I have to go now. I'm not feeling great. I think I need another meeting."

"Do you need me to go with you?"

"Nah, I'm OK." She stood there for a moment, doing the same finger-clicking thing she'd been doing earlier. Mason wondered what she was so keyed up about. Then she said goodbye and left. Mason walked her out and came back into the office in time to join a spirited debate.

"Maybe speed?" Will was saying.

Julia shrugged. "Not coke?"

He shook his head. "I don't think so."

"What on earth are you talking about?" asked Mason.

"We think Alexa was on something, don't you?"

Mason was appalled. "No! Why, because of her hot flashes?"

"And the speed of her delivery, and the nervous energy, and the erratic thought patterns." Julia was calm.

"She's menopausal. It's normal," said Mason. "And her recollection of the night of the fire was straightforward and organized."

Will shrugged. "We could be wrong. She just seemed different than she did this morning. She was anxious to talk to the cops, but physically she was pretty calm and still. You know her better than we do."

"That's right," said Mason, pissed off. "She's not using; she's just stressed and maybe a bit hormonal. Jesus, someone's threatening her life, someone killed one sponsee and shot at another. Wouldn't you be a little riled up?"

"Keep your pants on, Mason."

"I don't like you dissing my sponsor."

"Clearly." Julia looked at Will. "We need to talk to Lisa Rawlings. I think she's key. And maybe Fuzzy, too." She looked at Mason. "And did you catch the inconsistency in her story?"

"No, which part?"

"She said she was outside with Dave and the others when the fire broke out. But when we spoke to Dave about that night, he said she just appeared, which clearly implies that she wasn't with him at first. So where was she?"

"It was a long time ago."

Julia was silent for a moment, then she said, "You know, Mason, it's laudable that you believe in your sponsor so much, but you might have to face the fact that she's lying about something. It doesn't make her a bad person; it just makes her a liar."

"She's not lying."

"She's not being forthcoming. I think she knows exactly what these notes are about and doesn't want to admit it."

Will clicked a few keys. "Just sent you the address for Lisa."

"We'll go in the morning. It's too late now."

THAT EVENING, MASON was in the kitchen talking to Claudia and Will when Julia walked in. She was wearing a deep purple dress that went to the floor, and a fluffy lamb's wool coat. She was clearly on her way out.

"Another date?" asked Mason.

Julia nodded. "Yes, although somewhat against my better judgment. Justin is back in Los Angeles for a couple of days, trying to sort out the debacle at Oficina. He had the rest of the batch of wine tested and nothing was wrong with any of it. It's interesting."

"So it's as much business as pleasure? Are you thinking of taking him on as a client?"

"Not at all," replied Julia, pouring herself a small glass of water. "But there's something there . . . I can't put my finger on it."

The doorbell rang and Claudia went to let Justin in. He walked into the kitchen and put two bottles down on the table.

"Grape juice," he said, "but better than any grape juice you've ever tasted. We started producing it last year, and it's selling very well. All organic and squeezed from the same grapes we make the wine from. Try it." He looked over at Julia and smiled. "You look beautiful. I hope you're hungry."

"Always," she replied, smiling back.

Claudia had opened one of the bottles and poured everyone some juice. Mason tried it—Justin had been right; it was unlike anything she'd ever had. Deeply sweet but without being cloying, and more complicated in flavor than she'd expected.

"Delicious," she said, pouring herself some more. "Thanks."

"My pleasure," he said. "I'm hoping you'll all come up to the vineyard one weekend. We do tours, we grow olives, and we raise goats for cheese, too; it's not just wine." He looked at Claudia. "Our goat cheese is phenomenal, if I say so myself. It's won several awards and is perfect for cooking with as well as simply eating. I'd be happy to bring you some on my next visit." He shot Julia a look. "But it would be even nicer if you came to the source."

"Claudia makes a phyllo tart with goat cheese that is sublime, and any excuse to request it is fine with me. We'll come and visit soon enough."

Mason raised an eyebrow. She wasn't used to compliant Julia.

"Hey, Julia said you're running for office in Ojai, is that right?"

He smiled at her. "Yes. Ojai has given me so much, I just want to give back."

"Did you grow up there?"

"No, in Northern California, but I've been in Ojai for several decades."

"Where in Northern California? I'm from Berkeley."

"Oh yeah? Nice. I'm from farther north."

Julia stood up. "Shall we go?"

"Yes." Justin was reaching for her arm when his phone rang. He flicked a look at his screen. "I'm so sorry—I need to answer this. It's my vineyard manager. He doesn't call unless it's serious."

"Of course, would you like more priv—" said Julia, but Justin had already answered the call.

"Hey there," he said, then went silent. Then, "When? Which section?" He listened some more, as his face changed from white to red in a matter of seconds. "OK, we'll call the CCOF in the morning." He paused. "No, we can't just rip them out. It will have spread. Everything will need to be tested." His face grew darker, his mouth twisted. "And I want everyone there in the morning. Every single person who might have had anything to do with it, or who fucked up and let it happen. It must have taken time; someone was asleep at the wheel. It's a fucking disgrace." He was furious, and Mason watched Julia observing his temper. This didn't bode well for their evening.

But then Justin ended the call and took a moment to compose himself. He turned to the group and apologized.

"I'm so sorry for that, so rude."

"What happened?" asked Julia.

"Nothing. Just vandalism at the vineyard. We'll get to the bottom of it." He ran his fingers through his hair, distractedly. "I can't catch a break right now. First the adulteration of the wine, and now this." He looked at Julia. "Someone sprayed a whole section of the vineyard with Roundup."

Julia frowned. "The weed killer? How do you know?"

"They didn't try to hide it. There were spray bottles of it left under the vines, which were covered in it."

"Why is that so bad?" asked Mason.

Justin sighed. "Because we're an organically certified vineyard. We use alternative methods always, for weed control, pest control, everything. There are no artificial fertilizers or chemicals used anywhere in the process. This could ruin us. We'll lose all those vines, of course, but the CCOF, the California Certified Organic Farmers, could easily discover the chemical spread through the earth and polluted everything. We might lose that whole parcel." He walked shakily over to the table and sat. "It's a disaster."

"Who would do such a thing?" asked Claudia.

"A competitor? Kids?"

"Seems a little sophisticated for kids, right? I can see them ripping out vines or stealing stuff, but pesticides . . ." Julia sounded thoughtful. "I assume you want to cancel dinner and head back up the coast?"

Justin sighed and looked at her again. "No. This trip has been far from successful. I'd like there to be one good thing . . . and dinner with you was always going to be the highlight."

Mason looked at Julia's face, which was unreadable, and then at Will, who was staring at the table with a look on his face she recognized. He was thinking, hard.

"Who has access to the vineyard?" he asked. "I assume there is some kind of security?"

Justin shrugged. "They chose a section of the vineyard that is farthest from the main buildings, and they must have done it either very early in the morning, before we start work, or sometime overnight. We have fences, of course, but no security patrol or anything like that." He paused. "At least, we've never had to before. Maybe now we do." He looked at his watch. "Alright, I'm going to put this out of my head for now. Let's go."

Julia smiled at him, and together they left the room.

Mason waited until she heard the front door close, then she turned to Will.

"Well, that's weird."

"Right?" he said. "Not his best week, not by a long shot."

Mason thought of Alexa. Of Iris. Of Archie.

"Yeah, it's been a tough week all around."

"Which is why," said Claudia, turning to the refrigerator, "I made a chocolate trifle." She pulled out a large footed glass dish. "There's nothing that isn't improved by chocolate cake, pudding and whipped cream. Everyone grab a spoon."

26

MASON DIDN'T HEAR Julia come home, but the next morning she was at breakfast.

"How was your dinner?" asked Mason.

"Delicious," replied her boss, but said nothing else.

"What time did you get home?"

"A little after none of your business and a few minutes before butt the fuck out," said Julia, reaching for more coffee. "Are you ready to talk to Lisa Rawlings?"

"Yes," said Mason. "Will gave me her rap sheet and potted history. You can read it in the car."

"I know it already," said Julia. "She was there the night of the fire. I want to know what she saw, if anything."

"Got it," said Mason. "We'll ask her about it."

"You'll stay out of it," said Julia, popping a piece of croissant in her mouth. "Just take notes and keep your mouth shut."

"How am I going to learn if you don't let me do things?" protested Mason.

"By observing a master at work," replied Julia. "Hurry up

and finish. I'm taking this opportunity to get my hair done by a very old friend in Vegas."

Mason raised her eyebrows. "Seriously? What about your fancy Beverly Hills guy? I thought you loved him?"

"I do, but Vern is a whole different ball game." She looked at Mason and grinned. "If you had more than half an inch of hair on your head, he'd transform you, too, but even Vern can't do anything with that."

"I like my hair this way," said Mason, running her hand over her buzz cut.

"Happy for you. Let's take the Porsche."

BROTHELS AREN'T LEGAL all over Nevada, only in certain counties. Lisa's business was in Pahrump, a town about four and a half hours away from LA and an hour from Vegas, which was apparently the main point of today's excursion. Pahrump is the home of the Chicken Ranch, a very famous brothel, and there were signs everywhere for it. Lisa's place, which was called, cunningly enough, Lisa's Place, had no such signage, but thanks to the miracle that is GPS, Mason pulled up in front with no problem.

Julia leaned down and looked at the front door, frowning. "Doesn't look like a brothel."

"What do you want, tits on the door?" Mason undid her seat belt and got ready to get out. "Come on. I can't wait to see you in a house of ill repute." She looked at Julia. "At least you dressed for it."

"I dressed for Vegas, for Vern. We're just here on the way." Julia was wearing a short print dress and white knee-high boots.

"Are you planning on dancing in a cage later?" asked Mason.

"I won't rule it out," replied Julia, getting out of the car. "What happens in Vegas stays in Vegas."

"If you end up cage dancing, it will NOT stay in Vegas," replied Mason. "There will be footage on the Internet within minutes." She locked the car. "I really like that dress, though."

"Mary Quant," replied Julia.

"Not so sure about the coat."

Julia was wearing an astrakhan jacket with a fur collar. "I don't really care what you think about my clothes," she said, "as you may have noticed." She looked Mason up and down. "I don't love your outfit, but seeing as you wear a variation on it every single day, I've at least gotten used to it."

"What do you mean? I wear a wide variety of clothes."

"No," said Julia, turning to walk up to the building. "You wear jeans, a T-shirt and boots almost every day. Sometimes the boots are brown, sometimes they are black, sometimes they are Converse high-tops, of which you own three pairs. Sometimes the jeans are ripped, sometimes they are skinny, occasionally on a very hot day they are shorts. Once or twice you've worn a miniskirt over ripped tights. You have maybe a dozen T-shirts. I think I've seen them all. You own a leather biker jacket, a vinyl biker jacket, a suede biker jacket, and a sheepskin flying-type jacket that I've seen once, when it was unseasonably cold. You own hooded sweatshirts, also. I imagine I'll see more of them when winter rolls around again."

Mason stared at her. "Wow. Someone's been paying attention."

"I like clothing. You do not." She raised her hand and rang the doorbell of Lisa's Place. "I imagine we will both be overdressed once we step through this door."

And she was right.

MASON WASN'T SURE what to expect at a legal brothel, but maybe something between a hotel and a strip joint. In some ways she was right: The enormous man who opened the door was reminiscent of a bouncer, insofar as he was almost as wide as the doorway and had an expression that suggested you were welcome to try it, and welcome to get your ass kicked as a result.

"We're here to see Lisa Rawlings," said Julia, evenly.

He grunted and stepped back.

The hallway they entered was well lit and clean, and as he led them farther into the house, Mason was surprised to be reminded of the few spas she'd been to. There was a smell of vanilla and eucalyptus, and there were candles everywhere, and enough soft cushions and throw blankets that they could have bedded down a busload of refugees without any trouble. Not that refugees were the common clientele. It was around lunchtime, and at first Mason thought they were the only visitors, but as they passed some closed doors, she heard men's voices and low laughter drifting through. Business was underway, albeit subtly.

The main room continued the coastal elegance vibe, with pale blue walls and white and cream furniture. Navy accents and green glass decorations everywhere made Mason think of Nancy Meyers's movies rather than hardcore porn, and the three young women sitting in the room were wearing luxurious terry cloth dressing gowns as though they'd just had a massage and were waiting for their hot stone facial appointment. They looked up and smiled happy smiles of welcome, and when Lisa Rawlings walked in, Mason had to almost physically hold her eyebrows down.

Lisa looked like your well-to-do aunt who'd married an investment banker and moved to Connecticut. Pale slacks, a navy cashmere sweater over a white button-down, a simple but well-cut blond bob . . . she could have been serving lemonade in the Hamptons. She smiled at her young women and then at Mason and Mann. President of the PTA, maybe. Or the owner of a homewares store where the prices attached on little stringed tags made you gasp.

But then she indicated they should sit, and said, "Are both of you ladies looking to get laid, or is this a pussy-watching-pussy situation?"

Which maybe gets said in the Hamptons more than you would think, but who knows?

"Neither," said Julia, calmly, "although we appreciate the options. We're here to talk to you, actually. We're friends of Alexa Rousso, and we're hoping you can help us to help her."

There was a momentary silence, as Lisa rifled through her mental Rolodex. Then, "Ah yes. I remember Alexa." She looked up at the bouncer. "Jeffrey, I'm going to take these ladies out back. Please call me if we have any actual customers."

Jeffrey nodded and turned back toward the front door.

"He's such a love," said Lisa, getting to her feet. "This way please." She looked at the young women. "Sorry to disturb you ladies."

"No worries," said one of them, as the three of them got up and walked out.

"Where are they going?" asked Mason, following Lisa.

"Back to their rooms, of course," said Lisa, looking over her shoulder. "They come out when a customer arrives, but other than that they spend their time privately. Many of them are students, working on various degrees, one or two of them are freelancers, and they work remotely from here . . . that kind of thing." She led them to a doorway and opened it. "What were you expecting, a red-lit viewing area?"

"I guess," said Mason, shrugging and entering what turned out to be a fairly ordinary kitchen. "I've never been to a brothel before."

Lisa smiled. "They're all different. Mine caters to a very discerning clientele, mostly businessmen who've come to Vegas for conventions or conferences, and for whom a more explicit environment would be off-putting. This feels like their orthodontist's office, or maybe their private banker's . . . much easier to spend money in."

"And how much do you charge them?"

"The minimum price for an hour of time with one of my young ladies is two thousand dollars, if what you're looking for is conversation and fairly vanilla sex. Anything more exciting than that and the price goes up." She laughed. "And it often goes up." She flicked on a kettle. "Tea?"

They shook their heads, then waited politely as Lisa boiled the kettle and made herself a cup of tea.

"Alright," she said, sitting down. "What can I do for you, or rather, for Alexa? I haven't thought of her in a very long time. Is she well?"

"She is," said Julia. "However, she's been receiving threatening letters that reference something that probably happened back when you two were friends."

"We weren't friends."

"You weren't?"

"No, we were addicts together. I don't know how much you know about addiction, but it's not a good bedrock for lasting friendship."

Julia shrugged. "I have many addicts as friends."

"Active addicts? Or sober ones?"

"Mostly sober."

"Well, when Alexa and I knew each other, we were both definitely active, and as I've been sober only on and off in the intervening years, I don't have many people I can really call friends." She took a sip of tea. "I've been sober nearly a decade now, but most of my friends from back then are dead, or in jail."

Mason nodded. "Congratulations." She paused. "On the sobriety, not the dead friends."

Lisa laughed. "I got it, don't worry."

"Alexa is sober, too," said Julia. "She got sober back then."

"I remember she went to rehab; that's the last I heard of her. It was a difficult time. I was not the woman I am now."

"Few of us are," said Julia.

"I wasn't even alive then," said Mason, then regretted it as they both swiveled to look at her.

After a moment, Julia said, "I wanted to ask you about the Albatross fire. What do you remember about that night?"

Lisa nodded. "Not a whole lot, although it was memorable for several unpleasant reasons. Primarily because I lost a girl in the fire. The police and her family got all up in my face, and I had to leave Oakland. Go somewhere with a little less heat, you know, if you'll pardon the phrase. And things got a little better, and then a little worse again."

"Did you go back to Tomales?"

"Yeah, but I got arrested and eventually sent away for a spell. I cleaned up in prison and stayed clean for a while afterward, but life got . . . lifey . . . and I picked up again." She sighed. "It's not been an easy road, but things are much better now." She gestured around at the kitchen. "I'm clean, I own this place, the girls are nice, the johns are far nicer than the ones I used to know . . . All in all, it's good."

"What do you remember about Alexa, back then?"

"She was gorgeous, I remember that. She could have made a load of money working for me, but she was never interested in that. She was married and then divorced and married again." Lisa laughed. "Never saw the point in marriage, myself. But she liked it. Maybe she was more of the picket fence type than you'd imagine. She had a beef with Fuzzy, I remember that." She looked at Julia. "Have you talked to Fuzzy? I know he's still around . . . well, not around, because he's in prison, but he's alive at least. He might remember what they fought about, because I certainly can't."

"Money? Drugs?"

Lisa shook her head. "No, it was more than that. I think it was about Birdman." She folded her arms on her laptop. "He was this guy Fuzzy worked for, a much bigger fish than we were. He had money and he liked to date my girls a lot; that's how I got to know him." She frowned. "He was rough with them, though, so I made him pay more." She sighed. "As I said, the clients I work with now are more pleasant, although you still get those that like to hurt women. I tend to intervene quickly these days. I don't need anyone's business that badly. My girls know I will protect them." She looked sad for a moment. "That wasn't always true."

"Of course," said Julia, calmly. "Do you remember his actual name?"

"Nope, never knew it. We all just called him Birdman. One

or two of my girls refused to go with him anymore—he was too much, you know?" She looked into her teacup, as if the past was playing there like a movie.

"Is that what Alexa and Fuzzy fought about?"

"I doubt it. Alexa didn't care about my girls, didn't poke her nose in my business."

"What else do you remember about the night of the fire?"

Lisa looked down at the table and into the past. She clearly didn't like the view, because when she raised her eyes back to Julia's, they were flat and cold. "Very little. I was extremely high. I wasn't inside when it started, obviously, because I'm still here."

"Do you remember where Alexa was?"

Lisa shook her head. "She wasn't with me. I was sitting outside with Fuzzy and, actually, Alexa's husband Dave. We were all pretty out of it, leaning against the wall of the building. I just remember that suddenly we were all running, and we could hear people screaming inside. There was a lot of smoke, even at the distance we ran to."

"Did you see all your girls?"

"All but the one that died. Eve, her name was. I don't think they ever found her body, but I don't know for sure. I just know she was there, then she wasn't, then she never was again."

"And after you ran, Alexa was with you?"

"Yeah. And then the next week she went south, to go to rehab, I think. I was back in Tomales by then, so I don't know. Fuzzy stayed in Oakland—you could ask him."

"We will."

"Give him my regards," said Lisa. "We were in love at one point, not that either of us knew what that meant at the time." She stood up. "I'll have Jeffrey show you to the door. I want to get back to work."

"You still work yourself?" said Mason, surprised.

"God, no," said Lisa. "I'm making a quilt."

JULIA OPENED THE car door and slid inside. "This case keeps going back to that fire. I think we need to dig a little deeper." She picked up her phone and called Will. "Hey, it's me. We're on our way to Vegas to get my hair done, then we'll come home. Can you get ready to tell us everything there is to know about the Albatross fire? I think it's the key."

"I'm already working on the slides," replied Will. "I'll be ready in the morning." There was a pause. "And Claudia baked a chocolate cake. I can smell it."

"Tell her to put some aside for me, will you?" said Julia, and hung up. She waved her hand at Mason. "Floor it—my hairdresser is temperamental. If I'm more than a few minutes late, he'll take it out on my bangs."

Mason floored it. And while Julia got her hair done, she played blackjack and won $378.

So, all in all, a pretty successful trip.

WILL HAD INDEED made a presentation, and early the next morning, he took them through it.

"OK, so the official report on the fire says it broke out just after eleven p.m. on the nineteenth of July, 2000. They estimate a crowd in and around the building of about five hundred people, give or take, with about fifty people inside the building. Twenty of those got out in the first three or four minutes after the fire broke out; the remaining thirty were trapped upstairs, or at the back of downstairs, and weren't able to escape. Due to very smoky conditions, most of the fatalities were caused by smoke inhalation, and the remaining ones were from the fire itself." He clicked to the next screen, which had a floor plan of the warehouse. "This is somewhat loose, because part of the problem was that the space was essentially one big open room, upstairs and down, and the residents created interior walls themselves, out of a wide variety of materials."

"Like store mannequins," said Mason, trying not to think of the imagery Alexa had put in her head.

"Exactly." Will clicked to some photos. "There aren't many interior photos available—this was before smartphones—but there were some Polaroids and individuals' photos of their work that showed some interior aspects." The images were essential mid-'90s—there were a lot of flannel shirts and posters of Nirvana around—but they were human and touching, nonetheless. Young people, in their twenties mostly, grinning for the camera, some splattered with paint, others showing their work, sculptures, graffiti, some clothing. They all looked happy, a little stoned maybe, but your typical young, artsy, hip crowd, with maybe the slight crust that comes from living someplace where hot running water isn't a given. Mason knew kids like these, had been a kid like this herself. She still was, mostly, just one who now had a paying gig and a nice place to live. She looked away from the images; they were making her chest hurt.

Will kept clicking. "Ten of the victims were all found together at the foot of a collapsed staircase from the upper floor. Others were still at the back of what was left of the upstairs, the rest on the lower floor. There were no fire escapes from the upper floor, and the lower floor had big loading doors at one end, and ordinary doors on the other three walls. The loading doors were where most of the people who escaped went out; two of the remaining doors were locked, and the last door was unlocked but apparently blocked by furniture of some kind. There was really only one way out, and if you hadn't been close to it when you first realized there was a fire, you were screwed." He clicked again. "This is a list of the fatalities."

Mason frowned. Next to the names were ages.

Twenty.

Twenty-two.

Twenty-four.

Eighteen.

She stopped reading.

Julia was tougher than she was. "All these people had friends and families, presumably, who were grief-stricken and angry and might still be. It's entirely possible that a survivor, or relative of one of the dead, is angry at Alexa and sending these notes."

"But what do they think she kept quiet about?"

Julia made a face. "Who knows? For all we know they could simply be angry that she survived when so many didn't."

"Should we question her again, see if anything here jogs her memory?" suggested Will.

"No," said Julia, shaking her head. "If she hasn't told us now, she probably won't open up unless we can use additional information as leverage. Let's go talk to these people."

"The dead?" Mason was confused.

"No," said Julia, calmly, "the ones they left behind."

After a pause, Will continued moving through his presentation. "In the end," he said, "it was determined that the fire was an accident, probably electrical in origin, with enough certainty to sue PG&E. Burn patterns were lost because of the wholesale destruction of the structure, and sadly, few witnesses survived. It was generally accepted that the electrical situation inside the Albatross was a nightmare, with people running cables everywhere and overloading circuits. Residents reported almost daily losses of power, fuses blowing all the time, that kind of thing." He clicked to an arrest photo, then another. "These were the two men ultimately deemed criminally responsible. Andy Carhart was the on-site super, insofar as he lived in the building and was the guy you'd report an issue to. People generally really liked him; he was gentle and friendly, and even the survivors hesitated to point the finger at him. But he was also the guy who locked the doors, and allowed the rampant misuse of electricity, that kind of thing. He was not good at confrontation, and this guy"—he indicated the second photo—"rode roughshod over him. He is Michael Harrison, and he was the liaison between the residents and the owner of the building, who was a guy who lived in San Francisco and who didn't pay much attention to the Albatross at all. He owned half a dozen warehouses in and around the Bay, as well as several other business properties, and he was the very definition of an absentee landlord. Harrison was the de facto landlord: He said yea or nay to potential residents, came by every week to collect rent—all of which was payable in cash—in theory paid the utilities, talked with the safety inspectors, et cetera. If Andy reported an issue, Harrison would tend to blow it off, and Andy found it hard to stand his ground. People said he basically did whatever Harrison told him to do, and that included locking the doors." Will shrugged. "People had zero problem pointing the finger at Harrison. He was a cocky bastard who ruled that building like a fiefdom, and preferred to have tenants who were young, attractive women he then creeped out. No one was very sad when he was found responsible and sent to jail. But they were sad when Andy was."

"Are they still in?" Julia asked.

"Nope," said Will. "Both served their time, seven years for Andy, nine for Harrison, and both are out. And before you ask"—he raised his hand—"yes, I attempted to find contact info for both and was only successful in the case of Andy. He's still living in Oakland. Harrison appears to have dropped off the face of the earth."

"Alright. I need you to go through the list of fatalities and pull together relatives, lawyers, any contact details for anyone who might still be harboring a grudge." Julia looked at Mason. "You'll be thrilled to hear that we're going back to the Bay Area. You can alert your family or not, as you see fit."

"I see fit not to," said Mason, "but I reserve the right to change my mind."

"Of course," said Julia. "And I reserve the right to force the issue, because I really did enjoy seeing you squirm."

Mason squinted at her. "I will enjoy inviting your sisters for Christmas, then."

"Good luck with that. I doubt you could track them down."

"Oh, I have their contact info," said Will, innocently. "You sent presents last year."

"I did?" asked Julia.

"Yes," he replied. "You sent flowers to Maybelle and a double-ended dildo to Phyllis."

"Hmm," said Julia. "Festive."

27

THIS TIME, JULIA and Mason flew into the San Francisco airport, then rented a car for the long drive into the city. Will had managed to turn up contact information for about a third of the list of those lost in the fire and was working on the rest. Many of them still lived in the Bay Area, and a majority were in the city. Plus, it turned out Julia had a fondness for the Fairmont, the stately and enormous hotel on the top of Nob Hill. Mason didn't argue; she was OK avoiding Berkeley for the time being, though she knew she was going to have to talk to her family at some point. She still hadn't decided how she felt about Louise's apology. It had been surprising, and touching, and on the one hand she wanted to accept it and maybe start trying to be friends, as well as sisters . . . and on the other she remembered all the petty comments and criticisms over the years and wanted to maintain the relationship's cool and distant vibe. Cool and distant she could handle; she wasn't sure she had the capacity for warm and fuzzy. As they walked into the palatial lobby of the Fairmont, she decided to punt the whole debate and see if her subconscious could sort it out for her.

"I had a great deal of fun here, over the years," Julia said. "We filmed a movie in the city one summer, and Jonathan and I rented the penthouse. Good times. Well, those parts of it I can remember." It always amazed Mason that Julia spoke of Jonathan so fondly, when his death had caused her so much trauma, both from the loss of him and from the resulting miscarriage of justice. Mason wondered idly if she'd ever love anyone like Julia had loved her late husband, and then she found herself thinking of Archie, and then she stopped thinking about it altogether, and just followed her boss into the elevator.

"Dammit," said Julia, walking down the hall past a woman carrying the world's smallest dog. "I forget they allow pets. I could have brought Lorre."

"Let's not spoil him any more than we already do," replied Mason. Julia's dog, who did have a distinct resemblance to the late actor, insofar as he had large, bulbous eyes and a diminutive stature, had lived for the first part of his life with a man who treated him like a king, and had then been adopted by Julia, who seemed the think he should be carried from place to place on a cushion and fed only the livers of nightingales, or some such thing. "He's gotten a little big for his britches lately."

"At least he doesn't cost me tens of thousands of dollars in broken glass," replied Julia airily. "And he does tricks, which Phil most certainly does not."

"Cats are not so much for tricks," said Mason, using the key card to open the hotel room door, then gasping as she stepped in. It was a suite, with a large balcony that overlooked San Francisco. It was stunning.

"Very nice," said Julia, following her in and tossing her bag on the bed.

Mason frowned. "Are we sharing a bed?"

"Perish the thought," replied Julia, looking horrified. "Your room is next door."

Mason went to investigate and discovered the suite had been connected to a very lovely room with an enormous bed. She stood there for a moment, looking out at the view (not as panoramic as the suite, but still mind-blowing), and marveled at the choices in her life that had led to this point. Yes, the decisions had been largely piss-poor, but somehow here she was. She enjoyed a moment of gratitude and was standing there smiling when Julia appeared at the adjoining door.

"Stop standing there like a village idiot who's totally lost the plot. Let's get going."

Mason closed her eyes for a moment, then turned. While it was good to be grateful, it was also good to remember that karma comes in many forms.

WILL HAD PUT together a PDF with the names and addresses of everyone Mason and Mann had come up to see. Their first stop was across the Bay, meeting with a retired fire inspector for the Oakland Fire Department. Will had set up the meeting and said the guy had seemed eager to talk. When they got to the address, that made more sense; it was a retirement home, and pretty grim.

It reminded Mason a little of the apartment where they'd met with Dave McGann—the same underlying smell of piss and desperation. That had been cat pee, this was clearly old people, and here the attempts to cover it up weren't helping.

The old man's name was John Hare. He'd been the lead fire investigator in Oakland for nearly forty years and was kind of a legend in the field. Right now, he was sitting in a chair that looked less comfortable than he might have liked, looking frequently at the walker sitting next to him. Mason wondered if he was ashamed of it, or just debating whether to begin the long process of getting to the bathroom. Old age seemed like a total bummer; she wasn't looking forward to it. Then she looked at Julia, who was of an age she used to consider old, and reminded herself that people age differently. She herself was going to kick ass the whole entire time. Hopefully.

"So," said Julia, settling herself across the table from John Hare, "thank you so much for making time to talk to us. I know it's been a long time since you thought about the case, but I'm hoping you remember it."

"Of course," said John. "The flesh may be weak, but the spirit is still sharp as a fucking tack. There are cases I wish I could forget, of course, but this isn't one of them. Arson investigation is usually pretty cut-and-dried, but this was tough, because there really wasn't a hell of a lot left to look at. Probably it was electrical, could have been candles, could have been a joint put down in the wrong place, who knows? Which is frustrating in itself. I like to put my finger on it, and usually I could. However, the high number of fatalities was due entirely to the landlord not giving a flying fuck about the safety of his tenants, and it pissed me off. I wanted to get him, and get him I did." He paused. "Fuckhead." He paused again. "Pardon my French."

"Duly pardoned," said Julia. "Why wasn't the building inspected?"

He laughed. "Oh, it was inspected. The Oakland fire chief knew all about it—everyone in the fucking department knew about it; they'd reported the shit out of it over and over again.

The whole problem was it wasn't fit to be inhabited, but no one cared about that. It was illegal from the get-go, right? No one was supposed to live there, but the people living there knew that and didn't care; they were those kinds of people, if you know what I mean. Artists and hippies and dropouts and young people who think they'll live forever . . ." He looked at Mason, suddenly, and his eyes were sharp. "Like you. Too cool for school."

Mason made a face. "I don't know that I'm too cool for school . . ."

But he wasn't paying attention to her. "We'd periodically tell the cops to raid the joint, and they would, and we'd clear it out, but then a week or two would go by and it'd fill up again. It was a busy time in Oakland, right? We had a serious crime problem, there was gang violence every night, murder rate was through the roof, it was chaos. A load of artists risking their shit in a warehouse was pretty low on the radar. We didn't like it—death traps like that make a firefighter's blood run cold—but there wasn't much we could do."

"So, no one was really surprised by what happened?"

"No." He shook his head. "Just surprised it hadn't happened earlier. And the way the fire spread was no surprise, either. Fire is a predictable animal. It hunts the same way every time: It follows the fuel and runs with the wind. Anyone walking through that place could tell you no one who wasn't standing in a doorway when the fire broke out would escape."

"How did you reconstruct the fire? I saw diagrams in the court papers, but the arguments suggested the interior moved and changed all the time, as people moved in and out and rearranged the space."

"Yeah," said the guy, "that was true. Every time we went to

inspect it, it would be different. At the time of the fire, there was an interior wall entirely made of store mannequins, right? Just a huge, interlaced pile of torsos and arms and legs, all woven into a separation. Cool to look at and a fucking nightmare in a fire, hot and poisonous." Again, he looked at Mason. "You see art, maybe, or something novel . . . I see fuel and smoke."

Mason tried to look neutral, but this guy was kind of pissed at her and she didn't know why.

"Most of the bodies were upstairs, just in a pile in the corner, where the staircase had been. The upstairs floor collapsed maybe thirty minutes after the fire broke out. No fucking chance. We got one lucky break: A tenant drew me a plan of the place as it had been the day before. She had it all in her head, and it helped us trace the path of the fire. Didn't help us nail the guy—it wasn't important for that—but it helped us see how the fire moved so fast."

"This girl, do you remember her name?"

He shook his head. "Nah. She was young, like you." Again, that barely held anger at Mason. "And she did it without really thinking. We were talking to people at the scene and I asked her if she could remember and she pulled a sketch pad or something from her bag, whatever shitty amount of crap she had left, and drew a floor plan right then and there. People's names, who was living with whom, where the shit plugged in, everything. I've never forgotten it. It was strange. And then she walked away with some loser guy she was with, and I never saw her again. They wanted her for the trial, but they couldn't find her." He sighed and drew a circle on the tabletop with his finger. "We didn't need her, because in the end no one was disputing how the fire had started or how it had spread; that was just presented at trial as settled fact. The issue was simply who to blame. They went with the most likely cause, electrical, and the one that led to the deepest pockets, PG&E."

Mason pulled her phone from her pocket and scrolled through her photos until she got to one of herself and Alexa, taken a few months before. She flipped it around to show him.

"Her?"

He looked, and a strange expression came over his face. Recognition, surprise . . . and something else. "Yes," he said. "She's older there, obviously, but I'd know her anywhere." He looked down, and then up at Mason and Mann. "She was real, then."

Julia raised an eyebrow. "Real?"

He looked embarrassed. "Honestly, there was a while there where I thought maybe she'd been a ghost. She was there, then she was gone." He shook his head. "No one else saw her but me, and the guys made fun of me for it. But I thought maybe she was one of the people who'd died, right? Hanging around like she was, all lost." He frowned. "Not really, of course, but it was weird. That whole scene was a nightmare, affected us all. There were people we never accounted for, you know that? Thirty people missing, twenty-nine bodies, but the fire burned so hot and some of those young women were tiny, maybe we missed one, or misattributed bone fragments." He looked at Mason and Mann. "It breaks your heart, pulling young bodies out of a fire, all that promise, burned up and wasted, all those years ahead to live, fall in love, have children of their own . . . it stays with you."

And Mason realized it wasn't anger he was directing at her. It was grief.

28

“WHAT’S NEXT?” ASKED Mason. They had driven back over the Bay Bridge and made their way through rush-hour traffic back to the hotel. It was early evening, and she was getting hungry. Yes, solving crime. Yes, helping one’s friends. But also, food.

“Well,” said Julia, “soon we will need dinner, but there’s someone we can go see first, I think. Will found a survivor from the fire who lives only a few blocks away, but he couldn’t dig up a number for him, just an address, so he might not be there. Might not have been there for years, in fact.”

Mason shrugged. “Alright, well, let’s go see. What’s the name?”

“Darren Olvera. He was a resident who’d been inside when the fire began, and who received fairly extensive burns, mostly on his hands and arms. He dragged several people out, but couldn’t go back in again because the smoke got too thick and the fire became too hot. He was one of the few people who came out of it looking like a hero.”

“Meeting a hero wasn’t on my bingo card for today,” said Mason, “but as long as it doesn’t take forever, I’m open to it.”

"It'll take what it takes," said Julia, somewhat caustically. "But I'm getting hungry, too, so don't panic." She looked at her phone where she'd pulled up the address. "Oh great, we can walk."

DARREN OLVERA LIVED on Filbert Street, one of the steepest streets in a city famous for vertiginous inclines. Julia had taken one look and sent Mason up to the address to see if the guy was even there. He was, but he also wasn't: He lived there, but he wasn't home, and his roommate was reluctant to give up his whereabouts until Mason forked over twenty dollars. Privacy is cheap, apparently. Such is life, thought Mason, as she clomped back down the hill to where Julia was waiting.

She leaned briefly against a wall for support and to catch her breath. "He's in a bar down the street. Do you want to leave it and try again tomorrow? He might be at home then."

"No, why? You scared to go in a bar?"

Mason made a face. "Not at all. I was being considerate of your age and level of tiredness. And my own hunger. It's getting dark."

"Gimme a break, let's go." Julia turned and headed carefully down the sloped street like a giraffe trying roller skates for the first time.

"I don't know how drunk the architects were who decided this hill was worth building on, but I'm glad I'm not drunk now. Getting down this street with all my faculties intact is hard enough." She leaned back, her high heels adding to the grade.

"The bar is on the flat part at the bottom, just around the corner."

"Great," sighed Julia. "I'm getting vertigo and my hamstrings are killing me."

It was a sports bar, and it took a minute for the sound to wash over Mason and separate itself into three or four different screens playing different games, and the noise from several dozen fans debating every play.

Mason walked up to the bar and leaned on it. The bartender was muscular, hot and not in the mood for bullshit, so Mason got to the point.

"I'm trying to find Darren Olvera. I don't suppose you know him?"

The bartender shrugged. "I might."

Mason sighed inwardly. What was with this neighborhood? Everyone was on the make. She pulled a twenty out of her pocket and placed it on the bar. "I'm not here to cause any trouble for him. I just want to ask him about a mutual friend. No problems, OK?"

The bartender took the twenty and slid it into her front pocket. "He's the guy in the corner on his own, red jacket." She inclined her head about a quarter of an inch in the right direction, and Mason took a look.

"Alright, thanks." She looked over at Julia, who had watched this whole exchange and was already moving toward Darren.

As the older woman approached him, Darren Olvera looked up. He saw her, and then saw Mason, tacking in his direction from the bar, and for some reason decided they weren't two probably harmless women, but were, instead, demons from a different, more deadly dimension. He literally flipped the table he was sitting at and took off at full speed toward the door, shoving Julia out of the way as he went.

"Hey!" called the bartender, clearly annoyed. "You said no problems!"

Mason didn't have time to shrug in response; she was busy righting Julia and charging out the door after Darren.

"Stop!" she shouted. "We just want to ask some questions."

But Darren wasn't interested.

Julia came out of the bar behind Mason. "Catch him," she called. "I'll wait here."

"Of course," muttered Mason, as Darren turned the corner onto Filbert Street.

Running full tilt is hard. Running full tilt up a street that Mason later discovered had a grade of around twenty-seven percent is incredibly hard. Luckily, it was just as hard for Darren as it was for Mason, and his house was more than halfway up the hill. Mason thanked her cardiovascular health and plowed up behind him, not having enough puff to shout, but trying to convey her harmlessness along with her determination to catch up with him.

"If you're heading home," she puffed, "I know where you're going . . ."

He said nothing, just kept pumping up the hill.

"We just want to ask some questions . . ."

Nothing. He'd reached his house and was fumbling for his key. Mason was right behind him and caught up before he'd gotten it in the door. He flipped around to face her and raised his fists.

"You're joking," said Mason, bending double and trying to catch her breath. "Now you wanna fight? I can barely breathe."

"What do you want?" he said. "I'm clean. Whatever it is, I didn't do it."

"Who the hell do you think I am?" asked Mason, her heart rate still pretty elevated.

"You're not the cops?"

Mason scoffed. "I'm insulted. Since when have cops dressed as well as her . . ." She pointed at Julia, who had clearly decided the party was worth joining, despite the hill, and was slowly and elegantly approaching them.

Darren considered this. "You're not the police?"

"No," said Julia, who had now reached them. "Why don't you want to talk to the cops?"

Darren looked embarrassed. "I was in some trouble . . . It doesn't matter."

"Well," said Julia, leaning against the wall, "I'm a lawyer, from Los Angeles. My name is Julia, and this is my associate Mason. We don't care what trouble you've been in. We just need to ask you some questions about the night of the Albatross fire. You were there, were you not?"

Darren Olvera pushed his sleeves down and nodded. "You're really not the police?"

"No, we're really not," said Julia firmly, "nor are we working with them. We're working for a private client, and anything you talk to us about will be kept confidential unless absolutely necessary." She smiled. "Mr. Olvera, I assure you everything is OK. I would appreciate going inside, though, as even just standing on this steep a hill is hurting the backs of my calves."

He relaxed, suddenly, and smiled back at her. "I'm sorry. I get a bit jumpy."

"I'm the one who had to run," muttered Mason, but she silently followed him and Julia as he opened the door and led them inside.

DARREN OLVERA HAD to be somewhere in his forties, but it was hard to place with any greater accuracy than that, because he had the well-tended good looks of many young men in San Francisco, and a muscular, athletic frame that could have been twenty-five. He was, however, very nervous.

Mason could feel it as soon as she entered the apartment. He was calmer than he'd been outside, but Darren still wasn't thrilled to be talking to them. However, he was doing his best, and offered them a drink as they entered the apartment.

"We didn't mean to freak you out," Mason said. "We couldn't find a phone number for you, thus no advance warning."

He shrugged, gave a small smile. "I lose my phone a lot," he said. "A number wouldn't have done you any good. How can I help you?"

Julia settled into the chair he'd indicated. "Were you a resident of the Albatross, or just visiting that night?"

"A resident," he said, "although not a very long-term one. I think I'd been there around a month at that point. I didn't know many people." He smiled again, but it hadn't gotten any bigger. "I got to know more of them afterward, to be honest, during the trial. There were cliques in that building, like anywhere, I guess. I wasn't that cool a kid. I mostly kept to myself."

"Did you know Alexa Rousso?" Mason asked.

"Yeah, I knew her, but she didn't know me . . . Her room was next to mine, and she was one of the cool kids, for sure. She and her husband knew everyone, were very friendly with the super."

"Andy Carhart?"

He nodded.

"What about the landlord's agent, Michael Harrison?"

"Nobody was very friendly with him. Andy was a good guy, a nice person. Harrison was a total dick. One of those guys who likes being powerful and likes to lord it over people. I barely exchanged a dozen words with him. I mostly dealt with Andy, everyone did." He squeezed his hands together. "I don't have much to tell you, honestly. The fire started, I got out, got a few other people out, that was basically it."

"When did you become aware that there was a fire?"

"I smelled it," he replied. "It didn't smell like the usual candle smell—people used candles a lot there, right, because the electrical in that building was a creative force, you know what I mean? Sometimes it worked, sometimes it didn't."

"And that's how the fire started? The electrical?"

Mason expected another nod, but Darren didn't do that. He shrugged.

Julia caught it. "You don't think that's how it started?"

Again, that sense of nervousness. "I guess. That's what they said at the trial."

"You don't think so?"

"I don't know. I'm no expert. Everyone seemed to agree that's how it was."

Julia watched him for a moment, as he squirmed a little in his chair. "Why don't you tell me what you remember about that night?"

He sighed. "You know, I said all this at the trial. You can read the transcripts."

She nodded. "Yes, but I'd like to hear it from you directly, if that's OK. I'm sorry if it makes you anxious to go over it."

"It doesn't." This was clearly a lie, but Julia was going to let it be. "Alright. There was this big party going on, right? Super noisy, people everywhere. It was kind of fun but also kind of overwhelming, so I'd gone inside to my space to, you know, chill out." He shot a look under his eyelashes. "And to get a little high, you know."

"Sure, you won't get any judgment from us. Could you hear the other people inside?"

"Some." He stopped.

"Go on," she said.

"I could hear people in the space next to mine pretty well. They were arguing, actually, so their voices were raised." He looked at Mason. "Your friend was there, Alexa. She has a very distinctive voice, and she was my neighbor, and she was . . ." He hesitated. ". . . gorgeous, so I knew her voice, anyway. She was arguing with someone. Two people, I think, because I could hear another girl's voice and a guy's voice, too."

"Do you remember what they were arguing about?"

"No. *They* had candles going, though. I could smell those. Alexa liked to burn these jasmine candles a lot, and incense, and I can remember that."

"Alright, and then what happened?"

"And then I got high and kind of dozed off a bit. I woke up because I could smell burning."

"Burning? Like smoke?"

He shook his head. "No, like burning things, like paper and fabric or whatever. Not a lot of smoke right then, just the smell. And I could hear people scrambling and calling out, and you can tell when there's something wrong, and there was clearly something wrong, so I got up and started sounding the alarm."

"Could you hear the fire?"

"Not at that point. And I started telling people to get out, and then there was a bigger sound, like something caught fire all at once, and *then* there was smoke. It got really bad, and I went back in and got another couple of people out, but then it got really hot really fast, and I couldn't do it anymore. I tried . . ." He raised his hands, unconsciously. "But it was too hot."

"Did you see Alexa get out?"

He shook his head. "No, but I know she did, because I saw her outside."

"What about the people she was with?"

He made a face. "No idea. I don't know who they were, so I don't know if they made it out or not. You can ask her."

"We will."

"Did you tell all this at the trial?" Mason asked.

"Some of it," he said. "I didn't remember about the smell of the candles, or about the argument. Back then things were worse, right? People had died, everyone was very upset, everyone said it was the electrical, so it didn't seem to matter if someone was having a drunken argument or not."

"They were drunken, the voices?"

He opened his mouth to answer and then shook his head. "They were loud, Alexa was angry, I could tell that much, but other than that I've got no idea." He wiped his hands on his pants, and said, "I don't remember anything else. Why are you asking about this now? It's all so long ago."

Julia shook her head. "We have a client and it's important to her. I can't say any more than that. Is there anyone else we should talk to?"

"I don't know," he said, hopelessly. "I'm not in touch with any of them anymore. I kind of drifted across the bay to here and tried to get on with my life. I try not to think about it very much."

Julia got to her feet, and Mason did the same. "Well, I appreciate you taking the time to do it now, for us."

"It's OK," he replied, shrugging. "When it comes up like this, it's hard for a few weeks and then it fades away again." He paused. "I wish it went away completely, but it never does." He tugged his sleeves down, obviously a habit. "Like any other scar, the best you can hope for is getting used to it."

29

MASON AND MANN made their way gingerly down Filbert and called a driverless cab to take them back to the hotel.

"You're not worried about the car having no driver?" asked Mason.

"Not at all," said Julia, looking out of the window. "I put my faith in strangers all the time. Putting my faith in a machine seems more sensible, if anything." She sighed. "People are far less predictable, plus they always want to chat." The car drew up in front of the hotel. "Let's get room service and call Will. We need to download and cogitate, and I do it better once I've eaten."

Two steak frites later, they video-called Will and propped Mason's laptop on the coffee table.

"I turned up something unexpected today," said Will. "I don't know what it means, but it's weird as hell."

Mason's phone rang. "Hold that thought," she said. "It's Alexa."

Julia looked at her sharply. "Don't ask her anything yet. I want some time to think."

Mason nodded and answered the call. "Hey there, what's up?"

Alexa sounded strange. Strangled. Trying not to lose her shit. Mason could tell all of that in the first few syllables.

"Jennifer is in the hospital. Where are you?"

"In San Francisco, with Julia," replied Mason. "What happened to Jennifer?" She turned to Julia and raised her eyebrows.

"Speaker?" mouthed her boss.

Mason interrupted Alexa. "Wait, can I put you on speaker? Julia's here, and Will's on the phone. It'll be easier than just repeating everything." She hit the button and laid the phone on the bed.

". . . and she has broken ribs and a big fat black eye," Alexa was saying, having clearly not heard Mason at all.

"Back up," said Mason. "Go over it again."

Alexa sighed, and everyone could hear the panic in her voice. "Someone pushed Jennifer into traffic. On the corner of Olive and First. She bounced off a taxi and hit the deck, got bruised up a lot, broke a couple ribs. She and I had been at a meeting together but split up afterward. I heard the sirens, but didn't pay any attention—there are always sirens, right?" She hiccuped. "At least you're safely in San Francisco."

"Did you already talk to Wilson and Brooks?" Mason frowned. "The detectives who are handling your case?"

"No," said Alexa. There was a long pause. "It's probably connected, right?"

"Julia here," said Julia, unnecessarily. "Of course it's connected. You got a threatening note, and someone sabotaged a major event and you got hurt. Then you got another note, and one of your sponsees was killed, then another note and someone shot at Mason and now attempted to kill Jennifer. It's all connected, it's all centered around you, and I think you know why and maybe even who." While her words were aggressive, her tone was not.

Mason looked at Julia and raised her eyebrows. "I thought you wanted time to think about it," she said softly.

"I thought about it," replied Julia. "Alexa, we spoke to someone today who remembers you being inside the Albatross shortly before the fire broke out, arguing with someone. Do you remember that?"

There was a long silence.

"Yes," said Alexa, eventually, and her voice was exhausted. "I do."

"You need to tell us what happened that night. I know it was a long time ago, but I think somehow it's the key to the whole thing."

Alexa sighed. "Alright, although I can't see how it's possibly connected . . . but OK. I was inside the building, hanging out with one of Lisa Rawlings's girls."

"Name?"

"I don't remember. I didn't know her all that well. We were just, you know, shooting the shit, getting high. I had candles going, I had incense lit, the usual thing for me. No big whoop. Then a client shows up for her, with Lisa. Lisa leaves right away, but the client seems to think he can maybe get a three-way for the price of a two-way, if you get me, and it took me a minute to dissuade him. That's what the person heard, I guess. I wouldn't call it an argument. It was more of a forceful clarification." She paused. "I didn't need to throw hands, but I would have."

"Fair enough. Then what happened?"

"Well, they left, and I lay down for a bit, to just chill."

"You were high?"

"Very."

Julia paused. "Will, you getting all this?"

His voice was clear. "Yeah, I got it. I have questions."

"For me?" Alexa asked.

Will's tone was firm. "Yeah. You said you didn't know the girl you were with all that well. Try harder. What was her name?"

"I don't . . ." Alexa sounded confused.

"I think you do know."

Alexa was quiet for a moment, then, "Eve. I don't think I ever knew her last name."

There was a pause, then Will said, "Eve Riley?"

"Maybe. It was first names only back then. It's not like we really knew each other." Her tone was diffident, dismissive, but there was an undercurrent of anxiety everyone in the room could hear.

"What's going on, Will?" asked Julia.

"This is the weird thing I was starting to tell you about earlier. A young woman named Eve Riley was listed among the dead from the fire, originally, and for many years. Her family, a sister and mother who lived in Petaluma, no dad listed, were among the class action plaintiffs, got part of the settlement, end of story, right?"

"Why do I think it isn't the end of the story?" said Julia.

Will looked grim. "Because the body of Eve Riley was discovered ten years later, buried in Tilden Park. Murdered."

Alexa made a noise on the phone, just a small sound. Maybe surprise, maybe fear—it was hard to tell.

Julia frowned. "But Alexa just said she was there that night."

"And Alexa's not alone. Several witnesses, including Lisa Rawlings, said she was there. She *was* there. And when her body wasn't conclusively identified among the remains, it was simply assumed it was an error of some kind, or that the intensity of the fire had obliterated her completely; it can happen in a mass casualty event like that. But the truth is that someone took her from the Albatross, saving her from the fire, and then killed her themselves, either that night or sometime afterward."

"And that means," said Julia, slowly, "that Alexa was potentially the last person to see her alive, and if she can remember the name of the client, then we might have a suspect, too."

Everyone looked at the phone, lying on the table.

"No," said Alexa.

"No?" asked Julia. "No, you don't remember his name?"

"I don't. I barely remember what he looked like. I'd never seen him before and we were talking for all of a minute." Alexa's voice wobbled. "Do you think it's him, the one who's sending the letters?"

Julia shook her head. "I don't know. I don't know why he would poke the hornet's nest so long after he'd gotten away with murder. I don't understand yet why this all started."

"I'm scared," said Alexa. "Scott is away again, and he took the dog."

"Will," said Julia, "go get Alexa, set her up in one of the guest rooms."

Will nodded.

"No," said Mason, "she can stay in my place. There are spare keys in the kitchen drawer."

"Fine," said Julia. "Alexa, can you be ready in about twenty minutes? Will is going to be on his way shortly."

"It's not necessary . . ." Alexa started to say, then they heard tears in her voice. "But thank you. I'll be ready."

"Try not to worry too much," said Julia. "I need you to remember as much as you can about the client you saw."

"I'll try. I'll get my stuff together."

"Will, I'll text you her address," said Mason.

Alexa dropped off the call, and Mason, Mann and Will looked at one another.

Slowly, Julia and Will smiled.

"I don't get it," said Mason. "Why are you two grinning like the cat that got the cream?"

Julia picked up the hotel phone. "Room service? Do you have ice cream?"

"Because," said Will, "a cold case murder popping up in the middle of our investigation? That's no coincidence. Half an hour ago we were nowhere, and now we have a big fat lead."

Julia hung up the phone. "Yes, indeed. Time to celebrate."

30

THE NEXT MORNING, Will sent over contact information for the detective who'd originally investigated Eve Riley's death back in the day. Detective Karneeva was probably younger than John Hare, the fire investigator, but they were clearly contemporaries. However, Karneeva was spry, there was no other word for it. And like the arson expert, his mind was as sharp as ever. When Julia had called him from the car, he'd been right on top of it.

"Eve Riley? Sure, happy to discuss it. Come now, I have time."

He lived in the flats of Berkeley, in a small, neat Craftsman house sitting in the middle of a wild garden that he clearly enjoyed (lots of bird feeders) but never tended (lots of weeds). The occasional, slightly feral tomato could be spotted, suggesting he'd made attempts at one point, but lacked commitment. Now he sat across from them, a cardboard file storage box of information on the table, a manila folder resting on top. The neatness of his files suggested he saved his commitment for his work.

"And why are we talking about this now?" he asked. His

eyes were bright, searching the faces across from him, but his hands lay calmly on the tabletop.

Julia smiled at him. "We're investigating a case in Los Angeles that seems to have connections to a variety of things up here. Firstly, the Albatross fire, and now, maybe, your old case."

"Really? We never solved it, you know. Anything you have to add would be very welcome. I mean, it's theoretically a closed case, but cases like this never fully close, not while I'm alive, anyway." He slapped the folder, then pushed it across the table. "Be warned, there are some less-than-pleasant photos in there."

Mason swallowed and opened the folder. At first she couldn't tell what she was looking at, just a long depression in the earth. But then she was able to make out the outlines of a body, the dull gleam of white bones. A shallow grave, with what was left of a woman in it.

"We couldn't get a lot of forensic evidence," said the detective, frowning. "The soil there, in Tilden, is highly acidic, and the body had a lot of decomposition. Teeth and bones were still good, so we could identify her from dental records, but there wasn't a lot of tissue, and all the clothing, if she'd been wearing any when she was buried, was gone. Analysis suggested she'd been there for around ten years, which tracked with her disappearance; that all tallied. But there wasn't much we could go on in terms of the perpetrator."

Mason thought about sitting in the meeting in Tilden and wondered how many other bodies might be buried within striking distance of the pumpkin loaf. She flipped through some more pictures, close-ups of jawbone, skull . . . and an arrest photo of Eve, who was young and blond, with a tousled mane of hair over a strong nose and a hawklike expression of disdain. She looked tough, but all that bravado hadn't been enough to save her from a determined killer. Mason looked carefully at all the photos, noting the clothes and accessories Eve had worn, trying to get a sense of who she had been. A tight T-shirt ripped and held together with safety pins, the silver matching the many bracelets and necklaces she wore. A charm bracelet, a bracelet with poppies and her initial, necklaces with dolphins, many earrings with skulls and flowers . . . She thought of the jewelry she'd worn herself at that age, the defiant mix of little girl cute and don't-fuck-with-me teen.

"Could you determine the cause of death?"

He nodded. "Massive skull fracture. The killer hit her with something heavy and rounded, like a bat, maybe, or a bottle, although that level of force would probably have broken a bottle and we'd have found glass fragments. It would have been quick, but we'll never know what happened to her in the hours before that." He pushed over an autopsy diagram, a sketched idea of the cross section of the weapon, a deeply curved and heavy implement. Various scratches and wounds marked on the outline of her body. He shrugged. "She put up quite a fight, but he got away with it. It bothers me to this day. And the funny thing is her family thought she'd died in the Albatross fire; several witnesses put her at the scene." He reached for the folder. "She was there with a woman called . . . hang on . . . Lisa Rawlings." He looked at the women. "Her pimp, basically. She wouldn't admit to it, of course, but she was known to us and had been arrested several times for soliciting herself. She'd had several young women with her that night, all accounted for except Eve."

Julia's eyebrows went up. "We've spoken to Lisa. She remembers the girl but still thinks she was lost in the fire. We got Eve's name from another source."

"Oh yeah? Who?"

"Alexa Rousso."

"Never heard of her. She saw Eve there?"

"Yes. And saw the man she was with, although she says she can't remember his name. So, once Eve's body showed up . . . Well, first, how did it show up?"

"Ironically, we'd had a season of small fire breakouts in Tilden, and fire workers raking over embers turned up a bone. They weren't expecting bodies, but they knew what it was and called us in. Didn't take us long to find the rest of her, and not much longer to identify her." He looked thoughtful. "She hadn't been reported missing originally, when she left home at fucking fifteen, but after the fire they ran stories in the local and state media, trying to pin down everyone who was there at the Albatross. There was a lot about it in the press. Some family member cared enough to get in touch with the Oakland PD. It was a sister, I think. Their mother died sometime after the fire. The sister came down to the city with photos, ready to identify her body, but of course after a fire like that there aren't bodies to be identified." He took the folder from Mason and rifled through it. "I have those photos around here somewhere. They show Eve in a better light than the arrest one . . . I'll send them to you when I find them. I wasn't involved right after the fire, of course; it wasn't a murder investigation, even though clearly someone was responsible for all those deaths. But it was criminal negligence, not arson, so I'd heard about the case, but knew nothing about the details. It was only once her body showed up that I got involved, and the connection to the Albatross came out in the course of the investigation." He looked at Julia. "Can I ask what you're investigating? Do you think it's connected to my case?"

Julia turned down the corners of her mouth. "I'm not sure. Our client is receiving threatening letters, implying she got away with something terrible in the past. We're trying to find out what that might be so we can work out who's sending them. She lived in Oakland and upstate California for most of her early life, and everything keeps leading back here. But so far we haven't found anything terrible, you know? She wasn't at her best when she was up here, but she got sober and pulled her life together." Mason watched Julia's face, the elegant expression giving nothing else away.

"Well, the past has a definite way of circling back around and hitting you upside the head, you know what I mean? I have four cases like Eve's, cases where the bodies of young women showed up just like hers did, and I probably turn over the evidence I have once or twice a month. I hate to think there are killers out there running around free, maybe even still killing." He looked at his hands. "Sometimes I think about how many people get away with murder and walk among us. The world is big, bodies are small; it's often a matter of chance that they're found, and we get an opportunity to avenge them. Eve could have stayed buried for decades, without fate taking a hand."

"You said four like Eve? Are you thinking they're connected? A serial killer?"

"No," he said firmly, "although we've had our share of those up here. These are simply young women who were killed and we never got to the bottom of it. And don't forget, literally thousands of people are reported missing in California every year, and who knows how many of those are killed. It's a forest, and these are just the trees we can see." He looked at the two women. "And your witness saw Eve that night with a man? Can she identify him?"

"She says not."

"Is she willing to look at pictures? It might be the break we need."

"I can ask my client, but I wouldn't hold out hope if I were you. She has only very foggy memories of that night." Julia looked at the detective. "But I'll try."

"OK." He put the folders back in the box. "I'm not giving up. The arm of justice is long and built for patience. Eventually, we'll get him. Then Eve will rest, and so will I."

31

DETECTIVE KARNEEVA LIVED on a slight rise, and when they stepped out of his place, Julia paused for a moment to take in the view. Or at least, she stood still for a moment, and Mason should have known better than to assume she was just sightseeing.

"How far away is Vacaville?" Julia asked her.

"About an hour or two, depending on traffic," replied Mason. "Why?"

"Because we need to go talk to Fuzzy, and he's at the state prison there."

"And you think we can just walk in?"

"No, of course not. Will has been working on it for the last week or so. He applied for visitation approval. We were added to Fuzzy's—sorry—Mike Jones's list of approved visitors, he made an appointment for us for today or tomorrow, and it's earlier than I thought, so maybe we can do it today."

Mason stared at her. "Why would Mike Jones agree to a visit from two people he's never heard of before?"

"Because his last visitor came to see him over three years ago and he's probably bored out of his mind. Prison's very dull, apart from the all-pervading fear of violence and the occasional bug in the food. Trust me, you'd hate it, not because it's scary, but because it's skull-crushingly boring."

"I have no intention of going to jail."

Julia laughed. "No one intends to go to jail, Mason, yet there they are." She gazed across the Bay. "It really is so pretty up here." She breathed the fresh, slightly salty air and sighed. "OK, let's go to prison. If we make good time, we'll get there just in time for visitation."

CALIFORNIA STATE PRISON Solano is a men-only medium-security facility near Vacaville, which is about forty-five miles from Oakland. They got lucky: Traffic was relatively humane, and they arrived at the prison with twenty minutes to spare before visitation.

Mason had never been to a prison before, but obviously Julia was painfully familiar with the process. She got very quiet as they signed in, showed ID, were searched and then escorted to the visitation area.

"Does it bother you being here?" Mason asked her in a low voice as they walked along a corridor. It reminded her a little of a hospital, the same smell of discomfort and disinfectant, and also something like a high school in session, as there was yelling and noise in the distance and the smell of a meat loaf that may or may not have contained actual meat.

"Yes," replied Julia, briefly. "But this is where he is, and so this is where we have to be. I'll manage."

Mason looked at her. "You could have given me a list of questions."

Julia shrugged. "I know where I'm going to start, but I have no idea where it's going to go, and that's hard to pin down on paper." She looked over at her young colleague. "Relax, Mason, it's been decades since I was in prison. I can handle it."

But then a door buzzed to let them in, and Mason saw her flinch.

MASON TOOK ONE look at Mike Jones and realized where he'd gotten his nickname. Although it was mostly gray now, his hair framed his head in a halo like a renaissance painting, huge and circular. On another man it would have been long; on him it was spherical. His face was calm, curious, and largely friendly. Maybe Julia had been right: He'd have taken a visit from anyone, just for the pleasure of something different to look at. As it was, he took one look at Julia and Mason and a broad grin split his face.

"Wow," he said, "they said you was lawyers. I wasn't expecting two good-looking women."

Julia smiled. "Women have been lawyers for a long time, Mr. Jones."

He nodded. "It's the good-looking part that's the surprise." He grinned at Mason. "But maybe I'm easily surprised."

She raised an eyebrow at him, as they all sat down at a table. She'd expected the glass partitions she'd seen so often on TV, but this was just a big room with many tables, and inmates and visitors moved about relatively freely. Then she remembered it was medium-security, and as she looked around, she realized further that most of the inmates were older than she'd expected. Nobody looks their best in an orange jumpsuit, though, to be fair.

"So, what's all this about?" Fuzzy asked. "I didn't recognize your name, although you"—here he pointed at Julia—"look like that old actress, who, now I think about it, had the same name, so you know, maybe I'm being slow on the uptake here. Are you her?"

"I am her," replied Julia. "I am the old actress. But I'm also a lawyer, although I'm not here to help you with your case."

He laughed. "There's nothing to help with. They got me for possession with intent to distribute, and seeing as I had more on me than anyone could reasonably expect to consume in a decade, and as I had prior convictions and had crossed state lines into Oregon, they kind of threw the book at me." He shrugged. "The first few years sucked ass, because I was over in Sacramento, max security, but I kept my head down and they moved me here. It's OK." He looked at Mason. "I haven't seen a beautiful young woman in about seven years, though, so you're kind of blowing my mind." He looked at Julia. "And you're no easier, it has to be said." He looked back at Mason. "You're kind of scary, to be honest."

Suddenly, Mason decided that she liked him. She wasn't sure why. She smiled. "Don't worry, I'll be gone soon."

"Not from here," he said, tapping his forehead. "You'll be here for a while."

"We want to talk about Alexa Rousso."

He frowned for a second. "Alexa? Haven't thought of her in ages. Is she OK?"

"She's fine. Someone's been threatening her. We're trying to find out why."

Fuzzy made a face. "Well, she never hesitated to get into a fight, I'll say that for her, so she probably pissed someone off.

It happens. But she was also one of the nicest friends I ever had, back in the day. Depending on where she was in the day, if you know what I mean."

"No, what do you mean?"

He leaned back in his chair and looked up at the high windows, each showing a sliver of California sunshine. "Well, depending on if she was high or waiting to get high. If she was feeling OK, if you get my drift, then she was good company, easygoing, funny, generous. If she was waiting to score, or couldn't score, she was a total bitch and would steal the ground out from under you if she thought she could trade it for a hit." He shrugged. "We were all the same, back then."

"We spoke to Lisa Rawlings. Do you remember her?"

"Remember her? We dated, on and off. Mostly on. She was gorgeous, sexy, trouble, you know? I loved her." He looked at Julia and smiled. "Is she OK? I haven't heard from her in twenty years."

"She's good," said Julia. "She's sober, she's living in Nevada, running a business."

His smile widened. "Oh, that's good to hear. I'd love to see her. I don't suppose I will. I doubt she ever makes it up here."

"I can pass on your address," said Julia, "if you like."

He started to nod but then shook his head. "She's better off without me," he said. "I was never a good idea for her. Got her hooked on smack, never treated her well." He paused. "I loved her, but I didn't really know what that meant, back then. Not sure I know what it means now, to be fair." He sighed. "But what about Alexa?"

"Lisa said you two had a beef?"

He looked surprised. "She did? I don't remember it. She saved my life, Alexa did, the night of that big fire."

"The Albatross?"

"Yeah. Me and her old man were sitting outside, with our backs against the wall of the building. Just minding our business, listening to the music, stoned, you know, the usual. And Alexa comes running out of the building all freaked out and sees us, and grabs us, and tells us to run. Two minutes later the place was on fire, and the wall where we were sitting came down right where we'd been. We would have been flattened." He made a face. "To be fair, we wouldn't have stayed sitting there, seeing as there were people burning to death on the other side of it, right? And the heat and smoke and everything, but whatever. I like to think she saved my life. That's how I remember it, anyway."

"Was Alexa alone when she came out?"

He nodded. "Yeah, although there were other people running out, too, but not with her, if you know what I mean. It was not a mellow vibe; it was chaos." He looked back at the windows, and Mason wondered how much time he got to spend outside. "Thirty-something people died that night. It was terrible."

"Did she have issues with anyone else?" asked Mason. "Anyone you remember?"

"She didn't get on with Birdman, that's for sure. She hated him."

Mason frowned to herself. That name kept popping up. They really needed to track him down.

Julia was on it. "No one else seems to remember much about him. Do you know his actual name?"

"Nah," said Fuzzy. "Nobody knew anyone's name back then. I didn't know his, he didn't know mine, and besides, he wasn't even around all that long. I think he was just slumming it with us, because his family had money, a poultry farm maybe, something like that, so I think he was just playing at being a baddie, if you follow me. I don't even remember where he got the nickname. He always had money to burn, and cases of fancy wine, and a car that actually worked. Occasionally, one would explode."

"The cars?" Mason frowned.

"No, the bottles of wine. They were fizzy, like champagne, you know? They weren't champagne, not strictly. I remember him lecturing me one night when I really wasn't in any fit state to take in new information, if you follow me. It's not champagne if it's not from one special part of France, or something like that. But it was like champagne, anyway. Bubbles."

"And he and Alexa didn't like each other?"

"I don't think he didn't like her—I think he liked her a lot, most of us guys did, she was pretty as hell and with cans to write home about." He looked at Mason and inexplicably apologized. "Sorry, but that's the truth."

"Don't mind me," said Mason. "She's got great cans."

"But she didn't like him. I think maybe he tried it on once and she wasn't having it. She was with that guy she married to start with, and then she was with that other guy . . ." He got lost in thought. "No, I don't remember his name."

"Dave McGann," said Mason.

Fuzzy's eyebrows shot up. "Yes! That's right, Dave. So, yeah, he never had a chance with her. He liked the girls, did old Birdy." He paused. "I heard he moved, but I don't remember where."

"We're trying to track him down."

"If he's still alive. He used to drink and do drugs like the rest of us, but he managed to never get hooked. Hated needles. He cleaned up his act, I guess."

Mason wondered how many people were saved by their fear of needles.

"And he was there, too, the night of the fire?"

"Yeah. Trying to get with some of Lisa's girls. Well, trying to get with any girls, but hers were more . . . available, right? He had no problem paying for it."

"Do you remember any of their names?"

"No." He rubbed his hand over his head, embarrassed. "I never paid much attention to them, to be honest. They changed all the time; she'd find new girls, others would drift off or meet someone who was going to change their life, whatever. It's not a job with a lot of consistency, hooking." He looked at Mason again, with that air of apology. "If you were considering it, you know."

"I wasn't," she replied.

"Did you see him afterward?" asked Julia.

"Afterward?"

"After you ran away from the fire?"

He shrugged. "Not that I remember, but like I said, it was chaotic, and I was high. Mind you, that sobered me up fast, all that running and people freaking out and the sirens and whatever." He frowned. "Not my best night, for sure."

"But he was there, along with Alexa, and Dave McGann, and Lisa."

"Yeah."

Julia fell silent, considering. Then she placed her hands on the table and pushed up. "OK, I think that's all. Can I call you if I think of anything else?"

"Yeah, of course. It'll be the highlight of my week." He laughed. "Or year, whatever. Not a lot happens here." He sat back as the two women gathered their jackets and put them on, watching their bodies unselfconsciously.

“Thanks, Mr. Jones, for agreeing to see us.”

“Call me Fuzzy. Everyone does.”

Julia nodded and headed toward the door. Mason hesitated, then grinned at the man sitting there.

“Bye, Fuzzy,” she said, then turned and walked slowly and swingingly away, giving him plenty to think of for later. Why not? It was no skin off her nose, and the thought of being trapped somewhere with only your own thoughts for company was terrifying. At the door she turned back to wave and found him grinning at her, fully understanding what she had done and why she had done it.

He raised his hand, winked, and waved at her. She did the same.

Friends for life.

32

IN THE CAR, Julia made calls while Mason got on the 80 and headed west.

First, she called Will.

"Hey, the rich kid we couldn't find a name for?"

"Yeah?"

"His family ran a poultry business. Near Petaluma."

Will cleared his throat. "Well, that narrows it down not at all. Poultry itself? Or eggs? There are dozens of chicken-related businesses in that area. I think I told you, it was . . ."

"Chickaluma, I remember. Look, I'm just giving you the information as I get it. Sometimes your mind makes connections mine doesn't. He always used to have cases of sparkling wine in his car. I doubt that's very helpful, either."

"Probably not," Will said, then coughed. "Did you know that the internal pressure in a champagne bottle is about five or six atmospheres, which is about the same as a car tire? The unusual shape helps to distribute the pressure, the punt in the bottom, the much thicker and heavier glass. They're an engineering marvel. We've all seen video of people christening ships by breaking a bottle of champagne on them, and how often they used to not break. These days they use a mechanical device to really give it a lot of force, making sure the bottle smashes in a satisfactory way."

"Not sure I've ever seen that," said Mason.

"I have," said Julia. "But then, I get around."

"By the way," added Will, "I have some unfortunate news." His voice got soft. "Phil got into trouble again."

"He broke something else?" Julia's voice was sharp.

"No . . . he tangled with a coyote."

"Is he dead?" asked Mason, feeling her heart contract, despite the firmness of her tone.

"No," said Will. "It seems to have been a surprisingly protracted fight, and Claudia heard the noise early this morning and ran out to investigate. She chased off the coyote and rushed Phil to the vet. He's in surgery now."

"Can I speak to Claudia?" asked Mason.

"No," said Will, and chuckled softly. "She's still there. She says she's not leaving till she sees he's OK."

"Since when is Claudia such a cat person?" asked Julia.

"Since Phil," said Mason. "He has that effect on people."

"Not me," said Julia. Then she paused. "I'll cover the costs of the surgery, of course."

Mason said nothing, as nothing needed to be said.

"You know," said Julia, "I'm starting to suspect Claudia was the one letting Phil into the house. A secret affair, going on right under my nose. I'm scandalized." But she was smiling.

"How's Archie, speaking of wounded soldiers?" said Mason.

"Recovering well," said Will. "He asked where you guys were, asked about Mason's safety, you know." Will laughed. "The way the two of you care about each other while pretending not to really care about each other is borderline adorable."

"Shut up," said Mason. She paused. "But he's OK?"

"I'm hanging up now," said Julia. "Go track down the rich kid."

"On it," said Will, and Julia ended the call.

Mason and Mann kept driving. Julia's phone rang, but she flipped the notification off the screen and silenced it. Mason looked at her.

"Who was that?"

"None of your business."

Mason frowned. "OK, well then it has to have been Justin Avermore, because if it was anyone else, you would have just told me."

"What makes you think you know everyone I know?"

"I don't, but if it was someone I didn't know, you would have said, 'no one you know,' or maybe 'nothing important,' and if it had been someone I know very well, you would have just answered. That suggests it was someone you didn't want to talk to in front of me, and right now the most likely candidate is Mr. Mayor himself."

"He's not the mayor yet. He's running for office."

"So, it was him."

"I don't like this snoopy thing you do."

"Ironic, seeing as you're the one who got me started on it."

"No, I think you were born snoopy." Julia sighed. "But you're right, I fully encourage it. Yes, it was Justin, and no, I didn't want to talk to him right now. Firstly, because you're in the car and can't be trusted, and secondly, because I was a little alarmed by how fast he lost his temper the other night."

Mason considered this. "I think most people would have been upset by someone vandalizing their precious vineyard."

"True." Julia gazed out of the window. "I'm not . . ." She tailed off.

"Not that into him?"

Julia didn't answer for a minute, then she said, "Not that interested in dating anyone. It's not him specifically. I like being single, I have no interest in sharing my life any more than it's already shared, and I don't need any more friends."

Mason grinned. "But you presumably have other needs?"

Julia made a face. "Your prurient interest is alarming, but sure, you're not wrong. I like men, I like the occasional dalliance, but, you know, I'm not desperate for it. Firstly, because most men my age aren't that compelling to me, and secondly, because there are other ways to get my physical needs met without having to have a conversation with either a boomer man who wants to explain shit to me or a younger man who wants to talk about Marvel movies."

"Do you even know about Marvel movies?" asked Mason, laughing.

"Of course. I watch movies. I enjoyed at least one of them." She paused. "I don't remember the title. There was a talking raccoon—I remember that."

They drove in silence for several miles, then Mason asked a question that had been buzzing around in her head for a few days.

"Do you think everyone lies?" she asked. "I thought of Alexa as a kind of paragon of sobriety, right? She's my sponsor, she's given me excellent advice for the last half decade, I trusted her completely, and now I'm not so sure. If she knows something that might have prevented Iris's death . . . if it IS related . . . or . . ." She paused and took a breath. "Someone shot at me, too, right? Archie could have been killed, and as it was, he was badly hurt. If she knows something that could help us, why isn't she spitting it out?"

Julia shrugged. "Beats me."

Mason kept her eyes on the freeway, trying to calm her emotions. "Teddy told me everyone lies. Big lies or small ones, but lies nonetheless. Do you think that's true?"

Julia made a face. "Probably. Teddy's a pretty good judge of the human condition. I think intention matters a lot when it comes to the truth. If you intend to hurt someone, you can do it with a lie or with unvarnished reality. If you intend to be kind, ditto."

"Isn't it always wrong to lie?"

"Of course not." Julia wound the window down a little and breathed in the cool, clean Sonoma air. She looked back at Mason. "I heard once in a meeting, *when my fear conspires with my pride, I lie* . . . I always remembered it. Alexa has pride, and it's not unreasonable. She's proud of the woman she is today, and ashamed of the woman she was before. Her pride wants her to remain inviolate in your eyes, and her fear is that if she told the truth about what she'd done, you would no longer respect her. Maybe you'd fire her as your sponsor. Maybe no longer be her friend. And that would hurt. And don't forget, we don't know that she's lying about anything. She might not have anything to tell us. She might be as confused as we are by what's happening. Or, she could be lying about not remembering much about that night. Or she could simply be hoping that what little she does remember has nothing to do with what's happening, that Iris's overdose is unrelated, that some random person shooting at you is just a weird coincidence . . ." She shrugged again. "We don't know what she's thinking, but your experience of her kindness and consideration should at least be a foundation for how you react to her now."

"But doesn't the fact that she is lying, right now, today, change who she is as a person?"

"I guess that depends on how you take it. You could try compassion."

Mason shrugged. "I guess. I don't know how I feel about it."

"That's OK. You don't always have to know. Feelings aren't facts; they change all the time. Just sit in it, let it sink in, and see what happens." Julia shook her head. "I'm going to close my eyes and think about how all this stuff fits together."

"Do you have any theories?"

"Yes. My theory is that the client Alexa saw with Eve was the guy who killed her. Either Alexa knows it for sure or strongly suspects it. And I suspect, in turn, that she knows his name and doesn't want to tell us. Why? I have no idea. It was a long time ago and hundreds of miles from where she is today, but there's still something about it that's keeping her quiet or making her lie about how much she remembers. Or maybe she really doesn't remember . . . Right now I don't know how it all fits together, or what is related to what, or who or why or when . . . I need to know more, and my immediate concern is the safety of Alexa and, by extension, you and her other sponsee." She stretched, then closed her eyes. "We'll go visit Jennifer in the hospital tomorrow, once we're back in LA. Wake me when we get to the hotel."

33

THE NEXT MORNING, they checked out and flew back to Los Angeles, and as they cruised down through the pale brown layer of pollution coming into the valley, Mason was grateful for every single piece of particulate. LA just felt right to her, in a way the Bay Area never had. They picked up the car and headed over to the hospital to visit Jennifer.

Mason was starting to get tired of the smell of institutions, the squeak of rubber shoes on linoleum, the coughing and muttering of people all around, the faint sense of imminent emotional breakdown. The atmosphere was better than it had been at the prison, but there was kinship there, for sure. Mason felt a flash of gratitude for her youth, her health and her ability to visit these places and then leave again. They took the elevator to the fourth floor and went looking for Jennifer's room.

Mason's fellow sponsee had definitely looked better. One eye was swollen shut, and she was bandaged and clearly somewhat sedated. The usual paraphernalia of a hospital stay covered the surfaces: magazines and grapes, Gatorade and paper cups, little tufts of cotton wool that should probably have been thrown away. A copy of the Big Book of Alcoholics Anonymous was on the nightstand, its familiar navy cover the only sign that this patient was slightly out of the ordinary.

Jennifer looked surprised to see Mason and smiled uncertainly at Julia, who was right behind her. Her long hair was pulled into a high ponytail that splayed out onto the pillow like a firework, making her look more festive than she probably felt.

"Hi there," she said, lifting her hand slightly from the blanket.

"Hi," said Mason. "We brought you something sweet." They'd stopped at the house to drop off their luggage, and Claudia had packed up what was left of the peanut butter cookies. "You're not allergic to nuts, are you?"

"Nope," replied Jennifer. "Most of my friends are nuts." She giggled.

Mason grinned. "Good drugs?"

Jennifer shrugged. "Turns out when you're actually in pain you don't get high, you just stop having pain. Which is fine with me." She winced. "I've also discovered broken ribs hurt a lot, and that shrugging isn't a good idea."

"You know Julia, of course," said Mason, as Julia took a seat on the far side of Jennifer's bed. "We'd like to ask you some questions about the accident."

"OK," said Jennifer. She looked at Julia. "It's a pleasure to see you again, albeit under strange circumstances."

"Circumstances are often strange," replied Julia. "I was sorry to hear about your accident."

"Oh, it wasn't an accident," said Jennifer. "No way. Someone pushed me."

"Tell us about it," said Julia, settling herself comfortably.

"There's not a huge amount to tell, honestly," replied Jennifer, shifting slightly in the bed and wincing again. "I was standing on the corner waiting to cross, and someone put both their hands between my shoulder blades and shoved. I was kind of in my head, listening to music and thinking about lunch, so I was completely unprepared and just went flying. Luckily, the light was changing, and the traffic was slowing down, so I went onto the hood of a taxicab and mostly rolled off, rather than getting hit, if you know what I mean. It still hurt like a motherfucker, though." She shifted again. "And I banged my head on the street and lost consciousness, so I got a concussion along with the broken ribs, which is why I'm still in here, I guess." She paused. "Such a headache you would not believe."

"Did they say anything to you? Were there any witnesses?"

"Well, if they did say something, I wouldn't have heard them: earbuds." Jennifer made a face. "I know you're supposed to have better situational awareness, but I really didn't think someone was going to try and throw me under a bus that day. And yeah, loads of witnesses in that I was standing in a crowd on a street corner, but I don't think anyone saw who it was. Or at least, the nice policeman who took a statement from me yesterday said they didn't have any leads." She smiled, suddenly. "I'm just grateful to be relatively unhurt. It's been a long time since I fell down, you know, and at least I wasn't drunk this time."

"Although," pointed out Mason, "it might have helped—you know, made your body more relaxed."

"I was pretty relaxed," said Jennifer. "I'd just come from a meeting and was thinking about sandwiches, so, you know . . ." She frowned at the two other women. "Alexa seemed to think it was something to do with her. I don't understand that."

Julia nodded. "How much did she tell you?"

"She said she thinks someone has it in for her, because of Iris." She looked at Mason. "And she said someone shot at you? What the hell?"

"My thoughts entirely," said Mason. "I'm against it. But they were a lousy shot and got my friend instead."

"They did? Are they OK?"

Mason nodded. "They will be."

"But why would someone want to hurt Alexa's friends? She's so nice." Jennifer looked confused. "At least, she's always been nice to me."

"And me," said Mason. "But she thinks it might have something to do with her past, when she was drinking."

Jennifer nodded. "OK. But why push me into traffic? Why not push her?"

"That's what we're trying to find out," said Julia. "How long have you known Alexa? Has she been your sponsor for long?"

Jennifer nodded. "I've known her for a few years, since I moved to Los Angeles."

"Where did you live before?"

"San Diego. I come from Northern California, but lived in San Diego for over a decade, got sober there. Work brought me up here, and I started going to meetings, met Alexa and lots of other people. Then last year I asked her to be my sponsor, and we started working together, you know, hanging out. I think she knows me better than I know her, you know what I mean? But I like her a lot." She looked questioningly at Julia. "What did she do, in the past?"

"Oh, the usual stuff. Drank too much, ruined things, you know."

"Relatable," said Jennifer, and they all nodded quietly.

Julia looked thoughtfully at Jennifer. "Did you ever nail down the source of the poisoning at your party? I understand you think it was the wine from Avermore."

"Yes," said Jennifer. "That's the conclusion we've reached. But he told me he tested the rest of the cases he brought down and none of them had any problem at all. It's a mystery." Her eyes widened suddenly. "You know, he knows Alexa, too. He might know something about her past."

Julia frowned. "He knows Alexa? How do you mean?"

"Well, that's how I met him. At the wedding in Ojai." She looked at Mason. "Remember? Alexa and I went to this wedding at Avermore Vineyard, and it was lovely, and then Justin was there, I guess, not at the wedding, but because it was his vineyard. He recognized Alexa and said hi and we got to talking about the restaurant, and I invited him to be part of it, you know, to supply wine to us. It was perfect: local, biodynamic wine that everyone at the wedding seemed to be enjoying a heck of a lot, judging by the hilarious dancing."

There was a short silence as Julia and Mason digested this.

Then Julia said, "How did Alexa know him?"

"Not sure," said Jennifer. "She said she'd known him when she was drinking. She was surprised he recognized her at all, it had been so long. She seemed unfazed, but then she got tired, and we left shortly afterward."

"OK," said Mason. "We'll ask him about it. And her. And if you remember anything else, let us know."

"I will," said Jennifer, frowning a little. "I can't imagine why anyone would want to hurt Alexa. Or the people close to her.

She might have done terrible things in her past, but we kind of all did, right? And she's not like that anymore."

"Some people find it hard to forgive," said Julia.

"Oh, I don't think it's forgiving," said Jennifer. "I think it's just hard for some people to forget." She reached out, carefully, and pulled a cookie from the bag. "Thanks for these."

"Of course," said Julia, turning to leave. "Get some rest. Feel better soon."

34

AS SOON AS they got in the car, Mason turned to Julia. "This might be a hot take, but I think we should look into Justin Avermore a little bit, don't you think? I mean, you've been out for dinner twice, but he's never mentioned Alexa, and Alexa has never mentioned him. That seems a little bit of an oversight."

"Why? He has no idea we know Alexa. Why would he mention her? Alexa had no idea we met him. She wasn't at the restaurant opening. And it's not like her name has come up in conversation over dinner." Julia was tapping away on her phone. "Having said that, I'm way ahead of you. Will's on the case. I'm sure he'll have a PowerPoint by the time we get home."

Mason slowed to pay for parking and wait for the gate to open. "Damn, it's expensive to park at the hospital. I guess they think people are so glad to be leaving they'll be ready to pay anything."

Mason slid the car into the traffic on Beverly Boulevard and came to a stop. "And another thing: Everything started after the wedding at his vineyard. I've been staring at Alexa's timeline, and I realized talking to Jennifer that it all fits: They went to the wedding and a week later the first letter arrived. I understand correlation is not causation, but it's right there."

Julia turned and looked at her. "Are you suggesting Avermore is the one sending the letters? Why would he?"

Mason frowned. "No, I'm not even sure how any of it fits in. I'm just pointing out that if on the night of the fire, Alexa saw the man who killed Eve, and Justin Avermore is someone she knows from that time, is it possible that either he's the man she saw or that maybe he knows the man she saw . . . ?" She ran her hands over her hair. "I don't know. The whole thing is confusing as hell."

"Agreed," said Julia. "Let's see what Will can dig up about Mr. Avermore before we go leaping to conclusions."

THEY WERE HEADING up to Sunset Boulevard when Will called them.

"As luck would have it, Avermore is in town right now," he said. "I started following his social media, and he posted from the Farmers Market on Third. He's delivering wine to some restaurants and paused to post pictures of Honeycrisp apples which were, admittedly, photogenic."

Mason frowned. "No wonder his vineyard is in trouble. He's never there."

"I'm sure it's not a one-person operation," said Julia, mildly. "But let's swing around to the Farmers Market and see if we can pick up his trail."

"Do we want to just ask him about Alexa?"

"I'm not sure. Let's see what he's up to and where he goes."

The Farmers Market on Third is a Los Angeles institution,

with dozens of vendors serving a wide variety of foods, along with fresh fruits and vegetables and several organic meat vendors. It's next door to the Grove, a modern outdoor mall that sees more visitors every year than Disneyland. Parking, as usual, was a bit of a pain, but the parking lot gave them a lucky break.

"Look," said Mason. She pointed to a van, an old-fashioned Chevy panel truck, with "Avermore Vineyards" painted on the side. "I like his vibe, not going to lie."

Julia nodded. "Great, so he's still here. Let's park and find a spot to watch the truck."

They got luckier still, when Avermore returned to the truck and instead of leaving, took a case of wine from the back and turned right around again.

"Off you go," said Julia. "After him. See where he goes."

"What about you?"

Julia scoffed. "If he sees me, it's all over," she said. "Yes, he's seen you, too, but it's not like he was looking all that closely."

"Hey," said Mason, slightly affronted. "I think I'm fairly recognizable and somewhat memorable."

"You're both of those things, but let's face it, he's been looking at me. Why are we still talking? Stay out of sight. Go!"

Mason sighed but slid out of the car and headed in the direction Avermore had gone. It was crowded, as it always was there, but he was tall and it only took her a moment to spot him. He didn't appear to be in any huge rush, and the crate of wine was probably pretty heavy. He put it down while waiting to cross the intersection outside the Farmers Market, and Mason had a moment to get a little closer. Remembering what Teddy had taught her, she had crossed to the other side of the street and was able to keep him in sight as he made his way away from the Farmers Market and along Third Street. He turned suddenly into a restaurant called the Black Cat, where presumably they were waiting for his delivery. Mason found a doorway opposite and waited. She wished she'd brought a hat. Teddy would be disappointed in her craft, but hey, she was a beginner.

Avermore appeared after a few minutes and headed back to the Farmers Market. On the one hand, this seemed like a fairly inefficient way to deliver wine, but on the other hand, moving and parking and reparking a truck in this neighborhood would be insanely time-consuming and likely to lead to a desire to kill oneself, so she got it.

She tailed him carefully and was surprised when he popped into a post office on the way, coming out after ten minutes carrying a couple of packages and some envelopes—why would he have mail delivered here? Shrugging inwardly, she stayed a little behind him and across the street and narrowly avoided being spotted when he got back to the truck and took out another case of wine. She sidled up to Julia's car and surprised her. Julia had clearly popped out to the market and was sitting in the front of the car eating from a container of fresh strawberries.

"Don't creep up on me," she said. "If I choke to death, you'll be out of a job."

"He's just delivering wine. This is boring."

"You have somewhere else to be?" asked Julia. "Quit your bitching." She waved her away.

Mason sighed but followed Avermore again. This time he headed through the Farmers Market and into the Grove, heading into a classic French bistro–style restaurant on the main square of the mall, next to the dancing fountain. Things didn't go as smoothly here.

Mason had taken up a spot on the far side of the fountain, and from there she watched Avermore approach a man who was presumably the manager. Strangely, the conversation took a turn almost immediately, when the guy started shaking his head as Justin Avermore approached. It didn't take a behavioral scientist to recognize he was refusing whatever it was Avermore was offering.

Words were exchanged, impossible to hear at this distance and over the fountain, but it didn't matter. Avermore was clearly insisting. The manager was clearly disagreeing. Hands waved. Paperwork was shaken. The crate of wine was deposited on a table, then lifted and handed back again. Avermore wanted the man to take the wine. The man did not want to take the wine. It was a master class in wordless communication, and Mason was happy to observe. Eventually, Avermore picked up the case of wine and stomped out of the restaurant. Mason followed him back to the truck, where he angrily replaced the crate of wine in the back and got in the driver's seat, pulling out of his parking space without really looking, and nearly squashing two Japanese tourists who were minding their own business and would doubtless have written a poor Yelp review, if you could Yelp review the driving of perfect strangers.

She quickly told Julia what she'd seen and raised her eyebrows. "What now?"

"Now we go home," said Julia. "Will is probably ready."

"Are we going to ask Alexa about Avermore?"

"I'm not sure," said Julia. "Let's take it one step at a time."

~~~

BUT WHEN THEY got home, Alexa wasn't even there. She'd left Mason a note saying she was out at a meeting and would see her when she returned. Mason looked around the guest-house for a second, realizing Alexa must have seen the time-line Mason had created for her, covering a portion of the living room wall. For a second she felt embarrassed . . . then realized that there was nothing on it that Alexa didn't already know about, seeing as she'd lived it. She sighed and looked again at the most recent part: The first letter had come only a few days after the wedding, then the second, then the fashion show . . . and so on. Somehow the wedding had kicked things off, and she couldn't help thinking Avermore must have something to do with it. But what it had to do with Iris, or the death of Eve over twenty years earlier, or the fire that had killed thirty people, or threatening letters, or flying enormous fruit, or if any of those things were even related to one another in any way . . . She sighed. So much information and all of it confusing as hell. Maybe she should give up private detection and become a nuclear physicist instead. Much simpler. She headed back to the office to see if Will was ready to explain everything. At least his presentations were linear, made sense, and had pleasing transitions and typefaces.

Not only was Will ready, but he also wasn't alone. Teddy was there, visiting Claudia, and all of them settled down in the office with a plate of oatmeal raisin cookies and a fresh pot of Italian hot chocolate.

"Alright," said Will, standing up and wielding the laser remote like, well, a laser remote. He went to his first slide, an image of one of Avermore's campaign posters. "Here is what
~~~

I've been able to dig up about Justin Avermore, although you only gave me an hour to do it, and I've barely scratched the surface."

Avermore had a nice face, Mason decided. Friendly, pleasant, unremarkable. Plenty of salt-and-pepper brown hair, deep-set eyes and a wide smile. Exactly the kind of guy who should be running for a small-town mayorship, in fact. His platform was equally approachable: more funding for the fire department, more economic support for biodynamic wineries (a little self-serving, but reasonable; his wasn't the only such winery in the area), an increase in after-school programs. Not a lot to argue with.

"Avermore was born in 1975, in a town called Cotati, near Petaluma." First slide, birth certificate. "His parents ran a farm supply business"—picture of Avermore Supply, complete with a tractor outside—"he had two brothers, and his childhood seems entirely unremarkable until the last year of high school, where he started to get into trouble."

Will switched slides, to a police booking photo of Avermore, taken some thirty-plus years earlier. The change was shocking. He was clearly under the influence of something; his eyes were heavy lidded and angry, his mouth set in a firm line of defiance, his arms folded with one middle finger very obviously in the upright and locked position.

"Arrested for public intoxication and petty larceny, after shoplifting a carton of cigarettes from a liquor store stockroom while the owner was taking care of other customers. Not done with any kind of panache; the owner spotted him coming out and locked the doors while the cops arrived. Avermore, according to the report, was belligerent and abusive."

"Was he charged?"

"Nope." Will clicked to another photo, maybe a few years later. "Nor was he charged in this incident, where he stole a car having supposedly mistaken it for his own. Apparently, he thought his own car needed to be hot-wired, so you would think a strong case could have been made, but in both cases the charges were dropped after a day or two." Will shrugged. "If I had to hazard a guess, I would imagine someone intervened on his behalf. Probably his family. It's not a big town, everyone knows everyone, that kind of thing."

"You can't be sure?"

"No, this was a long time ago, no one remembers any details and there are no court documents, obviously, because nothing went to trial."

"And these arrests were around the same time that he knew Alexa?"

"Unclear. He was arrested in Cotati. Alexa never lived there, but Petaluma isn't very far away at all." He shrugged. "But I found nothing connecting them."

"Unless . . ." Mason hesitated. "I realize this would be a hell of a coincidence, but he comes from near Petaluma, his family had money . . . could he be the Birdman?" Mason wasn't sure of herself but felt like it should be said.

Will shook his head. "I don't see it. His family was wealthy, but not outrageously so. They didn't run a poultry business, per se. And yes, he was trouble, but only the kind of small trouble teenagers get into. After high school there are no more arrests or problems, he went to UC Davis to study viticulture and agricultural economics, met his first wife, Angela, there, and moved to Ojai to open a vineyard. Since then, it's been business all the way, no kids, he and Angela got divorced a decade ago, seems like it was friendly, she still lives near Ojai . . . and now he's running for mayor." Will shrugged. "Until the food poisoning incident and the vandalism at the vineyard, he's been living a pretty stable life." He grinned. "And the fact that he's trying to date Julia should not be taken as a sign of instability."

"Thanks," said Julia, dryly.

Mason asked, "And do we think those incidents against him are politically motivated? Is that possible?"

"Because of the high-stakes international intrigue surrounding the mayorship of Ojai? Maybe a competitor? But for business, I would think, rather than politics. He's running against the incumbent who's held the position for over a decade and wants to retire. It's pretty low stakes."

"And the vineyard has been successful?"

Will nodded, flipping to another image, this time of a gorgeous home nestled in a valley. "It's growing and winning wine awards all over the place. Also open for weddings and events, with catering." He flipped to a website detailing options for special days of all kinds. "At a cursory count, dozens of proposals have taken place at the outlook point from their vineyard, with its sweeping views of the mountains." He clicked to an Instagram reel of someone getting engaged in the most picturesque fashion. "Pretty adorable." Another image. "They grow, as he reported, olives as well as grapes, both for eating and for oil, and there's a herd of very fancy goats who make cheese."

"The goats make the cheese?" Mason was giggling. "That *is* fancy."

"No," said Will, rolling his eyes at her. "Adult humans make the cheese."

"Why don't we just ask Alexa about him?" asked Mason.

"Wouldn't that be the simplest thing to do? She'll be back from her meeting soon."

Julia shook her head. "Probably, but not yet. I want to talk to him first. You said it yourself: Everything started after the wedding at his vineyard. The notes to Alexa. The sabotage of the fashion show, the break-in, Alexa acting weird, Iris OD'ing—maybe it's got nothing to do with it, but the timeline suggests it's at least worth asking some questions. And Alexa, to be honest, isn't in a very good place right now and isn't, I don't think, telling us the whole truth."

"There are public tours of the vineyard every day," said Will. "Why don't you just go to one of those? He's been asking you, right?"

"Sure." Julia picked up her phone. "I'll see if that works for him." She typed, then waited.

"He might still be driving around," said Mason, "angrily trying to deliver wine."

"He mentioned the other night that people were canceling orders. Jennifer's a pretty big name in the restaurant scene. If it's gotten out that it was his wine causing the food poisoning, people might get nervous. Reputation is everything." She looked at her phone. "OK, he said he'll be there tomorrow, he'd love to see me."

"Are you going alone?" Mason frowned. "I don't think that's a good idea."

"Neither do I," replied Julia. "You're coming with me."

35

IN THE END, it was quite the party. Will wanted to come, and so did Claudia, citing her interest in goat cheese and olive oil, which was considerable. Teddy came, too, citing his interest in Claudia. So it was with some misgivings that Mason pulled out the biggest car in Julia's collection, the Rolls Phantom V. This was not a decision Mason was happy about.

She was standing in the driveway feeling mildly nauseous when everyone else came out. She sighed.

"Are you sure you all need to come? Driving this is like driving a motor home, and the road to Ojai is twisty at the end. We could easily get stuck and then where would we be?"

"Well, wherever you stuck us, I guess," said Will, calmly. "We could go separately. You and Julia could take one car, and the three of us could take another. I don't mind."

Julia shook her head. "No, I want to make an entrance."

"You would make an entrance if you showed up on a bicycle," said Mason, pouting a little. "I would feel a lot more comfortable driving something less . . . immense."

"The Mercedes 450 also seats five in comfort," said Will.

"Yes," said Mason, "let's take the Benz."

"I said no," said Julia, opening the passenger door and gesturing for Will to get in. "I want to swoop up to the vineyard and make him wonder what head of state has just appeared. I want him to be a little bit overawed. A little bit cowed."

"That's a lot to ask of a car," said Claudia, clambering into the back seat.

"But this is absolutely the car to do it," added Teddy, following her, after taking a moment to admire the way she clambered.

"And just think of the comestibles we can fit in it," added Claudia. "We could take the Lamborghini, but then I'd only be able to bring back one log of goat cheese and a single olive."

"Fine," said Mason, capitulating. "If I lose control on one of those hilly hairpins and throw us all into a ditch, I apologize in advance." She got behind the wheel and cracked her knuckles.

"You'll be fine," said Julia, regally gazing out of the window. "Proceed."

And she actually waved a gloved hand as Mason, muttering, pulled out of the driveway.

THE JOURNEY FROM Los Angeles to Ojai takes about an hour and a half, without traffic, and God knows how long with. However, they made it onto the 101 without incident and then headed north with only minor swearing from Mason when she had to cross rows of traffic in order to switch freeways. Once they passed Ventura and took the 33, the road became both beautiful and twisty, and Mason started to sweat.

"I don't know what you're so nervous about," said Julia, looking at Mason in some confusion. "You've driven this car several times before."

"Yes, and never enjoyed it. It's a beautiful car, but it's the size of my first apartment."

"It has very responsive handling. It's often described as effortless."

"Not by me."

"We're nearly there, according to the GPS."

Mason flicked a glance at her phone screen. There was a right-hand turn coming up, and then a suspiciously thin and windy line leading to the vineyard itself. "Maybe we can park at the bottom and walk up?"

Frost formed on the interior of the windshield as Julia slowly turned to look at her.

"Yeah, never mind," said Mason, swinging the car into the turn.

"WOW," SAID CLAUDIA.

Julia was staring, too. She turned to Mason, who was just getting out of the car. "You know when you look at a building and you're like, sure, it's pretty, but there's something off about it, some imbalance, some ugly design choice, and it ruins the whole thing?"

Mason raised an eyebrow. "I'm not sure I've ever given it as much thought as you, but sure."

Julia frowned at her. "You say the stupidest things sometimes, Mason. I know there's an excellent brain under that too-severe haircut, I know you actually think very hard about most things you do, but sometimes you feign insouciance to a degree that's pathological. What did you first think when you saw my house?"

"That I'd walked into a movie."

"And why was that?"

Mason shrugged. "Because it looks like the kind of house you see in a movie?"

"And why is that? Jesus, interrogate your own mental processes, will you?"

"Do I have to? Isn't it enough that I have them?"

"No. Don't you wonder why you think the thoughts you have, feel the feelings you have?"

"Rarely." Mason paused, to humor her boss, and thought about it. "Because your house is special. It's impressive. It's stylish. It has an atmosphere."

"And there it is. That's right. Some buildings are well designed and built to the point that they have a character that transcends their literal construction. My house has it. And this place has it. In spades."

They both gazed up at the Tuscan-style buildings. Honey-colored stone, terra-cotta tiles, dark wood beams supporting the roof, archways and rambling vines. Large windows on the ground floor, smaller ones on the floor above, all of it on a grand scale probably not seen in the original inspiration. A main house, gazing down across the fields of vines that stretched in every direction, and then many smaller buildings, presumably housing the working areas of wine production.

"Yeah," said Mason, starting up the hill. "It's pretty."

"You're pretty," snorted Julia. "That's sublime."

JUSTIN HAD CLEARLY been waiting for Julia, and as they approached the entrance to the vineyard, he appeared. Mason was taken aback. Mr. Avermore had always been extremely well put together; it had been a defining feature. But now he was frazzled, his hair messy, his shirt untucked. Loose cargo pants ended in dusty clogs, and his expression suggested that although he'd known Julia was coming, he hadn't expected the entire squad.

"How lovely to see you all," he said, gamely. "I'm afraid I only prepared a limited brunch. I didn't . . ."

"Oh, they're here for the tour and the store," said Julia, quickly. "I couldn't stop them from coming. But they'll happily amuse themselves while we have brunch. That's totally fine."

Will chimed in, "I'm one hundred percent here for the tour," he said. "I have a lot of questions about small press technology. And the olive oil section promises to be fascinating. I read, on the way here, that you use a stone mill you imported from Spain that is over two hundred years old." He paused. "I imagine you've replaced the moving parts, I mean, obviously . . ."

"Obviously," said Claudia, Teddy and Mason, in unison.

"But the basalt stone parts are totally original, and who doesn't want to see that?"

Justin laughed. "You'd be surprised. But I'm glad you're so interested." He led the way up a little rise to a central area between the buildings, where a small crowd had formed. Maybe a dozen people, slightly more, all ready to tour a vineyard and drink wine at ten a.m. on a Wednesday.

The tour guide was a peppy young man wearing a down vest with the logo of the vineyard and a wireless microphone on the lapel.

"Welcome to Avermore Vineyards," he said, apparently thrilled to be here, in *this* moment, with *these* people. "We're going to begin by touring the outdoor areas of the vineyard, then the goat farm, then the olive grove, then we'll move inside to see the presses and cool rooms where we make everything. Sadly, not all the blocks are open right now—those are sections of the vineyard where we grow a specific variety—but there's still plenty to see."

Presumably, those areas affected by the vandalism were still closed, thought Mason. She looked around at the incredibly beautiful fields of vines, stretching into the distance. The whole scene was one of bucolic perfection, soft curving hills, distant mountains, the sound of a million bees and birds. Why would anyone want to destroy that? And destroy it so *specifically*... not just ripping it apart but poisoning it? She could see yellow tape roping off one large section of vines, and assumed that was where the pesticide had been sprayed. What a waste.

Claudia wasn't thinking about the case. She raised her hand. "Is there a shop?"

"Of course," said the young man. "There will be an opportunity to purchase wine, grape juice, olive oil and, of course, fresh goat cheese. There's also a café, which we open on tour days so you can all sample our wonderful products."

"Great," said Claudia, lowering her hand. She turned to the others. "I'm going to go find the store. You guys tour. I have shopping to do." Teddy trailed after her, of course.

The group set off, with Will pushing his way through to the front. Honestly, thought Mason, never had she met a man more thirsty for information. Bless his tiny socks.

"This south-facing grove is where we grow most of the olives we press for oil," said the guide. "We grow half a dozen varieties, some of which are used singly in oils, some of which we blend for specific flavor profiles." He pointed to one area. "Here, for example, are some Leccino olives, which we press for a very special single-variety oil, while over there is a broad swath of Pendolino, which not only press very well but also act as pollinator trees, useful because the other varieties we grow aren't as good at producing pollen but benefit from cross-pollination."

Mason felt a breeze as Will's hand flew up. He began to ask a question about rates of pollen production that had the rest of the group turning to stare at him, and Mason began to inch backward away from the group.

She slowly retraced her steps, separating from the crowd and heading up toward the main house. She spotted Julia and Justin sitting at a table on the terrace, clearly having what he hoped would be a romantic brunch. Julia was laughing and looking beautiful, Justin was looking smitten, so Mason gave them a wide berth and slipped around the side of the building.

She paused by a small coastal oak tree and surveyed the scene. She could see the tour group heading downhill through one of the olive groves, and spotted Claudia and Teddy through the window of what was presumably the shop. Teddy's arms were full of bottles of olive oil, and he had a long-suffering expression on his face. She smiled to herself and turned to look at the house.

Two sets of French doors stood open on the side closest to her, so she waited until the coast was clear and sidled in.

This was clearly Avermore's office. A huge fireplace was centered on one wall, a pair of crossed shotguns above it. There was a desk with a computer in front of the French doors, and a second desk with a printer, a scanner and a small electric typewriter. An old champagne bottle stood on a shelf, a series of awards on another. Mason was stepping toward the desk with the typewriter when she heard footsteps in the hallway.

A woman opened the door and gazed at Mason. She was wearing a gray uniform that suggested she was a housekeeper.

"Hello there," said Mason, smiling broadly. "I appear to have gotten lost. I was on the tour and went in search of a bathroom. These doors were open . . . I'm sorry."

The woman wasn't completely buying it, she could tell.

"The bathrooms are in the same building as the store. They're clearly signposted. You would have had to walk right past them."

"Oh, really? What a space cadet. Can you point me in the right direction?" Mason walked through the room toward the woman, but she held up her hand.

"Turn around and go back the way you came. It's quicker."

"Of course," said Mason, turning back and heading through the French doors. *Dammit,* she thought, walking around the corner of the house, *that wasn't as smooth as I would have liked.*

Fortunately, Julia spotted her sneaking back down the hill and called her name.

"Hey, Mason, why don't you join us?"

Mason pivoted on her bootheel and set off back up the hill. She looked at Justin, who appeared less than thrilled. But he smiled as she crossed the terrace. She could hardly blame him. She wasn't fond of third-wheeling, either, but what can you do?

"Did you enjoy the tour?" he asked, as she pulled out a chair and sat down.

"It was interesting," she said, and reached out to snag a slice of melon. She hesitated; she hadn't really been invited to this breakfast, and now she felt awkward.

Justin laughed. "Please, go ahead. I may have over-provisioned the brunch."

Certainly, the table was still groaning with food. Platters of fresh fruit, baskets of pastries, fresh butter and cream and syrup. Justin had pulled out all the stops.

Mason looked at Julia, who met her gaze squarely. "Justin is about to show me around the main house. Would you like to join us?"

Again, Mason flicked a glance at Justin. He was looking at Julia, a small smile on his face.

"Sure," she said, wondering what Julia was up to.

The house's interior was pleasantly cool after the sun and heat of outside, and it took Mason a second or two to adjust. A broad central entryway had two hallways leading from it, and Justin headed to the left. This put them on the right side for the office, and Mason wondered how easy it would be to break away and check out that typewriter.

Fortunately, Justin headed straight there, pushing the door open wide. "This is my office," he said, "where I do my best to run things." He laughed. "Although my vineyard manager does a lot of the heavy lifting." He pointed to the crossed guns. "I'm not a hunter at all, but those belonged to my great-grandfather."

"He was a big hunter?" asked Julia.

"He ran a farm and enjoyed the taste of rabbit. Those two things go very well together."

Julia looked interested. "Does a love of wine also run in your family?"

"It skipped a generation or two. My parents ran a farm supply store in the town where I grew up, and we had a little farm. Everybody did." He walked over to the wall opposite the fireplace, which was covered in large photographs. He pointed. "But these are my great-great-grandparents in their vineyard in Italy, and this is my great-grandfather in his vineyard in Napa. He was alone when he first bought land and planted the vines he'd brought over to America with him, but my great-grandmother soon joined him, and they grew the vineyard over the years. My grandparents sold it to a big conglomerate after the war, and my parents weren't all that interested in wine. But I was."

"And that's where you grew up? Napa?"

Justin shook his head. "No, Sonoma." He pointed to another set of photographs, large groups of workers posing in front of enormous harvests of grapes. "My mother remembers picking grapes as a child, but she never wanted that life for herself. She liked the money she inherited, but mostly she spent it on clothes and her birds."

"Birds?"

"Finches. She raised finches. We had enormous aviaries out behind the store."

"How interesting," said Julia. "And you wanted to open your own vineyard? Always?"

He nodded. "Yeah. And I was ready to leave Northern California and start over, you know?"

"Sure."

Mason pointed to the champagne bottle on the shelf. "Do you make sparkling wine here?"

He shook his head. "No, that's a very old bottle." He turned and smiled at Julia. "You ready to see the rest? The dining room was modeled after a Tuscan villa dating back to the sixteenth century. The frescoes are quite lovely."

"Of course," she replied, half turning to Mason. "Come on, Mason, keep up."

Mason cursed under her breath but followed her boss obediently.

"So, Justin," asked Julia, "how goes the search for your vandals? Any luck?"

He shook his head. "No. And we're going to lose that whole section of vines and need to scrape the topsoil for several feet. It's really terrible." He looked deeply troubled. "That and the food poisoning in Los Angeles has really hit us hard. I'm not sure what I did in a past life to deserve this misfortune, but it's not shaping up to be our best year, if you follow me. It was going so well, too."

"Have you considered suspending your campaign?"

He frowned and shook his head. "No . . . Well, yes, I've considered it. But so far people seem to be rallying around me. There's a good community here, of growers and wine enthusiasts, and bad luck happens to all of us at different times, right? Poor weather, pests, market forces, that kind of thing. I was worried about the restaurants in Los Angeles drying up, and they have quite a bit. Jennifer knows a lot of people down there. She's very connected and she seems determined to destroy me." He made a face. "I'm sorry, I know you two are friendly with her . . ."

Julia made a noncommittal gesture with her hands, and Justin continued.

"Fortunately, Los Angeles isn't our only source of business. We supply restaurants all over the Central Valley and farther north, and we're hanging on." He looked at Julia. "Not that I don't want as many reasons to visit Los Angeles as possible . . . but California is a big state, and it's a big country."

"When are the elections?"

"Six weeks from now. Anything can happen. It's not exactly a cutthroat contest. Mayoral elections here are nonpartisan, so we can dodge many of the big party issues. Plus, the incumbent has been in office for ages, and he's pretty tired. He doesn't love me. He'd rather have a generations-long Ojai native like himself running, otherwise I think he'd just retire and let me run unopposed."

He looked at his watch. "The tour will be over now. We should go and find everyone. Perhaps you'd join me later for dinner? Ojai has some wonderful restaurants, and it won't hurt my election chances to be seen with a beautiful screen legend."

"That would be lovely," said Julia, "although the word 'legend' makes me feel old, so perhaps you could rethink that."

"Goddess?"

"A little much, but better." She smiled at him, then turned to Mason. "Go round up the crew while I say goodbye to Mr. Avermore."

AS THEY ALL piled into the Rolls and pulled out of the parking lot, Julia turned to address them all.

"I'm very afraid to say that I think the charming Mr. Avermore needs to jump to the top of our suspect list."

"Really?" asked Will. "Suspected of what? The letters? The vegetables? Killing Iris? Killing Eve? Shooting at Mason?"

"Any and all, at this point."

"Dammit," said Claudia, opening her enormous shopping bag and viewing the contents. "If he ends up in jail, how am I going to get more of this olive oil?"

"Why?" asked Teddy.

Julia counted on her fingers. "He's the right age, he comes from Northern California, his mother had birds, the letters started after he and Alexa reunited at the wedding . . ."

"It's a bit of a major coincidence, isn't it?" asked Mason. "I mean, I'm happy to suspect him, but isn't it strange that your new boyfriend happens to be connected to the case we're working on?"

Julia shook her head. "One, he's in no way my boyfriend, and no, it's not a coincidence at all. We only know him *because* of Alexa. He and Jennifer met at the wedding because he recognized Alexa and spoke to her, or maybe the other way around, I'm not sure. And Jennifer invited him to supply the restaurant, which is where we met him. Everything starts at that wedding. And he and I are going out to dinner tonight, and you are going to break into the house and get a sample from that typewriter."

Mason swerved slightly on the road. "I am?"

"You are. Please focus on your driving. Teddy will go with you."

"Of course," said Teddy, from the back. His voice was somewhat indistinct; he was eating a piece of bread and goat cheese, which Claudia was putting together and handing around.

"I don't really understand what his motivation would be, though." Mason sounded petulant, even to herself. "And he seems so . . . harmless."

"I'm not sure, either," said Julia, "but your motivation is very clear: I'm telling you to do it, so you're going to do it. And I am not so harmless."

Mason said nothing, her lips tightening.

Steady munching from the back of the car kept everyone else silent.

MASON TRIED A couple of times to reach Alexa from the hotel, but she wasn't answering her phone. She had already left for work that morning when Mason got up, so they had yet to connect since Alexa had come to stay at the guesthouse. It was a little worrying, but also not entirely unprecedented. Alexa was always busy, and frequently hard to get hold of.

Teddy and Mason got ready alongside Julia. She wore a long, pale pink gown; they wore black from head to toe. Will fitted all three of them with the tiny earbuds he enjoyed so much, and added a microphone for Julia, hidden in a fold of her dress.

"I'll be in communication with all of you," he said, testing the system. "Julia, you'll let us know Justin's location at all times, as we need him away from the house for Mason and Teddy to do their job, which will take them no more than two minutes, ideally."

"What about alarm systems?" asked Teddy.

"I noticed today that all the outbuildings, the store, the presses, they all had alarm boxes on the outside, but the main house didn't."

"That's unusual."

"Yes, but lucky for us. Don't get cocky—just get in, type a quick sample and get out of there." He paused. "And if you think anyone else is in the house, just grab the cartridge or ribbon from the machine. I can get a sample from that."

"There's a housekeeper," said Mason. "We met this morning."

"OK, so on the off chance she lives in, grab the cartridge."

Mason nodded. Julia's phone chimed and she looked at it. "Justin's down in the lobby."

"OK, Operation Clickety-Clack is underway."

Everyone's eyebrows went up. "That's the name of this effort? Clickety-Clack?" Mason's tone was incredulous.

"Yes," he said defensively, "because of the typewriter objective."

Julia opened the hotel room door. "If we get caught, it will be because of that name. Worst name ever."

"What else would you suggest?" called Will, after her.

"I wouldn't," she replied, the door closing. "It doesn't need a name."

He stared at the back of the door, then turned to Mason and Teddy.

"Every operation needs a name, right?"

They shrugged, and Teddy clasped his shoulder warmly as they headed out after Julia.

"If you want to give it a name, you go ahead," he said.

They left, and Will turned to Claudia, who was sitting in an armchair flipping through a local magazine. She looked up at him.

"Wanna play cards?" she said.

He shook his head. "No. I still owe you a hundred bucks from last time."

36

DESPITE HER MISGIVINGS about the size of the Rolls, Mason couldn't deny the bugger was quiet. It slid to the side of the road like an orca in the deep ocean, silently going dark as she switched off the lights.

She got out and stood there for a moment, listening to the sound of insects and very distant surf, the gentle movement of a breeze in the trees, a faint smell of rosemary and lavender. This was going to be quick. In through the French doors, get the ribbon from the typewriter, back out, end of story.

"You ready?" Teddy's voice was soft.

She nodded, and the two of them headed up the driveway through the empty parking lot. The exteriors of the outbuildings were well lit, alarm boxes flashing their little lights, but no one appeared to be there, or working this late in the evening. All was quiet as they approached the house.

"Wait," said Teddy. "There's a light on in the kitchen. Let me go check." He disappeared silently around the corner and was swiftly back. "Just a side light, and he actually left the kitchen door unlocked. It's probably how he left the house. Not super security conscious, our guy."

"Maybe he's hopelessly naive."

"Or cocky as hell. After the vandalism in the vineyard, you'd think he'd be more careful, but some people think they're untouchable."

"The office French doors are locked. I checked," said Mason.

"I brought a cutter," said Teddy, pulling a tool from his pocket. "And some tape. If you're going to break and enter, you might as well do it as professionally as possible."

"I brought tape, too," said Mason, a trifle defensively. She paused. "I need to get a cutter, I guess."

"So many happy little tools," said Teddy. "Claudia bought me this one for Christmas a few years ago."

"She's the best," said Mason.

"She really is," replied Teddy, fondly. "She also bought me a laser cutter that could take a finger off at twenty feet, but that seemed like overkill for this."

"Bummer," said Mason. "Let's do it."

Teddy nodded and approached the glass doors. He quickly taped the pane just to the right of the handle, pulling out his cutter and efficiently cutting a large circle. Then, wrapping another long loop of tape around his hand, he folded a large piece onto the cut circle of glass and held it with one hand as he tapped it with the other end of the cutter. It snapped loose, but held, and Teddy unwound the tape from his hand as he lowered the piece quietly to the floor inside the room.

"Huh," whispered Mason. "Neat."

"Yeah," Teddy whispered back. "Claudia taught me that."

Mason fought a sudden urge to giggle, thinking of the couple breaking into and out of each other's apartments for fun. Was that what they did on dates? She pulled her focus back, as Teddy reached in and quietly opened the door.

Suddenly their earbuds buzzed into life.

"Dudes," said Will's voice, "I fucked up."

Mason and Teddy froze.

"There *is* an alarm system in the house, clearly, because Justin just got an alert on his phone and immediately got up and left the restaurant. Julia reports he said something about catching the vandals this time . . . You've got about four minutes to get the cartridge and get back to the car and then go the *other* way from town so he doesn't see the Rolls and get suspicious." He paused. "I knew we should have brought two cars."

Mason's blood ran cold, and she looked at Teddy. He shrugged.

"Hurry," he said.

Mason slipped into the room and scanned. The typewriter was where it had been, so that was a good first step. She started across the room, first checking back to see if Teddy was still there. He was, barely visible behind the edge of the doorframe. Holding back. Waiting. She reached the typewriter and took a firm hold of the ribbon cover, expecting it to hinge open like her dad's machine.

It was stuck. Fine. Plan B.

She looked around and found a sheet of printer paper; feeding it into the machine and typing "the quick brown fox jumps over the lazy dog" was the work of a minute.

She rolled the paper out and folded it into her pocket. She kind of wanted the ribbon . . .

Setting her feet, she took hold of the ribbon cover with both hands and yanked. It flew off, causing her to stumble backward and hit the bookshelves, setting the dusty champagne bottle rocking, its little metal label jingling. She turned as it toppled and managed to catch it before it hit the ground.

So. Heavy.

She hefted it in her hand, switching her grip to the neck and feeling the weight of it. Like a bat. And the metal label wasn't actually a label after all; it was a bracelet, with a flat engraved panel, the letter E, a twining of California poppies in enamel . . .

Suddenly, she thought of the pictures of Eve. The head wound the detective had pointed out. The silver bracelet in the booking photo.

This was the murder weapon.

The bracelet was a souvenir.

Justin was the man Alexa had seen.

Justin had killed Eve.

He'd hit her with this bottle, and the strength of the glass (thanks to all that internal pressure Will had told her about) meant it didn't even crack. The empty bottle was heavy enough; filled, it would have been worse, and Eve hadn't stood a chance. And then he'd taken her bracelet, hung it around the neck of the bottle, and put it up on a high shelf so he could look at it and remember.

Could Alexa have known? Could she have covered it up and helped him get away with it all these years? Was she as guilty as he was?

"Mason . . ." Teddy's voice from the doorway. "We're not going to have time to move the Rolls. He's going to be here any minute."

"Go move the car," she whispered back, the realization that she didn't know Alexa as well as she thought running over her like ice. "I'll hike up the road to find you."

"OK," he said, and disappeared.

Mason pulled her phone from her pocket and started

taking photos of the bottle. Noticing the smudges and marks all over it, the dark brown stains on the label. She thought about Detective Karneeva, thought about letting him run with what she'd discovered. Opened her messages and started looking for his number, ready to send him a photo of both bottle and bracelet. The clues he'd been hunting for all these years.

And that was when Justin Avermore came through the door.

37

AS HAS ALREADY been established, Mason was not great at impulse control. She probably could have made it out the French doors; they weren't that far across the room. She might have been able to take Justin in a brief fight; she was younger and more desperate than the middle-aged man, and he might not have been expecting any level of resistance. But instead, she held up the champagne bottle and said, "You killed Eve Riley, didn't you?"

Justin Avermore hadn't been expecting to see Mason. He might not even have expected anyone to be in the house. But he definitely wasn't expecting to get accused of a murder that took place three decades earlier.

Unfortunately, he was tougher than he looked.

"What on earth are you talking about?" He eyed the champagne bottle in Mason's hand. "Put that down. What are you even doing here? I'm calling the cops."

Instead, she held it up. "Go ahead. Call them. You took Eve from the Albatross, and somehow, either intentionally or by accident, she ended up dead. You hit her with this bottle, you buried her in Tilden Park, you took her bracelet. Why did you do that?"

There was a long pause as he considered his options.

Then he sighed, and reached up above the fireplace, taking down one of the long guns. His face, though still friendly, had taken on a coldness Mason hadn't seen before.

"No one is going to believe you," he said, breaking the gun open and checking it was loaded.

"Yes, they are." Mason took a step back and put the bottle down, freeing up her hands in case she needed to fight. "There are people who still care about this case, who care about Eve. It's going to come out."

"So what? It was an accident. The girl was freaked out by the fire. She begged me to take her away from there. We drove to the park. We conducted some business. But she was too upset . . . We got into an argument."

"And you hit her and then you buried her. That wasn't an accident. And you took her bracelet and kept the murder weapon. That wasn't an accident, either."

Justin stared at her and suddenly lost his temper. "You don't know anything about it. You weren't there. She was causing a scene. I had to shut her up."

"You buried her in Tilden to destroy any evidence," said Mason. "You chose that spot for the soil, right? You know about soil, don't you, and you knew that acidic soil would help to keep you safe. I'm going to tell the cops and it's all going to come out."

"No," said Justin, "it's not. Because there's going to be a terrible accident. I came home to what I thought was more vandalism underway, and it was only after I shot you that I realized what an awful mistake I had made." He raised the gun. “I might have to give up my run for mayor, but there are a lot of law-and-order voters around here, and everyone knows how much stress I’ve been under. I think I’ll get away with it.” He gestured with the gun. “I’ll give you a running start. It’s only fair.”

“I don’t think so,” said Teddy, stepping through the French doors.

Surprised and furious, Justin swung the gun in Teddy’s direction. Mason took two big steps, grabbed the typewriter, and threw it at Justin.

He pulled the trigger.

38

A PORTABLE ELECTRIC typewriter weighs about twenty pounds, and Mason was in more than good shape. She got a firm grip on it and gave it some serious, explosive effort. When it hit Justin in the head, he wasn't expecting it, and although he'd already pulled the trigger, Teddy had also been moving. They both hit the ground, but Teddy was the one who was ready to speak first.

"I'm hit," he shouted. "Run, Mason."

And Mason ran.

Through the French doors and down the hill toward the car. Roaring, bleeding from what was probably a broken nose, Justin Avermore came after her, carrying the shotgun. Mason eyeballed the distance to the car and veered away—she would be in plain sight the whole way and had nothing else to throw. She headed toward the vineyard, hitting top speed as she disappeared between the vines, and threw herself to the ground as she heard the shotgun go off behind her. It was dark now, and she needed to hide for a moment and contemplate a strategy. She touched her ear—she'd lost her earpiece at some point, and could only imagine Will was freaking out. Oh well, not much she could do about that now.

The vines were low, maybe three or four feet, and ran along wires strung between posts. Mason didn't know much about wine production, but she could see new light green shoots and leaves, stretching out beyond trunks and vines that looked more established. Every so often there were low metal . . . she wasn't sure what they were. Like lamps or tiny firepits, cold and empty now, but smelling vaguely of kerosene. Not that she was paying detailed attention; she was mostly trying to keep her head down so it wouldn't get shot off.

She ducked her head as the gun fired again, taking out a piece of post about six inches away from her.

Spitting dirt, she felt panic rise in her throat. Was Teddy going to make it? She needed to get back to the house, call for help. Get the other shotgun.

Justin was coming for her and getting closer. Wherever he was, he was moving silently.

She raised her head a little. The darkness was heavy, and the lights from the house were still dim. She couldn't see much at all. But then again, neither could he. Mason looked to the end of the rows of vines and saw she was close to the edge of the olive grove. More cover. She flipped over onto her back, which felt vulnerable but made it easier to push herself along with her bootheels, following the lines of wire-strung grapes toward greater safety.

"I know you're out here somewhere," Avermore said, much closer than she would have liked. "Your friend's bleeding to death up there, you can die out here, that's fine."

Thank goodness for the darkness, she thought.

"I really don't know why you're making such a fuss about this. She was just a girl . . . it was an accident. I've been so good ever since . . . She might not have deserved to die, but I definitely deserve to live . . ."

His voice drifted away for a moment, and Mason started going faster, flipping over, ready to get to her feet and run the last few yards into the olive grove. Once she was there, he really wouldn't be able to see her.

Which was when all those kerosene burners came on, all at once, designed to fight frost (she later discovered) and to aid workers picking grapes in the cool of the night. She was as lit as a performer in the footlights, and when she stood up to run, Avermore could see her as clearly as if it had been midday.

He raised the gun.

Mason ran toward the trees. She was nearly there . . .

Justin Avermore took aim, lit from below by the kerosene lanterns, shadows of the grape vines latticing his chest. He fired, once, and Mason spun around, feeling the buckshot graze the top of her shoulder, scalding it with flame.

She leapt then, full length into the shadows of the olive grove. Skidding on the ground, her face smashing up against a tree trunk, the pain in her shoulder and the concussion of the collision causing her to momentarily pass out.

Which was a terrible pity.

Because as Teddy drove the Rolls-Royce Phantom over the crest of the hill and silently mowed down Justin Avermore, Mason missed the entire thing.

39

IT TOOK THE ambulance and the cops ten more minutes to arrive, and during that time, Teddy located Mason in the olive grove and slid down a tree nearby to await assistance. When Mason came around, Teddy was the first thing she saw.

"You're alive. Oh, thank God. Claudia would have killed me."

Teddy laughed. "So it would seem. I am bleeding rather heavily, though, and she gave me this sweater, so you might still be in trouble. I think she might have knitted it herself."

But his voice was weak, and when Mason sat up and winced at her own injuries, she saw that he was covered in blood from the neck down.

"Shit, Teddy . . ." She scrambled to her knees and quickly assessed the damage. The edge of the shotgun blast had apparently hit him in the upper torso and neck, and there was a lot of blood and damage. Mason took off her shirt and blotted what she could.

She looked around. "Where's Avermore?"

"Under the car," replied Teddy. "I don't think he's dead, but he's probably not feeling great. I called 911 before I left the office." Indeed, sirens could be heard in the distance, getting closer. "You saved my life, lobbing that typewriter."

"Well, you still got shot. I'm sorry. And apparently you saved mine, too. I hope the car isn't a write-off. Julia's so fond of it." Mason wiped away some of the blood on Teddy's neck and saw a fresh supply oozing out. She pressed the T-shirt down hard, and Teddy jerked away.

"Careful there. You're bleeding, too, and you have the kind of goose egg on your forehead that is going to make Will queasy." He swallowed. "And fuck the car, it's too big to park in LA anyway. Julia can get another one."

Mason was feeling terrible, her head felt like it was going to implode, but the adrenaline was doing its job.

"Just hold on, Teddy. They'll be here soon." She looked up at the entrance to the vineyard. Where the hell was the ambulance? She turned back to Teddy, whose eyes were fluttering closed. "Teddy, stay with me."

"I'm here."

Mason's T-shirt was soaked, and Teddy's head lolled suddenly, as he lost consciousness.

"Teddy . . ." Mason shook him a little. "Teddy, stay awake." She slapped him a couple times, none too gently.

"Quit it," whispered Teddy. "I'll tell Claudia you were mean to me."

OK, thought Mason, *he's still in there.*

An ambulance raced into the vineyard, and Mason struggled to her feet and started waving.

40

"CLEARLY, I MADE an error. I should have brought an ambulance."

Archie was helping everyone into the Mercedes, somewhat carefully as he wasn't completely recovered yet. Teddy was bandaged pretty heavily, so he loaded him into the back corner. Claudia went next to him, clutching a collection of painkillers in a clear plastic bag. Then Will, who was undamaged but was trying to do something important on his tablet. And finally Mason, who was also bandaged (differently from Teddy, more of a one-armed sling situation) and seemed subdued and strangely quiet.

Archie turned to Julia. "Front seat for you, of course. You appear to have come out of all this entirely unscathed." He held the door open, the breeze carrying the scent of coastal oak and sagebrush, diminishing the smell of rubbing alcohol and emergency room that was pervading the car. The Mercedes 450 normally smells of leather and luxury, but today it smelled like Urgent Care.

"Apart from my date turning out to be a murderer, and two

of my operatives dodging death by a hair, yes, totally fine. Will, you making any progress?"

Will looked irritated. "I'm trying. We're a little in the back of beyond out here, and coverage is spotty. I'm trying to download massive files, and it keeps crashing the tablet. I knew I should have brought the laptop. Will I ever learn?" He literally pulled at his hair, and Julia raised her eyebrows.

"Sorry I asked," she said. She turned to Archie. "They wouldn't let him use his tablet at all at the hospital. It was very frustrating for him."

"Understood," said Archie. "And he couldn't do it at the hotel?"

"He refused to go back to the hotel. He felt responsible because he messed up about the alarm system."

"I did mess up," muttered Will. "They could have both been killed."

Archie closed the door. "But they weren't." He climbed into the driver's side and started the car. "In fact, it all turned out great, right?"

No one said anything, and he frowned, but focused on the driving for a moment, getting them onto the freeway back to Los Angeles before trying it again.

"I said, it all turned out great, correct? You caught the killer, you solved the crime, you were able to tell that detective he could close his cold case, there won't be any more notes . . ." He tailed off. "Why am I not getting a load of agreement noises?"

Teddy grimaced. "We're a little sore, firstly, and secondly, I don't think you're right."

"In what way?"

Julia sighed. "Mason, what do you think? Did we crack it?"

Mason shook her head. "No. We solved a crime, that part

is great, but we kind of answered a question we weren't asking, right? Justin Avermore killed Eve Riley, but that doesn't explain why he was sending threatening notes to Alexa."

Archie looked at her face in the rearview mirror. "She must have threatened to tell on him, at the wedding, no?"

"Why?" said Mason, shrugging. "Why now? We're assuming he was the man she saw Eve with, and that for some reason she's kept that to herself for thirty years. Why would she change her mind now? And why wouldn't she tell us all about it right away? All we know about the wedding is that they spoke. Jennifer didn't describe it as an argument, or anything like that." She looked at her hands, which curled into fists in her lap. "It doesn't hang together properly."

"What else?" asked Teddy, gently. "Think it all out loud, Mason. What else bothers you?"

Mason shifted in her seat and looked at him. "Why would he trash her event? Why would he kill Iris? Why would he shoot at me? Why plant alcohol at Alexa's house? Why push Jennifer in front of a taxi? Why any of that stuff? It's all so oblique—if she did threaten him at the wedding, and I'm not sure she did, why not just kill her? Why not just threaten her back, with immediate and overwhelming violence? I threatened to go to the cops, and he chased me with a shotgun."

Teddy was nodding. "Exactly. We don't know him all that well, but what we do know is decisive and self-protective. The attacks on Alexa don't fit. There's too much patience and subtlety."

Claudia snorted. "The giant vegetables weren't very subtle."

"True, my dove. When can I have another painkiller?"

"Two hours," she replied. "Do you need something to eat? I have fresh bread and olive tapenade with goat cheese left."

She rustled in her tote bag and pulled out a foil-wrapped sandwich. "I put them together at the hotel while they were picking buckshot out of you, in case you got peckish."

"You, my sweet, are a ministering angel."

"Wait till I get you home, baby. I'm going to nurse you real good."

Will made a furball noise.

Julia turned in the front seat and looked at her team. "There's a whole other part to it that doesn't make sense, either." She looked at Mason. "Did you get to that yet?"

"The attacks on him?" Mason nodded. "Yeah, that's also been bothering me. The poisoning at the restaurant could have been a one-off, a coincidence. But the pesticide at the vineyard, that's just too much. Someone was attacking him, too."

"Alexa?" Archie was perplexed. "Would she try and punish him that way?"

Mason shook her head. "I don't think so. Again, if she wanted to hurt him, all she needed to do was go to the police."

She thought about Detective Karneeva. How overjoyed he'd been when she'd called him, sent him the photos of the bottle and the bracelet. He'd reached out to the Ojai police, and she'd shared Wilson and Brooks's contact information. The wheels of justice were turning. Justin Avermore was going to pay for his crimes, thirty years after the fact. Karma is a patient, patient bitch.

"And why didn't she?" asked Claudia. "I don't get that part, either."

"I haven't been able to reach her," said Mason, pulling out her phone and hitting Alexa's number again. "It just goes to voicemail." She'd been trying for nearly twelve hours now, the whole time they were at the hospital. She wanted to let her sponsor know what had happened and also ask her . . . what the actual fuck? Had she known what Justin did? Had she kept it quiet for a good reason? Mason needed to know, because she was officially confused as hell about who Alexa even was.

She turned to Will. "Did you get anything from Karneeva, by the way? He said he was going to send us those additional photos of Eve he'd promised us when we were up there. I know I've seen that California poppy somewhere else, the one on the bracelet, but I can't remember where."

"Not yet," said Will, holding the edges of the tablet and hitting himself in the head with it. "I need new equipment, Julia. This tablet is several years old and it's just not . . ."

"OK," said Julia, mildly. "Don't have a coronary."

"And another thing," said Mason. "I know Justin was in Los Angeles a lot, but do we know for sure he was there on all the dates he would need to be to have been harassing Alexa the way someone was? I need to nail it all down."

"Another timeline to build," said Teddy. "So satisfying."

"Except that I think it's going to show that he couldn't . . ."

"Oh my fucking God," said Will, suddenly. "For ten seconds I had full bars and everything opened at once. Now I can finally . . ." He went silent, pulling the typewritten sheet Mason had given him from his pocket. The tablet was letting out a series of pings. "Oh . . . there's the email from Karneeva. I'll send it to your phone, Mason."

Mason pulled it from her pocket and opened her mail. "My phone's working, Will. Maybe there's something wrong with your tab . . ."

"It's fine!" Will frowned at her. "It just needed enough connectivity. Trying to concentrate here . . ."

Mason shot Julia a look, then opened the email from Karneeva. "He sent more photos . . . there's the bracelet in the booking photo, just like I remembered. And wait, here's one with her sister, the one he mentioned." She clicked on the image, and felt her blood run cold.

"Dammit," said Will. "Mother. Fucker."

"What is it?" asked Julia.

"The typewriter isn't a match. Not even close."

"I could have told you that," said Mason. "Because now I know who's been sending the notes." She flipped her phone around, holding it out for Julia to see.

Eve Riley. A little younger than she had been in the booking photo. Standing with her older sister, grinning at the camera. Masses of blond hair, strong profiles, don't-fuck-with-me attitudes. Safe, in the photo, happily protected by the curving arm of her older sister. A sister who'd never forgotten her, and who was now making sure she got the justice she deserved.

"Try Alexa again," said Julia, urgently. "And keep trying. We have to warn her." She turned to Archie. "Step on it and stay stepped until we get back to the city. No time to lose."

41

THEY SCREECHED UP the driveway to Julia's house forty minutes later, Archie having broken the speed limit the whole way.

Mason was out of the car and running to the guesthouse before the dust had even had time to settle on the car, let alone the ground.

"Alexa?" She threw open her door and ran in . . . Nothing. Her sponsor's jacket was gone, her purse, the spare set of keys. But her bag was there, clothes for a few days still next to the couch. So she hadn't gone home. But where?

Mason turned and headed back outside. Claudia was helping Teddy into the house. Will, Archie and Julia were standing by the car, waiting for her.

"Nothing?" Julia looked uncharacteristically worried.

"No." Mason pulled her phone out again. "I'll try . . ."

Her phone rang.

"Oh, thank God, it's her . . ." She answered, "Alexa? Where have you been?"

"I'm sorry, baby," her friend replied, her voice soft. "I've had my phone off, but I saw you called and called and called . . ." She laughed. "Sorry, sorry, sorry . . ."

"Are you OK?" Mason wasn't sure at first . . . Alexa's voice was . . . different.

"Oh, I'm better than OK. I'm fantastic. I got a terrible case of the fuck-its and decided it was time to relax and chill out and just, you know, drink. There's really been so much stress, am I right?" She laughed again. "I guess I'm going to have to start counting days again, but hey, it's OK. What's twenty-eight years between friends?" There was a clattering noise; she'd dropped the phone. "You can be *my* sponsor, if you like." More laughing.

"Where are you? I'll come and get you."

"No need, baby, we're all good here. I forgot how good it feels to drink, to let it all go." Her voice got dreamy. "I don't need to worry about anything now. I can just be right where I am, just be in the moment. It's all good. We're just driving around . . ."

"Who's we?" Mason's stomach started to sink.

"Oh, it's all good. Jennifer's here, she's looking after me." Another giggle. "She just went into the store to get more booze . . . so I took the chance to call you back. Oops, she's coming out. Talk soon, baby. Don't worry about a thing."

And she hung up.

"Fuck!" Mason called back but it went to voicemail again. "She's with Jennifer, and she's hammered."

Julia was confused. "Jennifer's hammered?"

"No, Alexa. No idea what state Jennifer is in, but I bet she's stone-cold sober. This whole time it's been her. She's the one with the patience to terrorize Alexa with those notes." Mason was pacing back and forth. "I knew I'd seen that poppy somewhere before. Jennifer has it tattooed on her wrist, along with an E for Eve, not for Edward, her ex-husband. I don't know how she found out that Justin killed her sister, but she did and she blames Alexa, and now she's got her and I have no idea where they are."

"Check the AirTag on her keys," said Will, calmly.

Mason stared at him. "What AirTag?"

"The AirTag I put on all the house keys. I did it last year when Julia was drinking; she lost her keys all the time, so I just did all of them while I was at it."

"There's an AirTag on the guesthouse keys?" Mason was being a bit dense, but Will took pity on her.

He nodded, navigating to the right screen on his tablet. He flipped it around. "See? She's . . ." He flipped it back again. ". . . in Griffith Park, for some reason." He watched the screen for a moment. "Huh, she's heading to the Observatory."

"Why?"

He looked at Mason. "How the hell would I know? I doubt she's driving, so you'd have to ask Jennifer."

"I will," said Mason, running back to the car, pausing to grab the tablet. "I know I can do this on my phone, but you've already got it up. Can I borrow it?"

"Sure. Don't drop it. I don't have a new one yet."

Mason ignored that. "Julia, you coming? I'm not one hundred percent certain Jennifer's going to kill Alexa, but I'm not one hundred percent certain she isn't."

"Not great odds," said Julia, climbing back into the car. "We really need Teddy, but I don't think he's up to it."

"I'm as good as Teddy," said Archie, getting behind the wheel. "I mean, he's a licensed, gun-carrying investigator and I bet he drives really well, but I'll get us there."

"Stop talking, start driving," said Mason. "Go, go, go . . ."

Julia wound down the window. "Call Wilson and Brooks," she yelled to Will. "Tell them everything, tell them to meet us at the Observatory . . ." She was thrown back in her seat as Archie hit the gas. "I'm pretty sure he heard that."

"He got it," said Mason, repeatedly dialing Alexa's number. "She's turned it off again. Hurry, Archie."

THE GRIFFITH OBSERVATORY was built by a man who rejoiced in the name Griffith J. Griffith, which was one of Mason's favorite facts about it. She also knew that he'd built it expressly for use by the public and that more people have looked through the telescope there than any other public telescope in the world. It was one of her favorite places in LA, and if it wasn't for the fact that she suspected Jennifer of wanting to kill Alexa, she would have been pretty stoked to be going there.

But all she could think about was the drop just past the front lawn of the Observatory, and how easy it would be for Jennifer to push Alexa over it. It wasn't a completely sheer drop, but it was steep enough that falling down it would cause major injury and possibly death. Pretty safe if you were sober . . . but Alexa was drunk. Very drunk. Pushing her over would be easy.

"Please hurry," she muttered.

"I'm going as fast as I can," replied Archie. "There's not much I can do about the traffic." They were moving along Sunset, and as it was midevening, there was plenty of traffic. But Archie kept going, and soon they passed the busiest area, headed into Los Feliz, and up onto Observatory Road.

"Try not to flip out," said Julia. "You don't know exactly where they were when you spoke to them. They could be only a little bit ahead of us."

But as they pulled into the turnaround in front of the Observatory, Mason's stomach sank.

"Well, fuck," said Julia. "I guess her patience ran out."

Jennifer and Alexa were silhouetted by the low stone wall that separates the front lawn of the Observatory from the plunging hillside. It's one of the best photo opportunities in the city, but at that moment the only two people standing there seemed to be fighting, rather than posing. Jennifer had Alexa by the shoulders and was dragging her over the wall toward the edge.

For the second time in less than an hour, Mason leapt out of the barely moving car and started running. Behind her, Julia was yelling at Jennifer, but at this close distance, Mason just focused on hitting her target and increasing her speed.

Jennifer turned at the last minute, pushing Alexa over the wall right as Mason slammed into her. Fortunately for Alexa, her drunken state meant she fell like a sack of potatoes and just lay there, but the momentum of Mason's run meant she and Jennifer flew over the wall and started sliding down the sloping, uneven few feet of ground that lay just beyond. Mason dug her boots and hands into the ground and managed to slow herself, but Jennifer was rolling dangerously fast toward the point where the ground dropped away much more steeply.

No . . . muttered Mason, *you're not getting away that easy* . . . She scrambled over the dusty ground and grabbed the back of Jennifer's shirt, slowing her progress just in time. Strangely, rather than being grateful, Jennifer reared up and swung for Mason's face, her own contorted with rage.

"How dare you stop me," she gasped. "I was nearly done . . ." She kept swinging, totally out of control.

Mason rolled onto her back and pulled Jennifer up and

over, slamming her into the ground. Then, getting on all fours, she hauled off and punched the other woman in the jaw, stunning her and at least slowing her down.

"It's . . . over . . ." she said, with each additional punch. "Stop fighting." Once Jennifer was still, Mason sat back on her heels and swiped her hand across her mouth.

Archie and Julia had reached them by then, and Julia was helping Alexa up and onto the low wall. She was very drunk, but she spotted Mason and smiled.

"Hi there, baby. When did you get here?" Her eyes were glassy, her gaze unfocused, but she leaned over toward Mason and almost toppled right back off the wall.

"I got her," said Julia, sitting next to Alexa, and resting her hand on the other woman's shoulder. "You just rest here a minute, OK?"

"OK . . ." said Alexa, her eyes closing. "I'm very tired now."

Archie climbed over the wall and bent down to check on Mason. "Are you OK?"

Panting, Mason nodded. She turned to Jennifer.

"Accept it," she said. "It's over. Justin Avermore is in custody. That's what you wanted, wasn't it?"

Jennifer lay there staring up at her for a long moment, then she closed her eyes. "He is? Really?"

"Yes. He confessed. He had the murder weapon. He's going to jail. There's no way he's going to get out of it. None."

Two tears slid from beneath Jennifer's eyelids, tracking clean streaks in the blood and dirt on her cheeks.

"Was it worth it?" asked Mason, angrily. "You could have just gone to the police."

Jennifer opened her eyes. "Do you have a sister, Mason?"

Mason was surprised, but nodded. "Yes. Older than me. We're not that close."

"Well, Eve and I were only seventeen months apart, Irish twins. She was the only good thing in my life, the single bright spot in a childhood that was unremittingly cold and violent. When she left for Oakland, she took my heart with her, but she wrote to me every week, telling me about the people she'd met, the things she was doing. She told me about Birdman, and I hated him for the pain he'd caused her. He was an animal. She told me about her boss, Lisa, and Fuzzy and all these other characters that felt so real to me. And then the fire happened, and we lost her. It nearly killed me. But I was determined to make her proud and I started building a life, learning my trade, moving up, right? And then they found her body, and I knew she hadn't just been lost, she'd been *taken*. And I did everything I could to help, but there wasn't much . . ." She looked over at Alexa. "And then the universe decided to take a hand. Isn't that right, Alexa?"

Alexa said nothing. She was resting on Julia's shoulder, largely unconscious.

"I picked Alexa as my sponsor because she was from Northern California, too, and because I heard her mention the Albatross fire in a meeting, telling her story. It sent her into rehab, turned her life around, or started to, anyway. And I fantasized that maybe she knew Eve, that maybe they'd been friends. It was just a dream."

"Years passed, and Alexa was wonderful to me, helpful and apparently honest. But then at the wedding we bumped into Avermore, and she clearly hated him. I asked her about him, on the way home, and she said he was a terrible person. That he used to hurt girls, that she thought maybe he'd done worse, that she'd seen him running away from the fire with a girl, a girl that later showed up dead. And then it happened: She called him Birdman and I realized I'd found him. And that she'd seen him taking Eve and did nothing about it." She looked at Mason. "Have you ever been disappointed in a person you'd thought was amazing?"

Mason nodded. She was disappointed in Alexa herself.

"I was gutted. But in that moment, in the dark on the Pacific Coast Highway, I realized the universe had given me a chance to make things right."

"Did you think maybe the universe wanted you to let the authorities handle it? Karneeva said you still call him occasionally. You could have told him."

Jennifer made a face. "I considered it. But I was so angry. I've been so angry for so long, and I wanted them to suffer."

"Not a super sober impulse."

Jennifer laughed. "Nope, not sober at all. I know what I did wasn't good . . . isn't good. But I wanted to ruin them both, like they ruined me. I wanted to take everything that mattered to them and destroy it. I knew how much Alexa cared for us, for her 'little chickies.' I wanted her to really know what it felt like, to love someone and not be able to protect them, to lose them. I wanted to ruin Justin's life, and hers. And thanks to you, I have. I knew when I told you Avermore and Alexa knew each other that you would find out who he was. That you and that nutty old lady you work with would finish the job."

"Hey," said Julia.

Jennifer ignored her. "I'd done my part already. I poisoned his wine at the opening. I told all my friends in the business to boycott him. I went to his vineyard and coated his shit with pesticides. I wanted to kill him piece by piece, take away everything he'd ever built, everything he loved. Like he took her from me."

"And what about Alexa? Why hurt her?"

"Because she knew about him but stayed silent. For decades. I don't even know why."

"I think I do." Mason stood up and turned to Alexa. "Hey, Lex . . . wake up."

"Wha . . . I'm tired . . ." But she woke up, sat up a little. "What is it?"

"You started the fire at the Albatross, didn't you? Those candles you were burning that night . . . and Justin knew, because he was there. I think when Eve's body was found, you told him you were going to the police, and he threatened you with exposure. And you were too scared of going to jail, and you thought it was too late . . . am I right?"

Alexa's eyes were so big, filling with tears. "How did you know? Nobody knows, just him."

Mason shrugged. "Because why else would you keep his secret? You wouldn't have held his secret all these years for no reason; you weren't friends, you didn't even like him. So there had to be a reason, and the best reason of all is fear—you taught me that. Fear makes us do terrible things. It makes us not do the right thing. And that's what you did—you simply didn't do what you should have done, and the years passed, and it got easier and easier to forget what was true. That's how secrets take on lives of their own. And then you ran into him at the wedding, and he thought his time was up, so he threatened you."

"I saw him and it all came back. I suddenly realized I needed to do the right thing, tell the truth. But he said he'd kill me. Kill Scott. Everyone I cared about. I was terrified."

"And on the way back from the wedding you were so shaken that you let slip just enough to Jennifer that she put it together."

"Really?" Alexa looked at Jennifer and smiled. "My sponsees are so clever." Then she lay back down on the wall and fell asleep.

There was a silence then, as all four of them stood there and listened to her breathe.

Mason said, "You sent the notes."

Jennifer nodded. "I knew he'd threatened her. I just went from there."

"You sabotaged the fashion show. I saw your dog outside after you said you'd left. You stole the control tablet and wreaked havoc."

"No one was hurt. I just wanted to ruin her career."

"You killed Iris," said Mason.

"No." Jennifer shook her head. "I told her a load of nonsense, told her Alexa thought she couldn't stay sober, worked on that little hard kernel of self-doubt we all have until she lost hope. I bought her drugs, I fixed the syringe, I handed it to her . . . but she made that final choice herself."

"I doubt the police would see it that way," said Julia, crisply. "You wiped the syringe, wiped your prints off it and put it in her hand . . . but you forgot to put her thumb on the plunger. At the very least you covered up your involvement in a crime. You are responsible for her death, emotionally, intellectually and, I believe, legally."

Jennifer shrugged. "You'll never prove it."

Mason thought about the night Alexa thought she was having a heart attack. The day in the office. Her increasing paranoia.

"You dosed Alexa with Adderall."

"Yup. It helps me stay focused, but Alexa's got a regular brain, so a big fat dose in her coffee made her think she was losing her mind."

"You planted alcohol at Alexa's house. You made us all doubt her sobriety."

"Sucks to be her. I was trying to ruin her serenity, make her question her own mind. It worked."

"You shot at me."

"Not very well. I missed on purpose."

Archie coughed.

"Not completely."

Jennifer looked over and seemed to notice Julia and Archie for the first time. "Sorry about that."

Archie nodded.

"You threw yourself in front of a car."

She nodded again. "I was willing to do whatever it took to punish Alexa for her silence."

"And to protect yourself. You made yourself look like just another victim."

"Sure," said Jennifer. "What are a few ribs to an avenging angel, right? I ruined her career, I hurt the people she cared about, I messed with her head and stole her fucking serenity and then I stole her sobriety." She looked over at Alexa and laughed. "And sure, if you hadn't shown up I would have been unable to stop a drunken friend from having a terrible accident and hopefully cracking her own skull on the way down, but I'm still going to count this as a win."

"Call it what you want," said Mason. "But now you're going to jail."

"Am I? For what? You're going to have a hard time proving any of this. I was careful."

"Not that careful," said Detective Brooks, emerging from the shadows. "We heard everything."

Jennifer gave a deep sigh and shrugged. "I've got an excellent lawyer and already got what I wanted. Do your worst. I doubt you'll get very far."

She got to her feet and shook the dust off herself. Walking toward the two waiting police detectives, she paused by Alexa and touched her on the head.

Alexa opened her eyes and smiled up at Jennifer, woozily.

"Hey there," she said. "Thanks for taking care of me."

"No problem," said Jennifer, walking away. "It was literally my pleasure."

42

A WEEK LATER, Mason was pretty pissed.

"She's going to get away with it. I can't fucking believe it."

Wilson and Brooks looked at each other, and then back at the team. "That's not what we're saying. We're just saying she's lawyered up with a really good lawyer, and there's not a lot of proof apart from what we all heard, all of which she's now denying. We couldn't find a typewriter at the restaurant that matched the notes. There's no proof that she sabotaged the show, no one saw her."

"I saw her dog outside!"

"She'll say it was a different dog, Mason. There's no connection between her and the drugs that killed Iris; there's literally no smoking gun in Archie's shooting . . ." Wilson shrugged. "We're just saying don't hold your breath. Be satisfied that Avermore is caught bang to rights and is going away for a considerable amount of time."

"I guess," said Mason, dubiously. "Now that Alexa's recovered from her relapse, she's helping the police make sure of it. She wanted to do the right thing all along . . . but with every year that passed, it got harder and harder. Now she can make amends."

Julia leaned back in her chair. "Life doesn't always work out the way you want it to, Mason. Some days you get the bear, some days the bear gets you."

Teddy spoke up. "If you become a PI, you'll see a lot of things that don't get resolved the way you want them to. You have to be OK with it."

"I don't know if I am OK with it," said Mason.

"You did a good job on this case, Mason," said Julia. "You worked out most of it yourself; you learned a lot. I'm proud of you."

Mason made a face. "Thanks. It definitely helped me decide that I want to finish my degree, by the way."

Will gave out a little cheer.

Julia nodded. "I thought you might. And the PI degree after?"

Mason shrugged. "I don't know. Probably." She looked at Teddy. "You seem to have come to terms with the various inherent contradictions. Maybe I will, too."

"I have flexible standards and a dubious moral character," said Teddy.

"I'm not saying that's common among PIs," said Wilson, "but it's not unusual."

"It's one of my favorite things about him," said Claudia.

"I like this job, as it is," said Mason, "but I'd like to have a gun."

"Oh shit," said Julia.

"Dear God," said Brooks.

Archie looked worried. "I'm not sure you're the right person to be carrying a firearm."

"Why not?" asked Mason. "I might get beaten up less."

"Huh," said Archie. "That's a good point. It is hard to see your poor face get walloped so frequently."

"He likes your face," said Claudia.

"He likes all of you," said Will.

Mason's phone rang. She answered. She listened for a moment, then stood up. "I have to take this. It's my sister. My dad's going back to work and our mom's throwing a fit."

She walked out of the room.

"Fifty dollars says she'll do the PI degree," said Teddy.

"I'll take that action," said Will, reaching for his wallet.

Archie shook his head. "I think she'll go to law school."

"I think she'll shoot herself in the foot," said Julia. "Or me." She looked at Archie. "You two are going out for dinner tonight, right? Maybe try and persuade her to pick up a new martial art instead."

"Not sure that's much better," he replied, dubiously.

The door pushed open, and after a moment Phil walked in. He was wearing a little collar like a sunflower to stop him from chewing his stitches, and he was cool enough to totally pull it off. He walked carefully across the room until he reached Julia's chair. Then he jumped up with the lightness of a breeze and stretched out his head to sniff her nose. She didn't say anything. So, he turned around on her lap and curled up like a croissant.

There was a long silence.

Julia reached out a hand and gently scratched his head.

"Damn," said Will, opening his wallet. He pulled out a twenty and handed it to Claudia. Archie did the same, as did Teddy.

"Suckers," said Claudia, pocketing the cash.

Epilogue

THE MAN WAS walking quickly, with his head down. He looked up briefly, as he prepared to cross the street, and Mason got a quick shot of his face. She took a second to put the photo in the right folder on her phone, then looked across at Teddy, who was lounging in a doorway halfway down the street. She nodded, and Teddy levered himself away from the wall and started to trail the guy, pretending to talk on his phone.

Mason kept pace on the opposite side of the street, dropping back a bit every so often, speeding up at other times. The man had no idea they were there, and if they did their job right, which they would, he would know nothing until they had what they needed, and it was too late for him.

It was evening, and as the light faded, the stars came out, scattered across the indigo sky. For a moment, between buildings, the bridge was visible, and in the clear air Mason smiled. *Keep walking, dude*, she thought to herself, *we've got all the time in the world.*

He did, he kept walking, and even though Mason knew where he was headed, she stayed alert. Teddy was ahead of the guy now, as they'd discussed, and when the guy sped up, suddenly, Teddy turned to look at a store window until he'd passed. Mason crossed the street, swapping places with Teddy, who dropped back and took the other side of the avenue. Mason pulled on a beanie, glad of the extra warmth and the additional layer of disguise. He'd never seen her, had no idea who she was, but she wanted to close this down tonight, and he'd be seeing her face before long.

Now there were girls ahead, their long legs bare, their skirts so short you could see their asses, their faces pinched with cold. Mason wished she could pay them all to sit in a coffee shop and warm the fuck up, but she couldn't. They wouldn't thank her for her pity, either. And tonight she needed them to be there, so she put her unease aside, and waited for the guy to approach them.

And he did.

Walking up to the first one.

Mason had her phone out. So did Teddy, who passed the man as he talked to the hooker, his phone held low but angled up, filming. The man didn't even register him, though the girl did, her eyes much more practiced at looking for danger than her potential client. She looked back at the guy and shook her head. Something wasn't right; she wasn't feeling it.

Mason wondered what he asked for. Made a face to herself, sped up to draw level with him, took a position in a doorway across the street and waited. The man approached another girl, oblivious to Mason's observation, unaware of the pictures she was taking, totally focused on getting what he wanted.

The second girl was younger, more amenable. Or maybe she was just cold, who knows, but she nodded, and the man turned to lead her away.

Mason knew where he was taking her—she and Teddy had watched this happen several times now—and Teddy was probably already outside the faded motel their quarry favored. No questions, rooms rented for cash, close to the freeway. Perfect for what he wanted, and probably a money-making machine. Mason followed the man and his new, temporary friend, and as they crossed the street to enter the motel, she saw Teddy, relaxed and in place. Their eyes met, and for a second he smiled. He knew she wanted this to be done, wanted to get it over with, and that tonight they'd gotten what they needed.

Shot of him in the lobby, renting the room.

Shot of the two of them, climbing the cement and metal staircase to the upper floor.

Shot of them unlocking the door, going into the room.

And now they waited.

THE MAN WALKED slower now, his evening activity completed, thinking about things other than his desire. Mason couldn't have cared less what he was thinking about; she had no empathy for him, and certainly no sympathy. He'd caused a problem, and she was going to fix it. How he reacted to it was entirely up to him.

She came up to him as he waited to cross back onto campus.

"Dr. Eberling?" she said, quietly.

He turned to look at her, saw a young woman who was almost certainly a student, standing here on the edge of the quad, presumably heading home from the library.

"Yes?" he said.

"I was wondering if you had a minute to talk."

He sighed and looked at his watch. He was in no hurry, but that didn't mean he had time for every sophomore who wanted to improve their grade. Although, he looked again; this was a very pretty girl, so who knows, maybe it would be worth his while.

"I can pause for a moment, but I'm very busy."

"Oh, I know," said the girl, and smiled. Somehow the smile was familiar, and for the first time a shiver of concern fluttered in his chest. She was confident, this girl. No deference at all.

"You can set up a time to come to office hours," he said, changing his mind. "I have to get home." The light changed; he went to step off the curb.

"Have to get back to your wife?" the girl asked. "The other Dr. Eberling. Denise. Zoology Department."

He stopped. "Yes . . ."

"Does she know where you go on your way home?" asked the girl, with a lightness that suggested she was asking about the weather, or his seminar on attachment disorders. "Does she know about your habit?"

"I have no idea what you're talking about," he said, gruffly. "Who are you?"

"It's not important," she replied. She pulled out her phone and opened her photos. "I've spent the last three nights following you closely, and I've taken some lovely photos of you with your young acquaintances. It's risky, don't you think?" Her tone stayed light. "To shop for friends so close to campus? I was surprised you didn't head into the city, but it would have made my job harder, so it's fine."

Eberling bent to look at the phone, his face going gray.

"Are you trying to blackmail me?"

"Not at all," said the girl, putting away her phone. "I'm just concerned about the faculty in your department. I would hate to see it lose the more seasoned members of staff. Do you get my meaning?"

He looked at her for a long moment.

"Are you talking about Dr. Mason?"

"He's an excellent teacher," replied the girl. "And if the rumors on campus are true, you're trying to push him out."

"They're just rumors."

"Really?" The girl looked at the phone in her hand again. "I'd love to see those quashed. I'd hate to have to share these with anyone."

"You wouldn't dare. I'd call the police. I'd get you thrown off campus."

"I'm not on campus. I'm not even local. I'm leaving here tonight, and you'll never see me again. If I hear that Dr. Mason is no longer in jeopardy, you will never hear from me again, either. But if I hear he's getting harassed, being threatened, or even worried about the future of his tenure, you will be explaining these pictures to your wife. I have friends here, and they'll be taking care of it."

The girl smiled at him suddenly, a smile of such angelic sweetness that without even thinking he smiled back at her.

"That's all," she said. "This is goodbye."

And then she turned and walked away.

ENTERING A COFFEE shop, Mason walked to where Louise was waiting and sat across from her.

Lou handed her a thumb drive, and Mason quickly uploaded the photos onto it.

"He didn't know who you were?"

"Nope," said Mason, handing over the thumb drive. "And you can take it from here, although I think we're probably done. Dad's back at work, right?"

"Yes. And hopefully this will cut Eberling off at the knees." She shrugged. "I tried doing it the right way, and I'm just glad you were ready to do it the wrong way." She hesitated. "Which turned out to be the right way . . . Oh, you know what I mean."

Mason grinned and nodded. "How much longer are you staying?"

"Another week," said Louise, raising her hand to call over the waitress. "Then I was thinking of swinging by Los Angeles on my way home."

"Sounds great to me," said Mason. She looked up at the waitress. "I'll have a grilled cheese and a chocolate malted," she said. Any diner can feel like home if you order the right thing.

And you have the right company.

LATER, DRIVING SOUTH, the Lamborghini eating up the miles with pleasure, Mason suddenly turned to Teddy and grinned.

"That was fun," she said. "Maybe being a PI would suit me after all. Perhaps my moral character is becoming more dubious."

Teddy laughed. "Oh good," he said. "I'll win my bet."

"With Julia?"

"No, with Claudia. When I wager with her, even if I lose, I win, if you follow my drift."

Mason giggled. "I wish I knew Claudia better. She's a bit terrifying and a bit wonderful."

"Just like you," said Teddy, affectionately. "You'll make an excellent PI. You were born to it."

They drove in silence for a few moments, then Mason turned to him again.

"So . . . how did you and Claudia reconnect?"

Teddy laughed. "Well, it all began with a missing painting and a counterfeit certificate of authenticity. It's a long story."

"It's a long drive." Mason settled down in her seat. "Start talking."

Photo © Dina Waxman

ABBI WAXMAN, the *USA Today* bestselling author of *Deadly Does It*, *One Death at a Time*, *Christa Comes Out of Her Shell*, *Adult Assembly Required*, *I Was Told It Would Get Easier*, *The Bookish Life of Nina Hill*, *Other People's Houses*, and *The Garden of Small Beginnings*, is a chocolate-loving, dog-loving woman who lies down as much as possible. She worked in advertising for many years, which is how she learned to write fiction. She lives in Los Angeles, California, with her three children, three dogs, and three cats.

VISIT ABBI WAXMAN ONLINE

AbbiWaxman.com

AbbiWaxman